Christmas came once a year.

And this year Maggie would embrace it. Trees, sledding, cookies. She was all in.

As if he read her mind, her son asked, "Can you come and help us pick out a tree, Finn?"

"I don't know if you heard," Finn said, "but I'm the best tree hunter in all of Alaska." To which her boy's face lit up with excitement.

There was no doubt about it. Oliver was blooming right before her eyes. And it had everything to do with Finn. She should know. He'd done the same for her when she was a child.

She told Finn when her son scampered off. Then warned, "I'm just worried he might get too attached to you. Oliver isn't looking for a father figure. He's looking for a father."

"No worries, Mags. We're buddies," Finn assured her. "Surely that can't be a bad thing."

"No, that's not a bad thing." Not for her son, she thought. But what about her? Was being Finn's buddy enough?

Belle Calhoune grew up in a small town in Massachusetts. Married to her college sweetheart, she is raising two lovely daughters in Connecticut. A dog lover, she has one mini poodle and a chocolate Lab. Writing for the Love Inspired line is a dream come true. Working at home in her pajamas is one of the best perks of the job. Belle enjoys summers in Cape Cod, traveling and reading.

Lois Richer loves traveling, swimming and quilting, but mostly she loves writing stories that show God's boundless love for His precious children. As she says, "His love never changes or gives up. It's always waiting for me. My stories feature imperfect characters learning that love doesn't mean attaining perfection. Love is about keeping on keeping on." You can contact Lois via email, loisricher@gmail.com, or on Facebook (loisricherauthor).

A Holiday Match

Belle Calhoune

&

Lois Richer

2 Uplifting Stories
An Alaskan Christmas and *North Country Dad*

LOVE INSPIRED
INSPIRATIONAL ROMANCE

LOVE INSPIRED®

INSPIRATIONAL ROMANCE

ISBN-13: 978-1-335-42987-2

A Holiday Match

Copyright © 2022 by Harlequin Enterprises ULC

An Alaskan Christmas
First published in 2017. This edition published in 2022.
Copyright © 2017 by Sandra Calhoune

North Country Dad
First published in 2014. This edition published in 2022.
Copyright © 2014 by Lois M. Richer

For questions and comments about the quality of this book, please contact us at CustomerService@Harlequin.com.

Love Inspired
22 Adelaide St. West, 41st Floor
Toronto, Ontario M5H 4E3, Canada
www.LoveInspired.com

Printed in U.S.A.

Recycling programs for this product may not exist in your area.

CONTENTS

AN ALASKAN CHRISTMAS

Belle Calhoune

For my brother, Stephen.
For introducing me to Steinbeck and *East of Eden*,
a book that changed my life.

Acknowledgments

For all the readers who have enjoyed the
Alaskan Grooms series and asked for more.

For editors Emily Rodmell and Giselle Regus, for
all their hard work and dedication on this project.

But they that wait upon the Lord
shall renew their strength;
they shall mount up with wings as eagles;
they shall run, and not be weary;
and they shall walk, and not faint.
—*Isaiah* 40:31

Chapter One

Finn O'Rourke paced back and forth in terminal 27A of the Anchorage airport. He looked around him, noticing the pine wreaths and red ribbons adorning the walls. The Christmas decorations provided a dose of holiday cheer. For the most part, airports were pretty stark places. He took a quick glance at his watch. His passengers should have met him here twenty minutes ago so he could fly them on the last leg of their journey to his hometown of Love, Alaska. A grumbling noise emanated from his stomach, and he knew it had nothing to do with hunger pains. Butterflies had been fluttering around in his belly ever since he landed in Anchorage. He didn't know why he felt so nervous.

Perhaps it had something to do with his client, Maggie Richards. Twenty years stood between himself and Maggie. A lifetime really. She was a mother now with a small child she was raising alone.

She'd hired his brother's company, O'Rourke Charters, and now he was flying her back to Love, where she would begin her new life, courtesy of her uncle, Tobias.

Tobias Richards. He was the reason Maggie and her son were relocating to Alaska from Massachusetts. There was nothing like an inheritance to turn a person's world upside down, Finn thought. Tobias had gone to glory with a few surprises up his sleeve. Finn had just found out he had also been named in Tobias's will. Receiving the paperwork last evening had been a mind-blowing experience.

Finn felt a twinge of sadness at the realization that his good friend was gone. He missed him terribly. Tobias had been one of the few people who'd truly understood Finn. And he'd gone out of his way to help him on multiple occasions. In fact, he was still aiding him from beyond the grave.

Finn let out a deep breath. After all these years he was going to come face-to-face with Tobias's niece, Maggie, his childhood friend. They had been as thick as thieves during her visits to Love when they were kids. Ancient history, he reminded himself. She probably wouldn't even remember him.

He grinned as memories of catching salamanders and skating at Deer Run Lake washed over him like a warm spring rain. They had shared secrets and explored caves and promised to be best friends forever. His friendship with Maggie had been special, and it had come to an abrupt end mere months before his entire childhood imploded. Perhaps it was the reason why those memories were engraved on his heart like a permanent tattoo.

All of a sudden a woman came walking toward terminal 27A with a small child in tow. She had dark hair and appeared to be struggling with a large-sized piece of luggage. Her tiny companion was dragging a rather large duffel bag behind him. A feeling of familiarity washed over Finn at the sight of her. As she came closer, there was no doubt in Finn's mind about her identity. It was Maggie!

Little Maggie Richards had matured into a beautiful woman, Finn realized. Despite the fact that he hadn't seen her in twenty years, Finn would have recognized her anywhere. Those stunning green eyes and the chestnut-colored hair set in a heart-shaped face were quite remarkable.

When she was within five feet of him, Maggie stopped in her tracks. Her eyes widened. "Finn? Is that you?"

Finn nodded. He smiled at her. All at once he felt like a little kid again. "One and the same," he drawled. "Hey, Maggie. It's nice to see you. Welcome back to Alaska."

He didn't know whether to hug her or shake her hand, so he did neither.

Maggie blinked and shook her head. "I can't believe it's you. I was expecting Declan."

"I work for O'Rourke Charters as one of the pilots," Finn explained. He didn't bother to mention he would soon be a co-owner of the company. Finn couldn't imagine her caring one way or the other. As a widow and single mother making a new life in Alaska, she had bigger fish to fry.

"You always did want to fly planes," Maggie said in a light voice. "Up to the wild blue yonder."

Hearing his grandfather's favorite expression tumble off Maggie's lips startled Finn. Killian O'Rourke had taught Finn and his younger brother Declan to fly. Finn's love of flying had come straight from his grandfather's heart. Killian had been a larger-than-life personality and the most loving man he'd ever known. The ache of yet another loss tugged at Finn. There wasn't a day in his life he didn't miss his grandfather and the man's steady influence and vast wisdom.

He inhaled a deep breath. Being back in Alaska after roaming around the country for several years meant having to deal with the past. So far, Finn wasn't sure he was doing such a good job of it. When he least expected it, old memories rose up to knock the breath right out of him. He shook the feelings off as he always did and focused on the here and now. Somehow he had to find a way to tell Maggie the specifics about his inheritance from Tobias. He prayed she wouldn't mind too much.

"Hi." The little voice startled him, serving as a reminder of Maggie's pint-size traveling companion.

"Hey. What's your name?" Finn asked, looking down at the small child standing beside Maggie.

Maggie tousled the boy's hair and said, "This is my son, Oliver. Oliver, this is Finn O'Rourke. A long time ago we were pals when I spent a few summers in Alaska with Uncle Tobias."

Finn stuck out his hand. Oliver looked up at his mother, then shook Finn's hand once Maggie nodded her approval. "Nice to meet you, Oliver."

"Are you our pilot?" Oliver asked, his expression full of wonder.

"Yep. I'm going to fly you and your mom to the best place to live in all of Alaska. There's moose and bears and fishing and reindeer pizza. Not to mention we have sled dogs and the northern lights."

Oliver's eyes grew big in his small face. "Whoa!"

"Are you excited about it?" Finn asked in a teasing voice.

Oliver nodded his head. "Mom says we're going to have our own house. We never had our own house before. And she's going to run a store." He rubbed his hands together. "And the best part is, she's going to find me a new father here in Alaska."

Finn felt his jaw drop. He swung his gaze toward Maggie. There was no doubt about it. Her expression showed utter mortification. He watched as she shot her son a look of annoyance. Oliver smiled up at her as if butter wouldn't melt in his mouth.

Finn reached out and grabbed Maggie's luggage and Oliver's bag. With a nod of his head he said, "Why don't we go board the seaplane and get ready for takeoff?" He winked at Oliver. "Love, Alaska, awaits you."

Once Maggie had settled Oliver into his seat on the seaplane, she sat down and buckled herself in. She couldn't remember ever having traveled in such a small plane before. She might have felt a little apprehensive if Finn O'Rourke hadn't been their pilot. Maggie knew instinctively they were in good hands. It was strange to feel that way since they hadn't been in each other's lives for quite some time, but Finn exuded an air of control and authority. And she knew he'd learned how to fly from the best—Killian O'Rourke.

As the plane took off, Maggie felt a burst of adrenaline race through her veins. They were really doing this! She and Oliver were on their way toward a brand-new life in the small hamlet of Love, Alaska. Maggie needed someone to pinch her. It was a surreal experience.

"Look, Mama. That mountain is ginormous!" Oliver's chubby, chocolate-stained finger pointed at a spot outside the window. She reached into her purse for a tissue, then wiped his fingers clean.

Maggie Richards chuckled at the excited tone of her son's voice as he pressed his face against the window of the seaplane. She leaned in and tousled his sandy head of hair, admiring his hazel eyes and infectious smile. No doubt she was biased, but Oliver was one adorable kid, even though he'd caused her a world of embarrassment with Finn at the airport. The look on Finn's face when Oliver had told him about getting a new father had been priceless. Finn hadn't known what to say and he'd looked at her with confusion etched on his too-handsome-for-his-own-good face.

Maggie hadn't bothered to explain her son's desire for a father in his life and her inability to convey to him that it wasn't something she could order on demand. Somehow Oliver had gotten it into his head that Maggie was going to find him a new father. Nothing she said or did could convince him otherwise even though the last thing Maggie wanted or needed was a husband. Been there. Done that.

Her heart ached a little bit as she observed her son. He'd been through so much in his young life. If she had one wish, it would be to build a stable, peaceful life for him. Maggie was determined to create a strong foundation for Oliver in Alaska, and she would do it on her own as a single mother.

"Oliver, I'm not sure *ginormous* is an actual word in the dictionary."

Oliver turned toward her with confusion radiating

from his eyes. He appeared crestfallen. "It's a word, Mommy. Honest."

She pressed a kiss against his cheek. "I believe you, sweetie." She reached for a napkin and wiped away the chocolate stains from the glass.

As she turned her head to peer out the window, Maggie let out a gasp as the majestic, snowcapped mountains came into view. Oliver was right. The mountains were ginormous. And magnificent. She couldn't remember ever seeing such a lovely vista in her entire life, even though she had traveled the world extensively before settling down to marriage and motherhood. How could she have forgotten this spectacular sight? Granted it had been twenty years ago, but some places deserved a lasting place in one's memory.

For most of the flight from the Anchorage airport, Maggie had been praying about this big move. Was she doing the right thing? By uprooting Oliver from their home in Boston she was taking him away from everything he'd ever known. On the other hand, she was determined to see her son grow up in a place where no one would judge him for his last name. Maggie had reverted back to her maiden name of Richards to avoid being blackballed. She had done the same for her son. He was now Oliver Richards. The town of Love wouldn't know their family history. They would be judged on their own merits and not based on news reports or local gossip.

Maggie let out a sigh. The last year had been devastating. Gut-wrenching. Her husband, Sam's death had left them reeling and trying to pick up the shattered pieces of their lives. Her beloved husband had been shot and killed while holding up a grocery store. In the aftermath, the bottom had truly fallen out of her world. Everything she'd thought about her life had been shattered in one devastating moment. To this day she still found it difficult to wrap her head around Sam's criminal actions or the fact that she'd been blind to them for so long.

But with this relocation to the other side of the country, a whole new world would be awaiting them. Uncle Tobias had bequeathed her his home in Love, as well as his shop, Keepsakes, and a nice sum of money. It would allow them to have a fresh start. That's what Maggie was calling it. She was relying on God to see them through the difficult weeks and months ahead. It wouldn't be easy to re-create a whole new life, but she knew it was important for Oliver's future and well-being.

Finn's voice buzzed in her ear through the headset.

"We're reaching our final descent. If you look out the window, you'll see beautiful Kachemak Bay stretched out as far as the eye can see. You might remember it from back in the day, Maggie. It's an Alaskan treasure."

Finn's voice was just as attractive as the man himself. It had been quite a shock for Maggie when she came face-to-face with her childhood buddy at the Anchorage airport. He was all grown-up now. With his dark brown hair and emerald-colored eyes, he was a serious looker. No wonder the town of Love had been luring women from all fifty states to their lovelorn town. If all the men looked like Finn O'Rourke, it was no small wonder Operation Love was such a successful campaign. Not that she wanted anything to do with it. Her dating days were over.

"It's awe inspiring," Maggie said into her mouthpiece. She turned and relayed the message to Oliver since he didn't have a headset on. "Pilot O'Rourke just reminded me of the name of the water down below. It's called Kachemak Bay."

Oliver wrinkled his nose. "Kacha what?" he asked. Maggie giggled at her son's attempts to pronounce the difficult word. Honestly, she could gaze at him all day long given the choice. This little boy was the joy of her life. She couldn't imagine how impossible it would have been to get through the past year without Oliver. Sam's death, and the circumstances surrounding it, had brought her to her knees. Her only saving grace had been Oliver. Sweet, funny Oliver.

"Kachemak Bay." She said the words slowly so Oliver could understand how to pronounce it. She listened as he repeated it several times in an attempt to get it right. "That's it," she said after the fourth try. "You said it perfectly."

"Yes! I did it." Oliver raised his fist in the air, his gesture full of triumph. A tight feeling spread across her chest. He seemed excited about their new journey. *Thank You, Lord. I've been so worried about him.*

Losing his father at five years old had been a catastrophic event for Oliver. She knew her son had a lot of emotions he'd bottled up inside him. And even though a year had passed, it wasn't a very long time for a child to grieve the loss of a parent. Oliver still struggled sometimes. He still asked for Sam. There were tears. And sadness. And tantrums. It broke Maggie's heart each and every time. Sam hadn't been a perfect father, but he had loved his son. And Oliver had been crazy about him.

Starting anew in Love, Alaska, might just be the very thing they both needed to get back on track and build a firm foundation for their future. They had been blessed by Uncle Tobias's generosity. The uncle she hadn't seen in twenty years had passed away four months ago. She had been remembered very generously in his will. Maggie felt a burst of joy at the realization that she was the owner of an establishment in a quaint Alaskan town. Between the shop and the house—it was so much more than she had ever dreamed of owning. Deep down inside, she didn't feel worthy of it all. But she would do her best to live up to Uncle Tobias's faith in her.

As the seaplane began to descend lower and lower toward the ground, Maggie gazed out the window and placed her arm around her son's shoulder. A shiver of excitement trickled through her. They were mere minutes away from landing in their new hometown. So much was riding on this brand-new adventure, particularly Oliver's happiness. Maggie hoped she'd made the right decision in bringing her child all the way to Love, Alaska.

Finn stood by the seaplane as Maggie and Oliver disembarked. He had grabbed their luggage and placed it on the pier for them. He looked around him at the familiar faces crowding around his two passengers. A small welcome committee had gathered to greet them at the pier, as was the custom when a newcomer arrived here in town. Finn smiled at the sight of the town mayor, Jasper Prescott, as he came toward them. With his long black coat and matching dark hat, Jasper cut a striking figure. Although he sported a gold cane, Finn knew it was purely an accessory. His wife, Hazel, walked by his side, her face lit up with a bright smile. Hazel and Jasper were newlyweds, having been married for less than a year. In many ways they were the heart and soul of Love.

Jasper reached out and wrapped Maggie up in a bear-like hug. "Howdy, Maggie."

He wasn't certain, but the look on Maggie's face seemed a bit overwhelmed by Jasper's enthusiasm. Or maybe Maggie was simply feeling the impact of this monumental move all the way across the country. He imagined having a kid added to the pressure.

This wasn't the first time a woman had come to Love with a child in tow. After all, Paige Reynolds had arrived a year and a half ago with sweet baby Emma in her arms—a big surprise no one had known about, including Emma's father, Cameron. It had all ended happily when Paige and Cameron walked down the aisle.

Maggie's son was a pretty cute kid, Finn reckoned. With his round face and hazel-colored eyes, he reminded Finn a little bit of himself at that age. He sure hoped Oliver's life was a lot more idyllic than his own had been. Although he had been a bit older when his mother passed away, the event had scarred him terribly and changed his life forever. Finn knew he'd never quite recovered from the trauma. Or the guilt.

Finn shook off the maudlin emotions. Things were looking up for him. He needed to be positive.

"Nice to see you again after all these years, Maggie," Hazel said in an enthusiastic tone. "Your uncle told us so much about you and Oliver over the years. He loved you very much." She reached out and enveloped Maggie in a tight bear hug.

Maggie's uncle Tobias had been a longtime resident of Love. He'd been an amiable man whose shop on Jarvis Street had always been popular. "Let her come up for air, Hazel," Jasper barked. Hazel let Maggie go, before turning toward her husband and scowling at him.

"Welcome back to Love," Jasper said in a booming voice. Maggie smiled at Jasper, which immediately lit up her face. With her delicate features, Maggie had a girl-next-door type of beauty.

Jasper turned his attention toward the little boy. "What's your name, son?" he asked in a robust voice. Finn let out a low chuckle at the look on Oliver's face. Much like everyone else who crossed paths with Jasper, Oliver seemed fascinated by his larger-than-life personality.

The boy looked up at Jasper with big eyes. "I'm Oliver."

Jasper stuck out his hand. "Hello there, Oliver. I'm Jasper Prescott, the mayor of this town. Everyone calls me Jasper though."

"Hi, Jasper." Oliver stared, then frowned. "Hey! You kind of look like Santa Claus."

Finn knew that Jasper—with his white hair, blue eyes and whiskers—had heard this a time or two. The town mayor threw his head back and roared with laughter. "I like your honesty, young man." He winked at Oliver. "To tell you the truth, I sometimes feel like him. I do tend to spread a lot of cheer around this town." He winked at him. "Especially during this time of year."

Finn stifled an impulse to burst out laughing at Jasper's comment as Hazel rolled her eyes and let out an indelicate snort. Jasper frowned at his wife, then turned back toward Oliver.

"Would you like to head over to my grandson's café for some peppermint hot chocolate and s'mores?" Jasper asked, eyebrows twitching.

Oliver's hazel eyes twinkled. "S'mores are my favorite!" he said with a squeal of glee. He turned toward his mother. "Can we please go?"

Maggie reached out and tweaked her son's nose. "Of course we can. S'mores are my favorite too."

Finn watched the interaction between mother and son. Their tight bond was evident. He looked away for a moment, casting his gaze at the fishing boats docked by the pier. The boats served as a distraction from the feelings bubbling up inside him. A wave of longing for his own mother washed over him in unrelenting waves. He'd lived without her for almost twenty years, but the pain of her loss still lingered. It still gutted him when he allowed himself to think about it.

He didn't know why, but lately the memories had been coming at him fast and furiously. And the guilt he felt over her death never seemed to let up.

"Finn!" Hazel called out. "Would you like to join us?"

Finn turned his attention back toward the group. "I have a few things to do, but I'll meet you over there in a little bit. Don't worry about the luggage. I'll bring it over to the Moose."

"Thanks, Finn," Maggie said with a nod of her head. "We really appreciate it."

Finn didn't say a word in response. He merely nodded his head. Something about seeing Maggie again after all these years made him feel tongue-tied. She was so polished and put together. There was a regal air about her, although she didn't seem like a snob. She was miles away from the tomboy who'd run around with skinned knees and untied shoelaces. He doubted whether they would even have a single thing in common.

"We'll see you later then," Jasper said, clapping Finn on the back.

Hazel clapped her hands together. "Well then. What are we waiting for?" she asked, motioning for everyone to follow her down the pier. Finn watched as they all walked toward Jasper's car. At one point Oliver turned back toward him and waved. The thoughtful gesture made Finn smile. He waved back at him, getting a kick out of the way the boy's face lit up with happiness.

Finn was glad they were traveling by car. Even though the Moose Café wasn't far, the ground was a bit slick from a recent snowfall. Maggie and Oliver weren't even wearing boots, he thought with a chuckle. Something told him it wouldn't take either of them long to figure out they were essential for Alaskan winters.

Once he was alone, his mind veered toward the pressing matter at hand—Tobias's bequest in his will. It couldn't have come at a better time. For weeks now he'd been in a financial bind. He'd needed to come up with a large amount of cash so he could buy into a partnership in O'Rourke Charters, his brother's business. So far his part-time job at the docks hadn't brought in much cash, and his hours spent working for O'Rourke Charters were few and far between. Living in a town recovering from a recession made finding a high-paying gig almost impossible. He was so close to achieving his dream of being his own boss. His financing had been approved, but for a lesser amount than he'd expected or needed.

Tobias had come to the rescue and left him a nice sum of money in his will. Although Tobias had placed a condition on receiving the funds, Finn couldn't be more thrilled about it. He clenched his jaw. Finn wasn't too sure how Maggie would feel about working side by side with him. Despite their past friendship, they hadn't been close in twenty years. The situation could prove to be very awkward. He no longer knew Maggie well enough to predict her reaction.

Just as the group departed in Jasper's car, another vehicle pulled up to the pier. It took only seconds for Finn to recognize it. He watched as his brother, Declan, got out and walked toward him. With his blond hair and movie-star good looks, Declan radiated charm. Until he'd married his wife, Annie, he'd been known around town as something of a ladies' man. Now he was enjoying the white picket fence and impending fatherhood. Although he was happy for Declan, Finn couldn't help but feel envious. That type of life wasn't meant for him.

"How'd it go?" Declan asked in an overly casual voice.

"Fine. Like always," Finn said in a curt voice. He didn't know why it bothered him so much to have Declan constantly checking on him. His brother must trust him since he employed him as one of his pilots. Yet, time and again, he gave Finn the feeling he was constantly peering over his shoulder. As the older brother, it didn't sit right with Finn. After all, for most of their young lives Declan had followed in his footsteps.

That was a long time ago, he reminded himself. Before he'd let Declan know he couldn't count on him.

Declan rocked back on his heels. "That's good," he said, quirking his mouth. Finn knew well enough by his brother's expression something was brewing. Declan was now shifting from one foot to another and clenching his teeth.

"What's going on? I know you didn't come down here just to say hello. Give it to me straight."

Declan quirked his mouth. "I need to firm up my plans regarding O'Rourke Charters. I know you said you were in, but I'm going to have to draw up contracts and take the final payment from you. Business has slid a bit even with the second plane, so I'd like to get moving on the purchase of a third one. I need for us to get moving on this partnership and secure more financing, as well as getting this infusion of cash from you."

Declan had been in a plane crash over a year ago. As a result, one of his planes—*Lucy*—had been damaged beyond repair. Because Declan had been trying to save money on his premiums on his insurance payments, he had reduced his coverage months before the crash. As a result, the policy hadn't fully covered the damages. Declan had managed to purchase a gently used seaplane a few months ago, but the company had taken a loss while operating with only one plane. Now his brother had his eye on a third plane in order to expand the business. Finn couldn't blame him for wanting to secure his company's future. Declan gave Finn flying hours as often as he could, but until he bought into O'Rourke Charters and they purchased another seaplane, Finn wouldn't be hired on as a salaried pilot. His dream of co-ownership would be on hold.

Finn scratched his jaw. "I know I've put you in a bind and I'm sorry about it."

Declan cut him off. "Finn, I'm not blaming you for not getting all the financing you needed, but I've been as patient as I can for the last few months. The bottom line is I've got to make some serious decisions about the future of O'Rourke Charters. If you want to join forces, I'm going to need us to sign a contract and have you make a substantial contribution to buy your way into the business."

"Declan, I'll be honest with you. I wasn't sure how I was going to come up with the last portion, but my prayers have been answered." Finn reached into his jacket pocket and pulled out the paperwork he'd received yesterday afternoon.

"What's this?" Declan asked as Finn handed him the documents.

"I got a visit yesterday from Lee Jamison. He's the executor for Tobias's will." He shook his head, still in disbelief over his windfall. "Believe it or not, Tobias left me a nice-sized sum of money."

Declan raised a brow. His eyes scanned the paperwork. He let out a low whistle as he swung his gaze up to meet Finn's. "Tobias was mighty generous. You know what this means right? There are conditions."

Finn nodded. "Yes. I'll have to help Maggie get the shop ready for its grand opening, then help her get it up and running for a total period of no less than four weeks. At such time the shop successfully opens, then

I'll get my inheritance." Finn repeated the terminology he'd memorized from the paperwork. "Then I can buy my way into O'Rourke Charters."

Declan let out a hearty chuckle. He slapped Finn on the back. "I can't believe it!" He grinned at Finn. "You always do land on your feet."

"Not always," Finn said, "but thanks to Tobias, we're going to be partners."

More than anything, Finn wanted to be a co-owner of O'Rourke Charters. He wanted it more than he'd desired anything in his life. For so long he had denied how great it felt to be up in the wild blue yonder flying a plane. But he couldn't stuff it down any longer. It was where he was meant to be and being a pilot was his destiny. From the very first time his grandfather had taken him up in the air and let him fly the plane, Finn had been a goner. Killian had told him it was his destiny. Being co-owner of O'Rourke Charters would give him stability and respectability. It would give him a purpose. It would allow him the opportunity to live out a lifelong dream. And even though his grandfather wasn't around any longer, perhaps he could still make him proud.

"Four weeks will be fine," Declan said with a nod. "I can work with that."

Finn grinned at his brother. It felt as if a huge weight had been lifted off his shoulders. "I appreciate it. And I'm not going to let you down this time. I promise."

"You better not," Declan said, his blue eyes flashing a warning. Finn knew he was referencing the countless times Finn had bailed on him in the past. Not this time, he vowed. He was no longer the man he used to be. Finn liked to believe he'd grown and matured over the past few years. He wasn't walking away from things anymore. Finn was done with running away from home and everything he held dear.

Declan turned back toward him. "I'm really happy for you, Finn. And for our future partnership. I really do want this to work out."

"Me too," Finn murmured as Declan turned away and continued back down the pier. Once his brother was out of earshot, Finn murmured, "Things are going to work out. They have to."

Now all he had to do was explain his inheritance from Tobias to Maggie and break it to her about the stipulation requiring him to work side by side with her at Keepsakes. Finn let out a deep breath. He wasn't sure what he would do if she objected. Would he still be eligible for his inheritance if she declined his help? His whole future now hung in the balance.

Chapter Two

Maggie found herself smiling as they pulled up in front of the Moose Café. As they'd driven down Jarvis Street, with its old-fashioned charm and festive holiday decorations, the quaint downtown area of Love had captivated her. Although she'd visited on three occasions as a child, her favorite had been during Christmastime. She'd been overjoyed to experience the town decked out in all its holiday glory. Those same feelings were rising up within her at this very moment. Nostalgia warmed her insides.

A fully decorated Christmas tree sat on the town green while pine wreaths and red ribbons graced every lamppost lining the street corners. This town was getting ready for the holiday, even though it was a month away.

She'd been a little surprised to see Uncle Tobias's shop all shuttered up as they drove by. It stood out amid all the other festively decorated shops. Keepsakes looked abandoned and neglected. Maggie didn't bother to point it out to Oliver. She didn't want him to be disappointed so soon after their arrival.

Poor Uncle Tobias, she thought. He had loved his shop so much. How she wished things hadn't been so tumultuous in her own life for such a long time. Perhaps she could have relocated to Love a year ago and helped out her uncle. Once Maggie entered the Moose Café alongside Jasper, Hazel and Oliver, the tinkling sound of the bell above the doorway welcomed her. As soon as she crossed the threshold, she noticed sprigs of holly dangling down from the ceiling. The interior of the establishment was decked out in Christmas decorations. Wreaths. A fully trimmed Christmas tree sitting in a corner. She noticed all of the waitstaff were wearing T-shirts with moose on them. Delectable odors assaulted her senses. Her stomach began to grumble, serving as a reminder that they hadn't eaten in several hours. And she wasn't sure the quick snack of pretzels and fruit they'd grabbed at the Anchorage airport even counted.

Oliver—her finicky eater—often needed to be encouraged to eat more. As it was, he practically lived on pizza, french fries and chicken nuggets. She looked down at him, eager to know his feelings at every point in their journey.

"This place is cool!" Oliver said, his voice brimming with enthusiasm. Maggie felt herself heave a little sigh of relief. It was so very important that Oliver embrace their new hometown. Maggie didn't think things would work out in Love if her son wasn't happy. After all he'd been through, Oliver deserved to be joyful.

And so do I, she reminded herself. Oliver wasn't the only one who had been put through the wringer.

As a mother it was easy to ignore her own needs, but she vowed to do better at being a more content, well-rounded person.

Maggie followed the trail of her son's gaze. He was looking at a pair of antlers hanging on the wall. He couldn't seem to take his eyes off them. Although the vibe of the Moose Café was rustic and a bit on the masculine side, Maggie could see a few feminine touches. Red-and-white carnations sat on each table. Soft, romantic paintings hung on the walls. It gave the establishment a nice, eclectic atmosphere.

"Thanks for the thumbs-up." A deep male voice heralded the appearance of a chocolate-haired, green-eyed man. He greeted them with a warm smile and patted Oliver on the back. "Those antlers are pretty awesome, aren't they?"

Oliver bobbed his head up and down in agreement. He flashed the man a gap-toothed smile.

"Cameron!" Jasper called out, addressing the dark-haired man. "We need a table for four, please." He gestured toward Maggie and Oliver. "This is Tobias's niece, Maggie Richards. You two might have met back when Maggie visited Love as a child." Jasper flashed her another pearly smile. "Maggie, this is my grandson, Cameron Prescott. He owns this delightful establishment." Pride rang out in Jasper's voice.

Cameron stuck out his hand by way of greeting. "Nice to see you again after all these years. It's been a long time. I'm happy to hear you'll be opening up Keepsakes soon."

"It's wonderful to be back," Maggie said. "And I'm very excited about the shop. Oliver and I have been very blessed by Uncle Tobias." Maggie didn't even have the words to express her gratitude about this opportunity. Her heart was filled almost to overflowing.

Maggie had vowed to be more courageous in her life. Fear had always been such a stumbling block. It was one of the reasons she'd stayed with Sam for so long and put up with his run-ins with the law and his inability to hold a job.

If anyone had told her a year ago that she would move to Alaska in order to run her uncle's shop, Maggie never would have believed them.

"And we're very grateful to have you back in Love," Hazel added. It had been Hazel who had called Maggie to tell her about her uncle's death. Then weeks later she'd called again to direct her to call the executor of her uncle's estate to inquire about her inheritance.

Upon hearing all the details about her inheritance, Maggie wanted to pinch herself. In one fell swoop, her entire life had changed. She grinned at Hazel. Maggie couldn't believe she was standing next to the impressive woman who had created the genuine Alaskan Lovely boots that had taken the country by storm. Uncle Tobias had told her all about Hazel's creation of the boots and the way the town of Love had set up a business to mass-produce them.

Maggie couldn't really put her gratitude into words without explaining about the major losses she'd endured and the shameful circumstances of Sam's death. It had cost her everything she'd worked so hard to build for her family. And she couldn't afford to talk about it to anyone in this town. She'd uprooted her entire life in order to start over here in Love. And she wasn't going to tarnish it by revealing her deepest, darkest shame.

Maggie wanted to be respected in this town. She wanted her son to be free of any stigma.

Maggie felt a tug on her sleeve. "Mommy. Can I go over to the jukebox?" She looked down at Oliver, who was pointing toward a tomato-red jukebox sitting in the corner of the room.

"Why don't I show you how it works?" Cameron suggested. "Make yourselves comfortable at any table you like."

Cameron walked away with Oliver at his side. Maggie watched them for a moment, feeling wistful about the lack of men in her son's life. It made her ache to remember how many nights Oliver had cried himself to sleep over his father.

"Tobias told us about the loss of your husband when it happened. He was heartbroken for you and Oliver." Jasper turned toward her and cleared his throat. "Maggie, Pastor Jack told us about the tragic circumstances."

Maggie felt her eyes widening. A wild thumping began in her chest. The jig was up. Her secret had been exposed. "How did he know about it?"

"He contacted the pastor at your church to find out if we could do anything to make your transition to Love any easier. Although we already knew you were a widow, we didn't know the specifics."

"W-what did Pastor Baxter tell him?" she asked, her heart in her throat. *Lord, please don't let everyone here in Love know already about Sam holding up the grocery store. I want to protect my son. He's innocent in*

all of this. It will be just like back home all over again.
Name-calling. Finger-pointing. Judgment.

Jasper looked at her with sad eyes, "He told Pastor Jack that your husband was killed in a grocery store holdup." He made a tutting sound. "It's so very tragic for your family." He began patting her on the back.

Maggie felt her shoulders slump in relief. She felt horrible for allowing this version of the story to go unchallenged, but for Oliver's sake she had to keep quiet. He'd endured enough. And he was just a little boy. She couldn't let the sins of the father be visited on the son.

"Grief is a process, Maggie. We know you're probably still trying to wrap your head around such a profound loss." Jasper's blue eyes became misty. "Never fear. We're here for you. We're going to make sure y'all have a joyful holiday season."

"Thank you, Jasper. I feel very blessed to receive such a warm welcome here in Love." Maggie blinked several times, doing her best to hold back the tide of tears.

Suddenly, Oliver came racing to her side. "Mom. Sophie said I can go in the kitchen and make my own pizza."

Sophie—the beautiful, Titian-haired waitress standing behind Oliver—was smiling down at her son as if he'd hung the moon. This town really was full of genuinely kind folks.

"Oliver is going to help me make a masterpiece," Sophie said with a grin. The Southern twang and the red-and-white Santa hat perched on her head only made her appear more adorable, Maggie realized.

"That sounds like fun," Jasper said with a nod. "I

think I'm going to come with you and take some notes so I can whip up a pizza at home."

Hazel let out a groan. "That's all I need," she groused. "I can already smell the burned pizza."

Jasper scowled at Hazel.

"Come on, Jasper," Oliver said, tugging at the mayor's sleeve.

The look etched on Oliver's face said it all. There hadn't been a lot of smiles or laughter in the last year. Lately, Oliver had begun to turn a corner, but his grief had been all consuming for such a long period of time. He had shrunken down into a quieter, less joyful version of himself. Maggie wanted the old Oliver back, the one who laughed with abandon and didn't seem afraid of the world around him. With Christmas coming in four weeks, she wanted Oliver to experience the wonder of an Alaskan Christmas.

At least for the moment her son seemed to be over the moon. She prayed this new adventure didn't get old. Love, Alaska, was a small, quaint town where everyone knew each other. Maybe over time they would be embraced by the townsfolk.

Once Oliver headed toward the kitchen with Jasper and Sophie, Hazel turned toward Maggie. Compassion flared in her eyes.

"There's no need to fret, Maggie. I'm the only one here in town who knows the truth about the holdup. And I'm not about to share your personal business with anyone, not even my husband," Hazel said in a reassuring tone. "It's not my story to tell."

Maggie looked over her shoulder to make sure no one might overhear her conversation. "Thank you, Hazel. I appreciate you keeping it in confidence. I really don't want everyone to know Sam was killed while holding up the store," Maggie said in a soft voice. "I just want a clean slate."

Hazel reached out and patted her on the shoulder. "Everyone deserves a shot at getting their life back on track. God loves you, Maggie. And pretty soon, this whole town will consider you and Oliver as one of our own."

One of our own. Just the idea of it caused tears to pool in Maggie's eyes. It was the very thing she hoped to establish for her son here in Love. She let out a sigh. Hazel knew her shameful secret, but thankfully she wasn't going to divulge it to anyone.

Rather than being an innocent victim, her husband, Sam, had been the gunman holding up the grocery store. And he'd been shot in the process, losing his life and making their son fatherless. The ensuing media attention had been a vicious whirlwind. Maggie had been the recipient of hate mail, harassing phone calls and even a few death threats. She had been fired from her job and they had lost their housing.

This opportunity for a fresh start was a blessing from God. And Uncle Tobias. He had loved Maggie so much he'd laid out all the groundwork for her to rebuild her life in his hometown.

Most people wouldn't believe it, but Maggie had been totally clueless about Sam's illegal activities. In the end, she had paid dearly for believing in her husband. For loving him so much she'd had blinders on.

"Never again," she murmured to herself as Hazel led her toward a table. In her humble opinion, love led to hurt and pain, loss and disillusionment. She had no interest in going down that road again. She was going to focus on her son and his well-being. She would be both mother and father for Oliver. Maggie wouldn't be looking for love in this small fishing village.

Romance could go knock on someone else's door.

Chapter Three

By the time Finn made his way to the Moose Café, his stomach was grumbling like a grizzly bear. Even though he was short on money these days, his belly hadn't gotten the message.

Finn tried to stuff down the feelings of frustration with himself. In many ways it felt as if the past year had been about starting over from scratch. Although he had made positive strides, he was still miles away from where he wanted to be in his life. He couldn't help but envy Declan.

While he'd been backpacking his way around the country and avoiding any hint of responsibility, Declan had been building up his company and cementing his ties here in Love. Now his younger brother was a newlywed and soon-to-be father. For a man like himself, who had always rejected the notion of settling down, Declan's life looked pretty idyllic.

You're not cut out for all that, he reminded himself. *It would all just fall apart, just like everything else.*

Finn smiled at the reindeer-and-candy-cane wreath

gracing the door of Cameron's establishment. He knew his friend had a zany sense of humor. Everyone in town had gone holiday crazy right after Thanksgiving, even though Christmas was still a few weeks away. He sauntered into the Moose Café, eager to grab a bite to eat. Although his stomach urged him to order a big meal, he knew his budget wouldn't allow it. Every extra nickel he had would go into his savings account.

The moment he entered Cameron's establishment, a warm feeling came over him. Even though the food was stellar, Finn knew he frequented the Moose Café for the cozy, down-home atmosphere. It was a feeling he'd been seeking his entire life but hadn't yet found on a personal level. A place to call home.

The sound of hearty laughter drew his attention to a table dead center in the dining area. His eyes went straight toward Maggie. She was laughing and he could see the graceful slope of her neck as she reared her head back.

Maggie was one of the most attractive women Finn had ever encountered. He felt a stab of discomfort as he realized she might soon be joining the ranks of Operation Love. After all, most women who arrived in the small fishing village came to town in the pursuit of a romantic match.

It didn't take a rocket scientist to figure out that men would line up in droves for an opportunity to date the beautiful single mother. Beauty was in the eye of the beholder, but in Finn's humble estimation, Maggie Richards was the most stunning woman who had ever stepped foot in Love, Alaska.

He shrugged off thoughts of Maggie. She was way

out of his league and he needed to keep his eye on the prize and not get distracted by thoughts of sweet-faced, green-eyed women. It had been a long time since he'd been romantically involved with anyone. Way too long according to Declan.

So far Finn himself had rejected the idea of being paired up with anyone. Although he didn't disapprove of Jasper's matchmaking program, Finn had learned a long time ago that he wasn't the home-and-hearth type. His fractured childhood was proof enough for him.

"Hey, Finn!" Hazel called out to him, waving him over toward her table. "Come over and join us."

Finn walked over to the table, greeting Sophie along the way as she gracefully carried a tray full of food and drinks. "I'll be right over to take your order, Finn," Sophie said with a nod.

"Just bring me a bowl of the soup of the day and a coffee," Finn said.

The only available seat at the table was right next to Maggie. Finn tried not to stare at her as he sat down. It was a near-impossible task. The light scent of her perfume rose to his nostrils. It smelled like vanilla and roses. He couldn't think of the last time a woman had sparked such a response in him. For so long now he'd just been going through the motions and avoiding getting close to anyone. Even his family.

Maggie leaned a bit toward him. Her voice flowed over him like a warm breeze. "I forgot my manners earlier, Finn. Thank you for getting us safely to Love on your seaplane. You're an amazing pilot."

He locked gazes with her, marveling at the deep green color of her eyes. "You're quite welcome. It was my pleasure. I think it's safe to say flying is in my DNA."

She grinned at him, showcasing dimples on either side of her mouth. "Your parents must be very proud, as well as your grandfather. Back when we were kids he really fawned over you and Declan. Killian thought the two of you had hung the moon."

Finn felt his face fall. Maggie had no idea about his mother's death or the circumstances surrounding it. He felt a little ache at the prospect of dredging up painful memories. There was no point in dodging it. Sooner or later, someone would tell Maggie about it and she would wonder why he hadn't mentioned it.

"My mother passed away quite a while ago. Actually, it was shortly after the last time you visited Love." He looked down at the table and began fiddling with his fingers. He might as well tell her everything. "My father left Love years ago. He pretty much fell apart after my mother died. And my grandfather passed on when we were in our late teens."

She let out a sharp gasp. "Oh, Finn. I'm so sorry to hear that. You've lost a lot over the years."

The sympathetic tone of her voice made him cringe. He didn't want to be the object of anyone's pity, especially not Maggie's.

"I had no idea," she continued. "My mother and Uncle Tobias had a falling-out not long after we left Alaska, so for many years there was an estrangement. I only got back in touch with him a few years ago. We were able to pick up right where we left off."

"He mentioned something about the falling-out. Tobias was really thrilled when you reached out to him. Your uncle and I became good friends over the years."

Maggie twisted her mouth. "I wish that I could have made it back to Love a long time ago." She let out a little sigh. "I'll always regret it."

"Tobias always dreamed of you coming back," Finn acknowledged, "but he understood you had your own life to live in Boston."

Oliver walked up to the table and stood close by his mother's chair.

Maggie nudged him in the side. "Sweetie, don't you have something to say to Mr. O'Rourke?" She shook her head. "I mean, Finn."

Oliver slowly moved closer to Finn. For a second it seemed as if he was having trouble looking Finn in the eye. When he did look up, his hazel eyes were full of wonder.

"Thanks for bringing us here." He chewed his lip for a moment. "I think one day I wanna be a pilot just like you."

"That's fantastic, buddy," Finn said, reaching out and tousling Oliver's hair. "One of these days I can take you up in one of the planes if your mom says it's all right. I can show you the local area."

Oliver's mouth hung open. Everyone at the table laughed. The sound of Maggie's tinkling laughter warmed Finn's insides. Much like the woman herself, it was charming.

"Can I go, Mom? Can I?" The pleading tone of Oliver's voice was endearing.

"It sounds like a fun excursion," Maggie conceded. "I think we can make it happen." Maggie sent Finn a grateful smile. Oliver let out a celebratory hoot as if he'd won a battle. His enthusiasm made Finn feel ten feet tall. He wasn't used to being viewed as important. That's how the kid made him feel. It was a nice change from thinking of himself as useless.

He stared blankly at the menu, trying to shake off the desire to look over in Maggie's direction. There was no sense in him denying it. He felt a pull in her direction. And what man wouldn't? he asked himself. She seemed like the whole package. Looks. Brains. And he knew from their past she had a lot of heart. But Finn had determined a long time ago he wasn't suited for romance. And it was clear from where he was sitting that a woman like Maggie was the sort you brought home to Sunday dinner with the folks. She wasn't one to be trifled with.

Just then Sophie appeared at the table with a tray of food. Thankfully it gave Finn something to focus on other than the woman seated to his right. She placed a bowl of soup down in front of him, along with a hearty-looking sandwich with kale chips on the side. Finn shot her a look of gratitude. Sophie winked at him. As his friend, she knew his financial situation was dodgy. This was her way of helping him out.

Finn took a huge bite of his sandwich, then sampled the lobster bisque, one of Cameron's specialties. He flashed Sophie a thumbs-up sign.

Instead of heading back to the kitchen, Sophie stood at the table with a concerned look etched on her pretty features.

"What's wrong, Sophie?" Jasper asked. "You look like you burned something in the kitchen," he teased.

Sophie's eyes darted over to Maggie. She bit her lip. "Agnes Muller just called. She knows it's Jasper's tradition to bring folks over to the Moose to welcome them to town, so she figured you might be here. She said she's been trying to reach Maggie since this morning."

Maggie looked down at her phone and let out a sound of frustration. "Oh, I had my ringer off. She's going to be Oliver's babysitter when he starts kindergarten in a few days. It'll only be for a few hours in the afternoon since he'll be in school till the early afternoon, but since I want to get the store up and running quickly, she'll be a big help." Maggie stood up. "Let me go call her back in case it's something important."

Finn's gaze trailed after Maggie as she walked over to a private area of the café to make her phone call. Even from a distance of twenty feet, Finn could tell something was wrong. Maggie's face crumpled. The look of distress stamped on her face was evident.

He looked away, reminding himself it was none of his business. The last thing he wanted to do was get wrapped up in somebody else's problems. The good Lord knew he had enough of his own to focus on.

"Did something happen to Agnes?" Hazel asked Sophie. Her brows were furrowed, eyes full of worry.

"She didn't say too much but she's at Liam's clinic," Sophie answered, referencing Dr. Liam Prescott, Jasper's grandson and brother to Cameron, Boone and Honor. "She wanted to talk to Maggie first, but she sounded pretty weak, if you ask me."

Hazel made a tutting sound. "Lots of folks have been coming down with the flu. I pray she rebounds quickly if that's what's ailing her."

All eyes were on Maggie as she returned to the table. It was evident something had happened to turn her sunny mood into a somber one.

"Is everything all right?" Finn asked, the question hurtling off his lips.

Maggie pushed her hair away from her face with a trembling hand. "Agnes took a bad fall this morning. She sprained her ankle and she's on crutches. There's no way she's going to be able to watch Oliver now while I'm working, which puts me in a real bind." Maggie threw her hands in the air. "I don't know what I'm going to do."

Maggie's stomach was tangled up in knots as she provided the explanation about Agnes's ankle. She felt a little numb. Her mind was whirling to try to come up with a plan B. Although she felt terribly for Agnes, she now had to worry about getting a replacement for the woman she'd hired as a sitter. Oliver was a great kid, but at his young age it would be hard to keep him entertained while she worked nonstop to get Keepsakes in tip-top shape. In order to capitalize on the Christmas season, Maggie needed to open up the shop as soon as possible. And after seeing the worn sign outside the shop, Maggie had the feeling her work was cut out for her.

The ramifications of the situation roared through her with a mighty force. Finding Agnes had been no easy task. This was a small town with few options for part-time childcare.

She sank back down into her seat and stared mindlessly at the table. She didn't want to panic about the situation, but she had no idea what she was going to do. Maggie needed the income from Keepsakes. Although Uncle Tobias had left her money in his will, she knew the importance of establishing a nest egg. She planned to stash most of the money in a bank account and live off her proceeds from the store.

Maggie glanced over at Oliver. Thankfully he was in his own world, munching on his pizza and seemingly oblivious to the unfolding drama. He was so sensitive these days. She didn't want him to worry about who would be taking care of him while she was at work.

"We'll just have to find somebody to fill in for Agnes," Hazel said. Maggie had the feeling Hazel was trying to sound chipper for her benefit.

"That might be easier said than done," Jasper responded with a frown. "Why don't you write down the particulars? Hours and salary. Anything you feel is pertinent to the position. I'll circulate it around town hall and see if anybody bites."

Maggie let out the breath she'd been holding. The mayor of Love was making it clear she wasn't alone in this. Gratitude rose up inside her. She'd felt so terribly isolated and alone for the last year. It was nice to know things in this town might be quite different for her and Oliver.

Maggie ferreted around inside her purse and pulled out a small notebook and a pen. When she was done writing, she ripped the page out and placed it down on the table before sliding it toward Jasper.

He looked up at Maggie and twitched his eyebrows. "Not many hours since it's an after-school position, but

I'll post it up. You might get a teenager looking for hours like this."

A teenager! How in the world could she leave her son with someone so young? Maggie knew it wasn't out of the ordinary, but in her world it was. Being overprotective of her son was a by-product of having her husband taken away from her in such a tragic way.

"I appreciate anything you can do. Problem is, I need to hire someone as soon as possible. I need to get this resolved so I can get the shop up and running." Maggie felt her voice becoming clogged with emotion. Everything had been working so smoothly until this rug had been pulled out from under her.

Anxiety grabbed ahold of her. Despite her desire to be courageous, she found herself faltering. For most of her life, Maggie had struggled with anxiety. It tended to rear its ugly head in times such as this one when she felt things were spiraling out of her control. Other times it just struck her out of the blue. She took slow breaths to steady herself, reminding herself that she wasn't dying or in danger, even though it felt like it when anxiety overwhelmed her.

"I think you need to get some rest, Maggie. You've been traveling all day and pretty soon jet lag is going to settle in." The rich timbre of Finn's voice startled her. For the most part he'd been sitting at the table as a quiet observer. His green eyes were sure and steady as they locked with her own. "I think a good night's rest will help you."

Maggie nodded, knowing his words were true. She wanted to check out their new house and unpack some of their things and take a hot shower before crashing.

Oliver needed a bath and a good night's sleep. "That's a good idea," she said, feeling grateful to Finn for sensing she was at her limit. She looked over at Oliver. His eyes were beginning to droop. She felt a twinge of guilt for not noticing how tired her son looked.

"I'd like to get going. Oliver is about to conk out. I'd appreciate a ride over to the house," Maggie said.

Jasper jumped to his feet. He bowed in Maggie's direction. "Jasper Prescott at your service. Get your coats on and I'll drive you over there."

Finn stood up from the table. "Why don't I drive them home, Jasper? I already have their luggage in my car," Finn suggested. "It's in the same direction as my house."

"Perfect!" Hazel said in a boisterous voice.

"Thanks, Finn," Jasper said, slapping Finn on the back. "There's a booster seat by the doorway. We picked it up the other day for Oliver based on Maggie's instructions."

"I'll grab it on my way out," Finn said.

"Let me just run to the kitchen," Hazel announced. "I've got a few pans of food I cooked for you and Oliver, Maggie. I hope you like lasagna, salmon and tuna casserole. You'll also find a few things at the house. Staples like pasta, cereal, milk and bread." She beamed at her. "This way you won't have to worry about grocery shopping or meals for a few days."

"That's really sweet of you, Hazel," Maggie said, feeling grateful for such generosity. She couldn't think of a single person in Massachusetts who would have gone out of their way for them. Despite the worry about finding a replacement for Agnes, Maggie had the feeling God had planted her and Oliver right where they needed to be.

Her son stood up and put his jacket on. Maggie reached down and zipped up his down coat. December in Alaska was frigid. Although Boston got cold, it couldn't compare to this type of biting weather. She reached into her purse and pulled out her son's hat. Before she could place it on Oliver, he'd moved away from her.

Maggie watched as he raced over to Finn. "What kind of car do you have?" Oliver asked, his face lit up with excitement. Her son seemed to have a sudden burst of energy. No doubt it was due to Finn.

Finn chuckled. "I drive an old truck. It's pretty cool though since it belonged to my grandfather. I fixed it up and got it back in running condition. Guess what color it is?"

Oliver scrunched up his face. "Um…baby blue like a robin's egg?"

"Nope. Not even close. It's as red as Santa Claus's suit."

"Whoa," Oliver exclaimed. "That must be awesome."

Something told Maggie that Oliver was developing a pretty strong case of hero worship. He seemed to think everything about Finn was cool. Finn had sealed the deal by offering to take Oliver up in one of his planes. She felt a twinge of envy. Maggie couldn't think of the last time Oliver thought she was the bee's knees.

"I'm going to go outside and warm up the car so it's not freezing inside. I'll meet you guys out front in a few minutes," Finn said. He held up his palm and Oliver high-fived him.

Maggie knew she should feel grateful for Finn's offer to drive them to their new house rather than worrying about Oliver's reaction to him. After all, Finn had already done his job by flying them to Love from Anchorage. She shivered as she watched her son's gaze trailing after Finn. A fatherless boy would look for father figures anywhere and everywhere. She didn't want Oliver to get any ideas about her childhood pal being his new daddy.

Finn. He'd sure grown up into an extremely good-looking man. She imagined he drew lots of interest from the females in town. Not that she was looking! Maggie had no interest in romance, which was ironic considering she was smack in the center of Operation Love territory. She was well aware of the program since she'd read the newspaper articles and seen the television shows highlighting Mayor Jasper Prescott's matchmaking campaign.

Love, Alaska, was Maggie's shot at redemption. God had blessed her by making her a mother. She owed Oliver a stable, loving home. It was her responsibility. Although her childhood buddy seemed like a nice guy, Maggie had no intention of getting fooled again by good looks and a smile. Romance wasn't on her agenda.

Love had certainly made a fool of her in the past. It had cost Maggie so very much. Her peace of mind. Dignity. Her reputation. Sam had betrayed her and Oliver. Now, she was solely focused on her son and creating a safe, emotionally healthy world for him. His needs came first. Oliver might want a father, but Maggie definitely didn't want a husband. She was determined to raise her son by herself and be both mother and father to him.

Maggie needed to keep her eyes on the prize. She had to focus on getting the shop ready for the grand opening and find a sitter for Oliver for the hours he wasn't in school. A whole new world was opening up for them. Maggie wasn't going to squander these opportunities.

Chapter Four

As he walked toward his truck Finn let the frigid blast of wintry air wash over him. He'd come outside so he could warm up the car for Maggie and Oliver and place the booster seat inside his truck, but it also provided him with him a few minutes by himself so he could reel in his thoughts.

Although the situation with Agnes was terrible for Maggie, he couldn't stop thinking about the timing. Tobias's will stipulated that he needed to help Maggie set up Keepsakes and provide assistance with the grand opening. Perhaps part of helping Maggie could be watching Oliver after school let out so he wouldn't be underfoot while she set up shop. He could be the part-time sitter.

Finn wasn't a childcare expert by any means, but he had ties to the community, a way with kids and a fun-loving personality. And for the next few weeks he could devote himself to the position, until such time as he could collect his inheritance from Tobias. While Oliver was in school he could help Maggie with setting up the store and ordering any inventory she needed, as well as doing any heavy lifting. By the time four weeks elapsed, Agnes could very well be on the mend.

It would be win-win for everyone.

The truck had considerably warmed up by the time Finn spotted Maggie and Oliver standing in the doorway of the Moose Café. Maggie held a large shopping bag in her hands. He imagined it contained the meals Hazel had prepared for the two of them. Finn stepped down from the driver's seat and walked Oliver and Maggie across the street to his truck. He helped Oliver step up into the cab, then took the bag from Maggie before lending her his hand, which felt so small in his larger one.

Once she was buckled in, Finn closed the door and made his way over to the driver's seat. As Finn began to drive down Jarvis Street, he found himself pointing out local places of interest. He could hear pride ringing out in his own voice.

"The sheriff's office is right across from the Moose Café," Finn said, gesturing toward the building. It had been festively decorated with wreaths and red ribbons.

"Is there really a sheriff who works there?" Oliver asked in an awestruck tone.

Finn nodded. "Of course there is. His name is Boone Prescott. He's Cameron's brother. And he happens to be a friend of mine in case you'd like to meet him."

"Whoa. I've never met a real-life sheriff before," Oliver said in a gushing tone. "I've only seen them in movies. I hope when I meet him he shows me his shiny gold badge."

Finn chuckled, enjoying seeing things through Oliver's fresh eyes. Love was a wonderful town, full of heart and connections and fortitude. The townsfolk had pluck and grit. For many years he hadn't appreciated his hometown. He'd been too busy trying to stuff down the painful aspects of his childhood. Running away and avoiding all the memories had been the easier path.

And in the process he'd also placed a wedge between himself and Declan. He wanted them to be close again, and they were slowly getting there.

"Oh, what a charming bookstore," Maggie said, turning to gaze out of the window at the Bookworm shop. "The holiday decorations really make the store come to life."

Finn nodded in agreement as he took a quick glance at the whimsical window display. Maisie had really gone overboard this year. Sugarplum fairies and dancing reindeer with glowing noses, as well as chubby snowmen and falling snowflakes. He wasn't usually sappy about Christmas, but there was something about the decorations that brought out his sentimental side. Finn couldn't help but think back on the wonderful holidays he'd spent with his family before the bottom had fallen out of their world.

His parents had always gone the extra mile to make sure they knew the true meaning of Christmas. The emphasis on the birth of Christ had been at the forefront, but there had always been surprises waiting for them under the Christmas tree—train sets and skateboards and dirt bikes. One year his father had gifted his mother with a toy poodle she'd named Pippin. Finn smiled at the memory of his mother squealing with joy.

"There's Keepsakes," Finn said, slowing down as

they passed the boarded-up shop. It would have been odd if he hadn't pointed it out. Truthfully, the shop had seen better days. Numerous townsfolk had deliberated over whether to fix up the exterior before Maggie arrived in town. In the end, it had been the general consensus that since Maggie was now the legal owner, only she could make the decision as to how Keepsakes should look.

He watched as a myriad of emotions crossed Maggie's face. Finn reached out and patted her hand. "Don't worry. All it needs is some spit and polish. You'll get it done in no time at all."

Although Maggie nodded in agreement, the look emanating from her eyes was full of trepidation. He wished there was something more he could say to make her feel confident about her new venture.

Finn continued to point out landmarks—the post office, the trading post, the newly opened hair salon, the toy store and the pawnshop. Finn slowed down as they approached the library.

"Right there is the Free Library of Love. My sister-in-law, Annie, works there as head librarian." He glanced over at Maggie. "They have a great children's section."

"It's beautiful," Maggie said. "I can't wait to explore this town at my leisure. There have been a lot of changes since I was last here."

"As you may remember, it's a small town," Finn conceded. "But it's full of treasures. I think you'll be very content here once you settle in."

Finn continued down the snow-covered streets, taking a left as he turned off toward the mountain road. It was bit more difficult to navigate than the main streets in town. Finn had learned to drive on these roads so he knew it wasn't anything he couldn't handle. But he worried about Maggie living out here and driving into town. He made a mental note to remind her about taking safety precautions and outfitting her vehicle properly with all-wheel drive and studded tires. Although she hadn't mentioned it, he assumed Maggie had also inherited Tobias's truck.

The sound of Oliver's chatter filled the silence once Finn ran out of things to say. He didn't know how to explain it, but there was something about Maggie that made him feel tongue-tied. That fact would probably make his brother laugh out loud since as a kid he'd always complained about Finn never shutting up.

Once he spotted the mailbox announcing they had reached Twelve Mountain Court, Finn turned down the long driveway and drove past tall snowcapped pine and spruce trees until he reached the house. The log cabin was a modest size. Perfect for a small family. In Maggie and Oliver's case it would be more than enough. He parked the car right in front, then jumped out of the car to grab the baggage.

"Can I help?" Oliver's little voice sounded just behind him.

He turned around and handed Oliver the smallest piece of luggage he could find. "Thanks for helping out." Finn walked behind Oliver. The corners of his mouth twitched as he watched the child using all his strength to carry the bag. This kid sure had pluck.

Maggie led the way to the front door, pulling out a set of keys and opening up the house for them. As they stepped over the threshold, the smell of cinnamon floated in the air. Finn placed their belongings down by the staircase.

On the hallway side table sat a bowl of pinecones emanating a wonderful scent. A big fruit basket sat next to it. A bowl full of candy canes sat nearby. Maggie walked over and reached for the card placed on the table. She began to read it out loud. "'Enjoy your new home. Blessings! Your new friends in Love.'" A small sound escaped her lips. To Finn's ears it sounded a little bit like a sob. Maggie wasn't facing him, but he could see her wiping at her eyes.

"Mommy, why are you crying?" Oliver asked. "I don't like to see you cry."

"Maggie, are you all right?" Finn asked as a strange tightening sensation spread across his chest. The thought of Maggie awash in tears deeply bothered him.

She turned around to face them, sniffing back tears. "I'm fine. I'm just a bit overwhelmed at their generosity. Everyone in Love has been so kind to us, including you, Finn." Gratitude shimmered in her eyes. "I'm very thankful."

"You're quite welcome," Finn said. "It's one of the things I love best about this town. The people here sure do know how to roll out the red carpet. I'm just glad those are happy tears."

Oliver looked up at Finn. "She cried a lot when my dad died."

An awkward silence settled over them. Finn didn't know how to respond to Oliver's innocent statement. Clearly, Maggie didn't either.

He knew from personal experience how devastating

it felt to lose a parent at such a tender age. His heart ached for Oliver…and Maggie.

"Oliver, why don't you head upstairs and check out your new bedroom?" Maggie suggested, steering the conversation away from the uncomfortable topic. Oliver took off and began racing up the stairs, the sound of his footsteps echoing in the silence.

"You two must be exhausted." Finn could see the slight shadows under Maggie's eyes. He needed to get out of her hair so she could explore her new digs and enjoy some downtime. A sigh slipped past Maggie's lips. "This day has been truly a blessing, but I am tired. It's a long way from Massachusetts to Alaska."

There wasn't any point in dragging his feet any longer. He'd been waiting for a moment alone with Maggie so he could broach the subject of Tobias's will. He needed to tell her about the stipulation whereby he would be assisting her with her new store.

"Maggie, I need to tell you something."

The serious tone of his voice caused a wrinkle to appear on her forehead.

"Okay. What is it?" she asked, her voice sounding tense.

"Tobias left me a sum of money in his will," he explained.

Maggie's features relaxed. She gifted him with a sweet smile. "That's wonderful, Finn. He was always crazy about you back when we were kids."

"Tobias believed in me. He made me feel I could do anything I put my mind to if I tried hard enough. Over the years he became an honorary grandfather to me." He shifted from one foot to another, then shoved his hands in his front pants pockets. "He loved you very much, Maggie. He talked about you all the time. I think that must be why he put a special stipulation in the will. In order to get the inheritance, I need to help you get the store up and running. Specifically, for a period no less than four weeks."

Maggie let out a surprised sound. She knit her brows together. "What? Why would Uncle Tobias have placed such a condition on his bequest?"

Finn ran his hand over his face. "I think he was worried about it being too much for you. He knew you'd been through a lot, having lost your husband last year and being a single mother. I believe he thought he would be making things better for you by giving you someone to help out with everything." Finn let out a ragged sigh. "And I know he was trying to help me. It's pretty humbling. Frankly, this couldn't have materialized at a better time for me. He knew that I needed an infusion of cash to buy into my brother's aviation business."

"That was Uncle Tobias's way, wasn't it? Even as a kid I remember all the times he tried to help Mama." She twisted her mouth. "She went from relationship to relationship, marriage to marriage—dragging me with her all across the country. Bless him. Uncle Tobias tried his best to turn things around for us, but it didn't work."

"He was a good man. And an even better friend." Finn missed Tobias more than mere words could convey. There hadn't been many people in his life who'd believed in him without reservation. It was because of his encouragement that Finn had approached Declan about becoming a partner in O'Rourke Charters. And now, thanks to Tobias's generosity, his long-held dream was within reach.

"I appreciate all of Uncle Tobias's efforts on our behalf," Maggie said. "To be perfectly honest, I'm going to need all the help I can get so Keepsakes can open as soon as possible." She made a tutting sound. "Leave it to Uncle Tobias to realize I couldn't do it all on my own."

"He believed in you. I know that for a fact," Finn said. "He said it all the time."

"Thanks for saying so. I don't ever want to let him down," Maggie said. "I want to do everything in my power to make Keepsakes successful."

"And I know you're looking for someone to watch your son while you're getting the shop up and running."

Maggie nodded. "Yes, I am. Do you happen to know of someone? I'm racing against the clock to find a reliable caregiver."

"I understand," Finn said, stroking his chin. "It's hard to focus on Keepsakes with an energetic six-year-old running around."

"If you know of anyone reliable to watch Oliver I'd be very grateful. As you can see, he's a sweet boy. A little high-spirited, but a good kid."

Finn cleared his throat. He shifted from one foot to the other. "Well, actually, I do know of someone."

Maggie's face lit up like sunshine. "You do? That's wonderful. Who is it? Maybe I can interview them tomorrow."

He gazed directly into Maggie's eyes, hoping she would see his sincerity. "It's me, Maggie. I could help watch Oliver."

* * *

Maggie wasn't certain she'd heard Finn correctly. "Did you say that you want the job? As Oliver's babysitter?"

"Yes," he said with a nod. "Not permanently or anything. I just figured since I'm already going to be helping you out at Keepsakes I could watch Oliver after he gets off from school. That way you would still be able to take care of business at the store and I would still technically be fulfilling the conditions of the will. I'd still be helping you with the store during the hours before Oliver gets out of school."

Maggie's head was spinning. Finn had thrown her a curveball. Although she knew Finn, so many years had passed by since they had truly known one another.

"What experience do you have with watching children?" she asked, wondering how she could let him down easy without hurting his feelings. She had never imagined hiring a man to watch her son. Finn didn't strike her as a babysitter.

"Not a lot really," Finn confessed. "But I used to be a head counselor at an overnight camp and I watch Cameron's daughter, Emma, from time to time. I'm honest and fun loving." Finn grinned. "Kids really like me. Just ask Hazel or Jasper. They can vouch for me."

She tugged at her shirt. "Well, that's all fine and good, but I need a qualified professional to watch my son while I'm working."

"*Need* being the operative word, Maggie. You're in a bind. Truthfully, so am I. I need to fulfill the terms of Tobias's will so I can partner up with my brother. That means we have to get Keepsakes in tip-top shape so it can open up as soon as is humanly possible. Working with your son underfoot could be problematic. This could be a mutually beneficial situation."

Maggie locked gazes with Finn. "I appreciate your offer, but I don't think it would work out."

He narrowed his gaze. "And why is that, Maggie? When you think about it, it's perfect. You've known me since we were kids. I'm not the bogeyman. Oliver already knows me. And he likes me. I'm trustworthy. You and your son's lives were in my hands when I flew you here from Anchorage. Surely you can see that?"

Suddenly, Maggie felt annoyed at Finn for putting her on the spot like this "It isn't about liking or not liking someone. Yes, that's important, but I need to find someone who's a good fit overall."

"I know you probably think a woman's touch is best, but you're wrong. Oliver could benefit from spending time with a man. It's written all over him."

Maggie bristled. Who did Finn think he was to tell her what her son needed? "Oliver is fine," she said in a crisp voice. "I give him lots of love. He isn't lacking anything. His father passed away quite suddenly a year ago. It's been hard wading our way through the shock and grief, but I've been acting as both mother and father for him. I've been doing the best I can."

Finn held up his hands. "It wasn't meant as an insult. I just know—I know what it's like to lose a parent at a young age." His voice softened. "I know what he's going through firsthand. It's a long process."

"I know," she said in a clipped tone. "I've been walking with him every step of the way." She hated the defensive tone of her voice, but it felt like Finn was telling her she wasn't doing a good job with Oliver. It hit her in her most vulnerable place—her fear of not being a decent mother to her son.

"You know what? Forget I said anything," Finn said. "I apologize for upsetting you. I just thought we both could make lemonade out of lemons. Forgive me. I shouldn't have brought it up."

He quickly moved toward the door, turning back to her from the threshold. "Good night, Maggie. If you want to hit the ground running with the store, I can meet you there first thing tomorrow morning. With four weeks until Christmas, we're really pressed for time. Ideally, if you can get the shop open in two weeks you can still rake in some great proceeds from holiday sales."

Maggie let out a squeak. "Two weeks?"

Finn nodded. "Keepsakes has always been a big holiday-themed shop on Jarvis Street. It's a Christmas staple here in town. The shop was shuttered last year a few months after the holidays. At the time no one knew Tobias was sick, so it perplexed a lot of folks."

She chewed on her lip. "I don't want to lose out on holiday sales, especially if people are anticipating it being open this year in time for Christmas. Why don't we meet at Keepsakes at nine? That way I can let Oliver sleep in and then get him breakfast before I head to town."

"Do you need me to swing by and pick you guys up?" Finn offered.

"Thanks for the offer, but Hazel gave me the key to Uncle Tobias's truck. I'll make sure to take it easy down the mountain road." Part of Maggie wanted Finn to come pick her up, but she knew it was important to start doing things for herself. She didn't want to take the easy way out. The thought of driving down the mountain road was a bit scary, but she was determined to face it head-on.

"Well then, I'll meet you in front of Keepsakes tomorrow morning. And welcome to Love." He opened the door and disappeared into the frosty Alaskan night.

"'Night," Maggie called out after him. She shut the door behind Finn and leaned against it. She felt completely exhausted after her long journey, the news about Agnes and her awkward discussion with Finn about Oliver. She let out a ragged breath.

"Why don't you want Finn to watch me?" She turned toward the sound of her son's voice. He was sitting at the bottom of the steps staring at her with big eyes.

"Oliver, what have I told you about eavesdropping on adult conversations?"

"I wasn't. At least not on purpose." There was a sheepish expression etched on Oliver's face. "I was thirsty, so I came back downstairs."

Maggie walked over to the staircase and reached for her son's hand. "Let's go get some water."

Once they were in the kitchen, Maggie went over to the cupboard and pulled out a mug. She turned the faucet on and filled it halfway. Oliver sat down at the kitchen table and Maggie handed him the water.

"Why don't you like Finn?" he asked before taking a generous sip of water.

Maggie gasped. "I do like Finn. We were friends when we were kids. And he's a really great pilot. But that doesn't mean I want him to be— "

"My manny?" Oliver asked.

Maggie couldn't help but giggle. "Manny? Where in the world did you hear that expression, Oliver?"

"Back home one of the kids in my class had one. *Manny* is a male nanny," he explained in a matter-of-fact tone.

"I know, Oliver. But I had no idea you would know."

"I know a lot of things. More than you think I know." Oliver's sad expression tugged at her heartstrings. Maggie wasn't sure she wanted to know what Oliver was talking about. Did he know more about Sam's death than she'd ever realized? She prayed it wasn't true. It was such a horrible thing for a little boy to wrap his head around.

"You're getting to be such a big boy," Maggie said, wishing she could turn back time to when Oliver was a little toddler in diapers. He was growing by leaps and bounds.

"I like Finn. A lot. It would be super cool if he could watch me while you're setting up our new store." Oliver was now pleading with her.

"It makes sense that you like him. But I need to have faith in the person who watches you. That doesn't come easily."

"He flew us all the way here in his seaplane. You trusted him to do that."

Sometimes Oliver's maturity shocked Maggie. He was wise beyond his years. There was nothing she could say to refute his statement. It was the truth.

"I appreciate your opinion, but this is something Mommy has to decide on her own. It's grown folks' business," Maggie said in a gentle voice.

Oliver rolled his eyes and groaned. "I hate when you say that."

Maggie chuckled at the look etched on her son's face. A feeling of immense love for Oliver hummed inside her heart.

As Maggie prepared for bed a little while later, thoughts of Finn's proposition continued to float through her mind. Was it really so out of the question? What had she really known about Agnes before she'd offered her the position? Surely she knew way more about Finn. After all, they'd been childhood playmates. More than that, she realized. They'd been besties.

Best friends forever. Hadn't they promised each other they would always be friends? And even though two decades had passed, she still felt as if she knew Finn. He seemed different, but deep down she sensed he was still the same comical, lovable boy. Would it be such a grand leap of faith to trust him to care for Oliver?

Oliver's pleas ran through her mind as she began to drift off to a peaceful sleep. Had she made a huge mistake in dismissing Finn's offer to watch Oliver?

Chapter Five

Bright and early the next morning, Maggie woke up to greet the first day of her new life in Alaska. While Oliver was eating a bowl of cereal, she went out on the back porch and took in the breathtaking vista stretched out before her. White-capped mountains loomed in the distance. Although the December air was frigid, it was clean and crisp. She let out a gasp as she spotted a majestic eagle soaring in the air. She couldn't look away from the bird's graceful moves. It made her feel centered and peaceful.

She shoved her hands in the pockets of her heavy winter coat. It was pretty cold out here, but she felt helpless to tear her gaze away from the view staring back at her. In all her life she had never seen such pristine land.

"I did it," she said in a triumphant voice. Despite all of her fears, Maggie had gathered up her courage and traveled all the way to this quaint fishing village. She was transforming her life. And she was now officially a business owner. Keepsakes might need some sprucing up, but from her childhood recollections, it had been a wonderful shop specializing in heartwarming treasures. It had always enjoyed a loyal, solid clientele.

She was going to be working side by side with Finn thanks to Uncle Tobias's directive in his will. Leave it to her uncle to protect her even after his passing. Maggie didn't have any friends in Love, and even though her friendship with Finn went back decades, she still felt connected to him. And she needed his friendship. He had always been a source of light and laughter. Maggie could sorely use it now as a newcomer to a town where everyone seemed to know each other. She and Oliver were basically strangers here in Love, despite their connection to Uncle Tobias.

The past year had been filled with an aching loneliness Maggie couldn't even put into words. Finding acceptance here in Love would be life altering. As she stood and stared out across her two acres of land, Maggie felt incredibly blessed. The past had been nightmarish, but the future felt hopeful.

Thank You, Lord. For blessings great and small. Even though I've doubted Your presence in the past, I know You must be here with me. I've felt You. At times it seemed like a push against my back, propelling me forward when I didn't even think I could get out of bed. At other times I felt this groundswell of confidence building up inside me.

A sudden rapping sound rang out behind her. When she turned around, Oliver had smashed his face against the glass patio window and was making funny faces at her. Maggie grinned at her son's goofiness. There was no question about it. Oliver seemed less stressed and

happier since they had arrived in Alaska. Maybe there
was something in the air here.

A half hour later, Maggie began the drive to town
from her new home. According to Hazel, Uncle Tobias's truck had recently been serviced by an auto body
shop. Maggie appreciated the gesture. Having reliable
transportation was of vital importance. The roads were
packed with snow and there were a few slick spots.
Maggie drove very gingerly. Thankfully, she was pro-
ficient at driving in wintry conditions due to the years
she'd lived in New England. She just needed to focus
on that aspect instead of giving in to her nerves about
Alaskan road conditions.

Oliver sat in his booster seat, pointing and gesturing toward anything of interest he spotted outside his
window. The toy store was of particular interest to him.

"Mom! Look at that toboggan! I'm putting it on my
Christmas list," he shouted, his voice brimming with
enthusiasm. "I could really fly on it."

Maggie smiled and made a mental note to purchase
the toboggan for Oliver. He deserved something spectacular.

She would make sure this Christmas was full of surprises and blessings and dreams come true for Oliver. A
toboggan would be really special for his first Christmas
in Alaska. Years ago Maggie and Finn had flown down
the mountain at Deer Run Lake on matching sleds. Finn
had surprised her by writing her name in indelible ink
on one of the sleds. Maggie chuckled at the memory
of how angry Declan had been about Finn giving his
sled to Maggie.

Thankfully, her phone's GPS had guided her perfectly to Uncle Tobias's shop. *My shop*, she corrected herself. It was hard to wrap her head around her new reality. In one fell swoop Maggie was a home owner, as well as the owner of a business and a truck. Her life had never been filled with so much promise.

Thank You, Lord, for all of these blessings.

Maggie felt startled by all of the spontaneous prayers she'd been uttering since arriving in Alaska. It was the second one today.

It had been a very long time since she had spoken on such a regular basis to God. They had come to a crossroads back when her life fell apart and Sam died in such a shocking manner. Maggie shivered as the memories of that terrible time crashed over her in unrelenting waves. It had felt as if the entire world had turned against her. Except for Uncle Tobias. He had soothed and comforted her, even though unbeknownst to her, he was dealing with his own terminal kidney issues and dialysis at the time. Her chest tightened as she remembered his invitation to come live with him in Alaska.

"Maggie, my door is always open for you and Oliver. Just say the word and I'll buy the plane tickets for you."

"That's very generous of you, Uncle Tobias. I'm wary of uprooting Oliver so soon after Sam's passing. But it's nice to know I have options," she'd told him.

"You'll always have a home here in Love," he'd told her in a voice clogged with emotion.

He had continued to invite her until his health condition had deteriorated. By the time Maggie discovered Uncle Tobias was so ill, he'd been in his last weeks of life. Maggie wasn't sure she would ever forgive herself for not being by Uncle Tobias's side in the last moments

An Alaskan Christmas

of his life. Why hadn't he told her about his illness? She
had the feeling he hadn't wanted her to go through another ordeal after what Sam had put them through. Maggie still wished she'd known Uncle Tobias was so sick.
It would have added an urgency to his invitation. For
all intents and purposes, he had been her closest family
member with the exception of Oliver. She couldn't even
count her mother, since their relationship was estranged.

A soft tapping on her window drew her out of her
thoughts. Finn was standing there with a determined
look on his face. In the clear light of day, she wasn't
sure how to feel about him helping her put the shop in
order. Although they had once been the best of friends,
they were now essentially strangers. *Doing it all by
myself would have felt empowering.* She prayed Finn
wasn't going to try to boss her around or take control
of things. Maggie had put up with a lot of that behavior
in her marriage to Sam. She wouldn't stand for it again!

She let out a sigh. She needed to stay positive and
stop blocking her blessings. Even though decades stood
between them, she knew Finn was a good person. Perhaps working side by side would help them get back to
a place in time where they'd been able to finish each
other's sentences. It would be nice to get her best friend
back. And if Finn overstepped with regards to the shop,
she wouldn't hesitate to tell him to take a step back.

"Finn!" Oliver cried out, unbuckling himself and
practically vaulting out of the car.

Maggie stepped down from the driver's seat, watching as her son threw himself against Finn. She winced
at the sight of it, filled with worry about Oliver getting

so attached so soon. It wasn't her son's way to be so demonstrative.

"Oliver! Give Finn some breathing room," Maggie said, gently pulling Oliver away.

"It's okay. No one ever gets this excited to see me except my dog, Boomer," Finn said with an easy grin.

Oliver looked up at Finn. "You have a dog? What kind?"

"He's a rescue. Part terrier and part Labrador. My friend Ruby Prescott pointed him in my direction. She trains search-and-rescue dogs."

"Do you think she could find one for us?" Oliver asked.

"Slow down, cowboy," Maggie said with a chuckle. "A dog is a big responsibility. We need to settle in first before we make such a big decision about a pet."

Oliver stuck his lip out and sent her a mournful look.

Finn, clearly seeking to distract Oliver, clapped his hands together. "Why don't we go check out the shop?" he asked. "I'm sure Uncle Tobias has plenty of things inside to capture your attention. Maps. Puzzles. Maybe even a periscope."

Oliver nodded enthusiastically, seemingly forgetting he was disgruntled with his mother. Maggie sent Finn a look of gratitude.

They began walking toward the storefront. Maggie stopped in her tracks and looked up at the shabby exterior. The windows were completely covered with heavy brown paper, making it impossible to see inside. The sign was weathered and worn, clearly in need of a fresh coat of paint. A long-ago memory tugged at her. A beautiful sign in a cherry-red color. It was a simple fix, she realized. One she could take care of herself with a fresh can of red paint and a ladder. She would make sure it was restored to its former glory. Thankfully, Hazel had made arrangements on her behalf to have the electricity turned on in the shop.

She turned toward Finn. "How long has the place been closed?" Maggie asked.

Finn shrugged. "About seven months, give or take. It was open last Christmas per usual. Tobias started feeling poorly and then lost the desire to keep the shop open. For a long time though no one knew he was ill. He kept it close to the vest."

A feeling of guilt swept over Maggie. If she had accepted Uncle Tobias's invitation to move to Alaska a year ago, perhaps she could have kept the store open and helped take care of her uncle. At the time she hadn't been ready to make such a major life change. It was a missed opportunity, one she would regret for the rest of her life.

Maggie took the keys out of her purse and dangled them in the air. "Here we go." She inserted the gold key in the lock. As soon as she turned the knob and pushed the door open, a musty scent filled Maggie's nostrils. The interior was dark. All she could see were shapes and stacks of things piled up. She let out a cough as dust tickled her nostrils.

"Let me turn the lights on." Finn's arm reached out and he fumbled along the wall for a few seconds before the lights came on. The shop was now flooded with light. Maggie let out a shocked gasp. The entire shop was one big mess. Not a single surface was clear.

Boxes had been strewed everywhere. Some were even piled up on top of each other.

"Oh my word," she said, raising a hand to her throat. Maggie blinked, hoping it was an optical illusion rather than reality staring her in the face.

The entire place was in disarray. As her gaze swung around the establishment, Maggie was finding it difficult to even make sense of the layout. She spotted a counter and a cash register but there were random items piled up along the space.

"What in the world?" Finn exclaimed. He was standing behind her with Oliver at his side. How she wished her son wasn't here to witness this.

"This place is a wreck!" Oliver said, walking past Maggie and peering around him.

Maggie reached for her son's arm to stop him from venturing around the store. Things were stacked up high. It was very possible something could fall on top of him and he could get hurt.

"No one's been in here since Tobias shut up the shop," Finn said. "I had no idea this place looked like this. It's probably why he shuttered up the windows." Finn had a stunned expression etched on his face.

Maggie shook her head. She felt sick to her stomach. "I —I don't know what to think. This place isn't even close to being ready for a grand opening." Tears pooled in her eyes. Once again, she felt as if the rug had been pulled out from under her. She hadn't expected the place to be in pristine, ready-to-go condition, but nothing had prepared Maggie for the ramshackle appearance of the store.

"I think Mommy is going to cry again," Oliver said to Finn in a loud whisper.

Finn met her gaze. She tried her best to blink away the tears. She felt a few tears slide down her face. It was embarrassing. Maggie wanted to be a courageous person. Not someone who broke down every time she came upon a roadblock.

"I'm not crying, Oliver," she said in a shaky voice. "I've just got a little dust in my eyes."

"It is dusty in here," Oliver said, scrunching up his face as if he smelled something rotten.

Suddenly, she felt Finn's arm around her shoulder. He pulled her close to his side and began patting her on her shoulder. It felt comforting and solid. It had been such a long time since she'd been held up by a man's strong arms. For the first time since she'd come back it seemed as if no time at all had passed since they'd been inseparable running buddies. Finn had always been good at drying her tears over skinned knees and squabbles with her mother.

"It's going to be all right, Mags," he said, using his childhood nickname for her. "All this means is that we have our work cut out for us. We can do this."

Her lips trembled. "B-but Christmas is only a month away. It's important that I hit the ground running so I can take advantage of holiday sales."

Finn nodded. "I agree. Those holiday sales are crucial, which means we've got to get this place in tip-top shape. Starting today."

She sniffled. "You're right. I'm just afraid it will all fall apart," she confessed. "I knew everything seemed too perfect."

"Be strong and courageous. Do not be afraid or terrified because of them. For the Lord, your God, goes
with you; He will never leave you nor forsake you,"
flowed from Finn's lips.

Maggie was familiar with the Bible verse, but it had
been quite some time since she had cracked open a
Bible. His words were comforting. They settled around
her like a warm, cozy blanket.

"I know this must seem overwhelming," Finn said,
"and I totally get it. You weren't expecting to see the
place look like this."

She shook her head, her hair swinging around her
shoulders. "I thought maybe there'd be a little dust and
a few cobwebs. A few boxes stashed in the corner."
She threw her arms wide. "But this! It seems a bit like
a hoarder's dream."

"It's not as bad as all that." Finn looked around the
shop. "This place needs some TLC. You're probably
an expert at that, right? You're a mom. You've changed
dirty diapers and wiped messy chins and faces. Mothers are warriors. Just think of this as taking care of a
child, one who is totally dependent on you."

Maggie chuckled. Taking care of a child was nothing like clearing up this tornado. But at least she could
find humor in it. Finn had made her laugh at a moment
when she felt deflated. Just like the old days. When
they'd been ten years old Finn had brought humor and
light to her life. The two summers and one Christmas
she'd spent in Love palling around with Finn had been
the best days of her life. He'd always had the ability to
make her laugh. After all of these years, he still did.

She took a steadying breath. Finn was right. This

place needed some serious TLC. Uncle Tobias had gifted her with a magnificent inheritance. He had made it possible for her to change her circumstances. She'd had to fight her whole life just to keep her head above water. And even though she was terrified, Maggie wasn't going to give up without a battle.

She placed her purse down on a nearby counter after wiping it down with a towel, pushing aside a few boxes in the process. She unzipped her down jacket and tossed it on a chair covered with plastic. She turned back toward Finn and Oliver then dramatically pushed up her sleeves.

"Let's get to work, boys. We need to get this place set up for the Christmas rush."

Finn let out a roar of approval. He raised his arm in the air in a triumphant gesture. Oliver, looking like a pint-size version of Finn, did the exact same thing. Maggie didn't have time to worry about Oliver's instant bond with Finn. Who wouldn't be crazy about the man? He was charming and funny and he had the cutest smile she'd ever seen.

Maggie looked away from the distracting sight of Finn O'Rourke. She had a job to do. She was laying the foundation for a solid future in this town. If they could get Keepsakes ready to open in two weeks, it would be the best Christmas present of all.

After a few hours of trying to make a clear path through the mess and organize some of the merchandise, Finn realized Oliver was fading fast. The kid was practically bouncing off the walls and desperate to leave the store. Every few minutes Maggie would have to stop what she was doing to see to Oliver's needs. At this rate, Finn figured, it would be Easter before the place was cleaned up.

It wasn't a fair situation for the kid, Finn reckoned. He was too little to help and too young to understand why he couldn't. Something needed to be done so they could focus without interruption on the shop. Finn's entire future was riding on the successful reopening of Keepsakes.

Finn excused himself for a few minutes, then placed a call to Ruby Prescott, his dear friend and wife to his childhood buddy Liam Prescott.

"Hey, Ruby. It's Finn. I need a huge favor."

"Name it," Ruby said.

Finn wasn't surprised by Ruby's quick response. She was easygoing and sweet by nature. Beloved by the whole town. Adored by her husband, Dr. Liam Prescott, and their son, Aidan.

"I was wondering if Aidan is available for a last-minute playdate. To make a long story short, I'm helping out Tobias Richard's niece, Maggie. She arrived in Love yesterday and we're down at Keepsakes trying to get it up and running. Her son, Oliver, is with us. He's right around Aidan's age. So I figured—"

The sound of Ruby's tinkling laughter came across the line. "Poor thing. I'm guessing he's bored silly."

"That's putting it mildly. And to be honest, this place is a bit of a wreck," Finn admitted. "He really shouldn't be here until we get things more organized."

"I guess that explains why the windows were shuttered. Poor Tobias was such a proud man. He probably just became overwhelmed." Ruby made a tutting sound.

"Why don't we drive down and meet you over at the Moose Café? Oliver can have lunch with us and then I'll bring him back to our house so the two boys can hang out together. You can swing by and pick him up later this afternoon. How does that sound?"

Finn exhaled. "Sounds like you're a lifesaver."

Once he hung up with Ruby, Finn pulled Maggie aside to tell her about his phone call. The moment he saw Maggie's expression, Finn worried that he'd made the wrong move. Maggie didn't seem so thrilled with his having set up a playdate for Oliver.

"I'm just not sure I'm comfortable leaving Oliver with someone I don't know."

"Well, Ruby's a good friend of mine. I trust her implicitly. And you and I are old friends, Maggie. You can trust my judgment."

Maggie bit her lip. Finn could see the concern swirling in her eyes.

He reached out for Maggie's hand. He squeezed it tightly. "Trust me. I wouldn't put Oliver in a dangerous situation."

"I get anxious about my son, Finn. He's all I have," Maggie said in a low voice. She turned and looked at Oliver, who was sitting down and playing with an electronic device.

"It may sound silly to you, but when we lost his father so suddenly it made me really fearful of something happening to Oliver. All at once, life seemed really fragile. I guess you could say I lost my courage." She made a face. "I suppose it's safe to say I haven't gotten it back yet."

Finn nodded. His throat felt clogged with emotion. "I

know what it's like to lose someone you love very suddenly. It throws you completely off balance. It makes you question everything. I think you need to remind yourself of how far you've come." He winked at her. "After all, you made a huge move to Alaska and you're about to open up your own shop. That's not for the faint of heart."

"I don't want Oliver to pick up on my fears." She cast another glance at her son. "He can go on the playdate. He needs to be a little boy. And making a new friend his own age will be good for him."

Finn grinned at Maggie. "He'll love Aidan. And Ruby's the best. Now you and I can start unpacking some of these boxes without worrying about something toppling down and hurting Oliver."

"Sounds like a party," she said in a teasing voice.

Finn smiled at her joke. He felt relieved she was loosening up a little bit. Although he could tell she was a fantastic mother, Finn sensed she was a little bit tightly wound. The fact that she had agreed to the playdate was a good sign. He admired her for having the pluck and grit to drastically alter her life by moving to Alaska. After what she'd been through, he knew it couldn't have been easy. The past had the power to get in the way of a person's future.

Even after all these years, Finn still struggled with his own past. Just when he thought he had moved beyond it, the memories rose up to cast a shadow over the present. He prayed Maggie would find a way to find closure and embrace her new life.

Not only for herself, but for Oliver as well.

* * *

Leaving Oliver with Ruby and Aidan wasn't easy for Maggie. But meeting Ruby Prescott had left Maggie with a warm feeling about the woman. With her dark hair and café au lait–colored skin, Ruby was a radiant beauty. She seemed down-to-earth and kind. And like Maggie, she was a mother to a young boy. Aidan seemed like an amiable, content little charmer. Oliver and Aidan had quickly warmed to one another. When she left the Moose Café in order to head back to the shop, the trio was ordering lunch and the boys were giggling over a shared joke. She didn't know whether to laugh or cry over the fact that Oliver didn't even seem to notice her departure.

Small steps, she reminded herself. Everything in Alaska was new to her and she needed to accept the fact that her little boy was growing up. He would always be her baby, but she needed to allow him to spread his wings.

"There's stuff in here that needs to be tossed," Finn noted. He was standing with his arms folded across his chest. He looked handsome and authoritative. Maggie felt thankful he had been here with her when she had first opened up the shop. It had been an absolute shock to see Keepsakes in such a shambles. Back when she'd been a kid, the store had been in pristine condition. Having Finn at her side had made it bearable. It was a comfort to know she wasn't alone in this. She still harbored childhood memories of helping Uncle Tobias stock shelves and playing with the cash register. Sweet, enduring memories etched on her heartstrings.

"Why don't we make a toss pile and a viable-merchandise pile?" Maggie suggested.

Finn wiped his arm across his brow. "Sounds like a plan. You also should start coming up with prices. Once everything gets settled you can look online and research how much the items are worth to make sure you're on track." He held up a silver frame. "Some of them still have tags on them."

Maggie nodded.

They began working in companionable silence. She could hear Finn rustling around by the back of the store. She was tackling an area by the front counter. So far she hadn't come across any of the Christmas items. She needed to get her hands on them so she could come up with a festive window display and set up the front of the store with seasonal items.

She looked over at the front window and envisioned creating a beautiful Christmas display to attract customers. Perhaps a lovely nativity scene or something with lots of bells and whistles.

After an hour of searching through boxes, Maggie finally hit pay dirt.

"Whoa. I think I just stumbled upon the Christmas merchandise." She lifted the lid off one box and began to poke around inside it. There was an abundance of items. Individually packaged ornaments. Tiny Christmas village display items. Christmas flags. Festive banners. Light-up lawn displays.

Maybe she could set up the Christmas village in the window. It would look beautiful with all the little houses lit up and blanketed with fake snow.

Finn wiped his brow with the back of his hand.

"That's great. All of that stuff needs to be front and center as soon as the shop opens."

Maggie tugged at another box. It was sitting off to the side with nothing placed on top of it. When she opened the lid she saw mounds of tissue paper. She reached in and gently began unveiling the items. She let out a cry of delight as she laid eyes on the delicate snow globe. Inside was a snowman and a little girl. She shook it a little and watched as snowflakes began to swirl around inside. Maggie let out a sigh. She'd always wanted a snow globe collection. Her mother had considered her request as too extravagant for a child, so her wish for one always fell on deaf ears. After all these years, she still loved the beauty and grace of the glass creations.

"Snow globes. This whole box is filled with them." She held one up for Finn to see. "Isn't this exquisite?"

"Nice," Finn said with a nod of approval. "Those will fly off the shelves."

Maggie ran her fingers over the smooth surface of the snow globe. It was so beautiful she almost wished she could keep it. But she couldn't get sentimental over the items. The whole point in owning a shop was to sell merchandise for a profit.

You're not a kid anymore, she reminded herself. It was silly to feel sad over a snow globe she had never received for Christmas.

"Are you a snow globe enthusiast? You can't take your eyes off that one," Finn said.

"I guess so," Maggie said with a nod of her head. "I've never owned one, although as a kid I found them fascinating."

"You seem to feel the same way as an adult," Finn teased.

"I suppose I've always been drawn to them." Maggie gently placed the snow globe back in its box. She imagined a customer would pay a good amount for it.

"So tell me about Operation Love," she called out to Finn, hoping to distract herself from bittersweet memories. "I read a little about it on the internet, but you've seen it up close and personal—the successes, the failures." Maggie had been invited to sign up for the program weeks ago, but it wasn't something she was considering. For someone who had been burned by love, joining the town mayor's matchmaking initiative would not be a prudent idea. Finding love was not her objective in Alaska, although she was still curious about the program.

"It's been great for this town. For so long there was a female shortage. The male-female ratio was really unbalanced. It still is, but it's not as bad. And there are lots of couples who've gotten engaged and walked down the aisle as a result. Do you remember Boone Prescott? Declan's best friend?"

Boone! Dark hair, intense eyes and a quiet disposition. Boone had been joined at the hip with Finn's brother, Declan. He'd been the type of kid who had sat back and watched everything around him. It didn't surprise her how he'd ended up in law enforcement.

"Boone met his wife, Grace, through the program." Finn chuckled. "Grace came here as a participant in Operation Love, although she was really working undercover as a journalist to write a story about the program and the townsfolk. They had a few bumps along the way, but they found their happily-ever-after."

"What about you? Have you signed up?" she asked, imagining Finn would be a big draw in this small Alaskan town.

"Nope. And I don't plan to either. I'm not looking to settle down," he said in a brusque tone. "I like being single and unattached."

Maggie felt as if her eyes might bulge out of her head. "Really?" The question slipped out of her mouth before she could rein it back in.

Hmm. How had the women in this town allowed an Alaskan hottie like Finn to stay single? It seemed as if he would be a hot commodity in Love.

"Is that so hard to believe?" he asked, raising his eyebrows in her direction.

"I'm just surprised. You have so much to offer. And the way you are with Oliver and Aidan, I can't imagine you not being a father."

"Some things just aren't meant to be. I don't relish that type of responsibility." The tone of Finn's voice sounded resigned.

"Is this about your father and the way he walked away from you and Declan?" she asked, shocking herself by asking the probing question. If Finn hadn't been a childhood pal she would never have dared. But she couldn't deny her curiosity about his family. Back in the day Maggie had been envious of his picture-perfect family. How had it all fallen apart so disastrously?

Finn looked startled for a moment. His jaw looked tight. He seemed to be struggling to answer her question. "Yes, I'm sure that has something to do with it.

I've always been aware that it comes with a huge responsibility—one I'm not looking to assume."

The forlorn tone of his voice made her wish she hadn't been so nosy. No doubt she'd stirred up painful issues from the past. How would she like it if someone started probing into Sam's death? All of her family skeletons would come tumbling out of the closet. If the truth came out it was possible the townsfolk would treat her like a pariah, just as they had in Boston. She shivered at the thought, knowing Oliver's future could be compromised if that happened.

"I'm sorry for asking. It's none of my business," she said in a brisk tone. "I didn't mean to open any old wounds."

Finn met her gaze from across the room. "You should know something. In a town this small you'll probably hear it at some point." Finn let out a ragged sigh. "My mother was killed accidentally by my father. They were fooling around in our backyard one night with a shotgun and they'd had a few too many beers. One minute they were joking around and the next moment the gun went off by mistake. She died right there at our house."

Maggie felt as if she'd been holding her breath the entire time Finn spoke. His revelation was shocking. Her heart broke for him and the entire O'Rourke family and all they'd lost because of such a senseless tragedy. This whole time she'd been wondering about the adult version of Finn and trying to pinpoint all the ways in which he had changed. Now it was all clear. The little boy who had been filled with such mischief and light and heart didn't exist anymore. Trauma had forever changed him.

"Finn! I'm so sorry you went through that heartache. I know how much you loved her. She was such a beautiful and kindhearted woman. And she loved you all so very much."

Maggie remembered Finn's mother. Cindy O'Rourke. She'd been gentle and kind and her laughter had filled up their home. She had baked peanut butter cookies and made rocky-road fudge. Maggie had often wished that her own mother could be a lot more like Finn's.

Maggie had experienced her own share of hard knocks in her childhood, but nothing like what Finn had endured. Loss after loss after loss. It was heartbreaking.

Finn broke eye contact with her and looked down at one of the boxes. "It was unimaginable. Truth to be told, losing her almost broke me. It definitely tore my father apart. He ran away from Love because he couldn't bear the pain of what happened. He ended up spending some time in jail for petty crimes." His voice softened. "I understand why he left us and why everything in his life fell apart. It still hurts though. To lose our mother and then our father—" His voice became clogged with emotion. He cleared his throat, then began to rummage around in one of the boxes.

"And then your grandfather passed," she said as memories of a sweet, round-faced man with a deep-throated laugh sprang to mind. Killian O'Rourke had been such a source of pride and inspiration. Everyone in town had adored him.

"Yep. It was like a domino effect," he said, his head still bowed. "That one nearly did me in. When he got sick I left town. It was too painful for me to stay here and watch him die."

Maggie felt a chill sweep across her back. She felt Finn's agony acutely. It was infused in his voice. It radiated from every pore on his body. "It must have been agonizing."

"And Declan had to deal with yet another loss. Only this time he was all alone. I bailed on him."

Maggie didn't know what to say to try to make it all better. Maggie had been widowed before she even turned thirty years old. So she kept quiet, knowing all too well some things couldn't be fixed or smoothed over.

"So you see, Maggie, I'm the last person who feels the need to get married and raise a family. I'm not exactly dependable. When Declan really needed me to help care for our grandfather, I was exploring Yosemite and backpacking my way through life." He let out a bitter-sounding laugh. "Nice, huh?"

She shrugged. "You did what you had to do to get by. No one has the right to judge you."

"Except myself," he muttered.

They both settled back into digging through inventory. Maggie tried to focus on the job at hand, but her thoughts kept veering back toward Finn and his tragic past. It made her chest tighten to imagine the ten-year-old Finn having to deal with such horror. Sam's death had put Oliver through the wringer, but Maggie had been by his side steadfastly throughout the whole ordeal.

She now knew a whole lot more about the adult Finn than she'd ever imagined discovering. He associated family with loss. Heartache. He hadn't put it into those exact words, but she sensed he was still running away.

Although he was physically here in his hometown, he was afraid to attach himself to anything significant.

She didn't blame him. Finn O'Rourke had lost a lot in his life. She imagined he didn't have a whole lot more to give of his heart. She knew a little bit about how it felt to feel so beaten down and jaded. Frankly it was a shame. Because something told her that like his childhood self, Finn had more heart and soul in his little pinkie than most had in their entire bodies.

Chapter Six

Finn loved Christmas. It was one of his most closely kept secrets. Although he hardly ever showed it, on the inside he was like a little kid bubbling with excitement in anticipation of the holiday season. Finn wasn't sure even Declan knew how much he loved the hoopla and the decorations and the feeling of goodwill toward humankind. As a man who had messed up a lot in his life, he deeply appreciated the idea of reconciliation at Christmas. It was the perfect time to embrace the Lord. He was deeply flawed, but God still loved him.

Ever since he was a kid, Finn had thought it was pretty awesome how he could mess up a million times, but it didn't change the way God felt about him.

I have loved thee with an everlasting love. The verse from Jeremiah had always stuck with him. It had sustained him during the worst moments of his life. Even though he was a sinner, he still had God's love.

And way past the age when kids believed in Santa, Finn had continued to believe with all his might. Although most people thought a little bit of the Christmas spirit evaporated once the secret of Santa was revealed, it had only made Finn more convinced of the beauty of this sacred time of year. Along with God, people were at the heart of Christmas.

On his way into town this morning he had cranked up the radio and rocked out to Christmas music. It didn't matter that he couldn't carry a tune. He could still belt out the lyrics about someone rocking around the Christmas tree. As he stood outside Keepsakes he stopped and looked up at the faded sign and the ramshackle exterior.

It needed to be spruced up before the snow came. The local weatherman had been reporting about a snowstorm hitting town in a few days. He made a mental note to mention it to Maggie and to remind her to stock up on household food and supplies by tomorrow.

Finn let himself into the shop with the key Maggie had given him. He flicked on the lights and surveyed the store. Although progress had been made, there was still lots to do before Keepsakes could open its doors. After about ten minutes of rooting around the shop, Finn heard the front door being opened. Maggie came in bundled up in a burgundy-colored coat and matching scarf. Both looked as if they'd seen better days.

"Good morning," Finn said.

Maggie grimaced. "'Morning."

Her normally friendly greeting was missing in action today. He studied her closely. Her eyes were red and it was clear to Finn she had been crying.

Finn frowned. "Wasn't today Oliver's first day of kindergarten?" Shouldn't Maggie be smiling?

Maggie nodded but didn't say a word.

"How'd it go?" he asked. He was being polite by asking. Finn didn't want to know the answer. He could see it all over her face. The idea of Maggie crying made him feel incredibly uncomfortable. He wouldn't know what to do to console her if she broke down in front of him. And the idea of her being in pain made his chest tighten uncomfortably.

"Terrible," she said in a mournful voice. "I walked him inside like all of the other parents and we stayed until the teacher rang the start of school bell." Maggie heaved out a deep breath. "Then all of the kids started waving to their parents and some of them were having a hard time saying goodbye."

Finn winced. "Let me guess. Oliver cried?"

Maggie put her hands on her hips. "No, he didn't cry. Nor did he wave or run up to me and give me a farewell kiss. He smiled, then turned around and joined the others for singing class. Seems they're putting on a little Christmas show and Oliver needs to memorize four songs."

"That's great. Sounds like he took to it like a duck to water."

Maggie nodded, lips trembling. "Yep. Oliver came through it with flying colors. Not so sure about Mom though. I feel as if I've been run over by a Mack truck. It's rough being the new kid in town."

"Maggie, you're going to be fine. Everyone knows that the first day at a new school is harder on the parents than on the kids. It's a thing."

"It is? You're not pulling my leg are you?" she asked in a wary voice.

"Of course not. And you should be really proud of yourself. Oliver is a well-adjusted kid, despite having lost a parent. Do you have any idea how incredible that is?"

A smile slowly crept across Maggie's face. Although he thought she was beautiful, a full-fledged smile transformed her into someone extraordinary. "It is pretty amazing now that you mention it." She ran her hand through her shoulder-length chestnut-colored hair and beamed.

"Hey! Look over there!" Finn cried out, pointing at a spot near the front counter.

"What is it?" Maggie asking, whipping around to see what had gotten Finn so excited.

"There's a clear spot over there. Can you believe it?" Finn asked.

Maggie shook her head and giggled. "It was bound to happen one of these days."

Finn enjoyed making Maggie laugh. He liked watching the way her eyes crinkled and her nose scrunched up. He had a feeling she had no idea of her appeal.

It was sad that they'd resorted to this type of humor, Finn realized, but seeing a clear spot in the shop felt like spectacular news. They had been working nonstop for days to get rid of heaps of items they'd deemed as trash and get the shop in decent order. For the first time it seemed as if there was a light at the end of the tunnel. With the holidays rapidly approaching, they needed to open as soon as possible.

A sudden knocking on the door halted their conversation.

Maggie looked at him with big eyes. "Someone's at the door."

He held his finger up to his lips.

"Hello," a masculine voice called out. "Maggie. Maggie Richards. It's Dwight. I've come to welcome you back to Love and to offer my condolences about Tobias."

Finn let out a soft groan and rolled his eyes.

"Dwight? As in Dwight Lewis?" she asked in a loud whisper. "The kid who used to wear bow ties and Bermuda shorts?"

"One and the same," Finn answered with a grin. "And in case you were wondering, he still wears those bow ties." Maggie started laughing, then clapped her hand over her mouth to silence herself.

It felt nice to have history with Maggie. They could share little inside jokes and memories from a time when his life had been idyllic.

Maggie scrunched up her nose. "Didn't we have a nickname for him?"

Finn smirked. "I think we had a few. If you open that door and let him in, word will travel around Love as fast as quicksilver about the state of things inside this shop."

Maggie's eyes widened. "That could be very bad for business," Maggie whispered. Finn wanted to laugh out loud at the outraged expression on her face, but he knew Dwight might hear him. Finn wouldn't be surprised if the town treasurer had his ear pressed up against the door.

"I'm heading over to the Moose to visit my fiancée, so if you'd like to come say hello I'll be across the way," Dwight said in a raised voice.

Finn rolled his eyes at Dwight's mention of his fiancée, Marta. Dwight had been single for a long time, but the minute he fell in love and got engaged to the chef at the Moose Café, he'd decided not to let anyone forget his status. For more reasons than one it rubbed Finn the wrong way.

Maggie and Finn huddled next to each other, waiting for any slight sound to indicate Dwight's presence. They were standing so close to one another Finn could see the golden flecks in her green eyes. He could also hear the shallow sound of her breathing.

"Do you think he's gone?" Maggie whispered. She was leaning so close to him her hair swung against his cheek.

"Mmm-hmm," Finn said, feeling slightly bowled over by his close proximity to Maggie. She smelled like flowers. Roses, perhaps. It was a heady scent. She was all kinds of pretty. There was an air of grace about her, he thought. She was soft and feminine, but there was strength at her core, even if she didn't seem to realize it. Losing a husband so tragically and at such a young age could harden a person, Finn imagined. But she didn't seem bitter at all. Maggie seemed determined to find stability for Oliver and to make the best of her inheritance from Tobias.

"I think we're safe," Finn said, reluctantly moving away from Maggie.

"Phew," Maggie said, swiping the back of her hand across her forehead. "He was persistent."

Finn made a face. "He's town treasurer now. You really have no idea. On any given day he's like a dog with a bone."

Maggie put her hands on her hips. "How about we stop for lunch and then tackle the shelving areas?"

"Sounds good, but I don't think we should go over to the Moose Café," Finn said, wiggling his eyebrows.

"Unless of course you want Dwight to know we were here the whole time."

She made a face. "No way. We can just pick up some sandwiches at the deli."

Finn cast his gaze around the store. With every hour he and Maggie spent clearing up the place, Finn was moving one step closer to his dream—co-ownership of O'Rourke Charters. Working side by side with his younger brother would be life altering. Finn still had a lot of work to do in order to show Declan he was back in Love for good.

Now that the shelves had been cleaned and polished, Keepsakes was beginning to look like an actual store. For the first time, Maggie knew they were out of the woods. She sat down on a crate and breathed in a deep sigh of relief. She cracked open a diet soda and raised it up in the air in a celebratory gesture. Although she never would have said it out loud to Finn, there had been many times when she'd doubted they would reach their goal in time. It wasn't very often she felt proud of herself, but in this moment she felt as if she had accomplished something monumental.

God was good. He had led her to this moment, and even though she had wavered many times in her faith, He was still showing her His grace.

A few minutes earlier Finn had volunteered to pick up Oliver at the bus stop then take him over to the Moose Café for a treat. Knowing Oliver would get a kick out of seeing Finn and spending time with him, Maggie agreed. Plus, it would give her the time to sit for a little bit and soak in the knowledge of the path she was about to walk down. Store ownership.

An hour later Finn walked through the door with her son at his side. Oliver had a chocolate mustache, no doubt from indulging in hot chocolate with Finn.

"Hey, buddy! How was your first day at school?" Maggie asked.

"It was great," Oliver said. "I made a lot of new friends."

Maggie felt as if her heart might jump out of her chest. All of her fears had been rattling around in her head. And now here Oliver stood looking as happy as a clam. She let out the breath she'd been holding ever since dropping Oliver off at school. Suddenly, all was right with her world.

Oliver began chattering about the goings-on at school.

"We were talking about Christmas at school. There's a big cookie exchange coming up where everyone makes cookies and then swaps so you end up with a whole bunch of cool holiday cookies. Aidan asked me to go sledding with him, so I also need a sled. And we need a Christmas tree, Mom. Everyone else has one." Oliver looked at her with pleading eyes.

"Oh, really now?" Maggie asked in a teasing voice. It tickled her to think her son was already in the thick of things with his classmates.

"Can we? Can we, please?" he begged, crossing his hands in front of him.

She leaned down and pressed a kiss against his temple. "Yes, my sweet. We most definitely can. I know the perfect place at home we can put it." There was no way Maggie could say no to the excitement bubbling up inside her son. She'd made a promise to herself. She was going to embrace Christmas and all it had to offer, if only to see the joy reflected in her son's eyes. Christmas trees! Sledding at Deer Run Lake! Participating in the town's Christmas cookie exchange. She was all in.

"Can you come and help us pick out a tree, Finn?" Oliver asked. There was something about the look emanating from Oliver's eyes that sent out warning signals. He was getting attached.

Finn playfully bowed to Oliver. "It would be my pleasure, Sir Oliver," he said in an exaggerated English accent.

Oliver giggled. "You sound funny." He turned toward Maggie. "When can we go to find the tree?"

"How about if we head over there tomorrow night?" Maggie suggested. "I have a few things to take care of around here. And I still have to figure out dinner."

"How does that sound, Finn?" Oliver asked, turning back toward Finn.

"Sounds like a plan," he said, holding up his palm so Oliver could high-five him. "I don't know if you heard," he said, bending down and speaking in a low voice to Oliver, "but I'm the best tree hunter in all of Alaska."

"Cool! We're going to get the best tree ever," Oliver said, his face lit up with excitement.

Maggie watched the interplay between Finn and Oliver. There was no doubt about it. They were getting along like a house on fire. Oliver was blossoming right before her eyes. And it had everything to do with Finn. She should know. He'd done the same thing for her when she was ten years old.

"Finn, can I talk to you for a second?" She waved him over so Oliver wouldn't overhear their conversation.

"Sure thing." He walked over to her, his eyes alight with curiosity. "What's up?"

"You asked me the other day about watching Oliver after school so I can focus on the shop."

Finn waved his hand at her. "Forget it. I know you weren't keen on the idea."

"I was being unreasonable," she admitted, feeling very humbled. Her overprotectiveness toward Oliver had clouded her judgment. "Your offer to watch Oliver was very generous. Honestly, he's crazy about you."

"So? Did you change your mind? Are you taking me up on my offer?"

She took a deep breath. "Yes, I am, if it's still on the table."

Finn graced her with a wide grin. "Hey! That's great. Of course it is."

Maggie chewed on her lip. "I think I was just worried he might get too attached to you. Oliver isn't just looking for a father figure, Finn. He's actually looking for a father. I just don't want him to get hurt or confused along the way."

"No worries, Mags. We're buddies," Finn assured her. "Surely that can't be a bad thing."

"No, that's not a bad thing," Maggie said, her eyes drifting back toward her son. He was still looking at Finn as if he was the greatest thing since sliced bread.

She felt relieved about the childcare situation being resolved. Finn had been right. It was the perfect solution. *Unless of course Oliver decides he wants Finn to be more than a buddy*, Maggie thought. She knew her son hadn't given up on the idea of finding a father here in Alaska. Something told her Finn would be at the top of Oliver's list.

Finn headed over to the Moose Café as soon as he and Maggie decided to call it day at Keepsakes. Since Annie was working late at the library, Declan had invited him to dinner. It would be nice to get together with his brother and talk over a good meal. It had been far too long since they'd spent downtime together.

The jangling of the bell heralded his arrival inside the eatery. Finn smiled as he looked around the place. Every time he walked in, it seemed as if Hazel and Cameron had added even more festive decorations. Yes, indeed. It was beginning to look a lot like Christmas.

"Hey, Finn. Are you looking for a table?" Sophie asked, coming up behind him.

"I'm looking for Declan. He's supposed to be meeting me here for an early dinner," Finn said.

"I haven't seen him yet, but I can find a table for the two of you," she said, waving him to follow after her. Finn trailed after her and sat down once Sophie placed two menus on a table set up for two.

"As soon as I spot him, I'll send him over."

"Thanks, Soph. Tell Noah I said hello, okay?"

At the sound of her husband's name, Sophie lit up like sunshine. "I sure will, Finn."

Sophie was a newlywed, having married Noah Catalano, a private investigator, after a whirlwind courtship. Folks in town were still grappling with Sophie's hidden identity as an heiress to a coffee empire. Her bank balance wasn't important. Sophie was well loved in this town.

Yep. Single folks were dropping like flies in this town, which meant it was only a matter of time until someone asked him about his status. An unattached male in Love who wasn't signed up for Operation Love was akin to a Bigfoot sighting. Everyone wanted the happy ending tied up with a big fancy bow.

"Where has Maggie been hiding?" Hazel asked with her hands on her hips as she made a sudden appearance at his table.

"Well, hello to you too, Hazel," Finn said in a dry tone.

She placed her hand on his shoulder. "Sorry, Finn. I don't know where my manners went," Hazel said in an apologetic tone. "How are things going over at the shop? Rumor has it you're helping out over there."

So far Finn had discussed his inheritance from Tobias only with his brother and Maggie. He knew Love like the back of his hand. Once word got out, he wouldn't have a moment's rest answering questions from the townsfolk. He loved Hazel, but for the time being he wasn't disclosing the particular reasons why he was helping out at Keepsakes. He was keeping his mouth shut about Tobias's will and his eyes on the prize.

"There's a lot of work to do. For the most part Maggie's been working to get the shop in running order." Finn made a face. "Don't repeat this, Hazel, but Tobias left that shop in really bad shape."

Hazel scratched her chin. "That's hard to fathom," Hazel said. "Tobias was such a meticulous person. I imagine he was overwhelmed when he got sick and made the decision to close up the store. It wasn't until much later that he took me into his confidence about his illness." She made a tutting sound. "It's frustrating because I can't imagine a single person in this town who wouldn't have helped out if he'd said one word about the shop."

Finn shrugged. "I was pretty close to Tobias and he didn't mention the shop, although he talked about Maggie all the time. He used to show me pictures of her and Oliver. It was pretty obvious he was crazy about them."

Hazel nodded. "He sure was. Tobias always hoped Maggie would make it back here." She shook her head. "I think he was a little brokenhearted he didn't see her again before he passed."

Finn straightened in his chair. "Hazel, could you make sure not to share that sentiment with Maggie? I think it would really wound her to know that particular bit of information."

"Me and my big mouth. I didn't mean it as a criticism of Maggie," Hazel said. "Tobias was such a kind and generous man. His death is such a big loss to this town."

"I know." Finn reached out and clasped Hazel's hand in his own. "I just want to make sure Maggie doesn't get hurt."

"You and Maggie have been spending a lot of time together," Hazel said, sending him a pointed look. "Don't think people haven't noticed. Are the two of you going to be the next It couple in this town?"

Finn waved his hand at her. "You've got it all wrong, Hazel. There's nothing romantic going on. We're just friends, just like back in the day."

"Finn is antiromance. Didn't you know, Hazel?" Declan came striding up to Finn's table. Obviously he'd heard the tail end of their conversation. Declan put his hands around Hazel's waist and placed a kiss on her cheek before sitting down across from Finn. Finn had to smile. As always, his brother knew how to make an entrance.

"Is that true, Finn?" Hazel barked. "There are lots of pretty gals here in Love looking for a God-fearing, handsome man like yourself." She tapped her fingers against her breastbone. "Look at me! I never imagined I'd be a newlywed at my age, but God has a plan for all of us. I learned not to question His timing."

Finn glared at Declan. "I'm not against romance." He shrugged. "I just don't want to settle down. It's not for me."

"Humph. And why not? It's not as if you haven't backpacked around the country and sowed your wild oats," Hazel muttered. "What are you waiting for? An engraved invitation to court someone?"

Declan sat back in his seat and chuckled. "That's what I'd like to know. With Annie expecting, it would be nice for my kids to have some cousins to rip and run with. At this rate they'll have to play among themselves."

Kids? A wife? Finn felt a twisting sensation in his stomach. Those weren't on his agenda. Not now. Not ever. Just the thought of it made him feel as if he couldn't breathe. It would be too much pressure for him. He'd promised God a long time ago he wouldn't even try to go down that road. That was his punishment for what he'd done to his family. A solitary life free of familial responsibilities. He had already destroyed one family. He wasn't going to risk tearing apart another one.

"We haven't seen hide nor hair of Maggie. Dwight was here asking about her. He said he went over to the shop but she didn't answer the door." Hazel tutted. "Poor thing is probably working herself to death. Maggie needs to get reacquainted with this town and the folks who live here."

As if from out of nowhere, Jasper sidled up to their table and stood next to Hazel. "Are you talking about Maggie? I keep wondering where she's hiding herself. Let's get her involved in town events. Maybe she'll want to join the PTA or the town council," Jasper suggested. "We actually have a position on the town council opening up in a few weeks."

Declan and Finn locked gazes. They both began to chuckle.

"What's so funny?" Jasper asked, his expression one of irritation. "Being on the town council is an honor."

"Those aren't exactly rip-roaring good times," Finn drawled.

"We don't want her to think Love is a snoozefest," Declan added. "How about the Christmas cookie exchange or the Deer Run Lake skating party?"

Finn snapped his fingers. "And what about the choral group who sings carols door-to-door?" Finn wanted Maggie and Oliver to experience the best of Love. The happier they were, the more likely they would stay in Love long-term. He felt a bit badly about not encouraging Maggie to participate more in town events. He had been so eager to finish work on the shop so he could collect his inheritance and buy into O'Rourke Charters.

He'd lost sight of the fact that Maggie needed to be exposed to a wide range of things in Love.

"Ooh," Hazel exclaimed. "I just found out there's a holiday mixer for Operation Love participants. Maggie's been invited even though she hasn't officially signed up yet for the program. There's still a female shortage in this town, so nobody minds bending the rules and allowing her to attend." Hazel jabbed Jasper in the side. "Something tells me the men of Love will be vying for Maggie. She's a good-looking woman."

"Sure is," Jasper said with enthusiasm. "I don't want to be indiscreet, but a few men have already asked about her." Jasper wiggled his eyebrows. "That holiday mixer would be great for Maggie to meet some eligible men." He rubbed his hands together. "Another Operation Love success story in the making."

"Don't count your chickens before they hatch," Hazel said, her lips pursed.

"What are you talking about?" Jasper asked. He puffed his chest out. "I'm an expert on the program and matchmaking in general. You should know that Maggie Richards will be the perfect partner for some fella in this town."

Finn felt himself grinding his teeth. He counted to ten slowly in his head. All this talk of Maggie and Operation Love was irritating. Finn didn't like the way Hazel was eyeballing him either. She was studying him like he was a biology exam.

"Let's leave these young 'uns alone so they can look at the menu. Come help me in the kitchen," Hazel said to Jasper in a blustery voice as she pulled her husband away from the table.

Finn felt himself tensing up. The idea of men fighting over Maggie wasn't a pleasant one. And even though Jasper wasn't giving up any names, Finn wanted to know who was asking about Maggie. There were a few men in Love who shouldn't even think about approaching Maggie. He could think of at least five off the top of his head.

Humph! They didn't even know her. Her likes and dislikes. Her favorite color. How she liked to spend her downtime. Did they even know she had a son?

"What's wrong? You look bent out of shape."

"Nothing. I just don't like the idea of some of these guys swarming over Maggie like bees to honey," he muttered.

Declan looked at Finn from over his menu. "Why not? If she finds the man of her dreams, won't it be a good thing?"

Finn clenched his jaw. A good thing? Yes. Maggie deserved to find happiness, but he couldn't deny the unsettled feeling in the pit of his stomach. She was a single mother and a widow who had lived through tragedy. She put on a brave front, but she was vulnerable in many ways. If Finn had anything to say about it, he wasn't going to let Maggie pair up with just anybody. The guy needed to be as solid as a rock.

Sophie appeared with two glasses of ice water and placed them down on the table. "I'll be back in a jiffy to take your order."

Finn looked down at the menu, studiously avoiding his brother's gaze. After what seemed like an eternity, he looked across at Declan, who was still staring at him. Finn let out an exaggerated sigh. "Just say it. I know you want to tell me something, hence the Darth Vader stare."

Declan's lips twitched at the Star Wars mention. "I know you're into Maggie. You can't fool me, Finn." The look on Declan's face spoke volumes. Sometimes his brother could be like a dog with a bone. He wasn't going to back down on this topic.

"Of course I like her. She's beautiful. And super sweet. You should see her with Oliver." He shook his head. "She's wonderful. But honestly, I'm not looking to romance her. I don't do serious. And I'm certainly not looking for a ready-made family." He let out a harsh laugh. "Seriously? Can you see me with a wife and a kid?"

Declan wasn't laughing. He narrowed his gaze and studied Finn. "Honestly, I can easily picture it, Finn. You're a good, honest man. You've made some missteps in the past, but who hasn't? You've really stepped up in the last year and come into your own. I think it's time you stopped beating yourself up about it."

Finn felt a huge lump in his throat. Declan's vote of confidence meant the world to him. But there were things his younger brother didn't know. He had no clue about Finn's role in their mother's death and the gradual dissolution of their family unit. Finn's worst fear was Declan finding out and casting Finn out of his life for good. Without Declan and Annie, Finn wouldn't have a family. He would be completely alone.

As Sophie came back to the table to take their order, Finn could barely concentrate on ordering his meal. Fear had grabbed hold of him.

All of these years he'd managed to keep his guilty

secret from Declan. A shudder went down his back at
the prospect of Declan finding out the truth about him
being responsible for the accident that had killed their
mother and the brutal aftermath—his father leaving the
family and Killian's death some years later. Finn had
lost most of the people in his life he held dear. He didn't
think he would able to bear it if he lost Declan too.

Chapter Seven

As Maggie peered around the thick brown paper still covering the storefront window she saw the gently falling snow. It looked so beautiful and serene. It truly resembled one of those idyllic images from a calendar. From this vantage point she could see the Moose Café, as well as other shops on Jarvis Street. She was counting down the days until they could rip down the paper and Keepsakes could join the other businesses in their holiday cheer.

Maggie couldn't remember a time in her life when she had worked so hard toward a goal. With the exception of her first few weeks as a mother to a newborn and the shocking circumstances of Sam's death, getting Keepsakes ready for business had become the most difficult endeavor in her life.

On the bright side, the shop was taking shape, and she could see all of the possibilities laid out before her. She had put aside items that she wanted to showcase in the front windows as a holiday display.

Day by day her friendship with Finn was strengthening. They were beginning to fall into old, familiar rhythms. He made her laugh with his corny jokes and she delighted him with tales of Oliver's antics. They chuckled over their childhood escapades and the fanciful dreams of their youth. It was nice to be friends with a man without romance messing things up. Although Finn was appealing on so many levels, Maggie couldn't see herself romantically involved with anyone. Sam had done enough damage to her heart to last a lifetime.

"You wanted to be a crime fighter," Finn had reminded her earlier that morning. "I vividly recall you talking about wearing a red cape and riding to the rescue."

"You wanted to be a pilot by day," Maggie recounted with a chuckle. "And a pizza maker by night."

"Sounds reasonable to me. Flying and pizza. Two of the finest things in life." Finn shook his head. "Such goals we had."

"We wanted to rule the world," Maggie said in a wistful tone.

They had been so innocent back then. At ten years old it had been easy to believe in happy endings and dreams come true. Both she and Finn had been exposed to darkness in their lives. Despite her belief that God hadn't been by her side through the tough times, Maggie now knew it wasn't true. He had seen her through the worst of it, and through Uncle Tobias, God had shown her grace and pointed her in a new direction.

Life tended to provide reality checks along the way. And then she'd had to switch up her dreams, Maggie realized, as she looked around the store. This place was her new dream. A feeling of gratitude threatened to overwhelm her. She'd never really allowed herself to imagine owning anything with such potential. Things were coming together.

She and Finn had arranged for a garbage disposal company to pick up the items in the shop deemed to be trash. At Finn's suggestion, they also had a pile of items they were donating to a charitable organization benefiting the homeless. In a few days a crew was coming in to help them give the place a top-to-bottom cleaning. They had a lot of work to do before then.

"Hey, Maggie." Finn's voice interrupted her thoughts. "I've been thinking. You've been working so hard here at the shop. It hasn't given you much time for socializing."

Maggie swung her gaze up from the front counter. Her mind felt blank. What was Finn talking about? The Operation Love campaign?

"Socializing?" she asked. It had been so long it felt like a foreign concept.

Finn chuckled. "Yes. As in getting to know the townsfolk. You're going to need their friendship and goodwill once the store opens. I'm one hundred percent certain you'll get their support, but it would be nice to have some established ties."

Maggie shrugged. "Well, I have you and Hazel. And there's Jasper and Declan." She was counting on her fingers. "And Ruby and Aidan."

Finn looked at her without saying a word. He didn't have to speak. His expression said it all.

She bit her lip. The town of Love was a small hamlet, but even she knew her numbers were pitiful. When was the last time she'd made an actual friend? Or ventured out of her comfort zone? Moving to Alaska had been a huge leap of faith, but it would be meaningless if she failed to connect with the townsfolk who lived here.

So much had been lost over the years, including her ability to connect with people.

"I did a little brainstorming last night about the grand opening. I think we should think big." He spread his arms wide. "Huge. We could make up flyers and host a holiday party here with eggnog and red velvet cake and lots of party favors."

Maggie smiled. She loved Finn's enthusiasm. Although it was crystal clear he was working with her in order to get his inheritance, he never hesitated to go the extra mile. He had a great attitude. It was no small wonder Oliver thought he'd hung the moon.

"That's a great idea," Maggie said. She rubbed her hands together. "Who doesn't adore eggnog?"

Finn looked at his watch. "I can man the store if you want to head over to the meeting for the carol singers. Pastor Jack would love to have you. They're meeting in the fellowship hall at the church at noon." He wagged his eyebrows at her. "I seem to remember you singing at church when we were kids, and I hear they're looking for a soprano."

"I do enjoy singing. It's been a while though," she said in a soft voice.

So many things had been watered down over the years due to Sam's problems. She had distanced herself from her church community due to the shame she'd felt after his death. How could she have walked into church after all the media attention and finger-pointing?

And she knew she hadn't really grieved Sam in the

proper way. Her anger and shock and embarrassment hadn't allowed her to fully mourn the man she'd loved but hadn't ever really known.

"I imagine it's like riding a sled down a mountain." Finn's eyes twinkled as he mentioned their favorite childhood pastime. "Something you never quite forget how to do."

Finn was right. She loved singing, especially in a group setting. Why had she given up something that gave her so much joy and brought her closer to God?

A sheepish feeling swept over her. Why was she feeling so reluctant to make friends in Love? She had been excited about making those connections, but now she felt nervous. There had been so much rejection back in Boston. Maggie almost felt wary of opening herself up to being hurt again by judgment and derision. It had been an incredibly painful experience to be shunned.

"Are you sure you can hold down the fort by yourself?" she asked. A part of her wanted him to tell her he couldn't handle dealing with the store by himself. That would give her a way out. Truthfully, the shop had become something of a cocoon for her. She spent all of her days at Keepsakes and her evenings were occupied by Oliver.

"I can definitely handle it, Mags. As they say, Rome wasn't built in a day. We're making great progress here. This place is starting to look terrific. Take a moment to stop and smell the forget-me-nots." Forget-me-nots were the official state flower of Alaska.

Although Finn's voice had a teasing tone, Maggie could sense he was serious. It hit her all at once. Finn cared about her. Despite all the years of separation, he still wanted the best for her. It made her feel all warm and fuzzy inside.

"Okay. Why not? I'm going to go meet up with the choral group." She sat down on a chair and pulled on her warm, fuzzy boots. She had splurged yesterday and bought a pair of Hazel's Alaskan Lovely boots. Maggie wasn't used to having new things. For so long she'd scrimped and saved to try to keep a roof over her family's heads and to see to Oliver's needs. Now, with this inheritance, she didn't have to constantly worry about every dime. She had even purchased a few items to put under the tree for Oliver. She couldn't wait to see the look on her son's face when he unwrapped the toboggan.

Finn nodded his approval. "Have a good time. I'll meet Oliver at the bus stop. No worries."

Maggie put her coat and hat on, then reached in her purse for her mittens. "I'll see you later." Strangely enough she felt like a child venturing out into the big bad world all by her lonesome.

"Hold on a minute," Finn called out. He walked up to her and reached out to zip up her jacket so her neck wasn't exposed. She looked up into his sea green eyes. "There. It's cold out there. We wouldn't want you to get sick." They locked gazes, and Finn smiled. Maggie felt the oddest sensation as she gazed into Finn's eyes. Butterflies soared in her belly. For a second she felt her palms moisten.

She shook off the feeling. Maybe she was coming down with something. Maggie gave herself a mental pep talk and headed toward the back entrance to Keepsakes. She turned around and waved at Finn, who was standing there staring at her as if she was a baby chick leaving the nest.

Step out of your comfort zone. Believe in yourself! Nothing ventured, nothing gained. She repeated these phrases in her head as she pushed open the back door and headed out into the wintry morning.

Although Maggie was trying to be brave, a part of her wanted to turn right back around and hide herself away in the shop. But she knew Finn wouldn't let her get away with it. And the truth was, she didn't want to disappoint him.

Finn didn't quite know what to do with himself while Maggie was gone. Although he kept himself busy hauling things outside to the back of the shop and doing a little online research about pricing for items, his mind kept wandering to Maggie. Was she having a good time with the choir? Had they welcomed her with open arms?

Maggie had looked so unsure of herself and nervous. He'd been torn between encouraging her and protecting her. He didn't remember her being so anxious. But they'd been ten years old. So much had happened in both of their lives since then.

By the time Oliver got off the school bus, Maggie still hadn't returned from her choir meeting. Oliver almost chatted his ear off, telling Finn stories about his kindergarten buddies and their antics. Finn loved seeing the boy's excitement and the innocent way in which he viewed the world around him. He felt a sudden need to make sure Oliver didn't lose his sense of wonder. Finn wanted to wrap a protective blanket around the kid so he wouldn't get jaded or hurt by life.

Stop it! You're not his father, he chided himself. *It's not your job to worry about Oliver. He has a mother, and no doubt he'll have a father soon.*

Operation Love tended to work pretty fast in Finn's estimation. Before too long Maggie would be paired up with one of the numerous men who'd signed up for the matchmaking program. Finn shouldn't feel annoyed about it, but he did. It was silly. Just because he'd decided not to enroll in the program didn't mean Maggie couldn't make the most of it. And if she did get married, they could still be friends. Somehow that thought didn't do anything to make him feel any better.

Maggie and Oliver were top notch. He let out a sigh. A man would have to be a fool not to see it.

Lord, please let Maggie find what she's looking for here in Love. If she somehow finds it through the Operation Love program, then so be it. I know Oliver wants a father, but I want Maggie to find her own happiness. She's been through a lot.

The door to the shop swung open and Maggie came bustling in, carrying a plastic tin. Oliver ran toward her and hugged her tightly around the waist.

"What a nice greeting. Seems like you missed me," Maggie said.

Oliver nodded and pressed his face against her. "Did you bring something for me?" Oliver asked, sniffing the tin.

"I brought some monkey bread. It's delicious," Maggie said. "You're going to love it."

"So, don't keep us in suspense. How was it?" Finn asked. He'd been on pins and needles since she'd left.

The smile on Maggie's face threatened to overtake

her entire face. "It was a lot of fun. I'm sorry I took so long, but I went for a hot chocolate with Ruby and some other ladies."

A sense of relief flooded him. "That's great. Who did you hang out with?"

She scrunched up her face. "Let's see. There was Paige and Grace and a Gretchen. I like them all a lot. And it felt so good to sing again."

"That's some fine company you were keeping. Those ladies are wonderful."

Oliver tugged at Maggie's sleeve. "Mom, you said we could go get the tree tonight. Remember?" The look on Oliver's face was hesitant, as if he was bracing for Maggie to say she'd forgotten all about it.

"Of course I do," Maggie said. She leaned down and pressed a kiss on Oliver's temple. "I've been looking forward to it all day."

"Mom, you're getting mushy again," Oliver said, dramatically swiping his hand across his forehead.

"Does tonight still work for you, Finn?" Maggie asked.

"It sure does," he said. "Why don't we grab something to eat across the street then head over to the town green? It's pizza night at the Moose Café. They'll be making ten different types of pizza. You name it. Pineapple pizza. Meatball pizza. Reindeer pizza. And the always popular, Heart of Love pizza. It has five kinds of cheese and it is literally the most delicious thing I've ever tasted in my life." Finn rubbed his stomach and made a funny face, much to Oliver's delight.

"Sounds like an artery-clogging experience," Maggie said, chuckling behind her hand.

"I know you love pizza," Finn said, shooting her a knowing look. "Come on. Admit it. You're going to have five slices of the artery-clogging, five-cheese pizza."

Oliver began giggling. "She usually just has two."

"Just you wait and see," Finn said with a wink. "She's going to devour this pizza."

"Can we go now?" Oliver asked, rubbing his stomach.

"Let me just make sure all of these boxes have been broken down and then we can head over," Finn said, his eyes scanning the shop. "I can't believe how good the place looks."

Maggie folded her arms across her chest and looked around her. "No, Finn. It looks great. I'm astounded by how nicely everything is shaping up. I think tomorrow I'm going to get started on the window display."

After a delicious pizza dinner at the Moose Café, Finn walked over to the town green with Oliver. Maggie drove her car down Jarvis Street and found a spot close to the tree stand in case they found a tree and needed to strap it on top to take it home.

Powdery snow was falling all around them. Oliver was running around with his head tilted back so he could catch snowflakes in his mouth. It was like a beautiful postcard of an Alaskan Christmas scene. Being here with Maggie and Oliver felt like a sweet privilege.

Thank You, Lord, for this beautiful moment. I'd almost forgotten the simple joy of looking for the perfect Christmas tree.

It had been far too long since Finn had participated in such a heartwarming outing. For far too many Christmases he had been roaming around the United States, far away from his hometown. He'd missed out on a lot of moments. This year would be very different. He was going to soak up as much as he could of the holiday festivities here in Love. And he was going to live in the moment and enjoy every single second of it.

There was a multitude of Christmas trees lined up in rows. Trees of all shapes and sizes. Finn inhaled deeply. The scent was one of his favorites. It brought to mind everything he loved about the season.

"See anything you like?" Finn asked Oliver.

When Oliver reached up and grabbed hold of his hand, a funny sensation spread across Finn's chest. It was such a simple thing, yet it made him feel like a rock star. He couldn't deny the raw emotions it brought up inside him. Suddenly, someone needed him. Was this what it felt like to be a father? If so, it was incredible. Oliver made him realize that he wasn't such a black sheep after all. He may have messed up a bunch of times, but in Oliver's eyes, he was still a pretty good guy. And that meant the world to Finn.

As they walked from tree to tree, Finn found his gaze straying to Maggie. Her tender interactions with Oliver demonstrated her loving nature. She was a wonderful mother. Every child should be so grateful as to have a mother like Maggie.

Joy hummed and pulsed in the air. Everything felt pure and serene. If there was such a thing as a perfect moment in time, Finn knew this was it.

Oliver began jumping up and down. He was pointing at a medium-sized pine tree. "Hey, guys. Isn't that a great tree?"

In Finn's opinion it looked a bit lopsided, but he

wasn't going to put a damper on Oliver's enthusiasm. If he wanted this slightly imperfect tree, then so be it.

Finn reached out and wrapped his hand around the base and then shook it. "It seems really solid."

"This is it!" Oliver said. "That's our tree."

"Are you sure?" Maggie asked. "Once we buy it and strap it to the top of the car, that's it. We're not coming back for another one."

"I'm absolutely one million percent sure," Oliver said, his expression solemn.

"Well, it doesn't get any better than that," Finn said, sharing a bemused look with Maggie. "Let's buy it."

Maggie began to dig around in her purse. Finn reached out and placed a gentle hand on her wrist. "The tree is on me. Consider it my welcome-to-Love gift to you and Oliver."

"That's not necessary, Finn. You're already doing so much to help out our family."

"Maggie, let me do this. Trust me. Tobias's inheritance is going to change my life in unimaginable ways." He ran a hand over his face. "I'm not sure I've wrapped my head around Tobias's generosity."

Maggie nodded. "I know the feeling. Oliver and I have been so incredibly blessed. Not only by Uncle Tobias, but by your friendship and the generosity of the people here in town. Jasper. Hazel. Ruby. This town really is something special."

Finn walked away from Oliver and Maggie, making his way toward the tent so he could purchase Oliver's tree.

"Hey, Al. I think we've decided on a tree," Finn said,

greeting Alan Pendergast, the owner of the tree stand. He reached out and handed Al a wad of cash.

"Hey, Finn. Good to see you. Which tree are you looking at buying?"

Finn turned around and pointed toward Maggie and Oliver. "The one right there beside the woman and the little boy."

Al nodded. "So is that Tobias's niece?"

"Yes, that's Maggie," Finn said. "And her son, Oliver. They're living out at Tobias's place."

Al let out a laugh. "I remember her as a little tyke. Tobias sure loved that girl."

Finn nodded. Tobias had been a devoted uncle to Maggie, even though a huge geographical distance separated them. He couldn't count the number of times Tobias had pulled out photos and letters from Maggie. Finn always had the impression Tobias viewed Maggie as his honorary daughter.

"He sure did," Finn acknowledged. "She's going to do him proud by running Keepsakes and carrying on his legacy here in Love."

Al jerked his head in the direction of Maggie and Oliver. "Who's the guy standing with them?" Al let out a chuckle. "You can't even turn your back in this town without someone trying to steal your lady."

Finn quickly turned around. From this distance he couldn't be certain, but it looked like Hank Jeffries had sidled up to Maggie in his absence. He had his palm up waiting for Oliver to give him a high five. Finn recognized his height and broad shoulders, as well as the red-and-black lumberjack coat he always wore. A feeling of irritation washed over him. Hank was a fireman.

Ladies loved firemen, although for some inexplicable reason, Hank was still single and available. And according to the rumor mill, he was looking to settle down.

Finn clenched his teeth. Hank was well regarded and a genuinely nice guy. It wasn't any of his business who courted Maggie or tried to make friends with Oliver. After all, hadn't Oliver spilled the beans about wanting to find a father in Love? Hank would fit the bill just fine, he imagined. He was heroic and strong and he didn't run away when things became too overwhelming.

Finn turned his back on the sight of Maggie, Hank and Oliver. The sudden appearance of Hank reminded him of his own unworthiness. He felt like a deflated balloon. Maggie and Hank made sense. He was the very definition of *reliable*. Steadfast. No doubt the whole town of Love would cheer them on.

"She's not my lady," he said in a curt voice to Al.

"Really? The two of you aren't the latest couple from Jasper's program?" Al asked, his brow furrowed in confusion.

For some reason, Al's question pricked at Finn. This whole evening had felt idyllic until reality had slapped him in the face. Hank's sudden appearance had been a jolt to the system, serving to remind him in no uncertain terms of his own inadequacy. He wasn't the type of man who could give Maggie and Oliver what they truly needed and deserved—stability.

"We're not dating," Finn snapped. "Maybe I should put a sticky note on my forehead saying we're just friends."

Al held up his hands. "Okay. I didn't mean to get you all riled up. It's just that you three look like a family.

And Declan settled down last year. Figured you might want to follow his lead."

He blew out a frustrated breath. "How many times do I have to tell everyone in this town? I'm not interested in Operation Love or getting married or starting a family. I don't want to be a father or a husband. I'm doing perfectly fine all by myself."

The moment the words tumbled off his tongue, Finn felt like a jerk. Al's hurt expression spoke volumes. Once again, Finn O'Rourke had messed up.

As Finn turned around to leave, he met Maggie's shocked gaze. She was standing directly behind him with wide eyes. He felt a sinking sensation in the pit of his stomach. There was no question about it. Maggie had overheard his rant.

He let out a ragged sigh. So much for their perfect evening.

Chapter Eight

Maggie's cheeks felt flushed as she stood awkwardly in the entranceway to the tent. Maggie had never heard such anger in Finn's voice. It had surprised her. For the most part, he always seemed so upbeat and content. And this evening had been so idyllic up to this point.

A thick tension hung in the air. She had no idea what to say to fill up the silence.

She'd been standing with Oliver when Hank Jeffries had come over and introduced himself to them. It had quickly become clear he had a romantic interest in her. Although he was handsome and friendly, Maggie had felt slightly uncomfortable. She'd been out of the dating game for quite some time. Even before she'd met Sam, Maggie had always felt awkward about dating. Clearly, nothing had changed.

On the pretext of asking Finn a question about the tree, Maggie had beat a fast path toward the tent. In the process, she'd stumbled upon a very revealing conversation.

Finn stood by silently, seemingly speechless.

"You must be Maggie." The older man came toward her and stuck out his hand. "I'm Al Pendergast. This is my Christmas tree stand. You probably don't remember me, but your uncle was a dear friend of mine. I met you once or twice when you were knee-high to a grasshopper."

Maggie shook his hand and shot him a shaky smile. "It's a pleasure to meet you again. You've got some beautiful trees here. My son is delighted."

"You sure know how to make an old man smile. I pride myself on top-quality Christmas trees." Al grinned. "Why don't we head back over to the trees and I'll wrap it up for you?"

As they walked back toward Oliver and the tree, Maggie couldn't help but notice Hank had disappeared. She felt a twinge of guilt about not being more receptive to him, but he'd caught her off guard. She probably didn't have to worry about him asking her out. She'd acted like a skittish newborn colt.

Mr. Pendergast placed the tree in a machine that wrapped it up in netting. Finn easily picked up the tree and strapped it to the top of Maggie's car.

"I'll follow behind the two of you in my car," Finn said. He'd barely said two words since she had surprised him in the tent. Maggie wasn't sure if he was embarrassed or annoyed with her for overhearing him. Either way, it felt awkward.

"Can I go in Finn's car?" Oliver asked, crossing his hands prayerfully in front of him.

Maggie tugged at his sleeve. "No, Oliver," she said in a sharp voice. "You're driving with me."

Ignoring her son's pout, Maggie got in the driver's

seat and revved the engine. Oliver was becoming entirely too enamored with Finn. Perhaps she needed to sit him down for a little talk about their friendship. Oliver wasn't shy about telling her he wanted her to find him a forever father. It wasn't too much of a leap for Oliver to imagine Finn in that role.

Lord, please protect my son. His heart is as wide and open as the great outdoors. I don't want him to get his feelings hurt. He's already been through so much.

As she drove home, Finn's words played back in her mind. *I'm doing perfectly fine all by myself.*

Maggie didn't know why it bothered her so much to have overheard Finn's harsh sounding words directed at Mr. Pendergast. It wasn't any of her business if he wasn't a proponent of the town mayor's matchmaking program. To be honest, neither was she. So what if he didn't want a wife and kids? It really didn't concern her. Finn was her friend, not a prospective mate. Because she felt so comfortable around him and she knew Oliver loved him, Maggie had allowed Finn a place in her life that wasn't strictly in the friendship zone.

If she was being really honest with herself, there was chemistry between her and Finn. The extensive amount of time she'd been spending in Finn's company had created a bond between them. But Maggie wasn't looking for love. She was seeking stability and a solid foundation. Although Oliver wanted a father, Maggie didn't need a man to help her give Oliver a bright future. She was fully capable of doing it on her own.

Finn had made things crystal clear about his wants and needs. He didn't need to spell it out any further. Finn liked having a solitary life. And he wasn't interested in changing. For the first time Maggie realized Finn had layers like an onion. On the surface he was jovial and full of zest, but underneath he was struggling with something. Maggie was certain of it. She knew from her own experience what it looked like when a person was keeping secrets.

Maggie had her own problems to deal with as a single mother making a new life for herself. Although Finn was a good friend, it wasn't her place to try to solve his issues. She already had her hands full trying to make sure Oliver was healthy and happy. The wounds from Sam's death were still so fresh.

When they arrived home, Finn carried the tree into the house, with a little assistance from Oliver. Maggie couldn't help but smile at the sight of her son carrying the tail end of the tree. He really wanted to be a mini version of Finn.

Once inside the house, Maggie directed Finn and Oliver toward the living room. Finn placed the tree in the tree stand right in front of their big bay window. She knew it would look spectacular when it was fully decked out with ornaments, lights and a shiny gold star on top. She could imagine it all, including gaily wrapped presents sitting under the tree.

"Thanks for helping us pick a tree, Finn," Oliver said with a wide grin. "And you were right. You are the best tree hunter in town. Maybe in all of Alaska."

"Thanks, kiddo," Finn said. "It was a real honor to be asked to join you and your mother. Finding the perfect Christmas tree is epic. You made my day!"

"You made mine too. It wouldn't have been half as fun without you." Oliver looked up at him. "I know you're super busy, but I really want to go flying with you."

The wistful tone in Oliver's voice made Maggie weak in the knees. One word from Finn and her son would be crushed. She found herself holding her breath. *Please, Finn*, she prayed. *Don't break his heart.*

"We can go on Saturday morning, bright and early." He locked gazes with Maggie. "Does that sound all right?"

There was no way in the world Maggie could say no, even if she'd wanted to. Oliver was looking at her with an expression of such hope shining forth in his eyes. "Sounds like a plan. I'll head into the store and set up the window display while you boys have your adventure."

Oliver let out a roar of approval. "This is the best day ever!" he yelled.

"I think it's time to head upstairs so you can get ready for a bath and bedtime. Say good-night to Finn," Maggie instructed.

"'Night, Finn," Oliver said, looking up at him with a shy expression etched on his face.

"See you later, gator," Finn said, tousling Oliver's hair.

"In a while, crocodile," Oliver shouted out as he raced toward the stairs.

Once they were alone, Finn walked over toward her. His hands were stuffed in his pockets and he had a sheepish expression etched on his face.

"About what you overheard back there at the tree stand," Finn began. "I don't want you to think I'm against people finding love or anything. I think it's great. And I'm not against Jasper's program. It's just not for me."

Maggie held up her hands. "You don't need to explain anything to me. I hope you don't think I would judge you for your opinions."

Finn quirked his mouth. "Maggie, I'm a single guy in a town full of bachelors who are all tripping over themselves to find a woman to settle down with." He shook his head. "I'm a bit of an anomaly."

"Glad to see nothing's changed since we were kids," Maggie teased. "You always were an outlier."

"That's a nice way of putting it." Finn chuckled. "Good night, Mags. I'll see you at the shop tomorrow."

Maggie saw Finn to the door and waved as he drove off into the dark Alaskan night. As soon as she shut the door, she leaned against it and pondered the events of the last few hours. Despite the slight tension at the Christmas tree stand, it had been an enjoyable evening, full of laughter, fellowship and discoveries. Oliver had thoroughly enjoyed himself with Finn. And Maggie had felt grateful for adult companionship.

If Maggie's past hadn't been filled with heartache and betrayal, she might be in a position to test the waters. Based on her research, Operation Love was a resounding success. Even Finn's own brother had found love through the program with Annie, who ran the Free Library in town. According to Ruby, Annie had come to Love in order to run the new library, then fallen in love with Declan O'Rourke, the pilot who had flown her to town. And her new friend Grace had met the sheriff of Love, Boone Prescott, through Jasper's matchmaking program as well. The list of successful matches was quite lengthy.

She'd heard so many romantic stories about Operation Love and people finding their true north. The truth was, Maggie was no longer looking for a fairy tale. She would be content to raise Oliver in a house filled with love and faith. She'd had her one love in a lifetime. Before everything had gone so horribly wrong, she and Sam had been a love story. Over time their marriage had buckled under the strain, but they had been a love match when they'd pledged forever to one another. Despite what people said, Maggie wasn't sure a person got two bites of the apple.

No matter how much she cared for Finn, there was no sense in hoping for something that would never happen. She and Finn actually had a similar outlook on romance. Finn was closed off to relationships and commitment. Maggie had been burned in the not-so-distant past by a husband who hadn't been on the same page with her or the lifestyle she wanted to lead. Right before her very eyes Sam had changed. And she hadn't been any the wiser until the bottom fell out of their world. There was no way she was going to set herself up for any more heartache. As it was, Sam's duplicity had brought her to his knees.

It was wise to keep Finn strictly in the friend zone and keep her heart strictly out-of-bounds.

Maggie's a friend and nothing more. Over and over again, Finn repeated the phrase until he felt certain it was seared into his brain.

He'd made a mistake by becoming too attached to the

beautiful single mother and her adorable son. He didn't have any romantic feelings toward Maggie, but he felt protective of her and Oliver. Being such a big part of their new lives in Love was dangerous to his decision not to form any lasting attachments. The night of the tree-hunting expedition, Finn had vowed to maintain a healthy distance from Oliver and Maggie. The lines were getting a little blurred, especially when people like Al started linking him romantically with Maggie.

Finn let out a snort. The tree stand owner had actually thought they were a couple. Finn stuffed down the little burst of joy he felt at being linked with his childhood friend.

Maintaining a distance from the Richards family was a difficult proposition since he was working with Maggie by day in the shop, then watching Oliver each weekday afternoon and some weekends. It seemed as if he couldn't manage to detach himself from their lives. And it was wreaking havoc on him. Despite his best intentions, Finn was finding it impossible to stay away from Oliver and his mother. He kept reminding himself that he didn't want to get too tangled up in their lives. Somewhere down the line Maggie might fall for someone here in town, and it wouldn't be fair to the man in question if Oliver's feelings toward Finn continued to blossom. It was very clear how Oliver felt about him—it was a very strong case of hero worship. Because Oliver was fatherless, Finn knew it was very possible Oliver had sought him out as a father figure.

Finn let out a sigh. The last thing he ever wanted to do was hurt Oliver. In some ways he reminded Finn of himself as a kid. Funny. Wise. And incredibly vulnerable. Finn could sense a lot behind Oliver's eyes.

For today he wasn't going to worry about building a little bit of a protective fire wall between them. Today was all about providing a wonderful flying experience for Oliver.

Finn O'Rourke didn't renege on promises. Especially not to six-year-old boys who made him feel as if he'd hung the sun, the stars and the moon.

Finn felt almost as excited as Oliver as he arrived at the airport hangar. He had arisen early this morning, bursting with enthusiasm about taking Oliver on a flying adventure. He stood outside and gazed out over Kachemak Bay. He couldn't have asked for better flying weather if he'd put in a special order for it.

As soon as he saw Oliver and Maggie walking toward him, Finn felt adrenaline racing through his veins. It was always like this before he flew —excitement pulsing through his body. It was a rush, pure and simple. The thrill of a lifetime.

Finn knew the moment Oliver saw him standing in the airport hangar. He started running toward him at breakneck speed, leaving Maggie in the dust.

"Welcome to O'Rourke Charters. Thanks for choosing to fly with us today, Oliver." Finn gestured toward the plane. "Please step inside and make yourself comfortable."

"Awesome!" Oliver practically tripped over himself making his way to Finn's side.

Finn placed his hand on Oliver's shoulder. "I think you're forgetting something," Finn said, jutting his chin in Maggie's direction. Finn could read Maggie's face like a book. She was fretting over her decision to let Oliver fly with him.

"'Bye, Mom," Oliver said, rushing toward Maggie and hugging her tightly around the waist. "Thanks for letting me do this."

Maggie's expression instantly transformed. She was smiling down at Oliver with an expression of joy etched on her face. Oliver's happiness was contagious.

"Be safe up there," she called out to them.

"Always," Finn said with a wave before helping Oliver into the plane. Oliver's eyes widened once he realized his seat was right in the cockpit next to Finn's seat. Once Finn was seated in the cockpit, he set Oliver up with a headset so they could talk over the roar of the plane.

"Up to the wild blue yonder," Finn called out as he worked the controls and began to ascend into the sky.

Oliver repeated Finn's words, reminding him of the way he and Declan had always recited those same words—their grandfather's mantra.

Once they were up in the air at a decent altitude, Finn began pointing out landmarks.

"This is my grandfather's plane," Finn explained. "I fixed it up a few months ago so it runs perfectly. It's called the *Killian* after him. He taught both Finn and me to fly on this plane."

"Wow. It must be old," Oliver said.

Finn let out a throaty laugh. "It is. We don't fly any customers in this plane. We reserve it for very special people."

"Like me?" Oliver asked, his grin threatening to split his face wide open.

"Exactly like you, Oliver." Finn turned toward Oliver. There was something about this kid that endeared him to Finn. He was curious and sweet and he had a zest for life unlike anyone else. Finn cared about Oliver in a way he couldn't even explain to himself. The kid brought up feelings inside him he'd never felt before. He could safely say he would take a bullet for Oliver.

"Look out the window! Do you see those trees covered with snow? That's Nottingham Woods."

"It looks so small from up here. Jasper said it was huge!" Oliver said, wrinkling his nose as he peered out the window. "They don't really look like trees."

"It's actually a really big forest like Jasper said. When we were kids my brother and I used to go cave hunting with our friends, the Prescott brothers. And guess what? Your mom came, too, whenever she visited."

"She did? Aw, man. I've never been in a cave," Oliver said in an awestruck voice. "Will you take me sometime?"

Finn grinned. Oliver was a boy after his own heart. He would have asked the same thing when he was Oliver's age. "If your mom says it's all right, I sure can," Finn said with a wink.

Finn steered the plane to the left, dipping it down low at an angle to give Oliver a thrill. Oliver let out a whoop of excitement. A few minutes later Finn spotted the glistening waters of Kachemak Bay down below. Patches of white reflected ice chunks on the surface. Finn loved looking down at the body of water. Its raw power was awe inspiring.

"Do you know what that is down below?" Finn asked.

"Kachemak Bay," Oliver said without hesitation.

"You're saying it perfectly. It takes most folks a while to learn the right way to pronounce it."

"Mom taught me on the ride over," Oliver said, his voice full of pride. Finn felt a little hitch in his heart at the sight of Maggie's son sitting beside him in the plane. He must be a resilient kid to have lost his father not so long ago and still be able to greet the world with a smile and optimism. He prayed Oliver's future wouldn't be hampered by the loss of his father. He knew all too well how those wounds festered.

As Finn made a final loop around Love, he looked out across the landscape of the hometown he adored. For so long he'd denied the pull of this town and what it meant to him. He glanced over at Oliver. He was sitting quietly, gazing out over the horizon with a look of satisfaction etched on his features.

"We're about to go into our descent and head back to the hangar," Finn announced. Truthfully, he could hang out in the sky for hours, but he knew Maggie needed him at the store for a few hours. He wanted to check out her window display and slap some red paint on the sign outside the shop. In a few days, the shop would be ready for the grand opening.

After landing the plane, Finn led Oliver inside the airplane hangar. A quick glance at his watch showed he was still within the time frame he'd promised Maggie. They could have a quick snack then head over to the shop.

"Hey, Oliver. There's a fridge out back. Why don't

you go grab a juice box or some chocolate milk? I've got some stashed back there."

"Okay," Oliver said in an agreeable voice before dashing off.

Declan was sitting at his desk poring over some paperwork. He swung his gaze up and focused on Finn.

"You're pretty crazy about Oliver, huh?" Declan asked. His blue eyes were twinkling with interest.

"He's a great kid," he said in a curt voice. Declan wasn't fooling him. He knew his brother was trying to stir something up about his feelings for Maggie and Oliver.

"You and Maggie seemed to have picked up right where you left off all those years ago. I remember the way the two of you were as thick as thieves."

"We're friends. You can tell Annie not to start planning a wedding shower," he said in a dry voice.

"Why would she do that? Word around town is that Hank Jeffries is interested in Maggie." Declan flashed him a smug look. "They're going out on a date."

Whoosh. Finn felt a jolt pass through him. Maggie hadn't mentioned anything about Hank or going out on a date. It wasn't as if she owed him that type of information, but Finn felt a little bit of a shock. He spent most days working side by side with Maggie. Why hadn't she confided in him about Hank?

"Seems to me if you're interested in Maggie you ought to speak up before she's taken." Although Declan tossed the words out casually, Finn knew his brother was trying to prod him into action.

"What part of *not interested* don't you understand? We're friends, just like in the old days."

"You two are like peanut butter and jelly. You finish each other's sentences. That's how it was when I met Annie. For a while I resisted what it meant. Don't be so stubborn, Finn. You're blocking your blessings."

"I'm not like you, Declan. Not everyone embraces marriage and kids with open arms. I knew at a young age I wasn't going to get the white picket fence and the house full of kids."

Declan frowned. "I understand, to an extent. Before I met Annie I had my doubts about happily-ever-after, but loving her helped me make peace with the past. I hope you see how it's possible. I'm living proof."

Just then Oliver came back into the room, juggling two small boxes of chocolate milk in one hand and some apple slices in the other. He grinned at Finn. "Look what I found. I got one for both of us." He handed a chocolate milk to Finn.

"We'll pick this conversation up later," Declan said, shooting Finn a glance filled with meaning. He smiled at Oliver. "I'm glad you had a good time today, Oliver."

"It was awesome," Oliver said. "Finn's the best pilot in all of Alaska."

Finn threw his head back and laughed. It was nice to hear a vote of confidence from Oliver.

The corners of Declan's mouth were twitching with mirth. "I see I'm outnumbered," he said.

Declan leaned across his desk and said in a loud whisper, "Don't tell Finn I said so, but I agree with you." He looked at his watch. "I better head off toward the pier. I'm making a run to Homer."

After Declan's departure, Finn sat down with Oliver so they could enjoy their chocolate milk and apple slices.

"So, what do you have planned for later on?" Finn asked. "Anything exciting for the weekend?"

He wrinkled his nose. "Mom has a date tonight," Oliver said in a soft voice. "I'm hanging out at Aidan's house."

Finn tensed up. Clearly, Declan's information had been correct. Even Oliver knew about it.

He made sure his voice sounded cheery. "Really? Well, that's nice."

Oliver frowned at him. "Do you really think so?"

"Sure. Why not?" he asked, hoping to inject a little positivity into the situation. Clearly, Oliver wasn't impressed with his mother's plans.

"Because if Mom goes out with this guy then they might get married. Aidan told me all about the Operation Love program," Oliver said, his voice trailing off. He bit his lip and stared at Finn with a troubled expression.

"Would that be such a bad thing?" Finn asked.

"Yes, it would," he said in a raised voice. "I don't want her to marry just anybody, Finn." His hazel eyes pooled with tears. "I want her to marry you."

Chapter Nine

Maggie cranked up the holiday music and did a little dance around the shop. Everything looked wonderful. The shelves had been painted a pristine white. The hardwood floors were glistening. Trash had been cleared. The charity organization had stopped by to pick up the donations. Stock had been delivered.

They still had some work to do, but it was night and day from when they had opened up the door and come face-to-face with a shop in disarray. That day Maggie had prayed for wisdom and strength to go the distance. With the help of Finn, Maggie was a few steps away from her goal of opening up Keepsakes in time for the holiday season.

Becoming a part of the fabric of this quaint town involved being seen. She didn't want to be a shadow anymore. It was the Christmas season. Celebrating the birth of Jesus meant rejoicing with your community. Locking herself away meant Maggie was living in fear. She didn't want to do that anymore. Not for herself or

Oliver. She wanted to embrace everything this town had to offer.

Maggie reached out and ripped down the brown paper from the windows. As light flowed into the shop, Maggie felt as if she was being embraced. She hoped Finn didn't mind her taking down the brown paper without him. She'd been caught up in a moment. It had felt right.

While she was setting up the window display, numerous townsfolk passed by the store. They smiled and waved at her. Some gave her the thumbs-up sign as they watched her set up the miniature Christmas tree and the snow globes on one side and the twinkling reindeer and the smiling snowman alongside it. Once she was done she stepped outside and surveyed it.

The sound of clapping interrupted her perusal of the display. Finn and Oliver were walking down Jarvis Street and straight toward her. Finn was clapping enthusiastically.

"It looks great!" Finn stepped closer to the windows and examined her displays. "I'd say this is the best holiday display on Jarvis Street."

"What do you think, Oliver?" Maggie asked. "Do you give it a thumbs-up?"

Oliver shrugged and pushed snow around on the pavement with the tip of his boot.

"What's wrong?" Maggie asked, reaching out and tilting Oliver's chin up so she could look him in the eyes.

"Nothing," he said in a short tone.

Maggie raised her eyebrows at Finn. She turned back

to Oliver. "Well, you better tell that to your lip. It's sticking out like a sore thumb."

Oliver rolled his eyes and walked past them, entering Keepsakes without saying anything further. Maggie's first instinct was to read Oliver the riot act. She had no intention of raising a brat with no manners.

"That attitude is unacceptable." Maggie frowned. "Did something happen?"

Finn sighed. "We had a great time flying, but afterward he began talking about your date."

Maggie gulped. "My date? With Hank?"

"Yes. He's not too keen on the idea of it."

"It's nothing. We met up at the mixer for Operation Love. We're just going out to dinner."

Finn held up his hands. "You don't need to explain a single thing to me."

Maggie's face crumpled. "I should cancel it. It's not worth upsetting Oliver."

"No, you shouldn't. Oliver is six. He's bound to try to put his foot down from time to time. I think they call it pushing the boundaries. If you let him have his way with this, you're going to create a little tyrant." He folded his arms across his chest. "Do you want that?"

"No, Finn. I most certainly do not. But maybe it's too soon," Maggie said. "He's just a little boy grappling with adult issues."

"Only you know if that's true or not. Keep in mind why you came here to Love in the first place. To change your life. You can't do that by standing on the sidelines."

"I need to talk to him, but what should I say?" Maggie asked. As a mother, Maggie usually had all the answers or at least a hunch about how to handle things. At the moment she felt clueless. She trusted Finn's advice.

"I think you should simply tell him you're meeting up with Hank because you're trying to get to know people here in town. Don't make too much of it. If you do, he'll pick up on it and freak out again."

Maggie nodded. "You're right. That sounds good."

On impulse, Maggie threw herself against Finn's chest and wrapped her arms around him. "Thank you. Not just for this advice, but for treating Oliver so well. Even though he's in a bit of a funk right now, you made one of his dreams come true today."

When she released Finn, she noticed he was staring at her with a strange expression on his face.

"What is it?" she asked, wondering if she had something stuck between her teeth.

"Nothing. It's just that…you're a fantastic mom, Maggie. Oliver is very blessed to have you. He's not at the age where he's going to say it to you in so many words, but I know he feels it. Right here," Finn said, tapping his chest.

Tears stung Maggie's eyes. The compliment from Finn meant everything to her. Every day she got up in the morning and put one foot in front of the other trying to do her best for her son. It felt gratifying to hear she was doing a decent job of it.

"Thanks, Finn," she said, her voice choked with emotion. She prayed he was right about Oliver. She felt so tangled up inside knowing he was upset about her plans with Hank. Being a mother wasn't all peaches and cream. It was tough, never-ending work, and not for the faint of heart.

She took a deep breath as she headed back into the store. Somehow she was going to have to find a way to talk to Oliver about her date with Hank.

Finn knew he'd blown things earlier with Oliver. When Oliver had spoken to him after their flying adventure about Maggie's date with Hank, he'd been completely shocked by Oliver's comment about wanting him to become his father. The comment had come out of the blue. In response, Finn had stumbled and fumbled, without a clue as to how to compassionately deal with a six-year-old boy's tender wishes.

He had deliberately withheld that information from Maggie when she'd asked him about what was bothering Oliver. It would have been awkward to tell her what Oliver had said to him. He was still wrapping his head around the six-year-old's comment and annoyed at himself for not responding well to it.

When he walked back into Keepsakes, Finn looked around the store for Oliver. He was sitting down at a little table Maggie had set up for him. His elbows were on the table and his head was slumped down next to the coloring book. He wasn't coloring or doing anything other than brooding.

A quick glance in Maggie's direction showed her distress over the situation. He didn't know what was bothering him more. Oliver's upset mood or Maggie's frame of mind.

"Hey, Oliver," he called out. "I've been thinking about something."

Oliver barely moved. "What?" he mumbled.

"You still haven't met Boomer yet," he said in a casual tone.

Oliver quickly raised his head up. His face lit up like a Christmas tree. "Boomer? Your dog?" Oliver's voice was infused with unbridled enthusiasm.

Finn folded his arms across his chest and rocked back on his heels. "Yep. One and the same. He gets really lonely when I'm away from the house. And he really likes visitors, especially kids your age."

"Really? Do you think he would like me?" Oliver asked. He stood up from his chair and walked over to Finn.

Finn laughed out loud. "Are you kidding me? He'd be crazy about you."

Finn shot a glance at Maggie, asking her a question with his eyes. She nodded discreetly.

"If you and your mom aren't busy tomorrow you could swing by and meet Boomer. If you think it's something you'd like to do, that is," Finn said.

"Yes! Of course I would," Oliver shouted, wrapping his arms around Finn's waist and giving him a tight bear hug. Finn felt certain no one had ever showered him with such enthusiasm in his entire life.

Maggie shook her head as Finn received the hug of a lifetime. Finn could see the relief etched on her face. It made him feel like a million dollars to have been able to do something to soothe Oliver and to provide comfort to Maggie. It troubled him a little bit. Never in his life had he felt this way before. And he didn't quite understand it. Why did it mean so much to him to be there for Maggie and Oliver?

He related to Oliver because of his own experience

with grief as a child. In some way he felt as if he was uniquely qualified to help the boy navigate his way through his terrible loss and the newness of their life in Alaska. If things had been different, it would have been a privilege to be Oliver's father.

He would have to settle for being Oliver's best friend and ally.

Pink and purple streaks of color stretched across the horizon. The rugged mountains popped out at her, making Maggie feel as if she could simply reach out her hands and touch them. If Maggie was a painter this would be her muse—the magnificent Alaskan landscape.

"Oh, it's a beautiful Alaskan morning," Maggie said as she gazed out of her bedroom window. "God sure did create a masterpiece when He made Alaska," she gushed. With each and every day, Maggie fell more in love with her surroundings.

Last night had been a pleasant evening in Hank's company. Although he had been a true gentleman, Maggie knew they could never be more than friends. Hank was looking for a wife and she didn't want to waste any more of his time. It wouldn't be fair to allow him to pursue her when she knew how she felt.

She heard Oliver rumbling around in his bedroom. Although they were due at church service in an hour, Maggie suspected Oliver had arisen early due to his excitement over meeting Boomer today at Finn's place. He had talked her ear off about it all afternoon and into the evening. She was fairly certain he had dreamed about it last night, she thought with a grin. That's how it should be for little boys. Dogs and trains and pilots with spar-kling green eyes and infectious smiles.

Her bedroom door burst open and Oliver stood in the doorway. "Is it time to go to Finn's house yet?"

"Not yet. We have church service first," Maggie re-minded him. "Don't you remember? I'm singing with the choral group."

"Aw," Oliver said in a loud voice.

Maggie didn't say a word. She sent her son a look full of reproach.

"Okay, I'm going to go get dressed for church," Oli-ver said in a chirpy voice. "I can't wait to hear you sing."

By the time they left the house half an hour later, both were dressed to impress. Maggie was wearing a cranberry-colored dress she had recently bought here in town. She had some high-heeled nude shoes she was going to slip on once they'd made it to the church. Navi-gating the snowy Alaskan weather dictated the use of boots. Oliver had put on his best pair of slacks and a dark blue sweater. She couldn't get over how mature he looked all of a sudden. He'd grown by leaps and bounds during the last year.

Maggie enjoyed singing with the choir at church. Oliver sat in the front pew and clapped along to the music. Although they were invited to stick around after the service for a pancake breakfast, Oliver practically dragged her out of the church.

"Oliver, we need to go change out of our church clothes," Maggie said.

"Why can't we just wear what we have on?" he asked with a groan.

"You can't play with Boomer in your Sunday best."

Oliver grumbled all the way back to the house, then practically vaulted out of the car when they reached home. Maggie was certain she'd never seen her son move so fast. It was as if his feet were on fire. She quickly changed into a pair of jeans and an oatmeal-colored sweater. Oliver was waiting impatiently for her at the door, wearing a sweatshirt and a pair of dark jeans.

Maggie drove the truck to town, navigating the snow-packed roads with a measure of confidence she hadn't felt when she'd first arrived in town. At moments like this Maggie wondered what Uncle Tobias might think of what she was doing. Hopefully, he would feel proud of his niece and the steps she had taken toward rebuilding her life.

As soon as the small, log-cabin house came into view on Swan Hollow Road, Maggie let out an admiring sigh. Finn's house was lovely. It was rustic and cozy. The house was nestled in a wooded area with a clear view of Kachemak Bay. It seemed like the perfect setting for Finn.

Right after they drove up, Finn walked outside, accompanied by a sweet-faced dog with black-and-white fur. He had a fancy red collar around his neck with rhinestones on it. Maggie thought he looked adorable.

"Boomer!" Oliver called out as he jumped out of the truck. The medium-sized dog ran toward Oliver and jumped up on him, knocking him to the snow.

"Down, Boomer!" Finn ordered. "Sorry about that. He tends to wear his heart on his sleeve."

"It's okay. He's just being friendly," Oliver said. "I don't mind."

Boomer's tail was wagging ferociously. Oliver threw

his arms around Boomer and hugged him. He began to pat him in a loving manner. Maggie had the feeling Oliver would once again be asking for a dog of his own.

"We got a present for you, Boomer." Oliver looked at Maggie. "Do you have it, Mom?"

"Sure thing," Maggie said, digging in her purse. "Here it is. Make sure it's okay with Finn to give it to him." She handed Oliver a bone wrapped up in a big red bow.

"Thanks, guys. He'll love it." He waved them toward the house. "Why don't we go inside and you can give Boomer the bone?"

Finn ushered Maggie and Oliver inside his home. The smell of pine wafted in the air. Another smell assailed her senses. It smelled like freshly baked cookies.

"Your house is lovely, Finn," Maggie remarked, looking around her at the sparsely decorated home.

"Thanks. I'm renting it, but I'm hoping to buy it from the owner. I'm crossing my fingers it all works out when I become co-owner of O'Rourke Charters. I'll be making a full-time income then and I can qualify for a mortgage."

Maggie's heart warmed at the possibility of Finn finally staking roots in Love. For so long he had been running away from making his hometown his permanent home. Surely this was a sign of growth and change, Maggie thought.

"Excellent," she said. "Inheriting Uncle Tobias's house has allowed us to own our first home. We were always renters. It's an amazing feeling."

Finn clapped his hands together. "Hey, can I offer

either of you something to drink? Hot chocolate? Tea? Cider? I have some cookies in the kitchen. They just came out of the oven."

"Mmm. They smell good," Oliver said, following Finn toward the kitchen.

"Aren't you full of surprises?" Maggie murmured as she spotted several racks of cookies sitting on the stove.

"I like baking," Finn said with a shrug. "Especially Christmas cookies. Most of these are for the winter carnival tomorrow night. Help yourselves though. I made more than enough."

Maggie reached over and grabbed a gingerbread cookie dusted with sprinkles. She took a bite and let out a sound of appreciation. "Hey, you're good at this, O'Rourke. This is delicious."

"Finn is good at everything," Oliver crowed, biting into a cookie.

Finn tousled his head and said, "Thanks, buddy."

"I guess I better pick up some snow pants for us so we can go to the winter carnival," Maggie said, thankful Finn had mentioned the event. With everything going on with the shop, Maggie had completely forgotten all about it.

As Maggie sipped a cup of green tea and watched the interplay between Oliver, Finn and Boomer, she couldn't help but wonder about Finn's determination to stay single and unattached. This house seemed perfect for a family. It was way too big for one person, and Finn seemed to enjoy being with people. He wasn't exactly a loner.

Finn O'Rourke was an enigma. The more she thought

she knew the man, the more she realized there were many aspects of him she might never be able to fully understand.

Having company over at his house wasn't something Finn was used to. He hadn't lived here very long, but lately the place had begun to feel like home. Inspired by Maggie and Oliver's Christmas tree, he'd even put up one of his own—a lovely balsam fir that towered over him. He still needed to buy a few more pieces of furniture. At the moment his style was minimalist. But, considering where he'd been little more than a year ago, his current situation represented major progress.

There was something so comfortable about having Maggie and Oliver hanging out with him at his house. It felt like family had stopped by. Conversation flowed easily. Finn didn't feel he had to do anything special to entertain them. Oliver was enamored with Boomer. And Boomer seemed to have fallen in love with Oliver as soon as he gave him the juicy bone.

"I think it's time I took Boomer for a walk. Want to come along, Oliver?" Finn asked.

"Sure thing," Oliver said, jumping up from his seat.

Finn hoped Maggie wouldn't offer to come along on the walk. Although he always enjoyed being around her, there were some things he needed to set straight with Oliver. And he thought it might be best if she wasn't around.

"I think I'll stay here and read the paper. Grace has an interesting article in here about making an Alaska bucket list," Maggie said, her nose buried in the local gazette.

Finn led Oliver out through the back door. He handed him Boomer's leash and began walking toward the woods.

In his excitement, Boomer was pulling at his leash.

"Don't let him lead you, Oliver. Just tug sharply on the leash to get him to walk beside you. If you let him get away with it, he'll try to do it every time he's taken for a walk."

Oliver listened intently and followed Finn's instructions. Within a matter of minutes, he'd gotten Boomer under control.

"Hey, buddy. I think we need to talk," Finn said, trying to make his voice sound casual.

Oliver looked up at him with big eyes. "Did I do something wrong?"

"No, little man. I think I might have done something wrong. Yesterday when we had our flying adventure you were upset about your mom going out on a date."

"It's okay, Finn. It doesn't matter. She went anyway," Oliver said with a shrug. Finn's lips twitched.

"You said something that surprised me. About wanting me to be your father."

"It's true. I do."

Finn felt as if his heart might crack wide-open. Oliver's little voice was filled with sincerity. It was amazing, Finn realized, how open and honest kids were. They laid it all out there, risking getting their hearts broken and their hopes dashed. Oliver's wide-open heart gutted Finn.

Finn reached out and clasped Oliver by the shoulder. "Oliver, that's the biggest and best compliment anyone has ever bestowed on me." He smiled at Oliver. "Life isn't as simple as we'd like it to be. Matter-of-fact, it's pretty complicated."

Oliver looked down and focused on Boomer. "So you don't want to be my dad, huh? I kind of figured."

"Hey, that's not it. I imagine being your dad would be the most awesome thing in the world."

Oliver looked at him, tears shimmering in his eyes. "Really?"

"Yes, really. But you can't just snap your fingers and pick a dad, Oliver. Your mom has a say in who your father's going to be. That's the way it works. And it's best when the mother and father are in love," Finn said, fighting past a lump in his throat. "Because a home filled with love is the best home of all."

"My dad used to say all the time that I was the best thing he'd ever done," Oliver said. He swiped away tears from his cheeks. "Sometimes I miss him so much it feels like I'm going to burst. I've been thinking if I found a new dad it wouldn't hurt as much."

"I know what it feels like to lose a parent. When my mom died it felt like the sun had been extinguished. For a long time, it seemed as if there was nothing good anywhere in this world."

Oliver nodded. "I felt the same way. It's been better since we moved here. I don't cry myself to sleep every night like I used to."

"Oliver, when we lose someone special there's an ache on our souls. It lessens over time but it never completely goes away. If you find a dad here in Love, that will be terrific. But it won't necessarily stop you from feeling sad about your dad."

"I guess you're right," Oliver said. "My mom cries

sometimes. She says it's like a rushing river when you lose someone."

"Your mom is one smart woman," Finn said with a nod of his head. Maggie was right. Grief was like a rushing river. It hit you when least expected. It could be wild and out of control. Unpredictable.

"I want to make sure you understand this one huge thing. You deserve an outstanding father because you're an incredible, loving, amazing boy. And if I had to guess, I'd say you're going to get your wish one of these days. Be patient."

"It's okay if you can't be my dad, Finn. 'Cause you're already my best friend."

Finn cleared his throat. Words eluded him. He wanted to grab Oliver and hug him for all he was worth. *His best friend.* Finn would accept that title with honor. And if he wasn't so afraid of messing up Oliver's life, Finn would fight to earn the title of father.

Chapter Ten

As soon as Maggie and Oliver arrived at the winter carnival on the town square, it felt to Maggie as if the entire town of Love embraced her. People approached her and introduced themselves, extending condolences to her about Uncle Tobias and welcoming her to town. Many expressed their enthusiasm about the grand opening of Keepsakes. It was nice to see all of the Prescott brothers —Cameron, Liam and Boone—happily settled down with their other halves. Their younger sister, Honor, who had been a toddler when Maggie had last seen her, was now a lovely young woman.

"Maggie Richards!" Maggie spun around at the sound of her name being called.

Dwight Lewis hadn't changed in two decades. He looked remarkably similar to the bespectacled, bow tie–wearing boy who had preferred math equations to chasing frogs in the Nottingham Woods. Seeing him after all these years served as a blast from the past.

"Dwight!" Maggie greeted him. He pulled her into a friendly hug. Maggie felt a groundswell of emotion.

Even though she and Finn had joked about Dwight the other day, it felt wonderful to see another childhood friend. She felt a little bad about hiding from him, although Keepsakes hadn't been ready for prying eyes.

A thin, dark-haired woman stood beside him. Dwight reached for the woman's hand and laced it with his own. "Maggie, I'd like to introduce you to Marta Svenson, my fiancée. Marta, this is my childhood pal Maggie Richards. She's come back to Love after a long absence."

Dwight was beaming with happiness. It bounced off him in waves. Maggie felt overjoyed for him and Marta. Finding love was truly a wonderful thing.

It felt nice to be in the thick of things. For too long she had burrowed herself in the shop and neglected making the acquaintances of the townsfolk. Many remembered her from her childhood visits to town. It was very humbling. And heartwarming.

Seeing the square lit up with holiday lights was a spectacular experience. Oliver's eyes were lit up with joy. As far as the eye could see were Christmas lights— colored lights, white lights, sparkling lights. They extended throughout the downtown area. Jarvis Street was lit up in spectacular fashion. It was a breathtaking sight to behold. The Free Library of Love was decked out in red and green flashing lights.

So far she hadn't seen Finn. Oliver kept asking for him over and over again as they explored the lights and ice sculptures. He had been looking forward to spending time with Finn this evening. As a diversion she sent him to play with Aidan and a few children from school. Maggie stood and watched from a distance as Oliver raced around the square with absolute abandon. Her chest tightened with pride. He was acclimating nicely to this wonderful town. A casual observer would never have known he was a newcomer to Love.

All of a sudden Maggie spotted a flash of red and a rugged frame. It was Finn! He had walked up to Oliver and lifted him up from behind. Finn was spinning him around in circles. Maggie didn't need to see Oliver's expression. She knew he was grinning from ear to ear.

"They're so sweet together." Ruby walked up beside her and jutted her chin in the direction of Finn and Oliver.

"They really are," Maggie acknowledged. "Oliver is Finn's biggest fan. And Finn is so attentive and caring. He's been a wonderful friend for both of us."

"Are the two of you…circling around each other?" Ruby's brown eyes were twinkling with interest.

"Not at all. We're just friends." She quirked her mouth. "Finn isn't looking for an instant family. Or a wife. And I need stability for Oliver." She made a face. "I actually caved and went out on a date with Hank Jeffries."

"How was it? Any sparks?" Ruby asked, curiosity glinting in her eyes. "I know you said you're not really looking for romance."

Maggie shook her head. "Hank is a nice man and dinner was delicious, but I can't really see anything developing between us. As much as Oliver has let it be known he wants a father, I'm not interested in a romantic relationship. I'm still dealing with my husband's death. Romance is the last thing on my list."

"Of course you're still grieving his loss, Maggie.

Losing a spouse is one of the most traumatic life events a person can go through. Not to mention you've moved all the way to an Alaskan fishing village far away from home. You have to give yourself time." Ruby patted her on the shoulder. "But, somewhere down the road you might be ready to open up your heart to the possibilities. Speaking as a mother, your life doesn't begin and end as a mom. You need to be happy too."

Maggie said. "That's very true. Everyone deserves to be content in their lives."

Happiness. For so long Maggie hadn't even considered her own joy. Back in Massachusetts she'd been so miserable in the aftermath of Sam's death. And if she was being honest with herself, her marriage had been rocky for quite some time prior to the tragic loss of her husband. Sam Daviano had put her through the ringer during their marriage. Arrests for petty crimes. Chronic unemployment. Verbal abuse. In the aftermath of his death she had even changed Oliver's last name to Richards in order to avoid the stigma associated with his father. In the end, there had been nothing left for them in Boston.

Moving to Alaska had transformed Maggie's life. Day by day, she was building a life for herself and Oliver. There were moments of pure happiness where she knew they were both healing. The residents of Love made Maggie feel as if she'd landed right where God intended her to be.

And it had everything to do with being in this small fishing village, her friendship with Finn and the remarkable people who were helping her find peace in Love.

* * *

After parting ways with Oliver, Finn headed over
to the concession stand. All of the proceeds from the
winter carnival event were going to a homeless shel-
ter in Homer. He surveyed the goodies. Sugar cookies. Cupcakes decorated with frosting reindeers. *Bûche
de Noël* cake. He had to admit his Christmas cookies
looked delectable. At least half of them had already sold.
He didn't have much of a sweet tooth, but these items
looked scrumptious. He imagined Oliver would get a
kick out of the whimsical baked goods.

Finn still hadn't come face-to-face with Maggie, although he'd spotted her from a distance. He was deliberately keeping away in case Hank and Maggie had come
here together this evening. Although he liked to think
he was taking the high road, it still irritated him that
Maggie and Hank could potentially be the next It couple
in town. He shook the feeling off, stuffing it down to a
place where he wouldn't have to examine his emotions.

"Your cookies look good. I'd recognize them anywhere." Declan's voice heralded his arrival before Finn
saw him.

"Thanks. Why aren't you out there at the dogsledding
track?" Finn asked, jutting his chin toward the dogsled
area. Declan had always been a huge fan of the sport.

"Annie was feeling a bit tuckered out, so I was keeping her company. I didn't want her to run the risk of
falling off the sled. Liam says fatigue is normal at this
stage of her pregnancy, so I'm trying not to worry."

"Makes sense. Liam wouldn't steer you wrong," Finn
said in a reassuring voice. He could see the worried
expression etched on Declan's face. To say Annie was

Declan's world was an understatement. "Speaking of Annie, where is your better half?" Finn asked, looking around the area for his sister-in-law.

"She's somewhere talking to Jasper about the town council vote on library funds. At which point I recused myself from the conversation," Declan said in a dry voice.

Finn chuckled. Knowing Annie, she was reading the town mayor the riot act. He almost wished he could witness it. Not many people could go head-to-head with Jasper.

Just then Finn caught sight of Maggie. She was wearing a puffy white coat with matching ski pants. On her head was a jaunty pink hat that was tilted to the side. Her cheeks were rosy and the tip of her nose was pink. He couldn't help smiling.

"Go on over, Finn. You know you want to talk to her," Declan said, jabbing him in the side.

He scowled at his brother. "Declan, will you give it a rest? Stop meddling. You're acting like you're twelve years old."

Declan held up his hands. "All right. I won't say another word." He held up his hand. "Scout's honor."

Finn couldn't help but chuckle. Declan always managed to make him laugh. "You were never a Boy Scout. Not even close."

Declan snorted. "Neither were you!" Finn smiled, enjoying the familiar rhythms of his relationship with his brother. He prayed they would continue to grow and strengthen as siblings.

"Finn! Finn!" Oliver was calling to him from across the way. Finn waved at him, then beckoned him over.

The boy grabbed Maggie by the hand and began pulling her toward Finn and Declan.

"I'm going to go find my lady," Declan said, crossing paths with Maggie and Oliver and exchanging pleasantries as they passed by. Declan turned back toward Finn and winked at him in an exaggerated manner.

"I've been looking for you everywhere," Oliver said as soon as he reached Finn's side. "I wanted to show you the dragon ice sculpture."

"You should have known I'd be over here by the snacks," Finn said in a teasing voice. He rubbed his stomach. "They've got some mouthwatering treats, including my very own gingerbread cookies."

Oliver rubbed his mittened hands together. "Ooh. I love gingerbread."

"Hi, Finn. How are you?" Maggie greeted him with a warm smile.

"I'm good. Are you having fun?" he asked.

She nodded her head. "This is a wonderful holiday event. Everyone is so down-to-earth and welcoming. They really know how to make a person feel at home."

"Are you here alone? Or…did Hank come with you?" Finn blurted out the question before he could reel himself in.

Maggie wrinkled her nose. "No, I didn't come with Hank tonight. Oliver and I came together."

"No?" he asked, as a feeling of relief swept over him. Thoughts of Hank being with Maggie had been gnawing at him. Suddenly, Finn felt on top of the world.

"Did you guys get a dogsled ride?"

Maggie bit her lip. "No. I haven't ridden on one since I was a kid."

"So what? It's like riding a bike. You'll be fine."

Maggie shook her head vehemently. "Nope. It's not going to happen. I don't need a broken ankle or a bruised hip if I fall off. Thank you very much. Those dogs go so fast."

"Come on, Mags. I'll ride with you and Oliver. I'll even hold your hand and keep you from falling off if that's what's worrying you." The image of them riding together made Finn feel like a kid all over again.

Maggie began to giggle. Finn loved seeing the way her eyes crinkled and the sides of her mouth twitched. He looked at Oliver, who was watching him watch Maggie. He had a glint in his eye and Finn had the strangest feeling wheels were turning in his six-year-old mind.

"Mom said she'll ride the dogsled," Oliver piped up. He was grinning from ear to ear.

Maggie held up her hand. "I said maybe. It wasn't a promise, Oliver."

"But, Mom, they're only here for the winter carnival." Oliver's face fell. "They came all the way from Nome."

"Oliver, I didn't buy any tickets. And the line is really long," Maggie said, pointing toward the team of huskies.

Finn didn't know if this was becoming a habit, but he found himself wanting to make everything right with Oliver's world. The kid had him wrapped around his little finger.

"Well, I just happen to have some pull with the person who brought the huskies to town." He turned to Maggie as Oliver began hooting and hollering.

"How about it, Maggie? Let's ride the dogsled for old times' sake."

* * *

Finn's invitation to take a ride on the dogsleds made Maggie feel like the ten-year-old version of herself. If she closed her eyes, she could picture them being led by the pack of huskies with the wind whipping against their faces and snow gently falling all around them. It had been pure joy.

"I have a surprise for your mother." Finn's huge grin threatened to overtake his face.

"What is it?" Oliver asked, jumping up and down with excitement.

"Why don't the two of you grab some hot chocolate? I'll be right back." Finn dashed off, leaving the two of them wondering what he was up to. Maggie walked to the concession stand with Oliver and bought two hot chocolates, as well as one of the reindeer cupcakes for Oliver. Before she knew it, Oliver had stuffed half of the cupcake in his mouth. He swigged it down with some gulps of hot chocolate. Maggie shook her head. She hoped Oliver wasn't going to be on too much of a sugar high.

Live in the moment, she reminded herself. Tonight was special and she wasn't going to ruin it by focusing too much on the sweets table. Her son was happier than she had seen him in well over a year. That in itself made Maggie feel like doing a jig.

Thank You for blessing us with this evening, Lord. For the fellowship and goodwill of this wonderful community. And thank You for bringing Finn back into my life and for allowing him to be a guiding light for Oliver. We are truly blessed.

By the time Oliver had finished the cupcake and hot

chocolate, Finn was walking back toward them with Aidan at his side. He was holding a bunch of tickets in his hand. "It's official. We have tickets for the dogsled."

Oliver began cheering. "Yippee!" he yelled.

"I told you I had a little surprise," Finn said. He pulled a sled from behind his back—an old-fashioned wooden one with red trim. Although the sled was worn down, Maggie instantly recognized it.

"Are you kidding me?" Maggie asked. She raised her mittened hands to cover her mouth.

"I wouldn't kid about this," Finn said. "This sled is a classic and a cherished memory."

Maggie reached out and traced the faded letters spelling out her name. "After all these years you still have it? I can't believe it."

"It's seen better days, but it's been sitting in the attic all this time."

Oliver frowned. "What's so special about it?"

"This was your mother's sled," Finn explained to Oliver. "She used to ride like the wind down Cupid's Hill over at Deer Run Lake. I'll have to take you there sometime so you can sled with Aidan."

"That would be awesome," Aidan said in an excited voice.

Oliver's jaw dropped. "Wow. You must have been cool back then, Mom."

Maggie and Finn began to laugh. Aidan giggled.

"We sure thought we were," Maggie said. "Finn was pretty mischievous. This sled actually belonged to Declan. Finn borrowed it then wrote my name on it. You should have seen the steam coming out of Declan's ears."

"No one ever accused me of being a choirboy," Finn said in a teasing voice.

"No, they never did," Maggie said in a low voice as memories of the first time she'd ever met Finn flashed into her mind. It had been straight after church service and he'd tried to frighten her by putting a frog down the back of her shirt. Maggie had chased after him and, after giving him a piece of her mind, she'd accepted an invitation to go salamander hunting with him. It had been an auspicious beginning to a wonderful friendship.

"So, Mom. Are you going to ride on the dogsled?" Oliver asked. "Aidan and I are going to head over there."

"I don't know, Oliver. It's been a long time," she said, suddenly feeling a little anxious. She wasn't a kid anymore. What business did she have racing around and being led by a pack of huskies?

Oliver shrugged and walked away with Aidan.

"That's unacceptable, Maggie Richards," Finn said in a scolding voice as soon as Oliver was gone. "I seem to recall you're saying you wanted to be brave. Am I right? What could be braver than racing like the wind on a dogsled and showing your son how it's done?"

Maggie rolled her eyes. "You're not going to give up on this, are you?"

Finn smirked and shook his head. "Nope. Absolutely not."

With a sigh of resignation, Maggie tucked her sled behind a bush for safekeeping and turned back toward Finn. "Let's do this," she said, motioning toward the area where the huskies were gathered to take people on rides.

When they got to the dogsled track, Maggie watched

as Aidan and Oliver stood together in line. Their little faces were full of excitement. Seeing their blossoming friendship reminded her of the way she and Finn had done the same dogsled run twenty years ago.

"Hold on tight!" Maggie called out as she watched the boys settle onto the dogsled with one of the mushers, then take off down the snowy path as the beautiful huskies exhibited their speed and power. She heard Olivier cry out with delight as they headed out of sight. When it was her turn to ride with Finn she held on tightly and prayed to make it back in one piece. Despite her nerves, it was an exhilarating feeling to fly across the snow-packed ground with the frosty air lashing against her cheeks. When they returned to the starting point she could hear Oliver and Aidan loudly cheering for them.

Gliding across the snow led by the team of huskies was a thrill ride for Maggie. She loved the exciting feeling of being pulled by the dogs at breakneck speed. After two rides, Maggie was chilled to the bone and done with dogsledding, although Oliver and Aidan wanted to continue to stand in line for another ride. Maggie chuckled. The boys didn't even seem to feel the cold.

"Why don't we go get something to drink to warm us up?" Finn suggested. He pointed at Oliver and Aidan. "These two will be fine. Something tells me they might go on a few more runs. I gave Oliver some extra tickets. He seems determined to use them."

"Oh, Finn, you're going to spoil him. I can't remember the last time we had so much fun," Maggie gushed. Even though her face felt slightly frozen, her teeth chattered and her wool mittens were slightly wet, Maggie wasn't about to complain. This evening had been stellar.

"This is one of my favorite town events," Finn said. "You can almost feel Christmas flowing in the air." He rubbed his hands together. "The lights are spectacular." He winked at Maggie. "I reckon they could spot us from space."

They made their way to the concession area where Finn bought two hot apple ciders and sugar cookies. Maggie didn't miss the curious glances thrown their way. She felt a moment of discomfort when she saw Hank watching them from across the way. She imagined everyone thought something romantic was brewing between her and Finn. Hazel began waving at her from behind the concession stand. She pointed toward Finn and gave Maggie a thumbs-up sign. Maggie frowned at Hazel and shook her head insistently, but Hazel continued to grin.

Maggie frowned. First Ruby. And now Hazel. She didn't want to have to explain to everyone later on about her platonic relationship with Finn. Was she sending out signals about wanting more than friendship? How could she expect Oliver not to get confused when most of the town seemed to be questioning their status?

"Don't mind the looks and the stares," Finn instructed. "In a place called Love, the residents are always looking for the next couple. Don't let it bother you."

"I'm sure they mean well, but it's a little nerve-racking."

"I grabbed a blanket from the warming area. If we sit over there you can keep an eye on Oliver without him seeing us," Finn suggested. "Plus, we won't have to be the object of any whispers."

Maggie nodded in agreement. She was fine with Oliver dogsledding, but she didn't mind watching him from a discreet distance. And Maggie had never enjoyed being stared at. Although the townsfolk of Love weren't being mean-spirited, she had endured enough stares in Boston to last a lifetime.

As they moved toward a quiet area with a clear view of the dogsled track, Finn found a perfect spot and took a moment to lay a blanket down on the ground. They both sat and got comfortable.

"I have some hand warmers if you need them," Finn said, patting his jacket pocket.

"I'm good for now. This cup is really warming up my hands."

They each sipped their warm ciders. With a full moon set amid an onyx sky, Maggie couldn't help but admire the beautiful surroundings. She felt so tranquil and relaxed. She knew it wasn't just the winter carnival or the townsfolk or Oliver's effusive joy.

"Do you think I've changed a lot?" Maggie asked Finn. Being here tonight at the winter carnival reminded her of the last time she'd been at a holiday event here in town. It had felt like a trip down memory lane. She had been ten years old. A lifetime ago for all intents and purposes. Sometimes she wished she still had a sense of childhood wonder. Back then she hadn't been nervous at all about riding a dogsled. Over the years she'd become more of an anxious person. Pushing past those fears was the best remedy for anxiety. She was trying really hard in all areas of her life to be braver than she felt.

"Not really. Maybe a little bit. Have I?" Finn asked. He ran his hand across his jaw. "Aside from growing into a ruggedly handsome man," he said in a teasing voice, "I think I'm still me."

"At first you seemed really different," Maggie said. She smirked at him. "But once I scratched the surface, you're the same old Finn."

"Thanks. I think," he said with a low-throated chuckle.

"I meant it as a compliment. Sometimes I feel like the best parts of me ended up being chewed up by life. You remind me of a time and place when I was a better version. I wasn't so anxious or jaded. And lately I've been wondering if I passed it on to Oliver. He can be a worrywart sometimes."

"I don't believe that, Maggie. Do you know why? Because of Oliver. That kid has more heart than anyone I know, except for his mother. Where do you think that came from?"

Maggie shook her head. "I'm not sure he got that from me. I've been so afraid, Finn. Afraid of taking chances. Afraid of the sky falling in." She shrugged. "Just plain afraid. I'm ashamed to admit it, but I get really anxious sometimes worrying about things that are out of my control."

He reached out and squeezed her mittened hand. "You have nothing to be embarrassed about. Everyone has fears. We all worry. Give yourself a break, Mags. You've been through a lot. That takes a toll on a person."

"You're right. It does," Maggie said. "I don't like the feeling of things being out of my control. But the reality is, life often is unpredictable."

"I get it. When my grandfather got sick I felt as if my world had tilted on its axis." He bowed his head. "My emotions were all over the place. Fear had me in its grip. I knew there was nothing I could do to keep him in this world and it made me panic. I ran away from the pain of losing him. In the process, I cut myself off from all the people I loved and who loved me in return." Finn cleared his throat. "I didn't get to say goodbye to him. Fear cost me that moment."

She reached out and placed her hand on Finn's knee. "I'm sorry you missed saying your final farewell to him. There was so much love between the two of you. I hope you've been able to hold on to that."

"It's been easier to focus on the good memories ever since I returned. Now that I'm no longer running I can finally breathe a little easier. There's something about being back home that's been healing in a lot of ways."

Maggie looked at Finn as surprise washed over her. She felt the same way about being in Love. There was something so special about this heartwarming Alaskan town. "Honestly, I've felt different ever since I stepped off that seaplane. I feel braver than I've felt in years. And hopeful."

Finn nodded. "Hope is a wonderful thing."

They locked gazes. "I'll tell you a secret, Mags. You were my first crush," Finn admitted.

Maggie let out a squeal. "Really?"

"Yes, ma'am. I used to wonder if you were crushing on me as well." He wiggled his eyebrows at her. "So? The moment of truth has arrived. Were you?"

Maggie ducked her head down. Her cheeks felt flushed. She shouldn't be embarrassed. This was Finn. Her childhood pal. But with his soulful green eyes and rugged good looks, Maggie was having a hard time keeping him strictly in the friend zone. Adrenaline did tend to course through her veins whenever he was in her orbit. As children, her feelings for Finn had been strictly platonic.

"To be honest, no, Finn. It wasn't until much later that I developed romantic feelings for anyone. I think I was sixteen. A late bloomer, I suppose. I think being around my mother made me wary of developing feelings for anyone. After all, she chased anything with a pulse. It didn't make for a very stable childhood." She met Finn's gaze head-on. "But I'll tell you one thing, Finn O'Rourke. I thought you were the best thing since sliced bread. You were the most impressive, courageous and wonderful boy I'd ever met. You showed me how to run freely and embrace everything the world has to offer. And you didn't treat me differently because I was a girl. You taught me not to be so fearful. And you changed me for the better. Every time I left Love I felt stronger and more confident. I owe you a debt of gratitude for that."

Finn placed his hand over his heart. "That means the world to me. I thought about you long after you left Love for the last time. I kept hoping you'd come back. But you never did."

"I thought we would come back too. When we left here that last time I never knew it would be twenty years before I came back to Love." She quirked her mouth. "My mother fought with Uncle Tobias over her lifestyle. He wanted us to stay in Love so I could have a stable upbringing." She shook her head as bitter memories rose to the surface. "She was always chasing the next best husband. So instead of coming back here we moved to

Arizona, then California and New Mexico before heading to New England."

Finn let out a low whistle. "That's a lot of moving around."

Maggie nodded. "It was rough. That's why I want Oliver to stay rooted in one place. Stability is important for children."

"Is your mom still around?" Finn asked.

"Yeah, she's living out in Las Vegas with a new husband. We're not close. There's no getting around it. My childhood was a train wreck."

"That's too bad," Finn said. "I guess both of us were going through a lot of dysfunction at the same time."

She squeezed his hand tightly. "I feel bad complaining when you lost so much."

Finn looked at her. A bittersweet expression was etched on his face. "Pain is pain, Maggie. It's hard to compare battle wounds. And you don't have to feel bad about anything. It's all right to feel whatever you're feeling."

"On a good day my feelings are all over the place," Maggie admitted.

"That's what I admire most about you. Your ability to be open and honest. So many people have a filter. You're genuine, Mags. You always have been."

Maggie felt her cheeks flush at Finn's compliment. Their faces were so close together and Finn was gazing into her eyes with such a tender look. Maggie looked up at him, wondering if she was misinterpreting what was about to happen next. Unless she was imagining things, Maggie was fairly certain she was about to kissed by Finn O'Rourke.

Chapter Eleven

Finn looked into Maggie's eyes and knew he was mere seconds away from kissing her. He tried his best to resist, knowing he was going against every vow he'd made about getting romantically involved with Maggie. He wasn't any good for her. She deserved someone solid. A father for Oliver. A man who could pledge eternity to her. He was filled with so much fear and anxiety about hurting the people he cared about. And if he was being honest with himself, he didn't trust himself to go the distance. In so many ways, Finn didn't fit the bill of what Maggie needed or wanted.

But in this moment everything stilled and hushed between them. It was just the two of them— him and his beautiful, sweet Mags. She was radiant in every single way imaginable. He reached out and stroked the line of her jaw with his fingers. She was so incredibly lovely. With her creamy skin and vivid eyes, Maggie was a knockout. Those same eyes were looking at him now with a mixture of anticipation and wonder.

"Maggie, I'm not sure I have the right to kiss you, but

if I'm being completely honest with you, there's nothing I'd rather do at this moment." His voice sounded raspy to his own ears. He wanted this more than he'd wanted anything in his entire life. That very thought worried him, but he stuffed the feeling down and focused on this interlude between him and Maggie. There was a lot to be said about living in the moment.

"I—I haven't been kissed in a long time, but I'd very much like for you to kiss me." Her voice was soft yet steady. It rang out with truth.

The raw honesty in Maggie's words propelled Finn forward. He lowered his head, letting out a sigh as his lips touched Maggie's. He placed his lips over hers in a tender, soaring kiss. She smelled like a mixture of the great outdoors and a light vanilla scent.

For Finn, this kiss was everything. It was friendship and romance and attraction. It was the ties binding the two of them together for decades. It represented new beginnings.

As the kiss ended, Finn knew with a deep certainty all kisses weren't created equal. He had kissed enough women in his life to realize this was special. Powerful. Spectacular. Seconds ticked by during which their foreheads touched and neither said a word. He could hear the low sound of his breathing and see the rapid rise and fall of her chest. At the same time, he knew he'd just made a colossal mistake.

"Finn, what does this mean?" Maggie asked, her voice full of uncertainty. "For us? I don't want to lose our friendship or put a strain on it."

"I don't know, but I do know I'm at my best when I'm with you, Maggie. I feel more like me than I ever do with anyone else," Finn admitted. He didn't know exactly how to put into words the way he was feeling. But he knew it felt right when Maggie was in his arms. She was rapidly becoming his best friend all over again. Finn cared so very much about her well-being. As a result, he couldn't stuff down the niggling feelings of doubt roaring through him. He wanted to try with Maggie. He yearned to be the man who could make her and Oliver happy, but he worried about hurting both of them. If he harmed either one of them, he would never forgive himself.

Finn opened his mouth to tell Maggie his truth. Kissing her had been a mistake. It had been a selfish move on his part since he knew it couldn't go anywhere. Maggie wasn't the type of woman a man should trifle with.

"Hey, Mom! There you are!" Oliver's chirpy voice interrupted them as he suddenly appeared in front of them. His cheeks were flushed with cold and his snow pants were damp. "I was looking for you everywhere."

Maggie grinned at her son. "I think it's time we headed home, Oliver. Your eyes are getting a little droopy and your cheeks are as red as a berry." Finn jumped up and lent a hand to Maggie, pulling her to her feet. For a moment their eyes locked. Something crackled in the air between them.

"C'mon," Oliver said, his voice full of fatigue. "I want to say goodbye to Aidan."

As they walked back toward the concession stand where the residents were gathered, Finn's mind was full of regrets. Even though kissing Maggie had been a moment of pure tenderness and connection, Finn couldn't allow himself to believe in a happy ending.

Sharing this precious time with Maggie hadn't changed a single thing. He still felt unworthy of a happily-ever-after.

Maggie had been fretting about the kiss she'd shared with Finn ever since the night of the winter carnival. She'd tried not to focus on it, but it felt like the elephant in the room whenever she and Finn were in the same area. She didn't know if she was imagining it or not, but things felt slightly awkward. Maggie wasn't used to kissing a man she wasn't attached to romantically. Although the past few days had been filled with completing the final days of setup for Keepsakes, she was preoccupied by her conversation with Finn the other night. He had praised her for being open and honest. Forthright. It bothered her to think she was keeping secrets from him, especially when he had been so transparent about his mother's accidental death.

Maggie couldn't hold off any longer. She wanted to tell Finn the truth about the circumstances of Sam's death. At this point, it felt like a lie to withhold such information. It was weighing her down like an anchor. Finn was her best friend here in town. It would feel therapeutic to get it off her chest.

Lord, please help me get the words right. I don't want Finn to think I've lied to him about Sam. And I pray he'll understand why I kept silent. I know Finn's heart—he's a strong, good man.

Maggie cooked that evening for her, Finn and Oliver. It was her specialty—spaghetti Bolognese with garlic bread and salad. Oliver had put both her and Finn on the spot by begging Finn to come for dinner. Maggie didn't mind since she'd been searching for an opportunity to have a private conversation with Finn. After tucking her son into bed, she stood at the sink and washed the dinner dishes, with Finn drying and putting them back on the shelves.

"Everything okay?" Finn asked. "You seem a bit preoccupied. I hope you're not worrying about the grand opening. We're in great shape."

Maggie shook her head. "It's not the shop." She bit her lip. "You've been so honest with me about your mother's death. It's made me feel a little bit ashamed."

Finn raised an eyebrow. "Ashamed? Of what?"

"I haven't been completely straightforward about my husband's death."

Finn frowned. His handsome features were creased in confusion. "What do you mean?"

Maggie took a deep breath. "He wasn't the victim of a store robbery. The truth is he was holding it up for money." Her voice quivered. "The store owner shot and killed him in self-defense."

Finn's jaw dropped. He stumbled for something to say in response to Maggie's confession. His mind whirled with the reality of her situation. Not only was she a widowed single mother, but she had been traumatized by the extreme circumstances of her husband's death. Her husband had single-handedly destroyed their family with his actions.

Finn's heart began to pound like crazy in his chest.

Maggie wiped away a tear. "Sam lived a double life. He had gotten into trouble with the law from time to time over the years, but mostly for small things." She let out a harsh-sounding laugh. "Not that it didn't matter, but I had no idea he was robbing stores. He grew up in really abusive foster homes, so I think I made a lot of excuses for him. I can honestly say I didn't see it coming."

"When the police came to my door that night I was in utter shock. I kept thinking Sam was the victim of the robbery because it was the only thing I could fathom. Then it became agonizingly clear he was a very troubled man. One I'd been married to for seven years."

Finn's heart was breaking for her and Oliver. It must have rocked their world to its core to have been blindsided in such a shocking way. "Maggie, I'm so sorry you went through all of that. It must have been agonizing."

"We went through a lot in the aftermath." Maggie ducked her head. "People weren't very nice."

Finn gritted his teeth. "What did they do?"

"I lost my job. We got phone calls and harassing letters. Our landlord kicked us out. Even our church community turned their backs on us. Most of the parents of Oliver's friends wouldn't allow their children to have playdates with him. We lost everything all at once."

Her voice faltered. "What I'll never understand is why people were so cruel to us. Why they blamed us. We were victims too. We lost our lives." Maggie's voice was laced with agony.

"It makes no sense as to why people choose to act in such a mean-spirited way. It's the very opposite of the way we're supposed to treat each other. I'll never understand it, but I do know good people outweigh the bad in this world." Finn deeply believed it. His faith taught him to do unto others and love one another.

"You're right, Finn. That's a good way to look at things," Maggie said with a nod.

There was no doubt as to how much she and Oliver had suffered due to her ex-husband. Maggie had been terribly wounded by her husband's actions and subsequent death. His heart bled for Maggie and Oliver. To suffer the condemnation of one's community after such a tragedy was shocking. He stuffed down a desire to head to Boston and deal with those small-minded people who had hurt Maggie. He'd like to give them a piece of his mind and a dose of their own medicine.

He hated cruelty, especially toward a defenseless and grief-stricken mother and child. It was the very opposite of the way he wanted to live his life.

"Why were you afraid to come clean about it here in Love?" he asked, hating how Maggie had been so consumed with worry about her past. Finn prayed she would put all of it to rest so she could focus on her future.

"Because of all the judgment we endured. Coming here was about making a fresh start. I couldn't risk losing the goodwill of the people here before we even stepped into town."

"That would never happen," Finn said, wanting Maggie to understand this town was different. It was far from perfect, but he knew without a shadow of a doubt the townsfolk would extend Maggie grace and brotherly love.

"I know that now, but at the time I didn't. I could take it for me, but not for Oliver. He's just a child. And God knows he's innocent in all of this. Children shouldn't suffer the sins of the father." Her voice broke and she began to sob.

Finn placed an arm around Maggie and pulled her close. "He won't, Maggie. Oliver is happy and thriving here in Love. You did the very best thing you could for him. You stepped out on a limb of faith and came back to Alaska. You seized an opportunity to make a better life for yourself and Oliver. Those are commendable things."

A hint of a smile appeared on her face. "Thank you for saying so, Finn. I'm very grateful to be here in Alaska. I just felt a little funny about not coming clean with you. You've been so open and honest with me."

"Maggie, you don't owe the town or me an explanation of your past. If you wish to share that information, then so be it."

"I'm grateful for your listening ears, Finn. And for accepting me, warts and all."

As Finn drove home, his thoughts swirled with thoughts of Maggie and all she'd endured because of her ex-husband. It made his chest tighten painfully. And he knew with a sinking feeling in his gut that the information he'd learned tonight confirmed everything he felt about the possibility of building something with Maggie. It just wasn't possible.

There was no way he could risk subjecting Maggie to any more hurt. He didn't trust himself not to mess everything up. What if he did something to hurt them? What if he destroyed them the same way he had torn apart his own family? What if he did worse damage than Sam had done?

How could he risk it? Maggie and Oliver had already

been through so much. Way more than he had ever imagined or could even bear to think about. Finn felt sick to his stomach. By kissing Maggie, he may have led her to believe a relationship was possible between them when he knew it wasn't. He should have just left well enough alone and let Maggie develop something with Hank. A man like Hank wouldn't let Maggie down in the clutch. With one impulsive kiss he had complicated things. His timing couldn't have been worse. They were on the cusp of the grand opening for Keepsakes. His future as a co-owner of O'Rourke Charters was just within reach. It was the one dream he'd allowed himself to hold on to through the years.

Any hopes of being with Maggie and Oliver weren't realistic. One way or another, he feared he was going to hurt them. And the very thought of doing so made him feel like the worst person in the world.

Maggie felt as excited as she had always felt as a kid on Christmas morning. She was going caroling with her choir group and Finn had been invited to come along with them. The group was in dire need of altos. Maggie had to laugh. Although Finn loved to sing, he tended to sing off-key. It didn't matter, she thought. Caroling was about spreading Christmas cheer and goodwill. It was all about heart. Finn had plenty of it. And he sang with unbridled enthusiasm.

At seven o'clock sharp the carolers met on the town green. They were all dressed in old-fashioned burgundy cloaks and the women wore fur hand muffs. Snow was gently falling and there was a frost in the air.

"Where's Finn?" Oliver asked, looking around him.

Maggie frowned. Finn should have been here by now. "I don't know, love. Maybe he's going to join us or something came up with O'Rourke Charters." She made a face at Oliver. "You know he wouldn't miss this unless it was something important."

Maggie checked her phone. There were no messages from Finn. She'd been with him a few hours earlier at the shop. He'd been a little quiet, but when she had reminded him about the caroling event, he'd been on board with it. Where could he be?

They went caroling door-to-door, singing Christmas hymns and spreading the joy of the season as they walked around town. Despite her disappointment about Finn, Maggie had a fantastic time. It was a great opportunity to bond with her fellow choral singers and the residents of Love. Having Oliver by her side had provided a good opportunity to show her son the real heart of Love, Alaska.

As the event ended, a large number of the carolers headed over to the Moose Café. Much to Oliver's delight, Maggie decided to join the group. Once they entered, Maggie immediately spotted Finn. While Oliver was distracted by a few of his school friends, Maggie made a beeline over to him.

"Finn! What happened to you? We were expecting you to go caroling with us."

Finn raked his hand through his hair. He seemed to be looking everywhere but in her direction. "Hey, Maggie. I'm sorry. I had to do some paperwork for O'Rourke Charters. There's lots to do before I become Declan's partner."

"We had a good time," Maggie said, not asking Finn why he hadn't bothered to call her.

"That's good," he said in a clipped tone.

"Something's wrong," Maggie said. "What is it?" She knew Finn like the back of her hand. The expression on his face seemed distant. Something was off.

"Can we go outside for a minute?" Finn asked, his features creased with worry.

"Of course," Maggie said, following after Finn as he took the lead and headed outside.

With snowflakes swirling all around them, Finn began to speak.

"I don't want to hurt you, Maggie."

"W-what are you talking about?" she asked. Her mouth suddenly felt as dry as sandpaper.

"Us. That kiss we shared at the winter carnival. It should never have happened." He tapped his fingers against his chest. "It was all my fault for allowing it to happen. We could ruin a really good friendship. For me, it's not a risk I want to take."

Maggie felt a bit stunned. All she could do was nod. She had been hoping their kiss meant Finn had changed his mind about being in a relationship. That, combined with his clear affection for Oliver, had allowed her to have hope.

Stupid, stupid, she chided herself. Finn hadn't made her any promises. In this instance, a kiss had just been a kiss. Maggie didn't dare allow Finn to see her disappointment. Or her heartbreak.

"I understand," she murmured. Heat burned her cheeks. She'd been so foolish to believe Finn wanted something lasting with her. Hadn't he told her over and over again he wasn't interested in relationships? How could she have been so naive?

"We want different things," Finn continued. "At some point down the road you're going to want a father for Oliver. Who knows? It could be months from now or years. And I can't blame you. He deserves one after everything he's been through. And not just anyone. A great one. That can't be me. I'm not—" He fumbled with his words and his voice trailed off.

Hurt flared through her. Sharing a kiss with Finn had felt like coming home. Why was it so easy for him to push her away? Oliver's face flashed before her eyes. The way he felt about Finn was epic. He thought Finn was better and stronger than any superhero. His little heart was vulnerable. Finn was right. She couldn't risk her son being burned. She knew he wouldn't do it on purpose, but the fallout would still be the same. It was far better to end things before they even got started. She felt grateful Oliver hadn't gotten his hopes up and thankful she hadn't allowed Oliver to see how she felt about Finn. When it came to Finn, her son wore his heart on his sleeve.

"You're right. We got a little carried away with the kiss. The bottom line is I need to focus on my future. Oliver's future. My goals haven't changed. My son needs stability, and perhaps down the line a father. As you said, that can't be you."

She saw something flicker in the depths of Finn's green eyes. It looked a little bit like hurt, but she had to be mistaken. After all, Finn himself kept making the same point. He wasn't built for the long haul.

"I'm sorry to be so blunt, Maggie. I know it might

sound trite, but I never in a million years want to hurt you. Or Oliver."

As if through a fog, Maggie heard Finn say goodnight before he turned on his heel and walked off into the Alaskan evening. She steeled herself against the painful feelings ricocheting through her. She blinked away the tears and steadied herself to go back inside the Moose Café.

Eyes on the prize. Finn was Alaskan eye candy, but he wasn't the marrying kind. Or the settling-down kind. He could make her laugh like nobody's business, but he didn't want to assume the role and responsibilities of a husband and father. If nothing else, Sam had taught her to doubt love everlasting. She had promised herself a long time ago that she wasn't going to allow a man into her life. Been there, done that. Her goal had been to create a stable life for Oliver. He was her world. But then Finn had crept his way into her heart.

He'd given it to her straight. Finn didn't want entanglements. Maggie was trying to be brave, but tears burned her eyes as his words washed over her. *We want different things.* He hadn't meant to be cruel. It was just the way things were. For a little while she had forgotten her own resolve to not allow her head to rule her heart. With a few little words Finn had reminded her that she didn't need a man in her life. God had given her the best gift of all by allowing her to be a mother. She didn't need any more than that in this life. Oliver was enough!

Maggie headed back inside, plastering a smile on her face so she didn't upset Oliver. He was sitting at a table acting like the life of the party with his school friends. She might be nursing a bruised heart, but at least her son was happy. She took deep little breaths and counted to ten before joining some of her friends at a nearby table. Maggie had no intention of letting anyone see her wounds.

Life had taught Maggie well. Finn might have hurt her, but she was used to love making a fool out of her. All she could do now was hold her head up high and carry on. Not just for herself, but for Oliver as well.

Chapter Twelve

Finn couldn't remember a time when he had felt so poorly. He'd left Keepsakes early today, not wanting either Maggie or Oliver to catch whatever was ailing him. His body ached and he felt feverish. He was fairly certain he was coming down with something. Maybe the flu. Or some random stomach bug. He let out a groan, wishing he could be taken out of his misery.

A part of him knew he wasn't really sick. Or at least he wasn't ill with a virus. He was aching from the reality of his situation with Maggie. For one brief moment he'd nurtured a hope about being the type of guy who could be in a normal relationship. Maggie had inspired him to feel that way. He had clung to her goodness as a way of convincing himself it was possible. Then everything had blown up in his face. Reality had come crashing down on him. It was one thing to tell yourself you weren't worthy of a loving relationship and quite another to deal with the impact of it.

Although Maggie had tried to hide it, Finn knew he'd

hurt her. And it pained him to realize he'd wounded a person he deeply cared about. Maggie didn't deserve it.

The door to his house crashed open. Finn jumped up from his couch at the jarring sound. Break-ins were unheard-of in Love. He hoped a tree branch hadn't fallen on his home.

Declan came charging toward him, his striking features etched in anger.

"What do you think you're doing?" he barked. "Why did you give up on you and Maggie? According to Hazel, you stopped things before they even got started."

Finn let out a groan. "Excuse you. You can't just come barging in to my house."

"Gimme a break, Finn. Stop trying to divert my attention. I saw the two of you at the winter carnival. It was obvious there were feelings brewing between you. You looked like a couple. Why did you bail on Maggie?"

Finn let out a groan. "I didn't bail on anyone. Not that it's any of your business, but things between Maggie and me got complicated. We're better off as friends. I'm actually doing her a favor."

Declan let out a snort. "Women are complicated, Finn. It's not rocket science."

"I'm not cut out for relationships. There! Are you happy now?"

"You love her, Finn. It's written all over your face. You show it every time you glance in her direction. Ever since Maggie's been back in Love I've seen a different side of you. One I thought was gone forever. You're happier. Your soul is lighter. You laugh more. That's because of her." Tears pooled in Declan's eyes. "I know how much it hurt you when Mom died. It was agonizing. You've always tried to hide your hurts, but I saw your pain. You haven't been the same since then."

"What do you want me to say, Declan?" He let out a groan. "Yes, I love her. But I'm not cut out— " Finn stopped midsentence and shook his head. The words were stuck in his throat. How could he explain himself without revealing the truth about the night their mother died? And if he did, Declan might hate him for the rest of his life. He couldn't bear the thought of losing his brother. He'd already lost so many people in his life. Losing him would gut Finn.

"Don't run away from what you're feeling for Maggie. Stay. For once in your life stick around and face things."

Finn shrugged. "Who says I'm running? Maybe I'm just walking away."

"From the woman you love? Why would you do that?" Declan asked.

"Because I don't deserve her or Oliver or a nice house with a white picket fence. I don't want to hurt them."

Declan winced. "Why would you say something like that? You deserve it all, Finn."

"No, I don't. Don't you get it? It was all my fault. All of it. Every loss our family endured. It was all because of me. And I'm scared to death I'm going to do something to hurt Maggie and Oliver."

"What are you talking about?" Declan asked, his voice sounding raw and wounded. Finn knew he was hurting Declan and it killed him.

Finn swiped away tears with the back of his hand. "I can't do this. Please. Just leave it alone."

"No way. You can't say something like that and then backtrack."

Finn heaved in a ragged breath. He'd avoided this conversation for two decades. Finn felt tired. He was so incredibly weary. For so long he had carried this heavy weight on his shoulders. He was close to the breaking point.

"It was me. All me. I put the bullets in the shot-gun. When I was home alone I did some shooting prac-tice in the backyard even though I knew we weren't supposed to touch the shotgun without adult supervi-sion. I replaced the gun right where I'd found it, but I didn't empty the shells." Finn couldn't bear to look at his brother. He didn't want to see the look of disgust on his face.

Declan let out a blast of air. "And you've been car-rying this around on your shoulders for twenty years? Blaming yourself?"

"How could I not? I knew what I'd done, but I didn't tell anyone. And Dad took the blame for it. He took off and stayed gone. He even served a prison sentence after running on the wrong side of the law. If you ask me, Gramps died from a broken heart. He couldn't take all of those losses."

Declan met his gaze head-on. "That's nonsense. He died of emphysema. He'd been dealing with it for years."

"The facts don't lie. I was the one who put the bul-lets in the rifle. That afternoon I was home alone...ten years old and eager to try something I knew was for-bidden. We were taught to always empty the shotgun. I didn't do that."

"And so what if you did? You were ten years old,

Finn. A child! I was eight. It could easily have been me who played around with the shotgun."

Finn shook his head. A part of him knew Declan was right, but another part of him still couldn't let himself off the hook.

"But it wasn't you who did it! It was me!" Finn exploded.

Declan shook his head. "Finn, you've got to find a way to put this to rest once and for all. You're giving up your future! I'm not going to let you do this to yourself. Do you hear me? I won't allow you to sabotage your happiness."

Finn watched as Declan stormed away from him and out of his house. He loved his brother for trying to lift him up, but there was still so much resting on his heart. It felt as if someone had placed a heavy anchor on his chest. Try as he might, Finn still didn't think he was worthy of being with a woman like Maggie.

Chapter Thirteen

A feeling of euphoria seized Maggie as she stood outside Keepsakes and looked up at the beautiful sign. A few days ago Finn had painted it a brilliant red against a backdrop of white. "I hope we've made you proud, Uncle Tobias," Maggie murmured as she scanned the display windows. Everything looked so festive and beautiful.

After feeling down in the dumps for several days about Finn, Maggie had convinced herself to snap out of it. As Oliver's mother, she couldn't allow herself to feel disheartened for too long. And she certainly wasn't going to allow Oliver to see her mope around like a wounded bird. She was going to keep her chin up and keep moving forward. If there was any awkwardness between her and Finn, Oliver would be the one to suffer for it. She was determined to treat Finn with nothing but kindness and friendship.

When she walked back inside the shop, Finn and Oliver were playing a game of checkers. She had to smile at the sight of them. They were strong competitors. Neither one wanted to lose the match to the other. Despite what had gone down between her and Finn, she didn't want anything to change for Oliver. Finn was still a very good man. So it was best to stuff down her heartache and act like a grown-up.

Maggie looked at her watch. "We're half an hour away from launch."

Finn said something in a low voice to Oliver, who quickly began to put away the game. As Oliver tidied up, Finn walked over to the front counter and pulled something from the shelves underneath.

"I have something for you," Finn said, holding out a gaily wrapped present. His expression was sheepish.

"What? Is this for me?" Maggie asked. She felt a little bit awkward about accepting a gift from Finn after things had fizzled out between them.

Finn nodded and pushed the gift toward her. "Today's a big day. I'm happy for you, Maggie. It's been a pleasure working side by side with you to get the shop up and running. Tobias would be over the moon."

"Should I open it now?" she asked.

"Go for it," Finn said with a grin.

Maggie began unwrapping the gift, marveling at Finn's mastery of gift wrapping. Once she'd ripped away the paper, Maggie took off the top from the square box. The moment she laid eyes on the rounded glass orb, she let out a squeal.

"Oh, Finn. It's magnificent," she said. She pulled the snow globe out of the box. It was a beautiful winter scene of a skating party at a lake. She shook the snow globe, admiring the delicate flakes that floated down on the scene.

"I could tell by the way you've been admiring the snow globes here in the store they were something you really admired. I also knew it wasn't something you would buy for yourself. You always think of others first."

"Do you like it, Mom?" Oliver asked. "Finn ordered it all the way from Montana."

Maggie reached down and tweaked Oliver's nose. "I don't just like it. I love it." She met Finn's gaze. "I'll treasure it forever."

The magnitude of Finn's gift lifted Maggie up to the stratosphere. Only Finn could have figured out her life-long love of snow globes. Only Finn would have had the foresight to order her such a meaningful gift and present it to her on such a special day.

As they locked gazes, a buzz of electricity passed between them. Awareness flared in the air. She didn't know what else to say without sounding sappy. Maggie hoped she wasn't wearing her heart on her sleeve, because at this moment the love she felt for Finn threatened to burst out of her heart.

She loved him. And she couldn't imagine not loving him. Not ever. Even though she knew they couldn't be together, that knowledge did nothing to change the way she felt.

A rapping noise echoed on the door. The sound of the doorknob rattling soon followed. Maggie felt her palms moisten with nervousness. It was hard to believe the moment had arrived. Keepsakes was about to open its doors.

"I think we have our first customers," Finn drawled. He looked at his watch. "And ten minutes early no less."

"Can I open the door?" Oliver asked.

"Why don't we do it together?" Maggie suggested, placing the snow globe back in its box and tucking it away behind the counter. With a deep breath, she headed toward the door with Oliver by her side and pulled it wide open, letting out a shocked sound as she saw a line of people waiting for entry. In all of her wildest dreams, she'd never imagined so many people showing up all at once.

"Welcome to Keepsakes," Maggie said in a cheerful voice.

"Thanks for coming," Oliver chirped, a big smile plastered on his face.

Excitement hummed and pulsed in the air as the townsfolk poured through the doors of Keepsakes. A little bell jangled every time a customer walked in. The smell of peppermint wafted in the air thanks to an essential oils diffuser. They had set up a little sidebar table with eggnog and apple cider doughnuts. Every customer was given a raffle ticket for a chance to win holiday prizes. A festive vibe radiated in the shop.

Hope floated in the air around them. She prayed her efforts to bring Keepsakes back to life would make Uncle Tobias proud.

Maggie greeted each and every customer. She felt very grateful for the bustling crowd. Finn was working the register and using his charm to sell additional items to customers once they were at the counter, checking out. Despite what had transpired between them the other night, they were working together to ensure the success of the grand opening.

At Finn's suggestion, Maggie had framed a black-

and-white photo of Uncle Tobias and hung it in a prominent place on the wall behind the cash register. It brought tears to her eyes to acknowledge how her uncle's kindness and generosity had affected so many lives. Maggie couldn't count the number of townsfolk who had approached her and recounted heartwarming stories about him.

With only an hour to go until the shop closed, a tall, good-looking man with gray-blue eyes walked in and a hush fell over the store. Maggie frowned as she looked around her. Hazel's jaw was practically on the floor. People were whispering and talking behind their hands. She swung her gaze to Finn. A myriad of expressions crossed his face—shock, recognition, joy.

Suddenly it hit Maggie like a ton of bricks. Although twenty years had passed since she'd last seen him, she felt fairly certain about the man's identity.

It was Colin O'Rourke, Finn's absentee father.

When Finn swung his gaze up from the cash register and spotted his father walking through the doorway, it felt as if he was having an out-of-body experience. He blinked once, then twice. He hadn't been mistaken. Colin O'Rourke had finally returned to Love, Alaska. The years had been kind to his dad. He was still a man who could turn heads by walking into a room.

Finn stepped from behind the cash register. In a few easy strides, he'd managed to intercept his father. They were the same height, Finn realized with surprise. For some reason, he always thought of his father from a child's vantage point. Taller. Stronger. Bigger.

"W-what are you doing here?" he asked in a low

voice. Even though he wanted to kick his father out on his ear, he didn't want to do anything to hurt sales or ruin the grand opening of Keepsakes. Maggie had worked tirelessly to pull this off. So far, they were knocking it out of the park.

Out of nowhere, Declan appeared at his father's side. "He's here for you, Finn."

Finn felt a stab of betrayal as he locked gazes with Declan. He'd known his father was going to show up here today! And he'd allowed Finn to be blindsided. He couldn't remember ever feeling so disappointed in his brother.

Finn swung his gaze around the store. Maggie was looking at him with wide eyes. He quickly walked over to her. "I need a few minutes. Can you man the cash register?"

She bobbed her head. "Of course. Take as much time as you need."

He made his way back to his father and brother. "We can't do this here. Let's go in the back room." Without waiting for an answer, Finn strode toward the back of the store and down a small hallway. He jerked open the office door and stormed inside, followed by Colin and Declan.

He felt as if steam was coming out of his ears. This was Maggie's grand opening. It wasn't the time or place for his father to show up out of the blue.

He scowled at his brother. "Declan! What did you do?" His question came out like a ferocious roar.

"I did what needed to be done," Declan said, his expression unapologetic. "I reached out to him."

"Son, we need to talk and it needed to be face-to-face. Man-to-man. I'm not leaving until we air things out." Colin's voice was firm, brooking no argument.

Finn let out a bitter-sounding chuckle. "Now? After all this time?"

"You're right," Colin said, shaking his head. "We're way overdue. And I apologize. To both of you. I bailed on our family. There's no excuse for the things I've done. Back then I didn't have the tools to talk openly to you about your mother's death." He winced. "Honestly, I'm not sure I do now."

Anger rose up inside Finn. "You've been gone in one way or another ever since then."

"Finn, I know there's no excuse, but my heart was broken. I'm not strong like you and Declan. And to make matters worse, it was my fault." Agony rang out in his voice. "She was my best friend. The very best of me. And when she left us, I crumbled. I lost sight of everything I held dear."

Maggie's face flashed before Finn's eyes. How would he feel if through his actions Maggie was taken from this world? He couldn't even imagine the utter devastation.

Colin frowned at him. "Declan told me you've been blaming yourself all this time," his father said.

Finn gritted his teeth. "I put the bullets in the shotgun. I went against everything I'd ever been told by you and Mom in our household." He wiped away tears with the back of his palm. He let out a groan. "Boredom set in while I was home alone. I put the bullets in and then I shot off a few rounds in the backyard. I'd lined up some cans and I wanted to see if I could hit them.

"I kept telling myself to take the bullets out so I

wouldn't get in any trouble, so no one would know what I'd done. But I forgot. And then that night you were in the backyard joking around. The gun went off. We lost our whole world. Because of me."

"And you never said a word, did you? You bottled it all up inside you and let it fester." Declan's face looked tortured.

"No. How could I?" he asked in an agonized voice. "I didn't want to lose the rest of my family. I didn't want all of you to hate me."

"So instead you hated yourself." His father's words hung in the air like a grenade. Finn had never thought about it like that before. It was true. He had been struggling with feelings of poor self-worth ever since.

Finn hung his head. He didn't know what to say. How could he put into words the guilt of a child over something so monumental? How to put into words the devastation of having your father unravel and leave the family who had so desperately needed him?

His chest tightened. "We lost so much. It was a lot to bear."

"You are not responsible!" Colin said in a raised voice. "No matter what you think you know about that night, you're wrong."

"You need to listen, Finn," Declan said. "Just listen."

"At the time I was as honest as I thought I should be about that night. You two were so young I didn't want to overwhelm you with the details. I didn't know it would be important." Colin raked his hand through his hair. "I never imagined you would blame yourself, Finn. How could I when I was the one at fault? Finn, you know how meticulous your mother was to detail. Cindy was like a bloodhound." Colin let out a sharp laugh. "Much the same way as she knew when you sneaked freshly baked peanut butter cookies from the tray, she knew you'd been playing around with the shotgun. That same day she emptied it when she realized what you'd been doing when we weren't home. We were planning to sit you down and talk to you about it, but then—" His voice trailed off.

"She died." Finn's voice sounded flat to his own ears.

"Yes, Finn, she passed. And there's not a day that goes by without my thinking of her. Mourning her. And wishing I'd never refilled the shotgun with bullets. Your mother and I had just enjoyed a wonderful night. We had dinner out at The Bay, then we came back here and drank some wine and a few beers. I was joking around with her about finally getting rid of that raccoon who kept messing with our trash." Colin's shoulders shuddered and he let out a sob. "To be honest, it all happened so fast. Like a flash. She was laughing and she lunged to take away the weapon. It was like an explosion."

For a few minutes everything was silent.

His father cleared his throat. "So you can't blame yourself, Finn. If you have to place all of this on someone's shoulders, pick mine. I'll gladly shoulder it if it brings you peace."

Finn felt as if he'd been blind for the last two decades and now he could suddenly see clearly. His father was a broken man. The death of his wife had gutted him. He'd spiraled out of control and, due to guilt and pain, abandoned his family. For many years Finn had harbored negative feelings toward the man who had given him life. But now—seeing him so shattered—it hit Finn hard. At this moment all he felt was compassion. And gratitude. It couldn't have been easy to come back after all this time and confess the truth of that night.

It was time to move past his mother's death. In Finn's opinion she had been the most loving, wonderful person in the world. Never in a million years would she have wanted her family to be eaten up by her death. She would have told them all to get a grip on themselves. Cindy O'Rourke would have hated all this angst and guilt and divisiveness.

He wanted to honor his mother. The way he was living his life wasn't doing justice to the woman who had given him life. He was throwing away every hope and dream for the future she'd worked so hard to build for him. Feeling overwhelmed, Finn bowed his head.

Lord, I need Your grace. I'm at a crossroads in my life. For so long I've been carrying all this guilt around on my shoulders. I can't carry it anymore. I'm incredibly weary. I'm not an unworthy person. I've made a lot of mistakes, but I'm still worthy of happiness. I've got to lay these burdens aside. I need to have forgiveness in my heart for my father. I've been so angry at him for something out of his control. He loved my mother more than anyone or anything. And I love Maggie. And Oliver. I need peace in my life so I can move forward and claim my future. Thank You, Lord, for allowing me to see clearly what's been in front of me all of this time.

When he opened his eyes he saw both Declan and Colin bowing their heads in prayer. He walked closer, bridging the distance between them. Without saying a word, Finn stood between them and clasped their hands in his.

"Lord, please bring us together as a family," Finn said. "Let the pain of the past be healed. Open our hearts and minds to all the possibilities stretched out before us. I ask this in Your name."

As soon as Finn stopped speaking he found himself enveloped in a hug by his father and Declan. His shoulders heaved as all of the years of painful separation and heartache melted away in the loving embrace of his family.

Chapter Fourteen

Maggie was trying not to worry about what was happening in the back room of the store. They had been sequestered for quite some time. Oliver was serving as her official greeter while she manned the cash register. There were only a few minutes left until the shop closed. They were all supposed to head over to the Moose Café, where Cameron had offered to host a small holiday party in Keepsakes's honor. Oliver was excited about having hot chocolate and s'mores and hanging out with his best buddy, Aidan.

Maggie's mind was whirling with the possibilities about the sudden appearance of Colin O'Rourke. Perhaps Colin had come back due an illness? Oh dear. She hoped it wasn't anything terrible. Or maybe he was trying to make amends at Christmas. It would be such a blessing for Finn and Declan if that was the case. The best gift of all.

When it was time to close up shop, Ruby took Oliver over to the Moose Café with her family. Maggie promised to meet up with them in a little while. She couldn't imagine what was going on in the back room. And the longer they stayed out of sight, the more she fretted. She prayed Finn was okay.

After what seemed like an eternity, Finn, Colin and Declan all emerged from the back room. Colin approached her and they exchanged pleasantries before he departed with Declan. Finn stood quietly in their wake. He was staring at the door his father and brother had just walked through.

"Finn, are you all right?" Although Maggie had accepted the fact that she and Finn didn't have a future together, she still cared about him. There was no denying it. She loved him. But she could never profess her love for him, because he didn't want it. He'd made that fact quite apparent.

"I—I think so." A dazed expression was stamped on his face.

"What was your father doing here?" Maggie asked. Finn had told her about Colin's disappearing act from his hometown. She couldn't imagine what had brought him back after all this time.

"He came to set me free," Finn said. A slow smile began to break out over his face.

Maggie wrinkled her nose. "I don't understand." She waved her hand at him. "Never mind. It's none of my business." She had promised herself to maintain a healthy emotional distance from Finn. It was the only way of protecting her heart from being smashed into pieces. She loved Finn, but she knew there was no hope of him loving her in return. Finn didn't want the same things as she did. He'd made it painfully clear to her.

And if nothing else, the past had taught her to guard her heart wisely.

"Yes, it is, Maggie. Or at least I hope it is. I'm praying you care enough about me to make it your business."

Maggie's lips trembled. "I—I did care. I do care. But you made it pretty obvious you don't want me to." *Don't cry*, she reminded herself. *Be strong.*

Finn took a few steps toward her, bridging the gap between them. Maggie sucked in a deep breath at his close proximity. It was dangerous for her equilibrium to be so close to Finn. Before she could take a step backward, he reached out and placed her face between his palms.

"Maggie, I love you," he said. The expression on his face was heartfelt. Tears misted in his green eyes.

She let out a gasp. His words had almost made her knees buckle. "What did you say?" she asked, wondering if she'd misheard him. Hope soared within her heart.

He grinned at her, then dipped his head down to place a tender kiss on her lips. Being kissed by Finn was a sweet surprise. She had been under the belief such a kiss would never happen again.

"I am head over heels in love with you, Mags. I have been for a while, but I was so busy running from things that happened a long time ago I didn't feel worthy of you and Oliver. I couldn't risk causing any more pain. When you told me about Sam, it tore me up inside. I knew you'd already suffered so much."

Maggie could read between the lines about Finn's past. But she needed to hear it directly from his lips. If there was even a shot at them being together, she needed to understand so they could move forward. Not just for herself, but for Oliver as well.

Finn took a deep breath and began to tell Maggie about the night of his mother's death and the guilt he had been carrying around for twenty years.

Maggie listened intently to every word. She tried to hold back the tide of tears, but they were soon streaming down her face. She cried for the little boy who had assumed ownership of something so devastating and life altering.

"Declan brought my dad here so he could help me understand things. We finally talked about the night of my mother's death." He shook his head, appearing incredulous. "After all of these years, we finally broke through the wall of silence and dealt with the facts. It wasn't my fault, Maggie. And the truth is, it wasn't my father's fault either. It was an accident. And he's suffered because of it ever since."

"Oh, Finn," Maggie cried out, dabbing at her eyes. "My heart breaks for what your family has endured. I'm so thankful you can put this to rest."

"Me too. I don't know how to put it into words, but my soul feels lighter."

"God is good," Maggie said. "It's amazing, isn't it?"

"For some reason, I always had God in my life. No matter how bad things were, I knew He always walked with me. It prevented me from giving in to total despair. It kept me putting one foot in front of the other and moving forward."

"Oh, Finn. I love you so much. I love your strength and how you lead with love. Despite the pain you've been dealing with, you always treat others with so much grace. You've been courageous this whole time. And incredibly selfless."

Finn ran his palm over her cheek. "Maggie, you make it so very easy to adore you. I can't imagine a life without you and Oliver in it. And I know God sent you back here so we could fall in love. Just in time for Christmas."

"Oh, Finn. This feels like a dream. I never thought God would bless me twice in a lifetime. I truly loved my husband, but our life together wasn't very happy. For a long time I was angry at him, but I've come to realize his problems were so deep-rooted he couldn't fix them. I feel so blessed to be loved by you and to love you in return."

"I thought I would be walking by myself through life. For so long I didn't think I deserved anything wonderful. I thought my mother's death fell on my shoulders. I came from a family that didn't discuss our pain. We never really talked about how my mother died. We were all just stumbling around trying to make sense of it and stuffing down the pain."

Maggie nodded. "It was such a tragic loss. But it was an accident. None of us are perfect people, but that's the beauty of being loved by God. His love is perfect, so we don't need to be."

"Yes. You're right," Finn said with a nod. "I think the grief for my mother led me to feel as if I was responsible. We lived in a house where things were left unspoken. My mother was the one who bridged those gaps and without her everything fell apart. A mother is truly the heart of a home. It's made me realize how important it is not to keep secrets."

Maggie grazed her hand across Finn's cheek. "I'm so sorry you blamed yourself for all of these years."

"I truly thought the blame was on my shoulders. And I believed if I told anyone, I'd lose everyone I cared about. So I stayed silent over the years. And it was slowly eating me up inside."

"You make a great point about secrets. I've known for a long time now that keeping this secret about the circumstances of Sam's death isn't right. It's weighing me down. In order to move forward I need to be honest about the past. And it might cause Oliver pain, but I have to find a way to tell him the truth. Maybe not today or tomorrow, but somewhere down the line I will." She took a steadying breath. "I think he's resilient enough to deal with it."

"That's why I reacted the way I did when you told me about Sam. I retreated. How could I risk hurting you and Oliver after finding out how badly you'd been wounded by Sam's flaws? That was the reason I never wanted a family of my own. I didn't trust myself not to royally mess everything up."

"Finn, you're not going to mess anything up. I hope you fully realize how strong and loving you are. The love you've shown me and Oliver demonstrates the strength of your heart. Never lose sight of it. It's the very core of who you are."

"From the moment you came back to Love, I knew my heart was shifting." He placed his hand over his heart. "I could feel it. But it scared me. It's frightening to believe you're going to hurt the very people you love the most. You and Oliver are my touchstones. Without you, my life would be a dull shade of gray. With the two of you in it, it pops with color. You make the ordinary things feel extraordinary."

"Oh, Finn. That's beautiful. We came to Love for a fresh start and a new life. From the very start you felt like family to us. I kept worrying about Oliver becoming too attached to you, but he knew right from the start we belonged together."

"Smart kid," Finn said with a chuckle. "He was right all along, wasn't he?"

"He sure was," Maggie said, grabbing Finn by the collar and pulling him toward her so she could place a triumphant kiss on his lips.

"Where are you taking me?" Maggie asked as she peered out the window of Finn's truck. Snow was gently falling past her window. She grinned as she spotted moose-crossing signs. It was now run-of-the-mill to see these signs, and on the rare occasion, she'd actually seen a moose or two crossing the road. She had settled in to her life in this heartwarming town and she loved experiencing everything the town of Love had to offer. Not a day went by that she didn't take the time to thank God and Uncle Tobias for blessing her so abundantly.

"I wanted us to have some alone time," Finn said, turning his gaze away from the road to wink at her.

"Keep your eyes on the road, hotshot," Maggie said with a laugh, moving closer to Finn so she could snuggle against him.

"We're almost there. Right down this road." Finn expertly navigated his truck down the road heavily packed with snow. A sign announcing the Nottingham Woods came into view. He drove down the lane and pulled his car into the lot. They both got out and began walking toward the forested area, hand in hand.

"I thought it would be nice to bring you to a place where my parents used to take Declan and me when were kids. Did you know they met each other around the same age as we did? They were kids themselves."

"No, Finn. I don't think you ever told me that before." She smiled. "That's really sweet. They were a real love story."

"Just like we are," Finn said, lowering his head and placing a sweet kiss on Maggie's cold lips. Her nose was tingling with cold due to the frigid weather.

Her lips began chattering. She wrapped her arms around herself. "Finn, it's super cold outside. Can we head back to town soon? I'm dreaming of sipping a peppermint hot chocolate at the Moose Café before opening up the shop."

"Hold on for a few minutes, beautiful. I've got something to say." He reached out for her mittened hands and entwined them with his own. "Maggie, I know this might seem fast, but in some ways I think we've known each other for a lifetime. We were best friends when we were ten years old and we still are. I think we both know the importance of seizing the day. Tomorrow isn't promised." He sucked in a huge breath. "I love you, Maggie." Finn quickly lowered himself to one knee in the snow. He looked up at her with love emanating from his eyes. Maggie felt out of breath. Time seemed to stand still as she watched Finn reach into his jacket pocket and pull out a wooden box.

Finn popped the lid open to reveal a sparkling solitaire diamond surrounded on either side by smaller emcralds. They were the same color as her eyes. Maggie let out a squeal then covered her mouth with her mittened hands. She locked gazes with Finn and let out a sob as she saw the love shining forth in his eyes. "Will you marry me, Maggie? I honestly never thought those words would ever come out of my mouth. I was convinced I'd live out my days alone. Until you. Until Oliver. You made me want to face the past and become a better man. You inspired me to believe I was worthy of happiness."

"Oh, Finn, of course I'll marry you. I adore you. I always have. And you deserve a happy ending more than anyone I know. I'm so blessed you chose me to be a part of it."

Maggie pulled Finn to his feet and helped him brush the snow off his pants.

Maggie continued. "When we were kids you always pushed me out of my comfort zone. And ever since I came back to Love, you've been encouraging me to be more courageous in my life. Your bravery has inspired me. You laid your soul bare about your past and your feelings of guilt. In doing so, you set me free, Finn. You made me realize how I needed to deal with my own issues. And I'll always be thankful for it. My heart is filled to overflowing. I never dared to dream about finding my happy ending. Honestly, I never imagined finding a spouse here in Love. I didn't want one. I was focused on Oliver and wanting his happiness to come first."

He reached for her chin and tilted it up so he could look into her eyes. "You're a wonderful mother, Maggie.

You deserve to be happy, and I am so blessed to be the man who gets to spend the rest of his days at your side."

Maggie grinned. "When I left Massachusetts to come to Love, I promised myself two things. I would make a wonderful life here in Alaska for Oliver. And I would be brave. I think I've managed to achieve both of my goals."

"Yes, you have, my love. I'm very proud of you. We're going to have a wonderful life," he promised. He dipped his head down and placed his lips over Maggie's in a tender and triumphant kiss. The kiss celebrated their love and the bright future awaiting them.

"What do you think Oliver will say?" Finn asked. "Do you think he'll be all right with sharing his mother with me?"

Maggie threw her head back and laughed. "Are you kidding? He'll be shouting the news from the rooftops." At the thought of it, Maggie felt tears pool in her eyes. "He loves you just as much as I do. That little boy came to Alaska with a mission. To find a father. I wasn't sure I could give him what he was looking for because even though I tried to be sensitive to his needs, I never really wanted or intended to open up my heart again."

"I'm so glad you changed your mind about that," Finn said in a teasing voice.

"How could I resist the devastatingly charming Finn O'Rourke?" Maggie asked.

Finn reached out and grabbed Maggie by the waist and twirled her around. "I can't wait to tell Oliver his mission has been accomplished," he called out. "I'm going to be the best husband and father in all of Alaska. You've got my word on that."

Maggie reached up and tugged Finn by the collar so she could place a kiss on his lips. "You've already got it in the bag, O'Rourke. What a merry Christmas this will be."

"It sure will." Finn nuzzled his nose against Maggie's and looked deeply into her eyes. "Merry Christmas, my love."

Epilogue

Christmas Day

A feeling of utter peace swept over Maggie. She didn't feel even a hint of anxiety. Her emotions were as calm as a lake in summer. Today promised to be one of the most wonderful days of her life. She was going to become Mrs. Finn O'Rourke. It was the most precious Christmas gift of all. Maggie was prepared to pledge eternity to her childhood best friend and soul mate.

The best things in life came to fruition when you trusted in God's plan and gave your heart wholeheartedly to another human being. With love, faith and trust, anything was possible.

Thank You, Lord, for seeing me through the storms of life. And for pointing me toward the rainbows. Finn is my happily-ever-after, the one I'd stopped hoping for. And he's going to be the best father in the world to Oliver. Thank You for blessing all three of us.

As she sat at her vanity table, Maggie surveyed herself in the mirror. She had always dreamed of getting married in a beautiful ivory gown. It was stunning! She felt elegant and graceful. Since her first marriage had taken place at city hall, this was a real dream come true. A happily-ever-after moment.

A knocking sound at the door drew her attention away from her thoughts.

"Come in," she called out.

The door slowly opened. Her son stood there with a huge grin on his face dressed to the nines in his miniature black tux with the red bow tie.

"Oliver! You look so incredibly handsome." Pride burst inside her chest at the sight of him. Although she had promised herself no crying today, the sight of Oliver threatened her composure. Tears were misting in her eyes.

"Thanks, Mom. And you look like a movie star, only prettier." Oliver had one of his hands behind his back. "I have something for you."

"What is it?"

"I made it myself." Oliver pulled his arm from behind his back and held up a drawing. Maggie let out a gasp. It was a picture of a man, a woman and a little boy.

Oliver pointed to the picture and said, "This is me. And you and Finn. A family."

"Oh, Oliver. It's beautiful." She sniffed away tears. "My loving, creative son."

Maggie held open her arms. Oliver ran into them and hugged her.

"I want you to know, Oliver, how much I love you. Marrying Finn won't ever change the way I feel about you. We're going to be a family. I don't want you to ever forget your father. But I also want you to know that Finn wants to be your forever dad. He loves you so very much." Tears pooled in Maggie's eyes.

"I love him too, Mom. Thank you for bringing us here and for finding Finn. I won't forget Daddy, but I don't think he would mind me loving Finn and having a new dad since he's in Heaven now."

Maggie brushed tears away from her cheeks. "No, baby. He wouldn't mind one little bit. Matter-of-fact, I think he'd be really happy about it." For so long now, Maggie had been mad at Sam. Now, she had come to terms with her former husband's imperfections and his tragic death. In order to embrace her future with Finn, Maggie knew it was important to close the door on her past. Forgiveness was part of the journey.

A short while later she arrived at the church with Hazel, Ruby and Oliver at her side. She watched as her friends walked side by side toward the altar. When the wedding march began to play, Oliver looped his arm through hers, ready to walk her down the aisle toward the love of her life.

"Ready?" Oliver asked, his eyes twinkling as he looked over at her.

Maggie nodded, too overwhelmed with emotion to speak. They began to walk down the aisle strewn with forget-me-nots. She teared up as they walked past a multitude of smiling, supportive faces. There was no doubt in her mind about being a part of this community. The townsfolk of Love had accepted her and Oliver with open arms.

Jasper winked at her as she walked by. Aidan gave Oliver a thumbs-up as they marched by his pew. Dwight beamed at her from his aisle seat.

When they reached the altar, Finn was standing there looking swoon worthy in a black tuxedo and crisp white shirt. A red bow tie and cummerbund gave him a bit of holiday flair. Declan stood at his side. Finn reached out and took Maggie's hand, then raised it to his lips.

"You look breathtaking," he said in a low voice.

"Right back atcha," Maggie said, fighting back tears.

Oliver turned away from them to head toward the front pew.

"Wait, Oliver. I have something for you," Finn said. He reached into his tuxedo pocket and pulled out a scroll tied with a navy blue ribbon.

"For me?" Oliver asked, his face full of surprise.

"Yes," Finn said with a nod. "It's a proclamation from the town of Love that we're one big family. Mayor Jasper signed it, so it's official. I want you to be my son in every way possible. If it's okay with you, your mother and I want you to be Oliver O'Rourke. I want to officially adopt you."

"Really?" Oliver asked with a sob. He swiped at his eyes as tears overflowed his lids. "That means we'll all have the same last name."

Finn took him in his arms and reassured him. "Forever and always, Oliver. Just say the word and we'll get the paperwork started."

"How about today?" Oliver asked, causing a chorus of laughter to erupt in the church.

Finn reached out and tousled his hair, a huge grin etched on his face. "It's Christmas, Oliver. I'm pretty sure the office is closed today, but tomorrow, bright and early, I'll get the ball rolling."

Oliver smiled and clutched the scroll to his chest,

then made his way to the front pew where he sat down next to Ruby, Liam and Aidan.

Pastor Jack faced the congregation and said, "Welcome to this celebration of a mighty love. Finn and Maggie met as children right here in Love." Pastor Jack let out a chuckle. "As they say, God works in mysterious ways. Delight thyself also in the Lord; And He shall give thee the desires of thine heart. God has been good to this couple. He has given them the most fervent desires of their hearts." He nodded toward Finn. "I think Finn has a few words for his bride."

Finn reached out and joined hands with Maggie. "Before you came back I was doing okay. I was getting by. It didn't take me long to figure out you held the key to my future happiness. You brought out something in me I'd buried a long time ago. I was holding on to a heavy burden that weighed me down. Because of you, I was able to face the past and put it in perspective. I was able to break through my pain and embrace true, enduring love. Maggie, being loved by you humbles me. I will love you and Oliver until the end of my days."

Maggie reached out and wiped away the tears streaming down Finn's face.

She looked deeply into his eyes as she spoke. "I came to Love to start fresh and to build a solid foundation for Oliver. I never imagined I would find a love of a lifetime. Finn—you and Oliver are my world. I promise never to forsake you. I'll be by your side, no matter what challenges we might face."

As the ceremony continued, Pastor Jack pronounced Finn and Maggie as husband and wife. Finn dipped his head down and placed a tender kiss on his beloved's lips. Joy filled the small church as the guests began to clap thunderously.

Finn and Maggie, with Oliver right by their side, walked down the aisle and out of the church into the brilliant December afternoon. Oliver reached into his pocket and began to throw red rose petals at his parents. Laughter filled the air.

Life was just beginning. And the world was their oyster.

* * * * *

NORTH COUNTRY DAD

Lois Richer

To the wonderful folks in Churchill, Manitoba,
who make the north country so much fun.

But if we must keep trusting God
for something that hasn't happened yet,
it teaches us to wait patiently and confidently.
—*Romans* 8:25

Chapter One

"We're orphans, just like Cinderella."

Dahlia Wheatley had forgotten how cute kids were.

"Not quite," she said with a smile. "You've got a daddy."

"Oh, yeah." The auburn-haired twins glanced at the man sprawled out in the seat across the aisle, chin tucked into his chest, stubbled jaw barely visible. They smiled and went back to coloring.

They'd scooted across the aisle forty minutes ago for a visit. Dahlia had encouraged them to stay and color with her markers while their dad slept. He looked weary, like a father who'd used every last ounce of energy to entertain his two young daughters.

Dahlia could almost pretend she was part of their family. For a moment, she let herself imagine smoothing that unkempt hank of dark hair off his forehead, then she caught herself.

She didn't even know the man!

"I'm hungry." The wiggly twin, Glory, looked at Dahlia expectantly.

"Me, too." Grace handed Dahlia her marker. "When do we get to Churchill?"

"Not until tomorrow morning. It's a long train trip."

"Because Canada's so big." Glory nodded sagely. "I'll get something to eat out of Daddy's bag."

"Let's leave Daddy alone." Dahlia lowered her voice, not quite certain why it seemed so important to her that they not wake him up. "He looks very tired."

"That's 'cause he's not used to us," Glory said. Dahlia thought the words sounded like something she'd overheard an adult saying. "He hasn't been our daddy for very long. Our real daddy died."

"So did our mommy." Grace looked at Glory with the most woeful expression Dahlia had ever seen. "She's in heaven, with God."

"I see." Touched by their grief, worried the two waifs would burst into tears, Dahlia thought fast. "I have a couple of chocolate pudding cups. Would they do?"

"Yes, please." Glory released the paper she'd been coloring and climbed up to sit next to Dahlia. Grace flopped beside her half a second later.

Dahlia dug out the pudding cups she'd thrown in her bag before leaving Thompson to go back home to Churchill. Paying the high price for a plane ticket or enduring a lengthy train journey through Manitoba's north country were the only choices available to reach Churchill. It took stamina for adults to endure the seventeen-hour train ride. Undertaking the trip with two energetic kids was a gutsy move.

While the twins ate their pudding, Dahlia fell into a daydream about their sleeping father and the circumstances that had led to him becoming a father to the twins. A wet splat again her cheek snapped her back to reality.

"I'm sorry," Grace said, her blue eyes huge. "I was trying to scrape the bottom and the spoon snapped."

"You got it on her shirt." Glory reached out to dab the mess with a tissue. She ended up creating a huge smear.

"Thanks, sweetie, but I'll do it." Dahlia cleaned her shirt as best she could, knowing that the dark chocolate stain probably wouldn't come out of her favorite top. "All finished?" she asked, eager to get the plastic spoons and containers into the garbage.

"Yep." Grace licked her spoon, depositing a drop of pudding at the side of her rosebud mouth before she held out her cup. "Thank you." Her sister copied her.

"You're welcome." Dahlia stored the trash, then pulled out a pack of wipes. "Let's get cleaned up before your dad wakes up and wonders what happened to his cute girls."

As she wiped their grinning faces and tiny hands, the twins told her that they were moving to Churchill from a small town on the prairies where their stepfather had been a teacher. Dahlia wanted to know more about the handsome daddy, but the twins had other ideas.

"Can we call you Dally?" Glory asked. "It's a nickname. I like nicknames."

"My grandmother used to call me that," Dahlia told her. Memories swelled but she pushed them away. This wasn't the time.

"Will you tell us a story?" Grace asked as she snuggled against her sister. "Our mom used to tell us lots of stories. Sometimes Daddy reads them from a book."

She tilted her head, her blue eyes intense. "Do you know any stories, Dally?"

"I might be able to come up with one." Dahlia spread the small hand-quilted cover the twins had brought with them from their seats. When they were covered, she waited for them to settle.

This was what she used to dream about—kids, special sharing moments, someone on whom to shower the love she ached to give. Part of that dream had been a husband, of course. A man who'd love her as her ex-fiancé never had. A man perfectly comfortable with two little girls who couldn't sit still, for example.

At that moment, the man across the aisle opened his eyes—gray eyes that cool shade of hammered metal—and stared directly at her. A smile creased his full lips.

"Go ahead with your story," he said in a low, rumbly tone. "Don't mind me."

Dahlia swallowed. Most definitely a hunk.

"She's going to tell us a special story." Glory nudged her sharp little elbow into Dahlia's side. "Aren't you, Dally?"

"Sure." Dahlia swallowed to moisten her dry mouth and told herself to stop staring at the man across the aisle. *He wasn't smiling at you, silly. He was probably smiling because of a dream. You're dreaming, too.*

"Are you sleeping?" Grace reached up and turned Dahlia's head so she could examine it.

"No, honey, just thinking," Dahlia said, embarrassed to be caught in the act of admiring their father.

"Do you know Sleeping Beauty? We love Sleeping Beauty, don't we, Grace?" Glory bounced on the seat. "Tell us that story, Dally."

"Yeah," the man across the aisle said in that husky voice. "Tell us that one."

But Dahlia was hooked on his deep voice and beautiful gray eyes. She couldn't concentrate.

Then he cleared his throat and her good sense returned. Now was not the time for distractions. She had too much going on in her life. This was not the time to get sidetracked by nice eyes.

She forced her attention away from him and began her favorite fairy tale.

"Once upon a time—"

I need a wife. Someone like that woman.

Grant Adams glanced at the twins now asleep on either side of him, surprised he hadn't woken up when they'd moved back beside him. The woman across the way was an amazing storyteller, her voice soft, melodic, like a lullaby. He'd let it lure him back into his dream world where life wasn't so overwhelming.

But though it was late and the rest of the car was dozing, Grant wasn't sleepy now. He was nervous. They'd be in Churchill by morning and then his new life would begin. He couldn't shake the feeling that he was failing the twins by bringing them to such a distant place.

A wife would have brought enough activities to keep the twins from being bored during the train ride. She certainly wouldn't have let them bother other passengers, like the woman across the way. A wife would have known he'd need three times the snacks he'd packed.

A wife could show these children she loved them.

Not that Grant didn't care for the twins. He did. Dearly. But he didn't know how to be a father. He didn't have the fatherhood gene—that's why he'd avoided love and marriage. That's why he'd vowed never to have children. Because he didn't have what it took to be a dad.

He'd studied enough psychology to know his lack of skill had to do with his mom walking out on his seventh birthday and leaving Grant with an embittered, angry man who drank until he was abusive. Grant had quickly learned to keep out of his dad's way, to not cause a fuss. None of this had earned him that special bond other kids had with their fathers. After a while, he had given up trying to find it and left home with an empty spot inside that craved love. Two failed relationships later, Grant knew he couldn't love. He'd vowed never to marry, never to have kids and expose them to the loveless childhood he'd endured.

Until Eva.

Eva of the sunny laughter and ever-present smile. Eva of the strong, unquenchable faith in God. Eva the optimist. After an entire year of persuasion, he'd finally accepted her love and her assurance that she could teach him how to be a husband and father. How could Grant *not* have married her? How could he *not* have adopted her two adorable girls?

Pain pierced his battered heart. He'd been naive to believe God would let him have so much blessing in his life.

Eva's death from a brain aneurism just six months after their marriage had decimated Grant. He'd never imagined that God, the loving God Eva had talked about, would take the one person who'd finally loved him. Losing his job a few months later had stolen every scrap of faith Grant had left.

So how could God possibly expect *Grant* of all people to be a father?

"You look like you could use a cup of coffee."

Grant lifted his head and saw the woman from across the aisle who had told the twins a story full of princesses and happily-ever-after. This particular princess had long red-gold hair that tumbled in a riot of curls around her face and down her shoulders. He realized suddenly that it was the exact same shade as the twins'. She had pale features like those the Italian Renaissance masters had smoothed from rare alabaster. But it was her smile that captivated Grant—wide, generous and inviting, it chased away the chill on his spirit.

"Maybe you don't like coffee," she said when he didn't respond. Her smile faltered, a tiny frown line forming between her hazel eyes. "I'm sorry if I bothered you."

"You didn't." Grant smiled and eased one hand free. "I'd love a cup of coffee. Thank you."

"I hope you're not just saying that to make me feel better." Her smile returned when he shook his head. She handed him the cup with a twinkle in her eyes. "You've sure got your hands full. Your twins are adorable."

Grant took a sip of the coffee. Earlier, he'd noticed a dark stain on the woman's emerald-green shirt, and a smudge on Glory's check to match it. But she wore a blue top now. Grant felt a stab of guilt at the thought that she must have changed clothes. She looked refreshed and awake. Beside her, he felt sticky, tired and utterly weary. And he had hours to go until they finally arrived in Churchill.

"How old are they?" she asked.

"Five."

"Glory and Grace." She sank into her seat across the aisle. "Wonderful names."

"I didn't choose them," Grant admitted. "I'm just their stepfather. Grant Adams."

"Hi, Grant. I'm Dahlia Wheatley. I own the hardware store in Churchill."

"It's nice to meet you." He squeezed the words out, trying to hide his shock. *Hardware?* He could not think of a vocation less likely for this delicate-looking woman. Ballerina seemed more appropriate.

"I'll confess, I guessed why you're on the way to Churchill. Laurel Quinn is a friend of mine." Dahlia smiled at him. "She mentioned she'd soon have a new employee at her rehabilitation project. She's eager to have you start work. The boys seemed excited about you when she told them. But then I guess most preteens are excitable." She grinned.

"Lives Under Construction is a great name for a project for troubled boys." Grant wondered how involved Dahlia would be with his workplace. "I'll only be working there on a part-time basis, but I'm looking forward to getting started."

"It's a great project. Once the boys figure out that the court did them a favor by giving them a chance to straighten out their lives instead of being locked up in a jail, they usually come around. Laurel will be glad you're early," she added. "Her newest group has already arrived. You'll be able to meet with them before they start school."

"I wanted to get to Churchill before September because the twins will be starting school, too."

"They're both clever. They'll do well." Dahlia's face softened as she glanced at Grace and Glory. "Laurel's rehabilitation program for troubled boys —we call it Lives —has gained a lot of recognition in the Canadian legal system." Her voice proclaimed her pride. "There never seems to be a shortage of kids needing help. Fortunately that's what they get at Lives, and now you'll be part of it."

"I was surprised Lives is so far into Canadian north, but I suppose isolation is one of the reasons for the program's success," he mused.

"I guess it helps that the boys can't easily escape," she teased. "But Lives' success is mostly due to Laurel." Dahlia's hazel eyes glinted with gold as she studied him. "The building used to be an old army barracks. Her biggest asset though is the land. She can expand as Lives grows."

"So she has plans for the place?" he asked.

"A lot. Laurel mentioned you're a life skills coach?" When Grant nodded, Dahlia admitted, "I'm not sure I know what that means."

"It means I'll be coaching the boys to figure out what they want from their futures," he explained, "and hopefully help them discover how to get it without breaking the law again."

"I see." Dahlia nodded, but those hazel eyes telegraphed her reservation. "Is that what you did before you came to Churchill? The twins said you were a teacher."

"Teaching life skills was part of my job as a high school teacher and counselor in a little town on the prairies." Grant tried to keep his voice light, refusing to show how frustrated he was with God's timing. "When they closed the school, my job ended."

"I'm sorry. I've heard that's happening a lot lately in rural areas." Sympathy shone in those amazing eyes. "No family?"

"I'm afraid my stepdaughters are stuck with only me." Grant glanced down.

"I'm sure they're lucky to have you." A soft look washed over Dahlia's face when her glance again drifted to the sleeping children. Then her mouth tightened. "Though if family doesn't offer the support it should, sometimes it's better to be alone."

Though Grant totally agreed with her, Dahlia's voice held a note of longing that made him wonder how her family had let her down. In fact, he'd begun to wonder a lot of things about this beautiful woman.

"How did you happen to end up in the hardware business?" A shadow fell across her face. "If that's not prying," he added.

"It's not. Anyone in Churchill could tell you and probably will if you wait long enough. Everyone knows everyone's business." She looked completely comfortable with that, but Grant's worry hackles went up.

What if everyone noticed his shortcomings as a father? Maybe then they'd think he couldn't work with the boys at Lives.

He desperately needed that job.

"Actually I'm—I *was* an architect." She paused and he knew there was something she wasn't saying. "I came to Churchill to be closer to nature while I do something worthwhile with my life." Dahlia made a face. "Does that sound all noble and self-sacrificing?

It isn't meant to be. The truth is I left home after a split with my fiancé and my family. A friend told me about Churchill, and here I am."

Something about the way she said the words gave Grant the impression that there was a lot more to her story. He wanted to hear the rest, but he could hardly ask her to confide in him. They'd only just met.

"Judging by what I saw when I came for an interview last month, Churchill is an interesting place." Grant struggled to sound positive as a thousand doubts about this move plagued him again.

"Churchill is isolated, which makes it an expensive place to live," Dahlia conceded. "The winters are cold and long, and there aren't a lot of the conveniences people farther south take for granted. But there are tremendous benefits to living here."

"I'm sure," he murmured, while wondering what they were.

"We live with polar bears, belugas and a lot of other wildlife in gorgeous terrain," Dahlia bragged with a toss of her curls. "In case it doesn't show, I love Churchill. There's no place else I'd rather call home. If you give it a chance, I think you'll like it, too."

Since Grant and the twins didn't have anywhere else to go, he'd *have* to like the place.

"When we first left Thompson, I noticed you working on something." He hadn't wanted to ask before but now he glanced at the roll into which she'd stuffed her papers. "Blueprints?"

"Yes. Every year I sponsor a community project. This year I'm going hands-on with one at Lives." Her smile dazzled him. "Would you like to see my plans?"

She sounded so enthusiastic his curiosity grew.

Dahlia popped off the lid without waiting for an answer. Her hands almost caressed the vellum as she unrolled it. She shifted so Grant could look without moving and perhaps wakening the twins. He gave the drawings a cursory glance. Surprised he took a second look then blinked at Dahlia.

"A racetrack?"

"Close." Her hair shimmered under the dim lights. She grinned with excitement as she leaned near. "It's a go-kart track," she whispered, obviously not wanting the other passengers to hear.

"Go-karts?" Grant frowned. "For the town?"

She shook her head slowly. "For the boys at Lives Under Construction. And their guests," she amended.

"Good for you." He wasn't sure what else to say. From what he'd seen of the place a month ago, Lives Under Construction needed some work. But somehow he'd never thought go-karts would be a priority. "Very nice."

"Don't ever try to fake it, Grant. You are so not good at it." Laughter bubbled out of her. She clapped a hand over her mouth to smother it, her eyes wide as she scanned the car to see if she'd woken any sleeping passengers. When she spoke again, her soft voice brimmed with suppressed mirth. "I know what you think. Go-karts are frivolous and silly, and they are. But they're going to be so much fun!"

Grant didn't know how to respond and Dahlia noticed. Her face grew serious.

"You don't approve." She sighed. "The boys are sent to Lives by the justice system to do time for their crime.

And they should." She chose her words with care. "But many of them come from places where they've never been allowed to dream or imagine anything other than the life from which they've escaped." She gauged his reaction with those hazel eyes. "Do you know what I mean?"

"Fathers were in jail, mothers were in jail, kids follow the pattern." He nodded somberly.

"That, or they were beaten or abused, or forced onto the streets. Or any other horror you can name. Not that it excuses their crime." Dahlia's tone was firm. "But that's not my point."

Clearly Dahlia Wheatley had thought through her plan very carefully, but Grant couldn't figure her out. An architect running a hardware store who wanted to build a go-kart track for some problem kids.

Unusual didn't begin to describe this woman.

"I want to get the boys to dream, to visualize a future that they can create themselves." A wistful smile spread across her face. "I want these boys to reach for something more than what they've had."

"Why go-karts? I mean, how will go-karts help them do that?"

"I told you. It's a community project."

"But it's not really for the community, is it?" he pointed out quietly.

"In a way it's for the community." Her eyes darkened to forest-green, her frustration obvious. "I want to do it because there was a time someone helped me see beyond my present circumstances. And besides, this project will give the boys focus and keep them out of trouble."

"Has there been trouble?" In all his research about Laurel Quinn and Lives Under Construction, Grant had read nothing negative.

"Not so far," Dahlia admitted. "But the current group of boys is more troubled than previous residents at Lives have been. Especially one boy, Arlen."

As she nibbled off the last vestige of her pale pink lipstick, a thoughtful looked transformed her face.

"Arlen?" he asked.

"Yes." She slid the drawings back into the tube, then leaned forward. "Most of the kids in town have access to quads in summer and snow mobiles in winter."

"Quads? Oh, like all-terrain vehicles."

"Right. But the Lives boys aren't allowed to drive. Even if they could, Laurel can't have them taking off all over the countryside. She has to know where they are at all times. They are serving a sentence, after all."

"Right." Grant blinked at the intensity of her tone. She certainly was passionate about this project.

"A go-kart track would allow them some freedom as well as some fun," Dahlia added. "Lives sits on an old army base with a runway that I can clean up so it can be used as the track," she explained. "I've acquired some karts, too, but they'll need repair. The boys will have to figure out that part because I'm not very mechanical."

"I see." It wasn't a bad idea.

"When it's complete," Dahlia explained, a faraway look filling her eyes, "the boys could have a special day when they allow their town friends to use the track."

"Which would give them some esteem among their peers." At last he understood. "Clever. I like it."

"Then you'll help?" Dahlia said.

"Sure. If I can," Grant agreed, pleased to be part of something that didn't require making beds and trying to turn masses of red-gold auburn hair into what Eva had called French braids.

"Great! Thank you, Grant."

"I'm going to be busy." He glanced at the curly heads on either side of him. "There are these two, of course, and Lives. I'll also be working part-time as the school's guidance counselor."

"I'll be grateful for whatever time you can spare." Dahlia settled into her seat with a smile and sipped her coffee.

Grant let his gaze trail down her left arm to her hand. No ring. So Dahlia Wheatley was single.

If there were single women in Churchill, maybe he could find a wife. People still got married for convenience, didn't they?

Ordinarily Grant would have run a mile from the idea of remarrying. Eva had been his one and only shot at love and he'd lost her. But he wasn't looking for romance. He sure wouldn't marry to have children—he'd never bring a child into the world. But he needed a wife because he had no clue how to be a father. When it came to raising the twins, he was as hopeless as his old man. But the right wife would know how to fill in for his lack.

As Grant mulled over the idea of marriage, his eyes were busy admiring the lovely Dahlia. He wondered if she'd consider such a proposition. He had a hunch she was good with kids. After all, he'd slept for over three hours and yet somehow there'd been no catastrophe or complaints. Dahlia's doing, he was sure. The drawings tucked into the seat backs and the smudge of marker on Dahlia's hand were signs that she'd known exactly how to handle them.

"Grant?"

He blinked and refocused on Dahlia, glad she could have no idea of his thoughts—otherwise she'd probably flee the train.

"I was thinking that maybe I could babysit Grace and Glory once in a while, in exchange for your help with my project." Her gaze lingered on the girls before it lifted to meet his.

"That would be nice." It surprised Grant just how nice it sounded.

"Good." She smothered a yawn. "Sorry. I'm tired. I think I'd better get some sleep before we arrive." After smiling at him again, she turned sideways in her seat, pulled a blanket over her shoulders and closed her eyes.

Grant wasn't in the least bit sleepy. Maybe coming here hadn't been a mistake after all. Maybe God was finally answering his prayer.

Glory murmured something and shifted restlessly. He stayed as still as he could, even though pins and needles were now numbing his arm.

Don't let them wake up yet, he prayed silently. *I'll never get them back to sleep and they need sleep. Please?*

God answered his prayer as Grace automatically reached out and folded her hand over her twin's. Moments later, both little girls were still.

Grant glanced sideways at Dahlia Wheatley. He couldn't imagine anyone taking Eva's place. But neither was he capable of ensuring the girls had the home life their mother would have wanted for them.

Was Dahlia mother material?

He gave his head a shake. First things first. All he had to do right now was get to Churchill, and get their lives set up. He'd worry about Dahlia's part in their lives later.

Chapter Two

A face full of ice-cold water ended Dahlia's dream of a family of her own.

She jerked upright, lifting one hand to dash away the water droplets clinging to her chin. Grant's twins stood beside her with smiles on their chubby faces. "Girls, did you just throw water at me?"

"We saw that on television. Everybody laughed," Grace informed her. "The little boy behind you was crying so Glory said we should try to make him laugh."

Whoever was laughing, it certainly wasn't Dahlia.

"Please don't do that again. It isn't nice, okay?" She sat up and dried herself off as she best she could with her blanket.

"Where's your father?"

"He went to get us something to eat. We're hungry." The two looked at each other mournfully.

"Did your father tell you to stay in your seats?" Dahlia asked.

"Yes." Grace looked ashamed.

"Then you should obey him."

When they'd taken their seats, Dahlia dug through her overnight case and found a clean, *dry* T-shirt. She'd have to change. Again.

"What's inside that round thing, Dally?" Glory asked, pointing to the tube with her plans for the go-kart track. "Treasure?" Her blue eyes began to glow with curiosity.

"They're special papers." Dahlia looked down the aisle for Grant's return. She waited as long as she could, but her damp silk top made her shiver. Finally she rose. "You two stay in your seats until your father comes back, all right?"

They nodded solemnly but Dahlia could see the bloom of interest flare across their faces and vividly recalled their earlier mischievousness. She'd just have to change her top in record time and get back before they got up to something else.

Easier said than done, especially after she caught sight of her reflection in the bathroom mirror. She released her damp hair from its clips and bundled it on the top of her head. Then she hurried back to her seat.

And stopped in the aisle, aghast. Nothing in her dreams of parenting Arlen had prepared her for this. Maybe she wasn't cut out to be a mother.

The air left her lungs in a gust of dismay. Her go-kart blueprints, her precious drawings, were spread on the floor. And the two little girls were coloring them.

Glory looked up at her and beamed.

"We colored it for you. Grace likes red, but I think roads should be black." She brandished Dahlia's black marker. "I mostly stayed in the lines."

What lines? The renderings were now obscured by

every color of the rainbow, thanks to the markers Dahlia had allowed the girls to use earlier.

"I'm putting lines in the middle of the road," Grace said, the tip of her tongue sticking from the corner of her mouth as she drew long yellow stripes in what was once the middle of Dahlia's go-kart track. "Roads always have lines."

"What are these little things?" Glory dabbed at the icon for the go-karts with her marker, pressing so hard she went through the paper. Her bottom lip drooped as she saw the damage. "I broke it."

Grace carefully set her yellow marker on top of Dahlia's white jacket to embrace her sister.

"It's okay," she soothed, hugging Glory close. Then she looked up at Dahlia. "It's okay, isn't it?"

Dahlia took one look at those sad little faces and said, "Of course. It's fine, Glory. Now let's gather up my markers. We're going to be at Churchill soon."

She rolled up the blueprints and pushed them into the tube, pressing the lid on. Then she scooped the markers into their plastic case, ignoring the streak marring her white jacket. When the girls were once more settled in their seats, Dahlia scrounged through her bag and found two packs of crackers and cheese.

"I don't know where your dad is," she said, summoning a smile. "But why don't we have a picnic. A proper ladies' picnic," she emphasized when Grace began to climb down. "We have to sit nicely in our seats. Now we'll carefully open our snacks."

Of course the cheese and crackers didn't open properly and crumbs spilled everywhere. It seemed only seconds passed before the cheese and crackers disappeared—except for what covered their faces and hands.

"What's going on?" Grant stood in the aisle.

Dahlia noticed the lines of tiredness fanning out around his gray eyes. He was an exceptionally good-looking man despite his rumpled shirt and tousled brown hair. Not rail thin. Just nicely muscled with a dark shadow on his chin and cheeks. He wasn't as tall as some of her male friends in Churchill, which Dahlia liked. It always made her uncomfortable when someone loomed over her five-four frame.

"Um, what are you doing?"

Dahlia suddenly realized that they had the attention of all the other passengers. The morning was going from bad to worse. "They were hungry," she murmured.

"That's why I went to get them something to eat." He held up a bulging white bag, gray eyes cool as a northern snow sky

"I figured that, but the twins were getting restless," she murmured. "I didn't think you'd want them disturbing others, so I let them have some cheese and crackers."

"Thank you. That was very kind, Dahlia. It's just that their mother didn't feed them processed food." Suddenly his gray eyes narrowed. "That's not what you were wearing before, is it?"

"No, I changed." She caught sight of Glory's face, her blue eyes were wide with worry. "Because I, uh, spilled some water."

"*You* did?" Grant asked, a hint of suspicion flashing in his eyes. "Did you spill water on your hair, too?" When she nodded, he glanced at the twins, then back at her. "I see. Well, thanks for helping them."

"No problem." She waited, shifting under his intense scrutiny.

He turned his focus on the girls. "I brought you fruit juice and a roll with jam."

"Mommy doesn't let us eat jam," Grace said.

"Well, you'll have to eat it today. It's all I could get."

Before Grant turned away Dahlia saw red spots appear on his cheekbones. The poor guy was trying, but the twins looked mutinous.

"I don't want it." A sad look fell across Grace's face. "I want my mommy," she wailed in a tearful tone as Glory joined in.

Those tears tore at Dahlia—she wanted to gather the girls in her arms and comfort them. But Grant simply patted Grace's head and clung to the bag with their breakfast while gazing helplessly at his weeping daughters. Glory, her face now streaming with tears, hugged her sister close and murmured reassurance.

Dahlia couldn't figure out Grant's reaction. He cleared his throat but no words emerged. He seemed confused. What was going on?

When it became clear to Dahlia that, for whatever reason, Grant wasn't going to comfort the girls, she stepped in.

"Hey, you two. Let's go clean up and then you'll be ready to enjoy the breakfast your dad brought. Okay?" She lifted an eyebrow at Grant. For a moment Dahlia thought he'd refuse to let her escort them to the washroom. But before he could, the twins' sunny smiles returned and each grabbed her hand.

"Okay." They squeezed in front of her, heading down the aisle, chattering back and forth like young magpies.

Dahlia held the door open, then glanced back at Grant. He was still standing where she'd left him, a bewildered look on his face.

Then he lifted his head and looked straight at her. She'd never seen anyone look so lost, so overwhelmed.

That's when Dahlia made up her mind.

She was a graduate of the betrayed-by-someone-you-trust-school and she had no intention of opening herself up to that again. But someone had to help Grant, and it might as well be her.

She'd step in—but only for the twins' sake.

When they returned from the bathroom, Grant was still standing in the aisle. Dahlia suggested Glory and Grace sit together, leaving Grant to sit in the empty seat next to Dahlia. The two girls dug ravenously into what seemed to Dahlia pitifully small and not very nourishing breakfasts, but then, she was no expert on feeding children.

"Is that what they usually eat?" she asked.

"They usually have a large bowl of hot cereal. Eva, their mother, always fed them nutritious food. I've tried to maintain that, but—" He sighed. "I can't always find it."

"Was your wife a vegetarian?" Dahlia hoped that didn't sound nosey. "My brother was a vegan. The doctor told my mom to make sure he got enough protein. Otherwise he was always starving."

Grant considered that for a moment. "I brought soup along for supper last night, but it didn't seem to satisfy them. I guess you noticed they were awake several times through the night." He sighed. "I'm new to all this."

"How long have you been at it?" she asked curiously.

"Eva died six months ago. We'd only been married nine months." He turned to glance at the girls. "She was so good with them."

"She had five years to practice," Dahlia reminded him. "You've only been a dad for a short while. Give yourself time."

"I'm not cut out to be a father. I've always known that." Grant's voice grew introspective. "But I didn't know I was going to lose Eva and have to parent on my own."

"I'm so sorry," Dahlia whispered thinking he was lucky to have found love even though his voice betrayed the pain of his loss.

She thought he must have loved Eva deeply. She had seen the same kind of love between some of her friends in Churchill. But though she'd often longed for it, she'd never found that special kind of love for herself. Once she'd thought she had, but even then, even when she'd worn Charles's engagement ring, she'd never been certain he was the man God chose for her. And apparently she'd been right because Charles had quickly dumped her when she'd sold her shares in her family's architectural firm. He hadn't bothered to show up to say goodbye when she'd left Toronto either. No one had.

Eager to forget the past, she asked, "Was that why you came to Churchill, to get away from the memories?"

"I'll never get away from those." Grant glanced at the girls. "But at least in Churchill I'll have work."

It suddenly occurred to Dahlia that, because of his work as a counselor, Grant might be able to help with Arlen.

"Speaking of your work, can I ask you some questions about the boy I mentioned before—Arlen?"

"I'm not sure how much help I'll be since I don't even know him." Grant sounded guarded.

"Since you're a counselor, I thought you might have some insight. You see, Arlen's very troubled. Lives is his last chance," she explained. "If he doesn't get his act together in the next four months, he'll be moved into an adult facility."

"A penitentiary?" Grant frowned when she nodded. "What did he do?"

"Recently, he threatened some people, and vandalized their property. But before that he was a good kid." She looked at Grant closely. "I can't explain the connection I feel to this boy. I've prayed and prayed about him but—" She stopped, blushed. Grant was so easy to talk to. Perhaps—too easy?

"Go on," he encouraged.

"In your counseling—" Dahlia paused and summoned her courage. "Did you ever come across someone you thought was teetering on the edge, someone you were certain would tip one way or the other with the least provocation?"

"Yes." Grant's attention was totally focused on her now.

"You've run across someone like Arlen before?" she asked, relieved to hear he understood.

"The boy I'm thinking about became progressively more problematic for his teachers," Grant said. "He seemed almost driven to break the law."

At the sound of consternation from Glory, Grant excused himself and rose to mop up her spilled juice.

Dahlia watched, unable to contain her excitement. Here at last was someone she could really talk to about Arlen. Laurel couldn't discuss a client, of course, and Dahlia's other friends didn't sense the desperation in Arlen that she did. But Grant had not only seen it before, he'd dealt with it.

"So what did you do?"

"Talked," Grant said. "A lot."

The air rushed out of her lungs, taking her excitement with it. "I've tried talking to Arlen. He doesn't hear me."

"I didn't mean *you* should talk." For the first time a genuine smile lifted Grant's lips, producing dimples in both cheeks that Dahlia found she couldn't ignore.

"What I should have said was that he talked and I listened," Grant corrected. "I encouraged, I tried to draw him out, I pressed him to expand on things he mentioned. Anything to keep a channel open between us." He shrugged. "In his case, talking eventually worked. He'd been brooding about things that he'd never resolved. Once he got them worked out, he saw he had options and that gave him courage to push toward the future."

"That's helpful." Dahlia nodded thoughtfully. "Thank you."

Grant studied her. In fact, his thoughtful gaze rested on her for so long, Dahlia felt herself begin to blush.

"Is something wrong?" she asked.

"I'm curious." Grant paused. "Is your go-kart project specifically tailored toward this Arlen kid?"

"It's a community project. I do one every year," she repeated. His eyes narrowed, but he remained silent.

"Say what you're thinking." She knew she wouldn't like whatever was coming next.

"Maybe I made it sound easy to help that kid I told you about," Grant said. His serious gaze held hers. "It wasn't easy, Dahlia. It took months of work, for which I had trained. This Arlen——" He stopped, obviously uncertain as to whether he should voice his concerns.

"I am going to help him," she said with firm resolve. "I'm going to do whatever I can."

"That's good. He could probably use an adult on his side. But be careful." Grant laid his hand on her arm for emphasis. Immediately, a zing of reaction rippled through her and she caught her breath.

"You're not suggesting I back off?"

"No." He removed his hand. She edged away from his shoulder, hoping that would help her breathe more evenly. What was it about this guy that rattled her?

"I think you should be very careful. If he's smart, he's learned the system and mastered manipulation. He's probably figured out how to con his parents, probation officers, maybe even you. It might be too late for you to help him, Dahlia," he added in a soft tone.

"It can't be." She leaned back in her seat. She shouldn't have said anything. No one, not even her closest friends understood how desperately she needed to help Arlen. Why had she thought Grant Adams would?

A pair of giggles made her look across the aisle. Once, children like Glory and Grace had been what she'd longed for, what she'd prayed for every day. Someone to love. Someone who cared about her, whom she could care about. Someone to share with.

She'd had that connection with her brother. He'd always been the one she'd counted on to be there for her. But she hadn't been there for him. She'd let him down when he'd needed her most. He'd begged her to help him and she'd been too weak. Now he was gone. She missed him so much.

It was only since Arlen had come into her life that Dahlia had begun to hope again. She believed God would heal her hurting heart through caring for Arlen.

"Why is helping this boy so important to you?"

Those gray eyes of Grant's refused to let her avoid his question, but something in her knew that she could tell him the truth, that she could trust him.

"The reason it's so important to me to help Arlen," she began, "is because… I want to adopt him."

Grant wasn't sure he'd heard Dahlia correctly. "Adopt him? But I thought—that is, he's older than the usual age for adoption, isn't he?"

"He's thirteen," Dahlia said. "He's in trouble and needs someone who will be totally on his side."

A single woman adopting a troubled boy who was on the verge of becoming a teenager? There were so many ways in which this was a bad idea that Grant wasn't sure where to begin. He was about to voice his misgivings when he saw the sadness on her face.

Whatever Dahlia Wheatley's reason for helping this kid, he felt certain it stemmed from some emotional pain of her own, and he wanted to know what it was. He'd hardly known her an hour and yet already he wanted to make things better for her.

"Why does Arlen matter so much to you?" He hated the way her hazel eyes dimmed of joy. "Please tell me."

Dahlia glanced at the twins. Grant checked and noted they were playing one of the games they'd created together. He heard her inhale, gathering her courage.

"Because of my brother. Damon was my best friend. He was eighteen when he ran away from home."

"I'm sorry, Dahlia," he said, feeling the pain in those few words.

"He left because he couldn't live up to my parents' expectations." Her hazel eyes grew shiny with tears. "Even though Damon tried his best, he felt he could never be enough for them. They wanted an heir for their architectural firm, a prodigy. Damon wanted to paint."

"What happened?" Grant could tell there was more to the story just by looking at her.

"He was walking on the road at night. A car hit him. The driver left him there to die." As Dahlia exhaled, a sob escaped her lips. Then she dabbed at her eyes and sat up straight. She looked him in the eye. "It was my fault Damon left, my fault he died."

Grant resisted the urge to reach out and touch her, to comfort her. "How could it be your fault?" Grant knew this wound in her heart had festered for years.

"Damon died the night of my sixteenth birthday." A tear rolled down her cheek. "He'd had a big fight with my parents about his grades that afternoon. He asked me to talk to them, but I was too afraid to confront my parents." Her voice dropped with shame. "I was always too weak to stand up to them."

"Dahlia, there is no way a sixteen-year-old is responsible for her sibling. It wasn't your fault." But Grant knew he wasn't getting through to her. She simply gazed at him with that sad, weary smile.

"I was too weak to be there for Damon, but I *am* going to be there for Arlen." Her voice held fierce determination. "He's not going to be one of the lost ones. Not if I can help it."

Because they were getting close to Churchill, Grant decided to say nothing more. "I'm glad you told me, Dahlia," he said very quietly. "Your brother sounds like he was your best friend." She nodded. "Regarding Arlen, though, I need to think about the situation a bit before I give any advice. Okay?"

"I'd appreciate any advice you have to offer," she murmured. "Thanks for listening."

Grant nodded and moved back to his seat across the aisle while marveling at Dahlia's mother's heart. Then the girls cuddled against him, begging him to tell them again about their new home.

As Grant related what little he knew about the house Laurel had arranged for them, he was very aware of the woman across the aisle who was now gazing out the window as if she were a world away.

Grant wasn't sure exactly how, but he *was* going to talk to Dahlia again. He sensed she needed release from the pain of her past and he wanted to help her more than he'd wanted anything in a long time.

An architect. That fit. He could see her long delicate fingers drawing gorgeous houses or state of the art office towers. He could not see her weighing nails or discussing grades of oil.

Funny, but Grant could also see himself around her in the future, which disconcerted him. Still, there was definitely something special about Dahlia. Most women were bored to tears with him. They tried to get him to talk about himself, but Grant preferred to listen, mostly because it was safer.

But he had a sense that Dahlia was the kind of person who could get you to admit things before you even realized you had. He could see her as a wife, and as a mother. She was generous with the twins and made them laugh. That's what he wanted in a mother for Grace and Glory....

Grant shook himself out of his daydream. There were any number of reasons why he shouldn't be thinking of Dahlia in this way, not the least of which was she wanted to adopt this boy, Arlen. And if there was one thing Grant knew for sure about his new life in Churchill, it was that he wasn't going to subject any more kids to his parenting. Grace and Glory were all he could handle.

Chapter Three

"**Y**ou must behave and not bother anyone," Grant told the girls as he got them ready to go to Lives Under Construction.

He felt foolish for having thought it would be easy to find a babysitter for the girls after only a few days in town. It was a mistake Eva never would have made. Now he resigned himself to the difficulty of keeping them occupied during his first session with the boys at Lives.

At least his car had arrived on yesterday's train so he could drive. Lives was situated just far enough out of town that walking there with two five-year-olds would be impossible.

"We'll behave," Glory promised.

"Put your crayons and coloring pads in your backpacks. You can work on those, but you can't interrupt. Okay?"

"Okay, Daddy." They nodded with serious faces.

Daddy. Why did he always feel like an imposter

when they called him that? Maybe it had something to do with his most recent failures.

Today the twins had begun kindergarten. He'd been so busy setting up his office at the high school that he'd forgotten to buy their supplies. Eva would have made sure they were prepared, maybe even had their hair trimmed. Heaven knew Grant craved shorter hair for the twins. The endless combing, snarls, braids—all of it made him feel even more of a klutz. But he couldn't bring himself to cut those glorious curls.

Tomorrow he'd go to the northern general store and buy everything on the list the teacher had sent home for him. She'd been understanding, but Grant hated looking so incompetent. He doubted any of the other parents had sent their kids to school without supplies.

Then there were clothes. The twins were still wearing things they'd clearly grown out of. He should have stretched his funds, cut back more, done something in order to outfit them better, but he couldn't help that now. They'd have to make do until a paycheck came in, though everyone in town would probably be talking about the shredded knees of their pants. Add mending to the list of things he couldn't do.

When they got to Lives, the twins bounded out of the car, happy and excited. They'd taken to Laurel immediately when she'd appeared yesterday with a welcome cake, but Grant wasn't sure how Grace and Glory would react to the boys. Maybe he could get the girls to stay in the kitchen while he met with them.

"I thought we'd all sit around the kitchen table," Laurel told him, dashing his hopes as they walked in.

The boys were in the midst of enjoying a snack. Sllence fell when he entered with the girls. As usual, Grace and Glory won over their audience quickly, and it wasn't long before the boys were plying the twins with food. When they were finished, Grant thought he saw regret on the boys' faces when he situated the twins at a table in the corner to color.

"Remember now, no interrupting," he reminded softly.

"We won't, Daddy," they chirped together.

"I'm sorry," he apologized to Laurel. "I don't have a babysitter yet."

"They're no problem. Now, let me introduce you properly," Laurel said. "This is David, Marten, Arlen, Kris and Kent. They're all new to Lives. This is Rod—he's been here for a while."

"Nice to meet you," Grant said, taking in details about each of the boys.

David, Martin and Kent were towheaded preteens who looked nervous and scared. Grant guessed they'd been talked into committing some offense and had been sentenced to Lives with the hope that one term would be enough to straighten them out. Kris stood next to Arlen, and had adopted Arlen's bored expression. It was an expression Grant had seen many times before. Rod was the only boy who looked perfectly comfortable.

"I'm Grant. I hope we'll all work well together," he said with a smile.

"What exactly are *we* working toward?" Arlen made no effort to conceal his surliness.

"Lives operates on respect, Arlen," Laurel reminded quietly but firmly.

"So you're the resident shrink," Arlen said, ignoring her.

"Life skills coach, actually," Grant corrected in a bland tone. "I'm here to help you figure out what you want in your future."

"Money, power, fame," Arlen joked. He grinned when Kris snickered but his eyes never left Grant.

"That's all you want?" Grant held the boy's glare. "It shouldn't take us long then."

"You think it's that easy to get those?" Arlen barked a laugh then looked to the other boys. "Hey, this guy's got the secret to life."

"There's no secret, Arlen." Grant leaned back and studied the boy. "If you want money, you get a job. If you want fame, you do something notable. If you want power, you become a leader."

"Who gets rich from working a job?" Arlen sneered.

"Lots of people. They work, they save and they accumulate. Is money your goal, Arlen?"

"It's everybody's goal." Arlen stretched his legs out and leaned back in his chair.

"Actually, it isn't," a voice from behind Grant said.

Grant turned, surprised by the thrill he felt at the sight of Dahlia.

"Lots of people with money are very unhappy." Dahlia offered Grant an apologetic smile. "Sorry to interrupt."

The twins rushed to Dahlia, calling her name with glee. She hugged both of them, smoothed their hair and asked about the pictures they were creating.

"Hi, guys," she said to the boys. They all responded but one. "Hello, Arlen." She looked directly at the sullen boy. He ignored her. "I should have phoned first," Dahlia said, her gaze moving to Laurel. "I didn't realize you were having a session this evening."

"We're just talking." Laurel held up the coffeepot. "Want some?"

"No, thanks." Dahlia turned to Grant. "May I take the twins outside to play while you finish your discussion?"

"Sure." Grant noticed how ecstatic the twins were to be with Dahlia, how eagerly they followed her from the room. Was he giving them enough attention?

He waited for Dahlia to escort the girls outside before he steered the conversation back to money. The boys initiated a good discussion about the role of money in their lives, but Grant found he was distracted by the woman playing with the twins outside the big kitchen window.

After half an hour, Grant knew it was time to shut down the group session. He wasn't doing his best listening and the boys were tiring. He ended on a thinking point and after scribbling a couple of notes, Grant gathered his and the twins' belongings and said goodbye. When he stepped outside, squeals of laughter greeted him.

"You're it." Dahlia tapped him on the shoulder then raced away.

Grant stood in the twilight, a memory weighing him down. Games were not something his father had permitted. In fact, he'd downright disapproved of them. The one time Grant had tried to join a school football league, he'd been severely punished.

Keep your mind on your work, boy. You won't live here free forever.

Even now, the injustice of it burned inside. All through his childhood he'd slaved to keep the house clean and the yard tidy. He'd even learned to cook simple meals, which his father couldn't bother with once he'd gotten a bottle in his hand.

"Is something wrong?" Dahlia stood beside him, her face lifted as she searched his gaze.

Those eyes saw too much. He couldn't bear for her to glimpse that lost part of him that had never quite recovered from his father's brutality. He shook his head then touched her arm.

"You're it," he said.

Though Dahlia smiled, her hazel eyes didn't have their usual twinkle. They locked on to his and held as a fizzle of current zipped between them, freezing him in place.

"Would you like to go for a coffee?" she asked.

Grant was surprised by how much he wanted to say yes. But the twins danced at his side. "I should get them home to bed," he said.

"May I help?" The sparkle flashed back into her eyes.

"You want to help with bath time? You'll get soaked," he warned.

"It's happened before. I didn't melt." Dahlia teased. "As long as you don't mind sharing them for a while."

Mind? He was delighted. "Don't say I didn't warn you."

It turned out Dahlia had ridden her bicycle over to Lives, so Grant loaded it into his trunk. Then they headed home with the twins chattering all the way.

"I'm hungry," Glory announced to Dahlia. "We had beans for supper. They were yucky. Daddy forgot mommy's special spices."

"He burned my toast, too," Grace added with a baleful look. "Can I have not-burned toast before we go to bed?"

"We'll see," Grant said so that Dahlia wouldn't have to say anything. It was his favorite expression because he never actually had to promise anything. He didn't make promises anymore, not after promising Eva he'd raise her girls the way she wanted. Look how that was turning out.

"I'm not the world's greatest cook." Dahlia tossed Grant a smile. "But I can manage not-burned toast."

"Easy to say," he warned. "Just wait until you have helpers."

Dahlia laughed as if it was the best challenge he could have given her.

When they reached his house and she bounded out of the car, ready to face her test, Grant had two conflicting thoughts in his mind.

He liked this dynamic woman—a lot. And he'd be doing her a favor if he kept his distance.

Dahlia wasn't sure what she'd expected Grant's home to look like, but it wasn't this. An old sofa and a matching chair covered in a pretty chintz pattern framed a large coffee table, the perfect size for two little girls to sit at and color. In the corner a tidy desk nestled under the window. There was no dust and no mess, yet the room had a lived-in feel, as if people enjoyed each other here.

She allowed herself to be pulled through the house as the girls chattered about their first day at school. It was while Grace and Glory were showing her their room that Dahlia noticed how few clothes they had in their wardrobe. None of them looked warm enough for the cold northern winter that would soon arrive.

After a lively bath time, Dahlia made the girls cinnamon-sugar toast, which they devoured. Then she supervised toothbrushing, read them a story and tucked them into bed, conscious of Grant standing by, watching. As she was about to leave the room, she noticed that Grant seemed tense.

"Good night, girls," he said, his voice hesitant.

"Kisses first, Daddy," Glory reminded.

He dutifully bent so that each girl could embrace him, and waited patiently as they plastered kisses across his check. But when Grace tipped up her face for his return kiss, Dahlia's heart squeezed.

A look of pure panic spread across Grant's face. He hurriedly brushed his lips against Grace's cheek, and a second later, did the same with Glory. Then he quickly drew away.

A moment later, his composed mask was back in place. But Dahlia had seen the truth.

Grant Adams was scared of his daughters.

She couldn't think of a thing to say as they moved back into the living room. Grant made tea and poured it, carrying her cup to where she sat in the easy chair. After the silence stretched out too long, he tilted his head and studied her in a quizzical way.

"Why did you choose a hardware store?"

It was exactly the right thing to break the tension that had fallen between them. Dahlia burst out laughing.

"I'm serious. It's not at all what I'd have guessed you'd do," he said.

"It's not that far from architecture," she mused. "Once I drew plans to build things, now I sell goods to make plans come alive."

"But don't you miss the creative part of being an architect?"

"Not really," she said, only then realizing it was true. "I like the problem-solving aspect of running a hardware store." She looked directly at him. "Besides, I couldn't stay in the family firm anymore."

Dahlia knew he was waiting for an explanation, but she wasn't sure how much to tell him.

"You don't have to talk about it if it's painful," he assured her.

"It is quite painful." Dahlia cleared her throat, sipped her tea then began. "I trained as an architect because my parents expected me to join their architectural firm. They told me that since Damon was gone, I'd take over."

"You didn't want that?"

"I did, more than anything." She heard the fervency in her own voice and smiled sadly. "I had a lot of dreams for the company. My fiancé, Charles, and I used to talk about the things we'd change, how we'd grow the business." She looked down into her tea. "I had no idea my parents thought I was incompetent."

"But—" Grant raised an eyebrow.

"They wanted *Charles* as CEO. I would be a figure-head, to carry on the family name." The sting of it was as sharp as it had been four years ago. "I graduated top of my class, well ahead of Charles. I could have taken a fellowship with a prestigious Montréal firm. Instead I went home, because they 'needed' me."

Dahlia couldn't disguise the bitterness that shone through her words.

"Why would they do that?" Grant asked.

"Because I was too weak, or so they thought." Dahlia saw confusion on his face and decided to tell him the whole story. "I had cancer as a child. Despite the fact that I got better, my parents always considered me sickly. Fragile. The doctors said I was cured, but my parents never heard that. My entire childhood, they were always on the watch, protecting me from myself." She exhaled. "Thank goodness for my Granny Beverly."

Grant sat silently watching her, waiting. That's what made him good at his job, Dahlia decided. He didn't have to say a word because you could feel his interest in you.

"Granny Bev was a dragon. She suffered terribly from arthritis, but she came to see me every single day when I was in the hospital. And she always spoke the same message. 'You are strong, Dally. You can beat this. You can do whatever you put your mind to.'"

"Good ally to have," he murmured.

"The best." Dahlia swallowed the lump in her throat. "Because of her, I beat cancer *and* finished school on the honor roll, though I'd missed more than half the year. Because of Granny Bev, I ignored my parents' comments about being too delicate for gymnastics, too." She smiled. "I actually teach it now, twice a week. You should enroll the girls."

"Maybe I will," he said.

"I'm a pretty good teacher." Dahlia knew she sounded proud and she didn't care. It had been a long, hard road to silence those negative voices that had dragged her down, and she'd succeeded.

Almost.

"Tell me the rest of the story," Grant prodded.

"I fell in love with Charles at university. He said he loved me, gave me an engagement ring. I thought my life was on track." She made herself continue though she'd begun to wish she hadn't started this. Revealing personal details was not her usual style and defending herself even less so. "We both interned at my parents' firm. They loved Charles. They offered him a job when we finished school."

"Was he supportive of you?" Grant asked.

"At school, yes. And at first he was a great partner at work." She paused.

"And then?" Grant nudged.

"Then things began to change." The understanding in his eyes encouraged her to continue. "Meetings were changed without notifying me. My parents took me off three large commercial projects I'd brought in and gave them to Charles although his specialty had always been residential."

"You complained?"

"Vehemently. They said they were worried about my health. Charles didn't want me to be run-down for the wedding. To prove them all wrong, I went out and found three more major clients." She smiled wryly. "Didn't do me any good. I caught the flu, which turned into pneumonia. I was out of the office for a week. By the time

I came back to work, Charles was acting CEO. I had been given the title of assistant."

Grant whistled. Dahlia nodded.

"My parents' explanation was that in two months they would turn the company public so they could retire and travel. They felt Charles was a natural for CEO, but he needed time to prove himself before a new board came in. I was to be the company spokesperson and find new clients, *because I was so good at it*," she mocked. "I'd be a figurehead, but Charles was the boss."

"What did Charles do?"

"Charles pretended it was all a big surprise, that he hadn't put in a word here and there to make my parents doubt my ability. He'd always promised we'd run the company together, but from the first day I knew who was in charge and it wasn't me." She forced a smile. "He said to think of it as a merger that would be cemented when we married. Later I could stay at home and 'look after myself' while he ran things."

Grant tented his fingers under his chin but said nothing. Dahlia continued.

"It took just two weeks before my office was moved off the main floor and I lost all my clients. Charles said he was reorganizing, but I got organized right out. My parents wouldn't listen to me. In Charles they'd found the son they'd lost."

"So what did you do?" Grant asked.

"The day the company went public I bought as many shares as I could—enough to get me into the general meeting. The board suggested Charles as CEO. I publicly refused to support him and stated why. A vote was called. Granny Bev, who had also bought shares, voted with me. Charles lost."

"And your parents?"

"They were furious. I told them how disappointed I was that they'd treated me so poorly." She exhaled, brushed away a tear and continued. "I told them that I'd prove I am strong enough to build my life and that until they were ready to acknowledge me as a fully capable adult, I didn't want to see them again."

"And you haven't?" he asked when she paused.

"Granny Bev had a stroke the next day. I stayed with her until she died. As soon as her funeral was over, I left. I've never gone back." Dahlia had to stop for a moment. "Before she died, Granny Bev said to me, 'You are the strongest person I know. Live your life *your* way, Dally.' So that's what I'm doing."

He nodded, his eyes on her, watching, waiting.

"She left me her stock in my parents' company. I sold my stock to buy my store here. I've never regretted that," Dahlia added.

"And Charles?"

"I've regretted him many times, but I never heard from him again, which is just as well," she told him.

"So now you're determined to live by your grandmother's words," he mused. "You're proving you're smart and strong and capable."

"Yes." She frowned at him, hearing something underlying his words. "What's wrong with that?"

"Nothing at all. I'm just wondering if it's enough for you."

"What do you mean?" Dahlia found herself irritated by his words.

"I've seen you with the twins. I've listened to you talk about Arlen. You have a heart for kids. You love people. You *need* people." Grant paused, then quietly said, "Shutting out love because one man hurt you won't heal your heart."

"I have lots of love in my life," she replied defensively. "I have good friends. We support each other. And one day maybe I'll have a child, too. Perhaps Arlen."

"Will that prove your strength?" he asked quietly. "Will he be enough to heal the pain Charles and your parents caused?"

Dahlia stared at Grant. Images of the fairy-tale dream from her youth, one she'd never shared with anyone but Damon, played through her mind. A family, motherhood. A husband, laughter, love...

"I don't know what it will prove," Dahlia whispered. "I only know I can't give up everything I've worked for. I need to prove myself."

Grant didn't say anything for a long time. Tension stretched between them like a taut wire and finally, when Dahlia could stand it no more, she rose.

"I should go home. Thanks for sharing the twins' bath time with me. It was fun."

"Not a word I would have used to describe it, but you're welcome." He smiled as he escorted her to the door.

She started to say good-night, but instead, she asked, "After all I told you, aren't you going to say anything?"

"I'm not a judge, Dahlia. You have a right to live your life any way you want. I wonder though—" He paused, not taking his eyes off her.

"Yes?" Dahlia shifted under that stare.

"I wonder if you realize you just described love as making you vulnerable and weak."

Dahlia felt as if he'd somehow seen right into her heart. Without addressing his comment, she simply said good-night, took her bike from the driveway and rode away, aware that he stood there watching until she turned the corner. Her thoughts were on Grant and what he'd said.

She was embarrassed by how much she'd shared with him, but more than that, she was floored by his observation. Did she really see love as making her weak and vulnerable? She'd certainly been made to feel that way by her parents and Charles.

Then Dahlia wondered if Grant said that to her because he felt the same way.

She remembered the petrified look on his face when the girls were saying good-night to him and decided that whether he knew it or not, she wasn't the only one who needed help untangling feelings about love.

Perhaps they could actually help each other. Dahlia could offer him assistance with the twins, and he could help her get through to Arlen. Perhaps they could help each other get closer to love.

The question was, was it safe for her to spend time with a man who made her heart beat a little faster simply by studying her with those gray eyes that seemed to look right into her heart?

There was only one way to find out.

Chapter Four

"I guess I don't understand what Grant's doing," Dahlia admitted to Laurel. She glanced around Common Grounds, the local coffee hangout, relieved it was almost empty. She didn't want anyone to overhear. "He never says very much to them."

"Grant explained to me that he's trying to gain the boys' trust first, by listening," Laurel said. "It only seems like he's not doing anything."

"I didn't mean that." Dahlia shook her head. "I'm sure he knows exactly what he's doing with the boys. It's his daughters I'm referring to."

"The twins?" Her friend shook her head, her confusion evident. "Grant seems like a very conscientious father."

"He is. That isn't what I meant, either. It's just—" Dahlia sighed. Laurel was looking at her quizzically. "Don't you think he seems rather standoffish with the girls?"

"I haven't really seen him with them much but no, I've never thought that," Laurel said. Her forehead pleated in a frown. "Why? Do you think there's something wrong?"

"No, no." Dahlia wished she'd never said a word. "I've just noticed he doesn't show them much affection, though I suppose that could have something to do with his grieving process."

"Maybe he's not the affectionate type," her friend suggested. "It's obvious the twins love him dearly, so I doubt there's anything to worry about."

Dahlia didn't want to belabor the point, though her reservations remained. "I have to get back to work, but thanks for sharing coffee with me. I don't get out of the store in the afternoon very often."

"You should," Laurel encouraged. "You push yourself too hard."

"If I don't, who will?" Dahlia smiled, paid for their coffee, then hurried back to work. On the way she met Eddie Smart, one of the many miners who used Churchill as his home base.

"Hey, gorgeous. Are you free to have dinner with me tonight?" When she hesitated he added, "I'm going back up north to the mine in a couple of days."

"Oh, Eddie, I'm sorry. I'm tied up." Dahlia felt guilty for refusing again but she didn't want to add to the romantic thoughts she knew he harbored toward her. "Can I take a rain check?"

"Sure," he said good-naturedly. "I'll be back in time for the fall supper. How about we sit together at that?"

"I'll try," she told him, unwilling to commit. Eddie was sweet. She didn't want to hurt his feelings but she was not attracted to him.

As Dahlia walked toward her store, her thoughts returned as usual to her go-kart track. She decided to call Grant later to see if he could help her with it on Saturday. The weather was gorgeous but northern winters came hard and fast. She needed to get the project going.

As it turned out, Laurel took the twins leaf hunting for a school project early Saturday afternoon so Grant was free to accompany Dahlia on a survey of the road she wanted to use for the track.

"It looks in fair condition," he said as they walked the winding, paved road. "I wonder why it was made in a circle."

"I did some research on this old base." As they walked together in the warm sunshine, Dahlia basked in a sense of camaraderie. It was nice to have someone to help her with the go-kart project. Of course, Grant wasn't just *someone*.

"And you learned?" he prompted.

"There was a lot of suspicion in the fifties. Everyone feared invasion by the Russians so the airstrip here was maintained. When the base closed, they dismantled the long, straight runway so no enemy plane could land. I guess they figured this circular bit wouldn't be of use to anyone."

"It will make a good go-kart track," he said, studying the weeds and grasses that threatened to take over. "It's good that this area is fenced. No wandering polar bears. But it sure will need some cleanup."

"That's where the boys come in," she said with a grin. "They can put in some sweat equity. I'm hoping you'll help them see my vision." She winked at him then stopped, surprised by the freedom she felt with him.

"I'll try." Grant blinked then glanced away. He resumed walking, obviously preoccupied.

"Is something wrong, Grant?"

"I was just thinking that I need a better way to get through to the boys about what their futures will be like if they make no changes. Mere words don't seem to impress these guys."

Dahlia thought about it for a moment. "Have you seen Miss Piggy yet?" Dahlia told him.

"What is a Miss Piggy?" Grant laughed, looking dubious.

"Miss Piggy is a C-46 aircraft. She's called Miss Piggy because she was able to hold so much freight. Years ago she actually did transport pigs on board.

She was to fly from Churchill to Chesterfield Inlet but lost oil pressure in her left engine shortly after departing Churchill. She crash-landed, and Miss Piggy became a tourist attraction, sitting there gutted on the rocks."

"Interesting," he agreed. "But how does this teach the boys?"

"The load was probably too heavy. Later they speculated it wasn't properly checked. That's likely what caused the crash." She raised an eyebrow. "How would you like to be the guy who loaded that plane? A mistake like that—" She let it trail away.

"It could have cost lives," he finished, nodding. "I see where you're going," Grant said. "Being responsible in everything so you don't cost people their lives, doing your job in every detail, not sloughing off just to get a paycheck—it would be a good lesson for the boys." He checked his watch. "I'm supposed to meet with them in twenty minutes. Want to come?"

"You wouldn't mind?" she asked, thrilled to be included.

"Not at all. Are you done here?"

"I am. It'll be nice to have an excuse to go to Lives and see Arlen."

Grant was silent as they walked back to her vehicle. When they arrived, he stopped and laid his hand on her arm. Her skin began to tingle at his touch.

"I want to mention something, Dahlia. About Arlen."

The serious tone of his voice made Dahlia steel herself.

"Arlen's got a lot of pent-up emotions. He wants to lash out. You're making yourself a perfect target for his anger by being so available to him." Grant's eyes held hers.

"I just want to be his friend," she said, blushing under his scrutiny.

"Arlen may not be ready to be friends, with anybody." His gaze softened, chasing away the chill of the afternoon. "Dahlia, this kid—he's not in a place where he can appreciate that you're trying to help him. He's locked up in his own painful world. You might have to back off for a while."

"I care about him," she said stubbornly. "How can I not feel that?"

"I'm not saying don't care." Grant smiled. "Just protect yourself."

"How?" she demanded.

"Don't be so—" He searched for the right word. "Vulnerable," he said at last. "He's getting his kicks from seeing your disappointment when he slights you or ignores you. Don't focus on him alone. Treat him as one of the group and if he doesn't respond, ignore him."

Dahlia hated hearing those words and for a moment, she wanted to argue. But Grant was a counselor and part of her knew he was right. They got in her car and headed toward Lives.

"I don't want Arlen to hurt you," Grant said breaking the silence that had fallen between them. "But he seems to want to. For some reason I think hurting you helps him, maybe takes the focus off of what's really underneath all that pain."

"I'll try to be more blasé with him," she said at last. "But I'm not giving up. I still want to adopt him."

"I know, but—" Grant was obviously struggling with something. Finally, he said, "He has a mom, Dahlia."

Dahlia was surprised to hear this. She'd thought Arlen was all alone.

"She made him a ward of the court," Grant added.

"So he doesn't *really* have a family, and his mother obviously isn't meeting his needs," Dahlia argued. "So maybe I can be his refuge."

Grant frowned. He opened his mouth, but Dahlia cut him off.

"I *am* going to have this boy in my life. Somehow. And you can't talk me out of it."

Grant nodded, but his face grew very serious, as if he was deeply troubled by her words.

Everything Grant had said depressed her. But Arlen was exactly like her brother. He needed her and she was going to be there for him. She would not fail again. Grant made her feel as if her dream of adopting Arlen would never come true. And it *had* to. Because that was part of God's plan for her, that's why He'd laid this particular boy on her heart. She knew it just as she knew making the go-kart track was the task He'd given her to help the boys and prove herself strong.

When they pulled up to Lives, she stepped out of the truck and walked to the front door. She entered the building in front of Grant. All her apprehension melted at the sound of the boys' laughter and the twins' high-pitched squeals.

It was easy for Grant to warn her off—he had two amazing little girls in his life.

She had no one. But she would soon, somehow. She had to.

"How are you, Arlen?"

Grant gritted his teeth at the sound of Dahlia's ingratiating tone. Hadn't the woman heard anything he'd said? He held his breath, waiting for the boy's sour retort. Arlen didn't respond.

Grant stepped into the kitchen, wondering why. He caught his breath at the sight of Arlen seated at the table, with a twin on either side. He was folding paper into an airplane. A huge smile transformed his usually surly face. Grant caught his breath when Glory reached up to touch his cheek.

Don't hurt her, please don't hurt her.

But Arlen's smile only grew as he smoothed the mess of curls off her face. "Didn't you comb your hair this morning, Glory?" he said in a very tender voice.

"Daddy tried, but he's not very good at it."

Grant's face burned at this condemnation.

"She gets knots," Grace explained. "Daddy doesn't like hurting her so he bundles her hair up like that. But it never stays. Are you going to make me an airplane, too, Arlen?"

"Of course." The boy's grin made him look like a different kid. In seconds he made Grace's airplane and sent it zooming across the room. His grin disappeared when he saw Grant. "I'm not doing anything wrong," he said.

"No, you're not." Grant glanced around the room. "Where's Laurel?"

"Am I her keeper?" Arlen demanded.

"Arlen, make it fly again!" Grace called as she retrieved her plane.

"You got it." Arlen's surliness vanished. Then he looked at Grant. "Laurel's in her office, on the phone with someone named Teddy," he said in a more respectful voice.

"Dahlia, want to come find Laurel with me?" Grant didn't want her fawning over Arlen.

Dahlia nodded and left the room with him. "Arlen seems to have bonded with the twins."

"I noticed." Grant wasn't sure whether to be glad or worried. But he was pleased to see that the boy had a much softer side under that grumpiness. "Who is this Teddy he was talking about?"

"Teddy Stonechild. Kyle—have you met him? Lives' activities director?" She waited for his nod. "Kyle and his father used to own a guiding outfit. Teddy came to Churchill to go on a trip with them a long time ago and kept coming back. Now he stays longer because his son is taking over his hotel business in Vancouver."

"And he and Laurel are…?" He deliberately left the question hanging in the air.

"No one can quite figure out what's between them," Dahlia said with a smile. "They started out at each other's throats, but lately Teddy's always here when Laurel needs help, which seems to be quite a lot."

Laurel emerged from her office and stopped short. She glanced from Dahlia to Grant and arched a brow. "I hope you didn't mind me asking Arlen to watch the girls. He's got some kind of rapport with them. I thought it might be something we could build on."

"Good idea," Grant said, though he wasn't sure it was. Another thing about fatherhood that bugged him—there was no black and white. He stepped into the kitchen and stopped dead, astounded by what he saw in front of him.

"Don't we look nice, Daddy?" Grace said.

She turned so he could admire her perfectly French-braided hair. Glory's hair was the same but slightly off-side. Grant knew that was because she'd wiggled more than her sister.

"You both look very nice," he said, trying not to sound surprised. "Did Arlen do it for you?"

"Yes." Glory skipped toward him, took his hand on one side and Dahlia's on the other and swung herself. "He knows lots of ways to comb hair 'cause he used to do his sisters'."

Grant stared at his daughter. She'd learned more about this boy in the few minutes they'd been together than he'd managed in two sessions.

Arlen rose, looking everywhere but at them. "It was

getting in the way when they were trying to color so I braided it."

"Thank you." Grant glanced at Dahlia, who looked as amazed as he did.

"Maybe you could show Daddy how to braid," Grace said, her hand tucked inside Arlen's.

"No." Arlen's cheeks turned red. He shook his head and sat back down. "Are we having a session or not?" he asked in his usual cranky tone.

"We are. I have something to talk to you about," Grant said, clearing his throat. "Then I'd like us all to go on a field trip."

Laurel called the other boys to join them. Grant began by speaking about mistakes that changed lives. Once he mentioned the crashed plane, it didn't take much persuading to get them excited to go see it. Soon Grant was driving toward Miss Piggy with Dahlia giving him directions. The twins sat belted in the backseat, and Laurel followed in the van with the boys.

"They really do look cute with those braids," Dahlia said in a soft voice. Grant wondered if she'd also noticed their shabby clothes.

"I tried to get Grace and Glory some new clothes at the northern store," he explained. "But they don't have anything the twins' size."

"They don't generally carry many clothes. Most people stock up for their kids in Thompson. It's cheaper. I might have an idea about that. Give me a couple of days, okay?"

Grant felt a rush of gratitude but ignored the urge he had to reach out and take her hand. He was going to ask about her idea when she directed him to pull over.

They'd arrived at the site of a half-demolished plane rammed into a hill. He'd never seen anything like it.

"It's quite a sight, isn't it?" she asked.

To say the least. Grant acceded to the girls' demands to be freed of their seat belts. Worried about their safety as they gazed in awe at the metal body ripped open by the impact of the crash, he grabbed their hands, insisting they stay with him.

"It's easier if we go around this way." Dahlia pointed.

Grant followed her sure-footed steps over the slippery moss-covered rocks and remembered she'd said she taught gymnastics. As far as he could tell, Dahlia did everything well. A moment later she reached out a hand to Glory, and Grant couldn't help but enjoy the sight of this lovely woman looking after his daughter. He followed with Grace until they stood beside her.

"Go ahead and look around," Dahlia urged the boys who'd just arrived. That blazing smile spread across her face as she turned to Grant. "I can see all of you are going to need some inspection time. I'll watch the girls while you look."

Grant accepted the offer, realizing that he was perfectly comfortable leaving the twins in Dahlia's capable hands. It was an unfamiliar feeling, being comfortable leaving them with someone else. Of course, Dahlia was... Dahlia. She was special.

He shook off the thought and went to inspect the craft with the boys.

When they'd finished, Grant sat on a rock at the top of the hill and waited until, one by one, the boys flopped down around him. The light breeze off the bay kept the afternoon comfortable. It was the perfect setting for teaching, making him think of similar settings in which Jesus had often taught.

"The sign doesn't say much about why the plane crashed," Rod said with a frown. "I looked it up at the museum once. The cargo was too heavy and the grounds crew probably didn't check the weight."

"Bad mistake, huh?" Grant said. "Nobody died, but they could have."

Arlen sneered. "What were they—dummies?"

"I doubt it," Grant said. "It's more likely they had a busy day, they'd done it thousands of times and got careless. Could happen to anyone, right?"

"Not hardly," Arlen rushed in. "A job like that, you have to know what you're doing. You don't fake it."

Grant looked at Dahlia. She smiled, and he knew she was thinking that this was exactly the opportunity he'd wanted. He smiled back, trying to ignore the fact that something was happening between them, that he felt a connection to her that was undeniable. It concerned him.

But he decided he'd deal with that later. For now, it just felt good to have her on his side.

Dahlia sat beside the twins, spellbound by Grant's voice as he led the boys toward self-evaluation. He laughed and joked, teasing and gently encouraging until they considered their own situations and came up with changes they could make to improve their futures.

She couldn't believe the difference in Grant. This incredible coach seemed miles from the distant, self-effacing, almost helpless father she'd seen with the twins. He didn't falter, didn't question himself and didn't hesitate. Even Grace and Glory seemed to understand that this was a precious moment of learning for the Lives boys. They sat quietly, peeling moss from the rocks and piling it in small mounds.

"Everything, guys," Grant paused to emphasize his point. "Every single thing you do has consequences. You may not see them right away. But there is a result and it won't always be what you want or expect. That's why you have to be so careful about your choices."

All of the boys seemed to ponder Grant's words, except Arlen.

"What do you know about our choices?" the boy sneered.

"Everybody has to make them. It's part of life." Grant smiled at him. "So think carefully, because you are a result of the choices you make. Change your choices, change your life." Seconds passed and no one spoke. Grant rose, and brushed off his pants.

"If you're ready, guys, I think we should head back to Lives," Laurel said.

As the boys climbed into the van, Dahlia pulled Laurel aside.

"Can I present my go-kart idea after they've eaten?" she asked.

"Sure. I'll leave it to you to bring up the subject when you're ready."

Dahlia was on tenterhooks during the drive back to Lives. This was going to be a lot of work and she could only hope the boys wouldn't give up part way through the project. When they arrived, Grant gave her a sidelong look as the girls preceded him into Lives. He reached out and touched her arm.

"Remember, I'm here to help," he murmured.

"Thank you." His touch and those gentle words silenced the fear inside her.

This was what she was supposed to do.

The boys were quieter during dinner, obviously mulling over Grant's words. Arlen was the first to rise to leave the table.

"Can you wait a minute, please, Arlen? I want to talk to you all about something."

"Not another lecture," Arlen muttered.

"Not at all," she said, smiling at him even though her heart ached when he rolled his eyes. "It's an idea I have. I want to know if you're interested."

Slowly, she laid out her plan in clear terms, her heart filling with hope when the boys began to chat excitedly. Only Arlen looked unimpressed.

"Let me get this straight," he said, glaring at her with dark eyes. "You want us to slave out there in the elements to make this thing for you—"

"Oh, no," Dahlia interrupted with a firm shake of her head. "It's not for me. It's for you. All of you will be able to use the go-kart track when it's finished."

"How would we do this?" Rod asked, shooting Arlen a glance that Dahlia interpreted as "chill out."

"Here's my plan," Dahlia began. "First we'd have to clear the road. There are a few places where we'll need to do some minor repair on the asphalt." A rush of excitement filled her when heads began nodding. "Then we'll need to collect tires to put around the perimeter of the track."

"I've seen go-kart tracks where they paint the tires.

Maybe red and black?" Kris said. When Arlen glared at him, Kris quickly bowed his head.

"The colors will be up to you boys to choose together," she told them, encouraged by the looks on their faces. "I've found some go-karts, but they need work. We'll have to find someone in town who can help with the mechanical stuff."

"My dad's a mechanic. I grew up helping in his shop," David said, "I helped rebuild motors lots of times."

"That's a valuable skill." Grant's gaze locked with Dahlia's, and the smile on his face made her skin tingle. She focused on the six boys, delighted by their response. *Thank you, Lord.*

"Sounds like a lot of work," Arlen said in an obnoxious tone.

"Yes, it does," Laurel spoke up. "That's why each of you needs to decide whether or not you want to be part of this. I don't think it's fair to ask Dahlia to organize everything and then have us quit when it gets hard. If we say 'yes,' we're in it—together—until it's finished."

The boys stared at each other.

"Wouldn't the kids at school be impressed?" Rod asked, a tiny grin twitching at the corner of his mouth.

When Dahlia looked at Grant, he winked. Inside, a tiny ember flamed to life. What an encourager he was.

"Maybe when it's finished, you could invite some of the school kids out to see what you've created," Grant suggested.

"Like they'd come," Arlen said.

"Oh, I'm pretty sure they'd come." Grant grinned.

"They wouldn't be able to help themselves. After all, how many go-kart tracks are there in Churchill?"

"I'm in," Marten said to Dahlia. The other boys followed his lead—all but Arlen, who stayed silent.

"I'm so glad you're enthusiastic," she said with a smile. "But I want you to think about this until Monday. Then we'll take a vote. Okay?"

"I think that's a good idea." Laurel glanced around the table. "Any other thoughts?"

"Why don't we take a look at the road now?" Grant suggested. "That way, we'll all have a better idea of what will be involved in making this work."

Dahlia followed them outside, thrilled by their excitement yet still troubled.

"You've really engaged them with this plan of yours," Grant said, walking beside her as the twins surged ahead on either side of Arlen.

"All except Arlen," she reminded him. She tried to hide her hurt.

"Dahlia." Grant reached for her arm to stop her. "Give it time. Something in his past hurt him deeply. It won't heal overnight."

"I know." Wistfully, she lifted her head to search him out and faltered to a stop. Without thinking, she grabbed Grant's hand and squeezed it. "Look!" she whispered.

In front of them, the twins had each taken one of Arlen's hands and were dragging him to see a bird sitting on a boulder. He burst out laughing at something they said, but then his laughter died away. He murmured something to the girls and the three of them crouched down to study the obviously injured animal.

Dahlia's heart squeezed as the embittered boy gathered the tiny bird into his hands. Gently, tenderly he cradled it, showing the twins how to soothe it.

"I never knew he cared about birds," she whispered. Only then did Dahlia realize Grant's fingers had curled around hers, warming her hand.

And for the life of her, she could not make herself break contact.

Dahlia was supposed to be strong, in control. She had no desire to open her heart to another man after what had happened with Charles. But she couldn't deny that it felt good to relax in Grant's protective clasp, just for a moment.

He was becoming a great friend, but that's all it was. And that's all it could ever be. No matter how nice it felt to hold his hand.

Chapter Five

Grant stared as Dahlia lugged bags brimming with clothes inside his house. He'd been thinking about her all day and now here she was.

"What is all this?"

"Stuff for the girls." Dahlia chuckled as the twins raced over and threw their arms around her legs. "Want to have a fashion show?" she asked them.

The twins were delighted even though Grant was fairly certain they had no idea what a fashion show was. After explaining the concept to them, Dahlia ordered him to sit on the sofa and wait as she ushered the twins into their rooms.

After a few minutes of giggles followed by Dahlia's whispers to hush, Grant rose and poured himself a cup of coffee. He returned to his seat thinking about the unusual woman who kept appearing in his life. Not that he objected. Far from it.

In the three weeks since he'd arrived in Churchill, Dahlia had been his lifesaver many times. She'd introduced him to countless locals, brought over casseroles for dinner and helped him get a feel for the small town and for how things ran at Lives where he often ran into her.

"Ta da! Look, Daddy!" Glory pranced in front of him clad in a cute pair of blue jeans and a matching denim shirt. "Aren't they pretty?"

"Yes, they are," he agreed, surprised by how well the items fit. "You look lovely. And so do you," he said to Grace, who strutted out in a red jumper dress with a white blouse. "Where did you get these?" he asked Dahlia, who stood watching from the bedroom door, her face glowing.

"I made them," she said breezily, as if it were a simple thing.

"You made them?" Grant asked, incredulous.

Dahlia laughed at his surprise. "I love to sew, especially for kids. Come on, girls, time to change outfits."

The twins squealed as they scurried back into their bedroom.

Dahlia lingered, her smile warming him inside. "Don't move," she said.

Again and again, the twins modeled their new clothing, including Sunday dresses, school clothes and rough-and-tumble play outfits. There were also two winter coats, one a dark emerald-green, the other a softer shade of a pretty jade tone.

"Surely you didn't make the coats?" Grant said, watching the twins snuggle their faces into the fuzzy trim around the hoods. When Dahlia didn't answer, he searched her face.

"No," she finally admitted. "I ordered them online. They were on sale," she said defensively.

He was embarrassed. He'd known he had to get the girls new coats, but he just hadn't gotten around to ordering them. Not the kind of thing a proper father would do, he now realized. Clothing your kids was as basic as feeding them.

"I'll reimburse you."

"That's not necessary."

"I insist. For the fabric also," he added. She must have spent a lot on the buttons and trim that created the individual touches the girls loved.

"Grant, please don't," Dahlia begged. Her eyes glistened as she watched Glory and Grace trade jackets. "Making these few things has brought me so much joy."

He smiled when he saw a little heart-trimmed pocket on the backside of Glory's jeans. "This is more, much more, than any friend would do."

"I guess that depends on your friends." Her incredible eyes held his for a long moment. "I had such fun. Please."

Grant knew he couldn't push it. He couldn't stand to see those expressive eyes lose their glow.

When and how had Dahlia's happiness come to matter so much?

"Okay, Dahlia. I insist on repaying you for the coats, but for the rest—thank you," he said, hoping she realized how much her gift meant to him.

"Thank *you*." Dahlia smiled, and for a moment, Grant felt the urge to do whatever it took to keep that smile on her beautiful face.

She turned back to the twins and hunkered down to their level. "Can I ask you to do something for me?"

"Sure," Glory chirped. "You're our friend. We help our friends."

"Yes, we do." Dahlia tossed Grant a sideways glance, her lips twitching with amusement. "If someone asks you about your new clothes, could you just say a friend gave them to you? Don't say my name," Dahlia clarified. "Just say a friend."

"You don't want anyone to know." Grace frowned.

"How come?" Glory demanded.

"Because I don't want anyone to feel bad that I didn't make something special for them, too. I'm very busy right now. Your daddy and I are working on a project with the boys at Lives."

"Is it for Arlen?" Glory's serious blue eyes looked from Dahlia to Grant.

"Yes, for Arlen," Dahlia admitted. "And the other boys, too."

Grace's face suddenly fell. "Arlen's sad inside."

"What do you mean, Grace?" Grant knelt next to Dahlia to get closer to his daughter. "Did he tell you that?"

Grace shook her red-gold head. "I can feel it. Here," she said, laying a hand over her heart.

Grant looked at Dahlia, who was gazing at Grace in amazement.

"You have the kind of heart that sees pain inside a person, sweetie." Dahlia caressed Grace's cheek. "It's wonderful that you want Arlen to be happy. I do, too." She rose. "Now I need to ask your dad something in private. Maybe you can go hang up your new coats."

But Glory had another question. "Did you sew any

thing for Daddy?" she asked. "Sometimes his shirts don't have buttons."

"I'm sorry about that." Dahlia grinned at him, her eyes dancing. "Maybe I'll have to show him how to sew."

"I already know how to sew on a button, thanks." Grant's cheeks burned. "I'll get around to it when I get time. Go hang up your coats now."

Glory left, frowning. She and Grace were whispering as they went into their room. Grant heard laughter and turned. Dahlia's shoulders were shaking.

"Go ahead, laugh," he said. "It seems there's no end to the humiliation those two are willing to subject me to."

"I think it's adorable that they want me to make sure you're cared for. They're very thoughtful girls. You should be proud," Dahlia said.

"That was their mother's doing. I'm just the stand-in—"

"I really wish you'd stop doing that."

"Doing what?" he asked.

"Putting yourself down. You've kept them fed, healthy and housed. Why do you always negate that?" Dahlia shook her head, her glorious curls dancing. "You give them love. They need that far more than new clothes or a new winter coat."

"I do love them," he said quietly. "But I'm not sure they know it. When I was a kid—well, hugs, affection—that wasn't part of my life."

"Grant." Dahlia fingers closed over his. "Glory and Grace know you love them and it has nothing to do with whether or not you hug them. You heard what they said about Arlen. Those two can see into a person's heart. They can see into yours."

"I hope so," he said dubiously. "Was that what you wanted to talk to me about?"

"No." She got a strange look on her face. "I, uh, need your help."

"My help?" He stared at her in confusion. "With what?"

She took a deep breath.

"Okay, this is embarrassing." Dahlia inhaled, looked him straight in the eye and let the story out in a rush of words. "There's this guy, a nice guy, called Eddie Smart. He works up north in the mines. Every time he's about to leave town he asks me out and I always put him off and say, 'Next time.' Well, he wants next time to be tonight. He called to ask me to go with him to the fall supper. I didn't want to go with him, but I couldn't think of a good excuse so—well, I told him I was going with you and the twins."

Grant was so surprised he didn't know what to say. He'd never seen Dahlia so rattled.

"Eddie's not a bad guy, he just wants there to be something between us. There isn't, and there won't be," she said emphatically. "But I don't want to hurt him or to keep his hopes up. So will you go?"

"To this fall supper?" Grant finished. "With you?"

"Yes. One of the local service groups holds it every year to raise funds," she explained. "When a family has to take a child to Winnipeg for treatment, this group helps cover the cost of the parents' flights and lodging so they can be with their child."

"Nice." Grant noticed her pink cheeks. He almost

wanted to keep her in suspense just to see how pink they'd get so he didn't accept her invitation. Yet.

"I'll pay for your supper and the twins'," she assured him, the emerald tones in her eyes blazing. "In fact I already bought the tickets. I like to support local events."

"I see." Grant nodded, trying to keep a straight face. "But what about this Eddie? Am I going to have to fend him off?"

Dahlia laughed, a sound that Grant was discovering he liked a lot.

"No, no. That won't be an issue." The gold flecks in her eyes danced when she gave him a secretive little smile. "I've arranged for someone else to sit with him. Marni Parker, who owns Polar Bear Pizza, thinks Eddie's the best thing since sliced bread. But he doesn't notice her because he's got these silly daydreams about me." She blushed again, a beautiful rose tone that washed over her entire face and neck. "I thought if he saw me with you and Marni was there to console him…"

She had a finger in every pot. Sweet, conniving Dahlia Wheatley. The woman amazed him.

"You're asking me to share a meal I don't have to cook? How could I say no?" Grant chuckled when Dahlia let out a sigh of relief. "But aren't you worried that people will talk about us?" he teased.

Dahlia shook her head. "I think most people in town realize I'm not interested in getting married. I'm too independent."

Grant felt a rush of disappointment, and told himself he was being silly for all sorts of reasons. He wasn't interested in marriage either, not after everything that had happened. Plus, he barely knew Dahlia—why should her opinions about marriage have any effect on him?

The hall was decorated in a fall theme and filled with people, most of whom Grant didn't know. But Dahlia smiled at everyone. She introduced him to so many people that Grant gave up trying to remember their names.

"It's our turn to sit down," Dahlia said just as the twins began to fidget, a sure sign they were hungry.

They had just taken their seats when a brown-haired man pushed his way through the crowd and stopped in front of Dahlia.

"Hi there," he said, gazing at her with a sheepish look.

"Oh, hi, Eddie," Dahlia said graciously. "How are you?"

They exchanged pleasantries; then she introduced him to Grant and the girls. Grant could understand Eddie's injured look—it probably wasn't easy to realize you'd lost a chance with a woman like Dahlia.

"I have the other tickets but the numbers aren't together," Dahlia explained. "But I thought you might enjoy eating with Marni. She's just back from her trip to Banff. I know how you love that park, Eddie."

Grant watched in awe as Dahlia beckoned Marni over and facilitated a conversation between the two. Soon, the couple left to claim seats on the far side of the room. Grant chuckled.

"Nicely done, Ms. Matchmaker," he said.

"Oh, shush," she said with a grin. "Pastor Rick will say grace for everyone and then we can go up and fill our plates."

That was when Grant realized that he'd have to battle with the twins over their food selections in front of the entire town. Everyone would hear the twins' protest about food that wasn't like their mother's, and he'd look like an idiot.

But after grace, Dahlia led the girls through the buffet line, adding a bit of this, a spoonful of that to their plates. She deftly handled their questions, assuring them that roast turkey was every bit as good as tofu.

Grant got so caught up in Dahlia's handling of the situation that he paid little attention to his own plate until they returned to their table.

"You really like Brussels sprouts, huh?" Dahlia asked, gazing at his plate.

He looked down, dismayed by the huge serving on his plate. When he glanced up, Dahlia's eyebrows rose. "I won't tease you about Eddie if you don't ask about my Brussels sprouts," he told her.

"Deal!" She grinned, then tucked into her food. "Isn't this great? I love fall suppers."

"There's more than one?" he asked.

"There are four. One is all fish. Deep-fried, battered, baked or smoked. You'll love it." She tweaked Grace's nose. "So will you."

Grace smiled happily as if she'd never had an issue with food.

"They always have lots of leftovers," Dahlia said. "For a five dollar donation you get a takeout container with enough food for another meal. You order them from Jeff, the guy with the green apron and the funny hat."

When Jeff came near, Grant ordered several containers, minus the Brussels sprouts.

"Six?" Dahlia said, green eyes wide.

"Six meals I won't have to cook. Besides," he murmured with a sideways look. "I already know the twins like them."

"And your choice of vegetable?" Dahlia teased.

"Brussels sprouts don't refreeze well. Corn does."

"Right. That's the reason." She giggled. Her smile grew when a young couple stopped by to chat.

Grant took the twins to the pie table, leaving Dahlia to chat with her friends. Grace insisted lemon was Dahlia's favorite so he brought back a piece for her.

"Thank you," she said, savoring her first taste. "But you shouldn't have left. I would have introduced you to Elena and Higgins. They're just back from their honeymoon."

"Your work?" he asked, tongue in cheek.

"I might have introduced them," she said, tongue in cheek. "They did the rest themselves."

"Higgins is a miner, too?"

"There are a number of miners who live here but work up north. It's convenient for them to fly in and out of Churchill."

"I'm guessing Eddie isn't the only one who's asked you out."

Blushing but not answering him, Dahlia turned to the twins and begged them for a taste of their pie. Her eyes twinkled when she noticed his uneaten slice.

"You don't like pumpkin pie?" Dahlia reached out as if to take it and burst out laughing when he pulled it away. "Your daddy has a sweet tooth, I think," she whispered to Grace.

"Can I see it, Daddy?" Grace wiggled closer to him, trying to look into his mouth.

Once again, Dahlia hooted with laughter. Grant had never known anyone who laughed so much. It was a lovely sound.

"There are kids' games in that room over there," she told him. "We could take our coffee along while Grace and Glory try the fishing pond." Dahlia waited for his nod, then rose and led the way. At first, the girls held back, but once Dahlia showed them how the game worked, they were fully involved. "So cute," she murmured.

So was she, Grant thought. Cute and generous and amazing with the twins.

"Dahlia, is this the man you were telling me about?" A diminutive, silver-haired woman nudged her way between Grant and Dahlia. She smiled and thrust out an arthritic hand. "Hello. I'm Lucy Clow. This is my husband, Hector. I understand you need someone to watch the twins after school. I'd love to help."

For a moment, Grant couldn't say a word. Dahlia had done this, probably heard him tell Laurel his worry about leaving the girls in so many after-school programs. How had she known he'd hoped to find exactly this type of woman to watch the girls?

No wonder the miners of Churchill were all interested in Dahlia.

She was, quite simply, amazing.

Grant thought back to all the times he'd thought that Dahlia would be a wonderful mother, and he began to wonder if perhaps the marriage-of-convenience idea he'd first considered on the train that day wasn't so crazy after all.

Dahlia couldn't figure out why Grant suddenly seemed tongue-tied. She shared town news with Hector and Lucy for a moment. Finally she nudged Grant's arm and he seemed to snap back.

In a matter of minutes he and Lucy had arranged everything, he'd introduced her to the twins and they'd fawned all over the smiling grandmother. Beaming, Lucy fluttered a wave before she and Hector left.

"You don't want to check out Lucy before hiring her?" Dahlia asked.

"You and Laurel both talk about her so glowingly. That's good enough for me." The twins asked if they could go back to the games, and Grant nodded. "She mentions God a lot. Is she religious?"

"Lucy's faith is an intimate part of her life. In fact, she and Hector used to be missionaries to the Inuit. God is important to her."

"Maybe she's the answer to my prayer." Grant blinked as if startled he'd admitted that.

"How's that?"

"I need someone who'll be able to teach the twins Eva's faith," he said in a thoughtful tone. "Lucy sounds like the perfect woman to do that."

"I see," she said, but it was clear she didn't.

"You're probably thinking that's something I should do," he guessed. "But I can't. I don't have that rock-solid faith in God that Eva had. I was trying to learn before she died…" Grant trailed off and was silent for a moment. "Anyway, it sounds as if Lucy's faith is strong, like Eva's was."

"Lucy's faith *is* strong," assured Dahlia. "But faith is a learning curve for all of us." She smiled, feeling the wryness of her statement. "I'm going through a faith test myself."

The moment she said it, Dahlia wished she hadn't. Grant knew too much about her already. He drew her confidence so that she blurted out things she shouldn't, things she'd usually kept bottled up inside.

"Arlen?" Grant guessed. She nodded. "You're trying to have faith that you'll be able to adopt him?"

"I'm trying to trust that God will direct things," she corrected quietly. "But I'm also trying to be mindful that His way isn't always mine."

His gaze rested on her, a troubled cloud in its depths.

"I wouldn't want you to get hurt, Dahlia. Arlen has a lot of anger buried inside, though I think most of it is directed at himself."

Dahlia wanted to press Grant, but she could tell that he wouldn't reveal details. It was clear he felt his responsibility to the boys very keenly. So she changed the subject.

"See that group of men over there?" When he nodded, she smiled. "They're dads who bring their kids to my gymnastic class on Thursday evenings. It's for parents and kids. You're welcome to join us. I think the twins would love it, too."

Grant glanced from the men to the girls and back to her.

"They're nice guys," she assured him. "Want me to introduce you?"

"Thanks, but I'll need to think it over and see if I have time," he said.

"Is that the real reason?" she asked softly.

"What do you mean?"

"Churchill is a small town, but most of us try not to judge. Every one of us has problems," Dahlia told him. "If we can help our neighbor, we do. That's what makes this such a wonderful community. Join us, Grant. A little fun among friends might be just what you and the girls need."

By the end of the evening, Grant felt a lot more comfortable mixing with the community, and that was due to Dahlia. She laughed with everyone, drawing him into the conversation so he could join their discussions. When the twins ran up and threw their arms around her, Dahlia's face glowed with pride and love and Grant knew she'd make a wonderful mother.

He was pretty sure she'd take the cake in the "wife" division, too, but he'd think about that some other time. Tonight he'd decided to ask her for her help, even though he was positive it wasn't the kind of help she had in mind. When they were finally alone he touched her arm to get her attention.

"Dahlia, would you give me a hand getting the twins home and in bed? After that, I'd like to ask you something." For a moment he thought she could see inside him, that she had a clear view of all his insecurities. Then the warmth of her smile washed over him.

"I'd love to and you can ask me whatever you want." Her grin blazed; her laughter rang to the ceiling. Joy spilled from Dahlia Wheatley like an artesian well.

To have that in his life, in the twins' lives, would be about the best answer to prayer God could give him.

Now all Grant had to do was figure out the right way to ask Dahlia to marry him.

Chapter Six

"You're so blessed." Dahlia collapsed onto Grant's sofa with a sigh. "Those girls of yours are a delight. I haven't had so much fun in a long time."

"Well, they absolutely adore you."

"The feeling is mutual." Dahlia took a sip of her tea, noticing that Grant seemed preoccupied. When he sat down across from her, his face was very serious. A frisson of worry tickled up her spine. "Is anything wrong?"

"No. Not wrong." He kept watching her. "It's— Uh, I wanted to ask you something."

"Go ahead." She shifted under the intense scrutiny of those gray eyes, especially when she realized *he* was nervous, too. "What is it?" she demanded when the silence stretched too long.

Grant inhaled then coughed. He set down his cup and took one of her hands. An eerie sense of déjà vu struck Dahlia, but she couldn't imagine why. Until he spoke.

"Dahlia, do you think—that is, would you consider… marrying me?"

She pulled her hand away and reared back. "Are you joking?"

"Not at all," Grant said, his voice too calm.

"But—why?" A thousand things rushed through her head, primarily that she'd jumped from the frying pan with Eddie into the fire with Grant. "I mean, I… We're…not in love, so…" She let it trail away, waiting for him to explain.

"I'm not talking about a regular marriage," he explained. "You've already told me, in no uncertain terms, that you're not interested in that. I'm talking about a different kind of marriage."

"Grant, it might be better—" The words snagged in her throat as his hands closed around hers.

"Please, give me a chance to explain. Please?" he asked. Sincerity blazed from his eyes and begged her to hear him out. "I haven't told you much about my childhood. Let's just say it wasn't pleasant. My father cared only for himself. The only tenderness I ever knew came from my mother and she left when I was quite young."

"I'm sorry," she whispered, tears forming on her lashes at the thought of a young Grant suffering such a loss.

"It was ugly, but I survived. I made my own way, went to school, got a job and met someone. The relationship turned into disaster. She wanted me to love her and I couldn't give what I couldn't feel," he said. "I didn't know how to handle her emotional demands so it ended."

"That must have been hard."

"It was," he agreed, his lips pinched tight. "I moved, started over. When it happened the second time, I figured that if I got counseling, I could change things." He gave her a self-mocking smile. "I finally grasped that because of my past, I'm not able to get past my—" He paused, searching for the right word. "I guess you'd say inhibitions. I decided to stay single. I never wanted to put a child through what I went through."

Dahlia didn't understand. "But you did get married."

"To Eva." His smile was genuine. "Yes."

"So?"

"Eva persuaded me that I needed the right teacher to show me how to be a husband and a father. She insisted *she* was that teacher, that she could help me change." Grant met her eyes. "And something did change. I had never believed that I could be a husband and a father, but with Eva, because I loved her, I started to believe that I could. But then she died and left the girls in my care, and I realized that I needed more than belief to be a good father. I needed knowledge and experience, neither of which I had."

"But you've figured it out now," Dahlia said.

"No, I haven't. Every morning I wake up terrified I'm missing something that will ruin their lives. And every day I make some stupid mistake that makes them cry." He looked up. "You've come to our rescue so many times. You always know exactly what to do. So I thought, you want someone to love, that's why you're trying so hard to reach Arlen. And here are two little girls who adore you, desperately needing a mom."

"Grant—I can't," she sputtered, searching for a way to make him understand.

"I wouldn't place any demands on you. It would be

for the twins' sake, so that they could grow up happy and safe, knowing they are secure."

He made it sound so *sensible,* so easy. But Dahlia couldn't be drawn in to his plan.

"You're patient and tender and kind. You'd be an amazing mom, Dahlia."

His sweet words revived that inner longing to shower her love on someone, to build that strong, nurturing bond with another human. And yet—

"I can't marry you, Grant. You're a great guy, and I think you're an awesome dad no matter how many mistakes you make. You don't need me or anyone else. You're doing an amazing job."

"Dahlia," he said, peering into her eyes. "Nothing would have to change."

"Grant, no." She shook her head. "Listen. You think you need me, but you don't. You're learning every day, and the girls love you so much. You'll find your way, I promise. Besides, marriage isn't part of my plans."

"You keep saying that. Why?" Grant leaned back, his gaze intent as he studied her.

He'd bared his soul to her. The least she could do was return the favor.

"I told you I was once engaged," she began.

"Yes. To Charles, wasn't it?"

"So you understand why I'm not looking to get involved again." Dahlia lifted her gaze and saw Grant shaking his head.

"Not all men are like Charles," he said in that calm manner of his.

"It wasn't just Charles's betrayal." She exhaled. "Do you really need to hear this?"

"Yes. Please?" Grant sat there, quietly, patiently waiting for her to share.

Dahlia closed her eyes and the past filled her mind.

"I went on a mission trip to Haiti before my last semester at university. It helped me understand so many things. I'd been sheltered and protected for so long, I'd lost sight of who I was, of my purpose. But in Haiti I saw these very poor people, some of whom had lost everything, and they were happy, truly happy."

"So you decided to change your life," he finished for her.

Maybe he could understand after all.

"Yes. I came home full of possibilities. One by one, they were crushed. My parents, Charles, my work. When Granny Bev died, I finally saw that if I married Charles I'd never be free. I'd always be sickly Dahlia to them. I knew that if I didn't leave, I'd begin to believe it about myself."

"So you came here and started your store."

"Yes." She sighed. "Now I feel I'm finally regaining my personal power. I'm proving to myself, and to my parents, if they care enough to find out, that I am strong, capable and competent. And I'm able to give back the way I want."

"Marrying me would put you back in the box?" Grant tented his fingers as he waited for her response.

"Marriage, period. Because that's part of what marriage, of what any partnership, is. No matter how equal you want things to be, there has to be one voice that's stronger, one person who prevails. Right now, *I* have to be that person in my life."

"That's something a lot of people don't figure out until it's too late," Grant agreed in a soft voice.

"So you understand." Anxious to make sure there was no misunderstanding, Dahlia said, "If I thought God wanted me to marry, if I felt He'd chosen someone for me, I would rethink my position. But that's not the case. You want a marriage of convenience."

"I want a mother for the girls, someone who will cover all the gaffes I make so I don't ruin their lives."

Grant didn't pretend romance. She liked his honesty.

"But there's no guarantee a wife would do that," Dahlia warned. "Besides, you're in control of their happiness now. Your past is over. You're the best parent they could have right now."

"I wish I were as certain," he said. Suddenly a speculative glow filled his gaze. "But maybe you can help me another way, Dahlia."

"Such as?" she asked uncertainly.

"You put couples together. Eddie and Marni. Higgins and Elena." As Grant's gaze met hers, warning lights flashed deep inside Dahlia. "Maybe you can find me a wife."

Dahlia sagged against the sofa back, seeking its support. How had she gotten herself into this?

"You know everyone in town and you know the twins. You must know who would be the most suitable candidate."

Some sixth sense warned her to run, yet Grant's shining gray eyes told her he was utterly sincere. She had to hear him out.

"Please, Dahlia, find me a wife."

She stared at him in shock, surprised to feel a flicker

of envy pinch her heart. But how could she possibly be jealous of someone he didn't even know when she'd just refused his marriage proposal?

Grant couldn't remember the last time he'd felt so hopeful. Enlisting Dahlia's help was genius. *If* she agreed. He waited as a myriad of expressions chased across her face. Shock, of course, bewilderment, confusion, but then Dahlia seemed to consider his request.

"I won't put any demands on them except concerning the twins," he promised.

"But you want to avoid love?" Her scrutiny and especially the disbelief on her face irritated him. "The women around here are my friends, Grant. Most of them *want* love in their lives. They're looking for the fairy tale of happily-ever-after."

"Then don't introduce me to them," he said flatly. Dahlia seemed baffled.

"I guess."

"Something else is holding you back. What is it?"

"If I do this and something goes wrong, you'll blame me." She lifted her troubled gaze to meet his. "I like you, Grant. I don't want something to interfere with our friendship."

"I promise it won't." He meant it. Dahlia had become a good friend. He couldn't jeopardize that. "Just think about it. And, of course, if you don't want to do it, we'll still work together on the Lives project."

"Thank you." Relief filled her hazel eyes. Dahlia rose. "I must get home. I've got accounts to go over. Thanks for coming with me tonight."

"I enjoyed it." He grinned. "And my freezer's stocked up, too."

"Don't pretend you can't cook," she chided. "Glory told me all about that casserole you made. It sounded delicious."

"I can cook some things. What I haven't been able to master are Eva's recipes. They never turn out edible."

"Then don't make them anymore." She tilted her head to one side.

"But she was adamant the twins eat healthy food," he argued.

"There are lots of healthy recipes on the internet. Check them out." Her suggestion made him feel foolish.

"I know, but—" He sighed. "Eva had a system. I'm trying to honor that."

"Grant." Dahlia almost touched his arm but then quickly drew her hand back, leaving Grant to wonder what had stopped her. "You're striving to be both mom and dad to your kids," she continued. "That has to be frustrating. Besides, I doubt you have the time to master her system."

"No," he admitted ruefully. "I don't. But it was important to her."

"More important than the twins themselves?"

He hadn't thought of it that way. Still, guilt rose.

"But Eva would want—"

"—you to do your very best for her girls," Dahlia finished. "Wouldn't she?"

Grant slowly nodded.

"Stop beating yourself up. Eva wouldn't have wanted you to feel guilty for doing things differently," Dahlia insisted. "In fact, I'm sure she expected you would."

Eva hadn't been perfect and neither was he. She'd understand. A sense of relief washed through him thanks to the delicate-looking but tough woman in front of him. "You've made me see things from a new perspective. I appreciate that," Grant said. "So will you consider helping me, Dahlia?"

"Find a wife?" She studied him. "I have to pray about it, and you should, too."

"I will," he promised.

"Bring the girls to my gymnastics class. If you want to meet women that's a good place to go."

"I didn't exactly say I wanted to—" He loved it when she teased him.

He said good-night when she left, locked the door, cleaned up their tea things and then sat down to mull over the evening. A glow of hope flickered inside. Maybe soon he'd have someone to help with the twins.

Dahlia had told him to pray about it so Grant bowed his head and began to pray. But the funny thing was, whenever he tried to visualize a new mom for Glory and Grace, it was Dahlia's face he saw.

Chapter Seven

Dahlia adored her gymnastics students.

Full of hope and potential, they were willing to push themselves to achieve, and they were an inspiration to Dahlia. They also seemed to be inspiring Grace and Glory, who were having a great time.

Having not seen Grant for a week, Dahlia had felt a bump of satisfaction when he'd walked through the doors with Glory and Grace. She'd tried to ignore the question that buzzed in her head. *Was Grant here to meet a woman?*

"I'll have to spend some time showing our two new-bies and their dad the ropes," she told Rod, whom she'd hired as an assistant. "Can you keep the others busy running through their paces?"

"Sure." He immediately called the group to order and began the opening routine.

"Hi. Glad you came," Dahlia said, smiling at Grant after she'd hugged the twins.

"Thanks. So, I guess I come back in an hour?" He met her gaze.

"What? No!" She laughed. "Parents are required to stay and pitch in."

Grant glanced at the girls, then back at her. "Pitch in?"

"Yes." She raised one eyebrow. "Is that an issue?"

It seemed eons passed before he responded.

"It's fine."

"Great." Dahlia chuckled at the pained look on his face. "You can put your jackets over there if you like." Then she directed them to the beginner group. "Okay, folks, let's finish stretching."

Dahlia led everyone through the opening routine sequences, proud of the kids as they moved easily from station to station. She asked parents to stay partly to give those who were employed away from Churchill precious sharing moments with their kids.

Grant and the twins mimicked everyone else as they learned the routines. By break time, everyone was smiling, including Grant.

"Is everything okay?" she asked him. He nodded. She turned to the girls. "Are you having fun?" Their grins said it all. "There's coffee over there for your dad and juice boxes for you. The cookies are for everyone."

"Cookies?" The twins' expressive eyes begged Grant for permission. He nodded and they dashed away. He and Dahlia followed.

"I've been meaning to call you about the track," she said hopefully. "I have some time Saturday afternoon, after four. Would you be available to help?"

"That's good for me." He accepted the coffee she handed him. "What needs doing?"

"Weeding. But that should go quickly since Laurel's bringing the boys."

"Then what?" Grant asked.

"I've received a prefab hut, which I thought could be a starting point for the go-karts. It needs to be assembled." She saw his doubt. "It's not hard, but it takes several people."

Grant agreed, but Dahlia noticed that his attention was on a woman in a red shirt chatting with Grace.

"That's Enid Thompson," Dahlia offered. "She's a teacher. Her son, Ben, is the blond boy who's bouncing all over the place." Dahlia studied Grant. "Have you met her?"

"No," he said.

"She's single. Her husband divorced her and left Churchill just after Ben was born. She teaches fourth grade."

"Single, huh?" Grant sipped his coffee thoughtfully.

"Would you like me to introduce you?" A twinge of jealousy caught Dahlia off guard. She suppressed her dislike at the thought of Grant being interested in Enid. But he *was* looking for a mother for the twins, and Enid had experience with motherhood. "Enid," she called. "I'd like you to meet someone."

Enid was smiling at something Glory had said when she looked up. Dahlia had never thought about Enid's looks before, but at that moment, Dahlia realized Enid was lovely.

"This is Grant Adams. Those are his twin daughters you've been talking to."

"Hello," Enid said a bit shyly.

Dahlia forced herself not to stare as Grant suddenly

became gregarious and talkative—a total metamorphosis. She excused herself and went to help Rod rearrange the room.

"I've never seen Grant smile so much," Rod commented.

"Nor Enid. Since her husband left, she's opted out of a lot of things in the community. She always uses Ben as an excuse." Dahlia blinked when Grant's smile widened. "I should invite them both for dinner so they can get to know each other better."

"I thought Grant was *your*...friend," Rod said.

"He is. I am. I mean, we're just friends," Dahlia told him then faltered to a stop, realizing how flustered she sounded when Rod lifted an eyebrow. "I mean, Grant needs someone in his life." The more she insisted, the more misgiving bubbled inside her.

She wasn't interested in him, so why shouldn't he look for a wife elsewhere?

Perhaps because she *was* interested in him.

Dahlia pushed the thought away and went to organize the groups for tumbling, trampoline and parallel bars. As usual, Dahlia lost herself in teaching the moves she'd adored as a child. At the end of class, she went over to talk to Enid.

"I wonder if you and Ben would like to come for dinner tomorrow night?" she asked Enid as they stored equipment.

Enid looked slightly surprised. "That's kind of you, Dahlia. We'd love to come. Can I bring anything?"

They discussed the menu for a few minutes; then Enid went to collect Ben. Dahlia walked over to Grant, who was helping the twins with their jackets.

"Would you three like to come over for dinner tomorrow night?" she asked. The twins bounced with excitement, making her smile.

"We'd love to share dinner with you. Could I contribute something?" He gave her a droll smile. "Pickles, perhaps?"

"Pickles would be great. And bring an appetite. See you then."

"Dahlia," he said before she could walk away. She stopped. "Thanks for helping me tonight. Meeting people, getting involved—it just seems to take so much extra effort for me. But you've shown me that it's worth it," he said with a smile. "I had a great time tonight."

Dahlia's heart seemed to skip a beat. "Good. And you're welcome." She struggled to ignore her response to that smile.

"We'd better go. See you tomorrow." After Glory and Grace hugged her, he ushered them out.

Dahlia watched as he gave Enid a wave.

Maybe she should have talked to Laurel before she set this plan in motion.

As she walked home alone, Dahlia planned the menu for her guests. But no matter how she tried to take her mind off Grant, she couldn't seem to do it. Grant was helping her with the go-karts, she reminded herself. Helping him find the girls a mom was the least she could do to repay him.

After all, it didn't matter if she found Grant attractive, or kind, or anything else. She didn't want the kind of marriage he was offering.

So why did she now regret having introduced him to Enid?

* * *

Dahlia had clearly gone to a lot of work for what Grant had thought would be a simple dinner. He noticed the extra place settings.

"I hope you won't mind," Dahlia said as she hung their jackets in the closet. "I invited Kurt—a friend of mine—and Enid to join us."

"Another friend who needs a love life?" he teased.

"Kurt?" She chuckled as she shook her head. "Kurt's already happily married. His wife, Trina, is a nurse practitioner. She flies out to Arviat in Nunavut two or three times a week. Kurt hates to cook."

"So you have him over for dinner." She nodded and Grant thought, *typical Dahlia*. She gave a lot to her friends.

She asked the twins if they wanted to help her make a salad. Amid their jubilant responses, Dahlia invited Grant to have a seat and relax.

"I'd rather help you and the twins," he said. "I could cut the pickles if you like."

"You actually brought pickles?" She chuckled when he retrieved the big jar he'd set on the floor near the door. "Then you have yourself a job."

As Grant worked, he couldn't help marveling at the sense of camaraderie he felt working with Dahlia. Everything seemed fun. The twins, who'd whined earlier about leaving their dolls behind, now giggled as they chopped mushrooms with plastic knives.

"I invited Enid to join us because I noticed you two seemed to hit it off last night. Is that okay…or will it make things awkward?" she asked.

Grant looked at her. The hesitation in her voice seemed out of character.

"Sometimes it's easier to talk and get to know people in a homey situation," she added. A pink flush tinged her cheeks, adding to her beauty. Her upswept hair and a hint of makeup emphasized her hazel eyes.

In that moment, Grant was surprised to discover that he thought Dahlia was gorgeous. He was so startled, he started to backpedal immediately.

"I guess that's true, though it wasn't hard to talk to Enid," he said nonchalantly. "She seems very friendly."

"She's a lovely person. A little reserved, perhaps. She doesn't trust anyone easily."

"With her history, you can't blame her for not being interested in starting another relationship," Grant agreed.

"She told you she's not interested?" Dahlia asked, sounding shocked.

"Yes. Actually, I think that's why it was so easy to relax with her." Dahlia gave him a look he didn't understand. He mused on it as he took the knife from Glory before she could crush the life out of an innocent tomato.

"Good job, Glory," Dahlia said. She scooped the tomatoes into the salad as the doorbell rang. "That must be the others."

Enid, Ben and a tall, lean man Dahlia introduced as Kurt joined them.

"Everything is ready," Dahlia said once she'd stored their jackets. "Why don't we sit at the table?"

She asked Kurt to say grace. His low tones vibrated

with reverence as he asked a blessing on the food. Then Dahlia filled everyone's glasses with punch.

"So you're helping Dahlia with the go-karts," Kurt said to Grant. "That's great. I've been out over the track a couple of times, checking it out. I was an engineer before I retired." When Dahlia returned to the kitchen, he confided, "I'm a bit worried about that track."

"Why?" Grant kept his own voice low.

"I think it's going to take more money than Dahlia's budgeted," Kurt murmured. "I'll explain later. Great salad," he said as Dahlia returned to the table. "Some loving hands chopped those mushrooms."

"Grace and I did that." Glory held up her hands. "Daddy, do we have loving hands?"

Grant hesitated, uncertain how to answer.

"Hands that do things for others are always loving hands," Kurt told them with a wink.

Dahlia skillfully drew Enid and Ben into the conversation and kept everyone laughing with stories about some of her customers' requests. By the time she served dessert, Grant felt totally comfortable with Kurt.

"I'm sorry to hurry away," Enid said half an hour later. "I've a lot of papers to grade. But it's been so lovely, Dahlia. Thank you."

"Thank you for bringing the squash. I'm going to need your recipe." Dahlia waved them out, smiling at Ben's sudden shyness when the twins hugged him. "Coffee?" she asked as the twins returned to a game they'd begun.

"Love to, but I can't. I've got a web consult in twenty minutes," Kurt said, rising. "I might be formally retired, but I still work the odd private engineering job. Difference is, I choose which jobs." He enveloped Dahlia in a bear hug. "Thank you, sweet one. I loved it. Trina will be relieved I didn't touch the stove."

Grant watched Kurt give the giggling twins the same bear hug he'd lavished on Dahlia.

"Call me Uncle Kurt," he ordered. "One of these days I'm going to take you fishing, if your dad agrees."

The twins squealed with delight as he set them down. Kurt held out a hand.

"Nice to meet you, Grant."

"Likewise," he said, holding Kurt's gaze. "What we were talking about earlier—I had a couple of questions. Can you do coffee tomorrow at three? I promised Dahlia I'd help her with the track at four."

"Sounds good." Kurt left.

"Well, you two sure hit it off." Dahlia said, smiling when he moved to help her clear the table.

"He's great. I'm glad you introduced us." The truth was Grant could hardly wait to hear Kurt's opinion on the track. If there were issues, he wanted Dahlia to know about them before she went any further with her project.

"Sorry my plan with Enid didn't quite work out the way I'd hoped."

"It was nice of you to try." Without thinking, Grant reached out and touched her hand before she could grasp another dish.

The green of her eyes seemed to darken to match the emerald tone of the sheath she wore. "I'll think of someone else. Don't worry."

"Thank you."

"Don't thank me yet." She looked at him for a moment longer, then withdrew her hand when the twins called out for her to join their game.

"Go and play with them," he urged. "Let me clean this up." When she hesitated, he said, "They've been looking forward to playing with you all day."

She finally agreed. When he checked a few minutes later, Dahlia was sitting on the floor in her lovely dress, smiling from ear to ear as she played chutes and ladders, completely unaware that the twins had stuck a clown face on her back. Tiny auburn wisps framed her face in curls, one of which slipped down her cheek to rest against her slim white neck.

How lovely she was. How absolutely perfect she'd be as a mom.

As a mom—that was all he wanted from her, wasn't it?

Confused by his thoughts of his lovely hostess, Grant sighed and returned to loading the dishwasher. He had a hunch that whomever Dahlia found for him was not going to measure up to Dahlia herself.

The following day Grant shifted in the booth at Common Grounds, the local café.

"So tell me your concerns," he said, impatient to hear Kurt's opinion.

Kurt leaned back. "From what I've heard," Kurt said, "Dahlia was told that fixing old tires along the edge of the old road will suffice. It won't. The shoulders are crumbling and badly weathered. The whole thing needs to be resurfaced, but that won't happen."

"Why not?" Grant asked, his stomach dropping.

"Paving equipment and crews are in short supply

here because it's so expensive to bring everything by rail. Cement is out because the cost would be astronomical to remove the old surface."

Grant's heart sank at his words.

"I don't think she can afford to do major repairs, but without doing that preliminary work, there isn't much point in doing anything else." Kurt tented his fingers. "There's got to be a way to find some money. Dahlia's project is too worthwhile to give up."

"That means fund-raising?" Grant frowned. "Is that possible?"

"Oh, yeah." Kurt nodded. "This place is big on community. They'll come through. A prayer or two wouldn't hurt, either."

Grant raised an eyebrow.

"You don't believe in prayer?" Kurt asked.

"I haven't had much success with it," Grant admitted.

"Nobody ever said God would answer on our timetable, but if you're as concerned with Dahlia's project as you seem, it's time to ramp up your efforts." Kurt swallowed the last of his coffee, set down his cup and rose. "Because without some kind of heavenly intervention, I doubt her go-kart track is going to happen."

Grant rose, too, his head whirling. Dahlia would be devastated if she couldn't complete her project, especially since she felt she had so much to prove.

Grant said goodbye to Kurt and headed home. On the way he decided he'd look for an opportunity to tell her what he'd learned from Kurt.

"And I'll pray," he vowed. "I have to think of some way to help. It's her big dream. I don't want to see it fail."

She'd done so much for him, it seemed only fair he do what he could for her.

His heart warned that there was more to it than that, but Grant refused to stop and analyze what that might be.

He pulled up to the house, but before he could open his front door, Lucy raced outside, her face as white as her hair.

"Why don't you answer your phone?" she asked, tears streaming down her cheeks.

"What's wrong?" Dread clamped an icy hand around his throat. He raced inside but didn't see the twins. "Where are they?"

"I don't know," she said, her voice frantic. "Grace asked for a glass of milk. I went to get it. When I came back, she and Glory were gone. Hector went to look for them."

"How long ago?" he gasped.

"Fifteen minutes?" Lucy buried her face in her hands. Then, as if regaining strength, she threw back her shoulders. "I'll stay here and pray. You go look for them. I've already alerted the police."

Guilt swelled. He wanted to blame Lucy, but it was his fault this happened. He'd failed again, having coffee when he should have been here, at home, doing his duty as a father. He'd never felt more helpless.

"My phone is on now," he said. "Call me—"

Lucy nodded and said, "Go!"

But once inside his car, Grant wasn't sure where to go. Dahlia, he decided. She'd know. He pressed the gas and headed to her store.

And prayed with every fiber of his being.

Chapter Eight

"You haven't seen them?" Staff Sergeant Dave Cramer asked Dahlia as they stood at the counter in the hardware store.

"No," she said trying to understand. "Why would Grace and Glory come here?"

"We're not sure where they went." He explained Lucy's frantic call. "I've started a search."

"Those twins are as mischievous as they come and they love to play games." Dahlia struggled to suppress her worry. "Grant must be frantic."

"I am," Grant said as he strode into the store.

"Give me a minute and I'll go with you to look for them," she promised. "Dave, this is Grant Adams, the twins' father. Grant, this is Staff Sergeant Dave Cramer. He's already looking for the twins."

"We've been trying to reach you, Mr. Adams," Dave said.

Dahlia ducked away to ask her assistant to cover for her for the rest of the day. When she returned with her jacket and truck keys, Dave was gone and Grant was pacing.

"Let's go find them," she said.

"It's my fault they took off," he growled, berating himself. She led the way to her truck.

"Let's take mine. I have four-wheel drive. We might need that. Why is it your fault, Grant?"

"I'm supposed to keep track of them." He sounded angry. "Where do we start?"

"Let's head toward your place in case they're on their way back. Who knows what those two are up to."

"I should have known Lucy couldn't handle them."

"Stop it, Grant. Blame doesn't help." Dahlia wanted to say she was to blame since she'd facilitated the twins' care with Lucy. But that wouldn't help. She pulled onto the street, glancing right and left as she drove. "Do you know what they were wearing?"

"This morning they had on those polka-dot outfits you made. It's been so warm and they wanted to show them off and…" His voice trailed away as he looked at her. "I don't know if they took jackets or not. Lucy didn't say."

Dahlia called Lucy, who reported nothing missing from the coat closet. Dahlia then called Laurel and asked if the Lives boys could help search.

"Of course. I'll drive them in now. Keep me posted. We'll check the road on the way," she promised.

"There. We've got a lot of helpers looking," Dahlia told Grant. "Keep praying. We'll find them."

They drove in silence for several minutes toward the school. Suddenly, Grant grabbed her arm, startling her so much she slammed on the brakes.

"Sorry. I just thought of something," he explained. "Ben told the twins about a sod house the Lives boys helped build. The twins have been asking questions about it ever since."

Without another word, Dahlia wheeled the truck around and drove toward the sod house.

"Can't hurt to check it out," she said. Her heart melted at the look on Grant's face. She pressed his shoulder and let her fingers linger, trying to encourage him. She wanted to do more, to ease his burden somehow, but how?

When they arrived, they stepped out of the car and glanced around. A giggle floated to Dahlia on the breeze.

"Listen." Dahlia held her breath. It came again, faint but undeniable. Her gaze met Grant's and held.

"Be calm," she begged softly. "We don't want to terrify them. We can explain later that leaving as they did was wrong. For now let's just make sure they're safe."

His lips tightened but he nodded his agreement. Dahlia led the way. A few moments later, behind the sod house, they saw the twins crouched down in some very tall grass, playing with a black cat.

"Hello, girls," she said. "I see you've found a friend. What's his name?"

"I don't know." Glory glanced from Dahlia to her father. "Hi, Daddy. What are you doing here?"

"Daddy and I came to look for you," Dahlia said before Grant could answer. "Miss Lucy is very worried. She doesn't know where you are."

"But we left her a picture." Grace frowned. "We asked for some milk for this kitty. Miss Lucy was bringing it to us, but she took so long. This kitty started to leave so we followed it. But I drew a picture for Miss Lucy." Grace tilted her head to look at her father. "Maybe she doesn't know how to read my pictures. Do you think so, Daddy?"

"Yes, I think that's exactly right," Grant told her. "We should go home so she won't worry anymore. You don't want Miss Lucy to worry, do you?"

"Oh, no." The twins shook their heads in unison.

"What about him?" Glory said, looking at the cat. "He's hungry. He meows all the time."

"Let's bring him along, then." Dahlia reached out to pick up the cat, but it clawed at her, leaving long scratches on her arm. "Ow!"

"You have to be gentle with him, Dally." Glory frowned.

"We'll leave him here, then," Grant said. He was immediately inundated with howls of distress from the twins.

While Grant tried reasoning with his daughters, Dahlia called Dave Cramer. Then she called Lucy and finally Laurel.

"I'm sorry I dragged you and the boys out," she apologized.

"Nonsense. We all wanted to help. Since we aren't needed there, we might spend the next hour or so pulling weeds along the go-kart track." Laurel chuckled. "I take it you won't object?"

"Hardly." Dahlia was delighted that despite the emergency, they would make progress today. "I'll be there as soon as I can."

Grant motioned to Dahlia that he wanted to speak to Laurel.

"Hang on, Laurel. Grant wants to talk to you."

Dahlia held out her phone. As his fingers grazed hers, a tingle zipped up her arm. When he gave her a strange look, she wondered if Grant felt it, too. "She's on the line," she managed to squeak.

"Thanks." He cleared his throat. "Laurel," he said bringing the phone to his ear. "Would you have room at Lives for a cat? I wouldn't ask, but the twins seem to have adopted one and my rental doesn't allow pets."

Dahlia could hear Laurel laughing. After a few moments, Grant handed back the phone.

"She said, 'How can it hurt to add a cat to this menagerie?'" He turned to the twins. "We can't take it home. But we can take him to Lives. They already know him there. Laurel says his name is Tux because it looks like he's wearing a tuxedo." Before they could ask, Grant explained, "A tuxedo is a black suit with a white bow tie."

"Tux. That's a good name." Grace and Glory looked at each other then nodded. "Okay, Daddy."

Dahlia could barely hide her grin at his huff of relief.

"Before we can go to Lives, we have to go home. You need to apologize to Miss Lucy for leaving without telling her. She didn't understand your picture and she was very worried." His face tightened. Dahlia knew he was trying not to show how scared he'd been. "You know the rules, girls."

"No leaving without telling." Grace nodded. "We're sorry, Daddy."

"I know you are. But you need to tell Lucy."

"Okay." Glory hefted the cat into her arms and, with Grant's help, climbed into the truck. Grace followed close behind. Grant closed the door.

"I'm sorry I took you away from work, Dahlia," he said.

"Any excuse is a good one." She smiled at him. "You did a great job with them."

"Thanks. When I was talking to Laurel, she asked me to hold a group meeting at the go-kart track site. She thinks the boys need to talk." Grant got in the truck and remained silent amid the twins' chatter until she pulled up in front of his house.

"Thank you hardly seems enough," he said after he'd lifted the twins out and sent them inside to apologize to Lucy.

"Forget it." Dahlia smiled and shook her head. "I'm just glad they're safe. If you'll wait, I'll close up the store and come back to pick you up. We could go out to the track together."

He shook his head. "You don't have to—"

"I *want* to, Grant. Otherwise, I wouldn't have offered." She looked directly at him. Couldn't he tell how far she would go to help him and his sweet daughters? Dahlia didn't realize she'd been holding her breath until he finally nodded "Give me fifteen minutes?"

"Take however long you need. And thank you." He smiled. "I keep saying that to you."

"Let's keep it that way," she teased and drove off.

By the time Dahlia changed into jeans and a work jacket, packed a couple of thermoses filled with hot chocolate, gotten back into her car and pulled up in front of his house, twenty-five minutes had passed. It took several minutes more for the girls to settle the now fractious cat.

"Are we going on a picnic?" Grace asked, eyeing the basket.

"No. But it's hard work pulling weeds. I thought we might like a drink and some cookies. Do you like hot chocolate?" When the twins didn't immediately answer, she glanced at Grant.

"I don't know if they've ever had it," he told her. "Eva felt sugar was very bad for kids and cut it from their diet as completely as she could."

"Oh, why didn't you tell me? Here I gave them dessert and—"

"Dahlia." His eyes rested on her like a soothing caress. "I've accepted that while Eva's ways were good, I can't completely adhere to them. I think a few sips of hot chocolate and a bite of dessert are okay."

"Well, look at you," she said with a huge smile. "Here you are making fatherly decisions about your kids. I guess you have accepted that."

"Yes, I have," Grant said proudly as he returned her smile. They got in the car and drove to the track. "Oh, look," Dahlia exclaimed as they pulled up. "Teddy's here. We should be able to put up that hut in no time."

The girls bounded ahead of them, straight to Arlen, and handed him the cat. He set it down, grimacing when its claws scratched his arm. His frown vanished when the twins ordered him to bend down so they could hug him. To Dahlia's amazement, a soft look of yearning spread across Arlen's face and he gathered the girls close.

"You scared me," he said. "Why did you leave without telling anyone? That's dangerous."

For the first time since they'd found the twins, Dahlia saw chastened looks on their faces.

"We're sorry."

"Okay, but next time, don't leave before asking permission." Arlen's voice held a tightness that surprised Dahlia. "Promise?"

"We promise." The two faces remained solemn for about ten seconds before their charming smiles returned. "Can we help with Dally's go-kart track?"

"Do you mind when they call you Dally?" Grant asked.

"No," she said truthfully. But the sound of that nickname brought back so many memories. Tears welled.

"But you're crying." Grant turned her to face him.

"Happy tears," she whispered, wiping her tears with her sleeve. "That nickname brings back memories."

"Good ones, I hope." He took a tissue from his pocket and dabbed at her cheeks, his touch gentle, his gaze warm and comforting. "You must miss your grandmother and your parents a lot."

"Sometimes I do," she admitted. "I expect my parents to appear one day unannounced and insist on inspecting what I've been doing." Her shoulders went back defensively. "That's why I need to get this done. I need to show them this track in action. Maybe then they'll accept that I'm not their weak, helpless daughter anymore."

"Maybe they'll come to see *you,* because they miss you." His quiet, pensive voice soothed.

"Maybe," Dahlia agreed. But she doubted it.

How could Grant understand? Grant would never betray the twins as her parents had betrayed her. He was committed to doing his best for them. All her parents had wanted was for her to marry someone who could take over their empire.

As they approached Teddy Stonechild, he thrust out his hand and introduced himself to Grant. "Those two sweet things of yours must be a handful. I heard about their adventure this afternoon. Must have been hard on you." After Grant agreed Teddy turned to Dahlia. "So what can I help with?"

She told him about the hut and, as expected, Teddy organized the boys into crews to put it together. Almost two hours later, as dusk settled over the taiga, the hut was finished.

Grant had already met most of Lives' staff; Sara, Lives' head cook, and her husband, Kyle, who was the activities director at Lives. He'd also met Rick Salinger, the local minister, and his wife, Cassie, and their son, Noah, all of whom had arrived in time for Pastor Rick to say a blessing over the structure. Dahlia bowed her head, filled with gratitude that this part had gone so easily.

"I can't thank you all enough," she said. "We're one step closer to making this dream a reality."

"It's our dream, too," Laurel assured her with a smile. "The boys decided on that this afternoon."

A loud cheer went up, but Dahlia noticed that Arlen didn't join in.

"It's so warm I thought we could have a picnic," Laurel continued. "Sara and Kyle are bringing it. In the meantime, we'll help Rick build a fire by collecting some material we can burn in it."

Everyone began to scavenge brush. Dahlia moved closer to Grant and nudged him when Arlen squatted to show the twins what to pick up. The look he shared with her made Dahlia feel as if they were proud parents. Grant seemed comfortable with letting the twins stay with Arlen. She admired the growth he'd made as a father and savored the moment they shared together.

Sara and Kyle arrived and within minutes had set up a table and loaded it with hot-dog fixings. Dahlia added her thermoses of hot chocolate and her cookies. Then she held Sara's baby while the Lives' cook supervised.

Dahlia cuddled the small body close, savoring the scent of baby powder. She had so much love bottled up inside. If only God would touch Arlen's heart, let him accept the love she longed to give.

"Come and watch us, Dally," the twins called, dipping their hot dogs dangerously close to the flames of the fire. Fortunately Arlen was there to look after them.

"You're very good with them, Arlen," Dahlia told him sincerely. He gave her a sideways glance.

"They're just little. You have to watch them all the time at this age. They can get into so much trouble." Then, as if he'd said too much, Arlen clamped his lips together and turned away.

A moment later, Grant approached her, his gaze moving from the baby she cuddled to her face. "You're a natural, aren't you?" Dahlia blushed. Before she could answer, he continued, "Do you have a moment? I want to talk to you. Privately."

Grant's sober face worried Dahlia. But at that moment, just as Laurel asked the boys to gather round Grant, Sara came to take her baby. Though she was curious about Grant's need to talk, there was nothing for Dahlia to do but find a spot to sit and listen.

"This track you're transforming," Grant began. "It's old. It had another use in the past. Together you're remaking it, turning something useless and abandoned into something new and worthwhile. I want to warn you that there will be hardships along the way."

She knew he was talking to the boys, but Grant stared straight at her. Dahlia felt a frisson of worry build and climb up her spine. Something was wrong. She could feel it.

Oh, Lord, her heart begged. *Whatever it is, please don't let it end my dream.*

As Grant spoke, he grew very aware of Dahlia's tension. He hated seeing her so worried.

However, he'd come up with a possible solution to the problem Kurt had pointed out.

"Think about ways you can reshape problems in your past into opportunities for your future. All it takes is some planning and determination. If you want to talk to me, I'm available for you."

Laurel asked Rick to close off the evening with prayer then asked the boys to help Teddy extinguish the fire.

"That was a very inspiring talk," Dahlia said to Grant.

"I agree," Laurel said. "I believe some of the boys are beginning to realize this is the time to plan for when they leave here."

"I hope so." His gaze rested on Arlen, who sat nearby on a log, one sleeping twin on each knee.

"I don't know if he's had a breakthrough yet. His facade seems as tough as ever, but you never know what God is working on beneath that mask." Laurel smiled at Grant and Dahlia, then hurried away to get the van packed up.

"He still pushes me away," she said to Grant.

"I think it's because he doesn't want to admit he's not totally self-reliant," Grant explained. "To have to rely on someone else is a weakness he can't yet accept." The longing on her face touched him and he had to stop himself from comforting her physically "Can you collect the twins and take them to the truck? I want to speak to Teddy for a minute."

"Sure." Dahlia looked pleased by the opportunity to interact with Arlen and the twins.

Grant moved away, watching as she approached Arlen. He wanted to remind her that Arlen would respond better to firmness. But he stemmed the urge, mentally willing the boy not to hurt her.

"Grant wants me to get the twins in the truck, Arlen," she said softly. "Would you mind helping?"

"Okay." He glanced at the redheads nestled against either shoulder, eased their sleeping bodies a bit, then rose. "I can carry them."

"Are you sure?" When he nodded, Dahlia led the way to the truck.

Grant couldn't hear the rest of their conversation, but when the interior truck light came on, he saw yearning on her face. He also saw a softening in Arlen's hard eyes as he eased Glory onto the seat, leaving Dahlia to belt her in while he tenderly carried Grace to the other side. After fastening her seat belt, Arlen brushed his knuckles against her pink-flushed cheek then carefully closed the door.

Dahlia moved beside him. She said something and Arlen's mask slid back in place. He nodded, jerked away from the hand she'd placed on his shoulder and quickly strode to Laurel's van, a lonely figure in the faint light of the remaining coals. Dahlia gazed after his retreating figure, tears on her cheeks.

Laurel had said Teddy was deeply involved with Lives. Maybe he could help make Dahlia's dream come true. Grant arranged a meeting with Teddy.

Then back at Grant's place, Dahlia helped him put the twins to bed.

Grant gazed at their sleeping faces, reliving the terror that had filled him when they'd gone missing. It couldn't happen again. They needed him. He adored them as he'd never imagined he could. He could not lose them.

When he returned to the living room, Dahlia confronted him. "What did you want to talk to me about?"

Grant didn't soften what Kurt had told him. It was better she know the whole truth up front. He laid it out as plainly as he'd been told.

"If it's hopeless, why did you let us put up that hut tonight?" Her face showed the strain she usually hid. "If the track isn't going to happen—"

"Because I think it *can* happen," he emphasized.

"Grant, I don't have any more money. I'm already scraping the budget to get this track functional." She flopped into his armchair.

"So we'll fund-raise," he told her. "We'll plan some events to raise what you need to complete the project."

A rush of joy filled Grant when the stress lines around her eyes eased. Finally, this was something he could do for Dahlia.

"Thank you. You have no idea how much this means to me, Grant."

"Yes, I do," he said softly. Dahlia had never looked lovelier than she did now with her mussed hair, her face almost devoid of makeup. Grant was surprised by how much he wanted to kiss her.

"I promised I'd do my best and I intend to," he said, try to rid himself of the image of Dahlia in his arms.

Don't let me fail her.

Dahlia's green eyes locked on his then shifted. Surely she hadn't read his thoughts? But why did she seem so nervous.

"*I* promised to help you find a mom for the twins," Dahlia said, speaking quickly. Her smile didn't reach her eyes. "Come to the store tomorrow at five and I'll introduce you to Carolina."

Did he want to meet Carolina? And even if he did, how could she compare to Dahlia? Bemused by his thoughts, Grant followed her to the door.

"Thanks a lot for helping tonight." Her hazel eyes barely met his.

"Thanks for helping me look for the twins today. You're a good friend."

At the word *friend,* an odd expression flickered across her face. Then she said good-night and climbed into her truck. Grant watched her taillights disappear.

She *was* a good friend, but Dahlia Wheatley felt like a lot more than just a friend to Grant.

However, Grant couldn't afford to consider more than a business partnership with any woman, especially Dahlia. Sooner or later he'd fail her, and hurt her. His past was a guarantee of that.

And Dahlia was too special to be hurt by his inadequacies.

It was better if he end his wayward thoughts about her. They could only be friends. No matter how lovely she was.

Chapter Nine

"So let's review what we've got for the fund-raiser so far." A week later, Grant stood before the men he'd met at Lives, who he'd come to consider friends. "Kyle, you have a turkey shoot planned?"

"Adults and kids," Kyle confirmed. "Preceded by a barbecue chicken dinner supplied by Polar Bear Pizza. Half the tickets are already sold."

"Great. Now, Teddy. Your idea?" Grant was thrilled about how quickly people had come together to help Dahlia.

It certainly said a lot about how Churchill felt about her. Not that he was surprised.

"Free accommodation for six people over Christmas and New Year's at my hotel in Vancouver," Teddy said.

"That's very generous."

And on and on it went. Projects organized by men who saw opportunity in Dahlia's project. Humbled that they'd chosen him, the newcomer, as their leader, Grant thanked them.

"Dahlia's done a lot for Churchill. It's about time

we gave back to her." Kurt shared a grin with the other men. "I've arranged for the shoulders of that road to be built up. My company will cover materials, but we need contractors and equipment."

"I know a couple of guys who could do the work," someone volunteered. "But we'd have to pay for the equipment."

"Maybe we could rent the town's." Rick spoke from the back of the room. "The church's benevolent fund could cover that."

"So the road work can begin right away with Kurt in charge." Grant waited for his nod. "Any other ideas?"

A man Grant didn't know rose.

"Jack Campbell. My wife, Alicia, and I will sponsor a Thanksgiving Day dinner at Northern Lights Lodge. We'll ask for donations to the go-kart track."

"Great idea. Not having to cook a big meal on that day is probably a dream for lots of ladies," Grant enthused.

"I always said this is a community beyond all others," Dahlia spoke from the back of the room, startling many who hadn't realized she'd arrived. "You've all proven me right. Thank you so much."

"The question is, will all this raise enough money?" Teddy asked.

All eyes turned to Grant.

"There's no way to know that yet," he said. "But if we can't raise enough money to complete the track before freeze-up, we'll put everything on hold and continue to fund-raise through the winter."

"Oh, but—" Dahlia bit her lip, her disappointment obvious.

"The boys would have lots of time to get those karts you found operational—that is, if we could find a garage or shed where they could work, and a teacher," Grant said, hoping someone would have a solution.

"And if we can get them here," Kyle added.

"Anything else we need to discuss?" When no one responded, Grant rose. "Let's meet in a week to discuss our progress."

The group broke up. Grant looked for Dahlia but couldn't find her, so he hurried out of the town hall. He had less than fifteen minutes left in his lunch hour before starting his class at the high school and he hadn't yet eaten the peanut-butter sandwich he'd packed this morning. Then, his car door opened and Dahlia slid inside.

"I just wanted to say thanks again," she said. "And to bring you this." The unmistakable aroma of fried onions on a hamburger made his stomach rumble. "I figured you wouldn't have much time for lunch but I thought we could eat together. Okay?"

"Very okay," he agreed as he unwrapped the foil bundle. He opened it, took a bite and closed his eyes. "This tastes so good."

She grinned, took a bite of her own and then blinked. "I forgot," she mumbled and reached into her bag to produce two bottles of lemonade. "I brought these, too."

"Perfect." Grant savored the tang of his lemonade as it slid down his parched throat.

"I'm surprised you'll eat with me after my matchmaking failures. I truly had no idea that introducing you to Carolina would bring so many questions. Believe me,

I didn't know she was going through a third divorce. She never talks about her personal life."

"She was just being cautious," Grant said, suddenly not quite as hungry as he'd been. "But Ida—now that lady scared the daylights out of me."

"Me, too." Dahlia shuddered. "I was also very embarrassed."

"Why?" Grant grinned at the way Dahlia ducked her head and hid her eyes beneath her lashes. Her cheeks were hot pink.

"Ida seems like such a sweet, quiet woman. She adores her Sunday school kindergarten group so I thought she'd make a good candidate. But when I heard her pumping the twins for information about you, I could hardly believe it."

"Given her shock at the twins' answers, I guess I'm not the kind of father she expected." Grant burst out laughing.

"I'm sorry about asking you to meet those two ladies," she apologized again. "I know I promised I'd help you find someone, but—"

"Maybe we should give the whole matchmaking thing a rest for a while," he interrupted.

Dahlia's eyes darkened to emerald. The confusion he saw in them grabbed at his heart.

"I still want to find a mom for the girls." He struggled to find the right words. "But we both have so much on our plates right now. I want to help the Lives boys as much as I want to see your project succeed."

"And?" Dahlia waited.

"I have to work with the school students as well as ensure the twins properly settle into their lives here,"

Grant said. "Maybe this isn't the right time to be thinking about changing yet another part of their lives."

"And you said you didn't know anything about being a father." A faint smile tugged at Dahlia's lips. "Yet you make these responsible, well-thought-out decisions about your girls' welfare. Hate to tell you, Grant, but that *is* fatherhood."

"Those aren't the important decisions," he protested.

"Aren't they?" She gathered up their trash, then caught his gaze. "I don't believe there are any unimportant decisions when it comes to children. God blessed you with the twins. I'm pretty sure He knew what He was doing." She pushed open the door and stepped out of his car. "I'll see you later at Lives."

"Thanks for lunch," he said, marveling at the way Dahlia could cut right to the heart of the matter. "Will you be there by five o'clock?"

"Provided I can get away. I hope we finish with the last of those weeds today so Kurt can start on the road edges. Bring the twins."

"I'm not sure about that. Aren't the polar bears around right now?" Worry pricked at him. "I don't want to endanger them."

Dahlia shook her head as she chuckled. "Arlen's appointed himself the girls' personal protector. A bear wouldn't get within ten feet of the twins." With a wave she was gone.

Grant drove to the school.

Dahlia is so sure about You. Why is it I never feel sure of anything? Is it because I'm not as close to You as I should be?

The prayer slipped out without thought, surprising

Grant with how good it felt to confide in God again. He decided to get up half an hour earlier in the morning so he could return to reading his Bible before the day started, a habit he'd learned from Eva.

Maybe then God would help him gain assurance about his decisions.

Though Grant wondered if he'd ever reach Dahlia's level of certainty about God, past thoughts that had once reminded him that when he'd needed God as a child, God hadn't been there, were now coming less frequently.

Maybe if he kept trying, one day he'd get as comfortable with God as Dahlia.

Grant decided there was a lot he could learn from her. She never ceased to amaze him.

As Dahlia tugged at the remaining weeds along the old road, she hummed a little chorus from church. Every so often she glanced over her shoulder just to be sure no furry white polar bear crept up on her—and then mocked the silly fears Grant had raised. The bears hadn't yet returned to Churchill or a notice would have gone out. The unseasonably warm days seemed to have slowed everything, including their arrival. Anyway, the fence protected her.

After a while, she forgot about everything but the beauty of the day as she silently worshipped God.

"You're making great progress." She jumped and turned to find Grant studying her, a smile threading through his voice. "It doesn't look like you need me," he said with a grin.

"I'll take all the help I can get. Feel free to grab a

weed. There's no shortage." Her eyes widened when she noticed the girls trailing behind him, their faces sad. "What's up with those two? They're usually bouncing."

"They thought Arlen would be here," Grant explained. "They're crazy about him. I promised them that if they behaved they could come and see him. If he doesn't show, I'm in deep trouble."

"And here I thought I was their favorite person." Dahlia faked a frown. "Oh, well, as long as they pull weeds, I won't be offended."

"They might pull the tops off," he said. "But that's the most you should expect."

Dahlia couldn't stop the laughter that spilled out. Grant was such fun to be with. She couldn't remember feeling so comfortable with another person in a long time. His sense of humor matched hers, and she loved to make him laugh. She refused to think about the days after the project was complete when she wouldn't see him nearly as often.

"Here comes our help," she said as the Lives boys arrived.

Dahlia watched as Arlen joyfully embraced the twins, then showed them how to remove a few tiny weeds with the miniature spades he produced.

"I'm sorry, Dahlia. I imagine it must hurt to have him snub you."

"It does hurt. But I'm trying to leave it with God and let Him sort out the ways and means."

"It's as easy as that?" Grant took the huge weed she'd pulled, added his own to the pile in the middle of the road.

"Easy?" Dahlia took out her frustration on another

weed. "It's not easy at all," she huffed as the roots came free. "But trusting God means believing He will handle things for my best interest. If I worry, I'm second-guessing Him and that's not trust."

"I second-guess God all the time," Grant admitted, continuing to work beside her.

"It's an easy habit to fall into. We tend to fall back on the easiest route. If we'd only trust, we'd realize that's far easier than worrying."

"I'm beginning to realize that."

As Grant worked silently beside her, she realized that he was changing, gradually building the faith he'd once claimed he'd given up on. She prayed for him silently as they worked side by side for the next half hour. They paused only for occasional checks on the twins, who were enjoying their time with Arlen.

When the sun set and it grew too dim to work, Laurel coaxed everyone back to Lives, where they gathered around the big kitchen table to eat Sara's stew.

The boys joked about the go-kart track until Rod asked Laurel, "Is the track a sure thing? Or is there a chance we're doing all this work for nothing?" He frowned. "I've heard rumors."

"Grant and Dahlia are the project leaders," Laurel said. "Let's hear what they have to say."

"When I first began this project, I projected costs with the information I had." Dahlia met each boy's gaze directly. "At that point I had enough funds to complete the project. Since then I've been told more work is needed. Grant is spearheading a community group that is raising funds to meet expenses. Grant?"

Dahlia listened with burgeoning pride as he explained the fundraisers.

"You guys could help by making posters for advertising for the various events," he suggested. "If you could spare a few minutes to help out, we'd appreciate it. But you have to clear everything with Laurel first."

"What about the machines?" Arlen demanded from his place between Grace and Glory. "What's the point of doing all this work on the track if we haven't got anything to run on it?"

"There are used machines sitting in Thompson until we have funds to transport them here." Dahlia focused on Arlen. "We'll need a place to repair them. Perhaps you could ask around."

"Me?" He glared at her. "This is your project."

"No, it's a project designed to benefit those who come to Lives." With all eyes focused on her, Dahlia's cheeks warmed, but she refused to back down from Arlen's unspoken challenge. "It will take participation on your part to make it happen."

"I might not be here by the time it's working." He glared. "Why should I help?"

"Why wouldn't you?" Grant challenged. "Why should Dahlia stick her neck out to do this for *you*?"

Dahlia could see the boys were listening. *Keep going,* she mentally begged Grant.

"Let's think about this some more," he said. "What is the point of giving to others? Isn't it easier to grab for yourselves and let the other guy fend for himself?"

"Easier, maybe," Rod agreed. "But aren't people stronger when they work as a group?"

"Why?" Grant leaned back and waited.

"Because groups are always more powerful than a single person," Rod said. "That's why I got into a gang." The other boys laughed, but they knew what he meant.

Dahlia listened, fascinated by Grant's methods. He said little, yet he skillfully drew out each boy and then led them to the discovery that giving to others could make their own lives better.

"So," he said, drawing the discussion to a close. "We've got Dahlia getting this go-kart track up and running. A bunch of people in town are working to make it happen. I'm trying to help, though some might say I'm more a hindrance," he joked. "And you guys voted to go with this project. So besides pulling weeds, what will you contribute?"

Silence fell around the room as the boys risked a glance at their neighbor and then down.

"Maybe next time we talk, you'll have ideas of how you can play a bigger part in this project," he said. "Now I think I'd better take my girls home before Arlen's arms go to sleep holding them."

Laughter ended the session. It was the perfect note to finish on. Once they'd left Lives and tucked the girls into Grant's vehicle, Dahlia told him so.

"I don't know how you always hit the right note," she murmured. "But God has certainly gifted you. Those boys got the message loud and clear without you preaching at them."

"That's the best way." Grant smiled. "I'd better go. Morning comes earlier all the time."

"Want to bring the girls over tomorrow night? I'm making cookies for Thanksgiving."

"But that's a week away," Grant said in surprise.

"I'm making *a lot* of cookies," she said.

"I can certainly help eat them." He waggled his eyebrows, and Dahlia couldn't help but laugh.

"In exchange for your inexpert help, I'll throw in dinner. Six-thirty?"

He nodded and climbed in his car.

"Good night, girls," Dahlia said, sticking her head in Grant's window. The sleepy girls blew her kisses.

As she drew away, her face came within an inch of Grant's. Their gazes locked. Dahlia couldn't breathe. The slightest movement forward and they'd be kissing....

No!

Dahlia couldn't get sidetracked; couldn't weaken and let her heart get involved. A relationship meant being vulnerable to hurt and betrayal, and she didn't want to go through that again.

"Good night, Grant," she murmured and stepped back.

But as she pulled away, she felt something inside her cry out.

Why did being strong have to hurt so much?

"I can't believe you are actually encouraging them to make a mess." Grant felt his fingertips curl at the flour Glory had just dumped all over the counter.

"We can always clean up messes," Dahlia said as she scooped up the white powder. "The important thing about making cookies is to enjoy the process. Here." She handed him a cookie cutter in the shape of a turkey, then pointed to the slab of dough she'd rolled out. "Daddy should cut the first cookie, right?"

"Right." The twins grinned up at him, waiting.

"How do I do it?" Grant wished he'd made some excuse to leave the girls with Dahlia. Showing his utter ineptitude at making cookies was bad enough, but sooner or later, Dahlia would figure out he hated messes. And then she'd dig to find out why.

He did *not* want to go into that. Ever.

"Pick a spot and push the cutter into it." She smiled at him. "Easy."

Easy for her to say. He plunged it into the center of the dough, then quickly yanked it back out. Half of the dough stuck to his cutter. The rest remained on the counter.

Again his body tensed at the mess he'd created.

"You need more flour so it doesn't stick." Dahlia's hand closed over his, guided it to the flour container and carefully dipped it in. "Try again."

Stunned by how much he wanted her hand to remain on his, Grant froze.

Was he beginning to care for Dahlia?

Of course he cared about her. She was a good friend. She helped him meet people, helped with the twins. Of course he cared *about* her.

But care *for* her?

"What's wrong?" Dahlia's hazel eyes seemed to gaze right into his mind. The twins were staring, too.

"Where I should place it? There must be a method." He strove for a normal tone.

"In cookie-making, you find your own method." Dahlia's gaze remained on him. He knew she wasn't fooled by his offhand tone.

He shoved the cutter into the corner of the dough.

"Lift it slowly, Daddy." Now Grace placed her tiny hand on his. "So it doesn't break."

Grant drew the cutter slowly upward, revealing a perfect turkey.

"You did it, Daddy!" Glory cheered as if he'd just completed a marathon.

"It's an excellent turkey." Dahlia moved his work to a cookie sheet. "Now do some more. Try to get them a little closer together."

She nudged his hand slightly to the left. Again the spike of electricity flared.

"You're doing great." She smiled at him, then turned to the twins. "Your dad's ahead. Get cutting, you two."

Grace and Glory were experts compared to Grant. Wheat sheaves, scarecrows and horns of plenty multiplied beneath their small hands. There seemed no end to the dough.

"What are all of these for?" he asked.

"Every year I do a cookie-decorating afternoon at the nursing home," Dahlia explained.

"Surely a small place like Churchill doesn't have this many residents." Grant couldn't imagine how a few seniors would eat so many cookies.

"No," she conceded, a smile tugging the corners of her lovely mouth. "But we eat some, we break some, we give some to shut-ins and we use the rest at our Thanksgiving tea."

"Aren't *we* going to decorate any?" Glory asked, her face falling.

"Of course. But not tonight. Tonight is for making them and you're not finished yet." Dahlia rolled out yet another slab of dough. This time she handed him a pumpkin-shaped cutter. "You can do a few of these now that you're an expert," she teased with a wink.

This was the most family-oriented thing he and the girls had done since Eva had died. The mess still bothered Grant, but he'd begun to see Dahlia's method. She didn't obsess about a dusting of flour on the floor, bits of dough clinging to cupboard handles or the stack of dirty dishes in the sink because she knew she'd clean up when they were finished.

The twins beamed with happiness. That was worth a lot more than his inner angst over the memories of his father's obsessive-compulsive behavior.

"Did you make Thanksgiving cookies when you were a child, Dahlia?" he asked.

"With my grandmother." Dahlia pulled a pan of golden-edged cookies from the oven and slid them onto a rack. "She loved Thanksgiving. She celebrated God's generosity by making gift baskets brimming with homemade cookies. She'd deliver them along with a handmade card."

"To whom?"

Dahlia didn't immediately answer. Instead she helped the twins cut the rest of the dough, then lifted them off their stools and sent them to the bathroom to wash up. Then she answered.

"Granny Bev said she felt that God led her to those who should get her baskets." She lifted her head to meet his gaze. "I went with her every year to deliver them."

"The more I learn of your grandmother, the more amazing she sounds." Grant wished he could offer the twins the rich heritage of a loving, extended family.

"Granny Bev had a heart for God. Everything in her

life centered on Him. I want to be just like her—strong, focused, making a difference."

Didn't she know? Didn't she realize?

"You already are," Grant assured her.

"Not really. She was a woman of unbending faith. I'm not." She turned away, but Grant put a hand on her arm, forcing himself not to apologize for the flour mark he left there.

"Dahlia," he murmured. "You do so much for the community, not the least of which is the go-kart project. I've also heard about how you always give a discount to those who can't afford to pay full price and how you spend hours on customers' problems, even directing them elsewhere if you think they'll get a better deal. Your grandmother would be proud."

"Thanks." Her smile didn't reach her eyes. "But those are small things, nothing that would impress my parents."

"Why does that matter so much?" Grant asked then wondered if he should have when her face tightened.

"Because they don't see me as part of themselves, as part of the powerful, accomplished family they're so proud of." She stared at the floor. "I need to prove I'm not the weakest link."

"But you know you're not." Grant could see she didn't believe it. "Dahlia —"

"All that's left to do now is bake these." She smoothed a rubber blade over the counter, pushing the leftovers into a bowl. She placed the cutters and utensils, along with the mixing bowl, in the dishwasher and handed him a damp cloth. "Mind wiping the counters?"

He sensed that she'd deliberately cut him off because

she didn't like to show her vulnerability. If there was one thing Grant could understand it was that, so he didn't press her. He simply began scrubbing, his brain slipping back to his childhood.

"Grant?" Dahlia lifted the cloth from his hands. "I think it's clean now," she said in a gentle voice.

"Yes." He shook off the past. "The girls are nodding off. I think we should go. Thank you for this. We've had a wonderful time."

She didn't ask him to stay, solidifying his theory that she wanted to be alone. She helped him dress the twins in their outerwear then handed him a paper bag, insisting they take some of the cookies home. Grant suppressed his reaction to the brush of her fingers against his and shepherded the twins out the door.

"Thank you for everything," he said, staring into Dahlia's lovely face.

"Good night, Dally," Grace and Glory called until he closed the car door on their voices.

The twins fell silent on the drive home, as if they understood without being told that he couldn't talk to them right now, that he needed time to come to grips with Dahlia shutting him out so thoroughly. He did, but he also needed time to quash those hurtful memories he'd replayed in her kitchen.

When the girls were finally tucked in bed and the house was silent, Grant stood at the window staring into the dark night.

Memories of cleaning and polishing the cracked and tired yellow countertop in the kitchen of his childhood flooded back.

Do it again, boy. I'm not having my food prepared on this mess. Do it again with this!

Splash. He could feel the sting of the bleach on his reddened hands.

How could You possibly expect me to raise those two innocents? What if I'm like him?

For a moment, the awful horror of that possibility stuck and he couldn't break free. Then Dahlia's face with her shining hair, pure, clear eyes and genuine smile filled his mind.

"I could share the twins with her," a tiny voice in his head whispered. "We could raise them together."

As quickly as the thought came, he dismissed it. Wasn't it obvious after tonight that Dahlia didn't see him that way? Anyway, how could he be the man Dahlia deserved?

What if he hurt her? What if he only added to the pain she already carried?

Grant could never allow that. So he'd get on with his life and keep her as a friend, a very good friend whom he cared *about*. But that was all.

He *was* going to make her go-kart dream a reality, even though he had a hunch that neither completing the track nor winning Arlen's affection would erase the hurt she'd buried inside.

Grant blinked, surprised by how very much he wanted to give Dahlia everything she wanted.

Chapter Ten

"It's not going to happen," Arlen sneered. "So why are we killing ourselves to make this track useable?"

Dahlia had just explained that before they could resurface the track, they needed to fill the cracks. Rod and Arlen were doing that as she and Grant followed with the tar topcoat.

"Do you ever stop being a naysayer?" Rod's face was red from the exertion on this unusually warm day. "Let's just get on with it."

"Who made you the boss?" Arlen yelled.

"Guys, come on. Let's cut the fighting and work together so we can get this done. Okay?"

Dahlia was relieved Grant had intervened because she was running out of ways to reach Arlen.

"Where are the twins?" After Grant poured some of the tar on the surface, she spread it across the road. They worked well together. Like partners.

"Laurel took Glory and Grace to the beach." He waited until she'd finished one section before he started another. "They're choosing pebbles for a project. Laurel said it might be the last chance before winter blows in."

"We've been lucky with the weather." For the past three days Dahlia regretted ending their cookie-making session so abruptly. She'd done it because his presence in her home with the twins had engendered dreams she couldn't afford. She needed to stop dreaming and focus on her goal. The track.

Dahlia now sensed that something had changed between them, that he'd somehow withdrawn. There was nothing she could put her finger on. He was just— different toward her.

"The twins' birthday is Saturday," Grant murmured when Arlen and Rod had moved out of range.

"They'll be six?" A bump of envy grew in Dahlia's heart. How lucky he was to share this milestone with the precocious twins. Her first instinct was to offer to help so she could be involved in the celebration, but she wasn't sure that was a good idea given this distance she felt yawning between them. "I'll bet they're excited."

"That's the problem. They want to invite their entire class to a birthday party." Panic filled his gray eyes. "I can't handle that many kids."

Dahlia felt certain it wasn't only the number of kids he was worried about. Something else ate at him.

Stick to your decision to give him space, she reminded herself. She hoped doing so would help her quell these longings to be closer to him.

Dahlia jerked upright. Was that why she was helping Grant—to get closer to him?

"Would you be available to help?" His hesitation was painfully obvious.

She wanted to say yes immediately, but she reined herself in. "With what, exactly?"

"With whatever it is one does at a child's sixth birthday."

"You've never had a birthday party?" she teased, trying to make him laugh.

"No."

At first she thought he was joking. But his eyes remained blank.

"My father wasn't into parties," Grant said, his voice giving nothing away. "And he didn't allow me to attend them either. Eva handled the twins' parties, so I truly have no clue how to make the day special, apart from buying birthday cakes and supervising some games." For a moment, his eyes lit up. "I was hoping you'd tell me how your Granny Bev would celebrate."

Even though Dahlia wanted nothing more than to help Grant, she knew doing so would put her heart at risk.

However, he was out here sweating to help with *her* project. And how could she say no to a man who understood how deeply she valued her grandmother?

"Birthday parties aren't that hard," she said. "Especially for little girls. Wearing on adults, maybe. But not difficult."

"I'd be very grateful for any advice you can offer." His gaze held hers. "I hate to keep asking you for help."

"Don't be silly." She repressed a flicker of guilt. "It will be fun. But I said I'd be at Kyle's turkey shoot that night."

"I'm going, too. The party will be over by then." Grant frowned. "I really need to find the twins a sitter. I don't like to ask Lucy for even more of her time. I'm surprised she agreed to stay on as the twins' after-school sitter after they ran away. She tried to quit but I told her that could have happened to anyone."

"Why not ask him?" Dalia inclined her head toward Arlen. "I think he'd be great at it."

"Interesting idea." Grant emptied the last of the pail on the road. "Want to switch jobs with me?"

"I thought you'd never ask," Dahlia said, half laughing, half groaning as she rubbed her back. "I didn't realize this stuff would be quite so stiff to spread."

"Just be glad it's still warm. If the sun wasn't heating things up, it wouldn't spread at all." Grant handed her the pail, then adroitly used the spreader she'd struggled to wield.

By the time she and Grant reached Rod and Arlen, the two were sitting on upturned buckets, discussing football. Apparently their argument was over.

"You guys did a great job," she praised. "I'm so glad we could finish before it turns cold."

"I'm beginning to wonder if it ever gets cold here," Arlen scoffed. "Maybe all your talk of frigid weather is fantasy."

"You wish." Dahlia laughed. "The fantasy part is believing winter won't come. It will. This is the mildest fall I've known since I arrived and I won't object if God keeps the flurries back a little while."

"You really think God cares about stuff like that?" Arlen said.

"I *know* He cares about us." Dahlia winced at the pain clouding his eyes. "We're His children. Every dad wants to give his kid their heart's desires."

"My heart's desire is to not be here," Arlen snapped.

"Where would you rather be?"

Grant started talking to Rod, leading him away so she and Arlen could be alone.

"With my sisters." He looked straight at her and for the first time there was no enmity in his gaze, just a boatload of hurt. "But that isn't going to happen."

"You won't be here forever. You'll see them soon." She reached out to touch his arm, but he jerked out of reach. "If you need to talk to someone, I'm available. So is Grant. Please don't feel you're all alone."

"But I am. My sisters are dead and my mother doesn't ever want to see me again." His eyes bored into her. "I don't think you can fix that."

"No, I'm sorry. I can't," she whispered, aghast at the burden he carried.

Arlen turned and walked away. Tears rose to clog her throat as she finally accepted that reaching Arlen was impossible.

Grant must have read something in her expression because he broke off his discussion and walked toward her.

"Can I help?" he murmured.

"I have to go home."

Desolate, she was barely aware of what was happening as Grant took over. He took her keys and helped her into her seat. He dropped the boys at Lives, drove her home and put on the kettle without asking. When the tea was ready, he set a cup in her hands. Then he squatted in front of her, placing his hands atop hers.

"What's wrong, Dahlia?"

She looked into his eyes and gave voice to her painful acceptance of the truth she had to accept.

"I don't think God's going to answer my prayer for Arlen, Grant."

Dahlia's words knifed straight into Grant's heart. He could see defeat creeping in, taking over the woman who didn't do defeat. He couldn't stand it.

"You can't know that," he reminded her. "God could be working on him without you even realizing it."

"Do you think so?"

Dahlia's earnest, desperate question sent Grant off balance. He wasn't any more certain of God's intent for her life than he was of God's intent for his own. But surely God wouldn't disappoint a woman like Dahlia, who trusted Him so completely?

"I think you have to take your own advice. Trust," he said, recalling a past conversation they'd shared. "No second-guessing, remember?"

After a moment, her head lifted, her shoulders went back and she smiled. "Maybe you're right." She slipped one hand free to cover his and squeezed. "Maybe now isn't the time to lose faith. I have to keep trusting."

Grant couldn't help it. Her sweet smile, the blaze in her hazel eyes, the trusting way she looked at him —he leaned forward and pressed his lips to hers.

At first she startled, but then Dahlia leaned into the kiss. Her hand left his to slide around his neck, drawing him closer.

For Grant these moments were poignantly special. Possibilities loomed. Perhaps he *could* love someone,

Grant thought. Perhaps he wouldn't follow in his father's footsteps.

But he *was* like his dad. Eva had thought he wasn't, but she'd never known the bursts of anger that surged inside him, or his struggle to control them.

But Dahlia would know.

"I'm sorry. I shouldn't have done that." Gently, he eased away from her, anxious to put some distance between them.

"Why not?" Her hazel eyes brimmed with confusion.

"I can't get involved, Dahlia." He ignored his heart's yearning.

"But you're looking for a wife."

"I'm looking for a mother for the twins," he corrected gently. "I'm not…available for anything else."

She fell silent, her eyes searching his. Grant kept his expression as neutral as he could. Dahlia was good and sweet and lovely. It would be so easy to love her but he clung to his resolve.

"You're right," she whispered. "I can't afford to get sidetracked." She moved away from him. "We should talk about the twins' party."

Grant rose and sat opposite her. "You don't have to help, Dahlia."

"I want to, Grant. Truly."

She began listing things they could do for the girls. Grant scribbled notes, trying to forget what had just happened between them.

"Does that help?" She arched one eyebrow.

"Yes. Thanks." He checked his watch and rose. "I'd better get to work. Laurel will be bringing the girls back soon." If Dahlia realized he was eager to escape, she didn't show it.

"Thanks for helping with the track." She didn't look at him.

"That was fun. And at least Arlen revealed a little more about himself. That's progress." He waited. When she stood without looking at him, he wished he'd handled things differently. He hated the awkwardness that now loomed between them.

"Yes, it is." She walked him to the door. "I've got a big sale on Saturday at the store, but I should be able to sneak away if you need help with the party."

"No," he said in sudden decision. "You've done more than enough."

She did look at him then, surprise in her green eyes. "You're sure?"

"It's about time I do my job as a parent, don't you think?"

"You'll do fine, Grant," she said. "You love them. That's all they need."

He said good-night and left. But inside his head, a voice kept asking, *Is love really enough for the twins?*

In his heart he knew it was the only thing Dahlia wanted and he couldn't give it.

But oh, how wonderful to finally hold her in his arm, to kiss her as he'd longed to for so long. He drove home reliving every moment.

She shouldn't have done it.

But Dahlia could no more have stopped herself from peeking in on Glory and Grace's birthday party than fly to the moon.

Plus, she wanted to see Grant again.

She pulled into his driveway, trying to ignore the memory of his kiss. It was nothing, she kept telling herself, but unfortunately, her heart wasn't getting the message.

She couldn't waste time wishing otherwise. She glanced at her purse. Every nerve in her body tensed at what lay inside. A note she'd received yesterday, from her mother.

We want to see what you've accomplished up there, she'd written.

A thousand emotions raced through her. Seeing them again—would they finally accept that she was strong, capable even though the track wasn't yet finished? Had they forgiven her for leaving? Would they try to persuade her to return home?

Is she wanted their approval, Dahlia knew she had to get the track finished. She sighed, shut off her worries and walked to the house.

"Hi, Dally," the twins squealed when they opened the door.

"Happy birthday to both of you," she said, relishing their embraces. She handed each girl a gift bag.

"Thank you. We're going to open them later," Glory told her. "Right now we're having a party. Daddy made it."

"We have balloons and everything." Grace's blue eyes shone with excitement. "And Arlen's going to take us on a treasure hunt."

"Aren't you lucky." Dahlia held her smile when Grant appeared. He looked less frazzled than she'd expected. "How's it going?"

Arlen appeared. Before he ushered the twins back to their guests, he gave Dahlia a nod. She was astonished.

"It's going better than I thought it would." Grant grinned at her surprise. "I decided to do everything I always wanted and never had. A bit crazy maybe, but it seems to be working. Arlen's been great." Grant led her to the living room.

The room was party central. The pushed-back furniture allowed plenty of room for activities. Balloons covered the ceiling. One wall featured multicolored donkey tails, though the rest of the animal had disappeared. Through the patio door, she saw tiny boats floating in a paddling pool.

Grant grasped her arm, motioning to the circle of girls sitting on the floor, with Arlen between the twins.

"They're playing a whispering game. Come into the kitchen. I've got the coffeepot on."

"It's all fantastic, Grant. I don't know why you thought you needed help."

He motioned for her to sit at the table, which was covered with cupcakes.

"Those are for decorating later." He handed her a steaming cup of coffee and sat opposite her, his face beaming.

"I always thought you were a wonderful father, Grant," she told him, surprised by the tears filling her eyes "The twins couldn't be blessed with anyone better. You're amazing."

His eyes widened in surprise. "Thanks, Dahlia. That means a lot to me, coming from you.

She tried to gain control of her emotions, for his sake as much as hers. "How did you persuade Arlen to help?"

"He volunteered," Grant told her. "He showed up here this morning and took the twins on what he called a 'birthday walk' so I could get things ready. When I mentioned my idea of a treasure hunt, he said he knew exactly how to do it. I think being with the twins has been therapeutic for him."

"I'm sure." Dahlia wished she'd had some way to help Arlen. She was glad he'd found comfort with the twins but she knew he needed more. "Can I ask a favor? If you get a moment, can you sound out Arlen? When he told me about his sisters, I got the feeling that he's never really come to terms with their deaths."

"I've been thinking the same," Grant told her. "I've been waiting for the right opportunity to bring up the topic."

"Thank you," she said, a rush of relief filling her. Too bad she couldn't turn to Grant for answers about her parents. "So how can I help?"

"You can't. You're an invited guest," he insisted. "I didn't expect you until later. How's your sale going?"

"My staff have things well in control. I'm not needed." A burst of giggles echoed from the next room. She rose. "So what's next?"

"The treasure hunt. That's Arlen's idea," Grant told her as they walked into the living room. "I'm sure he wouldn't mind if we tag along. I want to take some pictures."

Dahlia watched as Grant snapped candid shots of the twins and their friends searching for treasure. The big surprise, however, came when Arlen mentioned how much his sisters had loved treasure hunts.

"Once I even put foil chocolate coins in a box and

buried it in the backyard," he murmured, watching the kids search for the last clue. "They loved it."

"Grace and Glory love you." Dahlia smiled at him. "It's kind of you to help Grant."

"He's a good dad." Arlen watched Grant climb a rock to get a better angle. "He doesn't think he is, though."

Curious to hear Arlen's viewpoint, she frowned. "Why do you say that?"

"Because he hesitates before he makes decisions just like my dad used to. He didn't think he could be a good father either."

"*Was* he a good father?" she asked as calmly as she could, hardly able to believe he was talking like this.

"My grandfather was mean," he said through clenched teeth. "My dad was afraid he'd turn out the same. My grandfather always said my dad was just like him. But it was a lie. Most of what my grandfather said was a lie." His voice dropped. "But not about me."

"What did he say about you?" Dahlia frowned.

"My grandfather said I killed my sisters. And he was right, I did. I didn't mean to but I did." Arlen angrily dashed the wetness from his eyes. "I loved them more than anything, but I killed them. That's why my mother never wants me to come home."

She stared at him, too shocked to summon words that would help him. He stood alone, a solitary figure in his pain, until Glory called his name.

For the rest of the afternoon, Dahlia studied Arlen.

When Grant approached her later, she pulled him aside. "I think you need to talk to Arlen sooner rather than later, Grant," she whispered. "He just told me he thinks he's responsible for his sisters' deaths."

Every time she looked at him now she was reminded of their kiss. And every time she had to quash the yearning for more.

"That is serious." Surprised, Grant nodded. "I'll make it a point to talk to him as soon as I can."

She should be keeping her distance from Grant, but asking Grant to help her with Arlen would make keeping that distance impossible.

But she had to do it because together she and Grant could make a difference in the life of this boy who so touched her heart.

Chapter Eleven

Utterly and totally exhausted from the birthday party that was still going, and his attempts at a private chat with Arlen, which kept getting interrupted, Grant's hope of peace crashed when he remembered Kyle's turkey shoot. Dahlia, by contrast, looked ready for the next activity.

"How do you do it? You worked at the store, raced all over town with Arlen's treasure hunt, and yet you look like you just woke from an afternoon nap."

"Naps are for wimps," she said, wrinkling her nose.

A sound from the living room made him look past Dahlia to where the twins were opening their gifts from Dahlia. Glory was crying. He hurried over to comfort her, wondering at the cause.

"Look, Daddy." Glory said between sniffs. "Dally gave us memory books just like the ones Mommy used to make."

"We miss Mommy," Grace wailed, tears rolling down her cheeks.

Very aware of Arlen and Dahlia watching him,

Grant pulled out a tissue and dabbed at the tears on their cheeks.

"You don't talk about Mommy," Grace said, her voice slightly accusing.

Glory's clear blue eyes gazed into his. "Don't you miss Mommy?"

What could he say? That he hadn't talked about Eva because he didn't want to remember all he'd lost? Because he didn't want them to remember the wonderful life they'd had with her and realize he wasn't measuring up? Because he didn't want to cause them pain?

"Tell them," Dahlia whispered, stuffing more tissues into his hand. "They need to hear."

"I remember your mom, Glory. I don't think I'll ever forget her." Grant took Dahlia's advice and began to share memories he'd kept private until now.

"The first time I saw your mom she was playing with you two in the park. You were going down the slide and you, Glory, were scared. She kept telling you not to be afraid."

"I like slides," Glory said, her tears dissipating.

"You do now, because she taught you how to go down, just like she taught you to try different things."

"Like pomegranates," Grace remembered. "Mommy got me to taste pomegranates."

"And onions," Glory added. Her nose wrinkled. "I don't like onions."

The other children loudly agreed.

"What else, Daddy?" Grace asked.

"I remember how your mom would hug you every night and put a special kiss on your forehead," he continued.

"I can't remember Mommy doing that." Glory's grin faded. "Why can't I remember, Daddy?"

Grant didn't have an answer to that. He felt every eye on him. The happiness on the twins' faces slowly faded and he knew it would only be moments until their tears returned. Why didn't he have the right words to say?

"Nobody remembers everything about the people who died." Arlen crouched down, his voice somber. "I can't remember everything about my sisters. But that doesn't mean I didn't love them or that they didn't love me."

Grace leaned her head on Arlen's shoulder. "How come?"

"Because people we love are tucked inside our hearts. Right here," he said, tapping his chest. "We can't remember everything, but every so often we remember something special like you did today when you opened those memory books. Maybe you can draw a picture in the book and that'll help you remember this birthday."

Glory looked at Grace. They nodded. Good humor restored, they thanked Dahlia for the books and the multicolored markers. "We like markers."

"I remember," Dahlia said with a chuckle.

Grant looked at her, suddenly recalling that first day on the train. He remembered seeing a yellow streak on the back of her jacket when they'd disembarked. Suddenly he knew the twins had a hand in making that yellow mark, though Dahlia had never said a word to him about it. What a lady.

"Do you want to open the rest of your gifts now?" The twins nodded, so Grant rose and moved out of the circle. Arlen followed. "Thank you," he said to the boy. "I appreciate you telling us about your sisters."

"You were right." Arlen followed him to the kitchen. "It does feel better to talk about my sisters. Maybe I'll tell you more someday."

"I'd be honored." Grant smiled, relieved that something had finally gotten through that tough shell. "Can you help the girls open the rest of their gifts now?"

Arlen nodded.

"You've had quite a day," Dahlia said, helping Grant restore the kitchen to order. "I wish he'd discuss his sisters more. I wonder what happened. He didn't tell you, did he?" She frowned when Grant shook his head.

"I think Glory is trying to find out." Grant lifted an eyebrow and tipped his head in the direction of the twins, who sat snuggled next to Arlen on the sofa. "Is it wrong to listen in?"

"Not when we're trying to help him." Dahlia set two chairs near the doorway, poured two cups of coffee and offered him one. Grant took it and sat beside her, very aware of her soft fragrance and the way her curls tumbled down her back. Sitting here beside her seemed so right. Then he heard Grace ask, "What were your sisters like, Arlen?"

Grant hoped the boy wouldn't brush off her question or hurt her feelings. He should have known better. Amusement threaded through Arlen's voice.

"Goofy. Just like you." He tweaked her pert nose. "Andrea and Priscilla loved to paint. They painted pictures of everything. I always gave them paints for their birthday and Christmas."

"Oh, no," Grant groaned in a whisper to Dahlia. "Now the twins will want to paint."

She smothered a laugh, her eyes dancing.

"Did you tell them bedtime stories?" Grace asked.

"All the time." His face looked vulnerable in the lamplight. "And they fell asleep in the middle of them, just like you do."

"And then they died," Glory said. "Like Mommy." Arlen nodded. "Did they get sick?"

"No." Arlen's voice tightened. "It was my fault."

"Why?" Glory asked.

"Because I didn't do my job and take care of them. I forgot because I was in a hurry."

"You forgot?" Grace touched his cheek, her voice very tender when he nodded. "That's okay. People forget lots of things. I forgot to tell Daddy I loved him last night."

A lump lodged in Grant's throat.

"I forgot to put the lid on Daddy's special pen," Glory added, not to be outdone by her sister. "Now it doesn't write anymore. That's my fault. But that's not like when your sisters went to heaven, is it?"

"Not quite." Arlen sounded as choked up as Grant felt. He glanced sideways and saw that Dahlia was also moved.

"Your sisters know you didn't mean to make a mistake." Grace tipped her head to one side. "One time, Glory hit me. I was mad, but Mommy told me that love forgives and that I should forgive Glory." She bent to look into his face. "That means I shouldn't be mad at her or blame her."

"I know." Arlen swallowed hard.

"It means you have to forgive *you*," Glory told him sternly.

"I'll try," Arlen promised, his voice choked.

A long silence stretched. Dahlia wiped a tear from her cheek, her smile tremulous. Grant couldn't take the tension any longer. He rose and stepped through the doorway. It was either that or kiss darling Dahlia again.

"I doubt if you two are hungry enough for a big supper," he said later. "How about I make cheese sandwiches?"

"Okay." Glory threw her arms around Arlen's neck. "And two for Arlen, 'cause he's big," she explained. "Dally, how many for you? Daddy makes them really good."

"He's a very special daddy, isn't he?" Dahlia smiled at Glory; then her gaze slipped to Grant. Her cheeks pinked. "And Arlen is your special friend. Do you know how lucky you girls are?"

"Yep!" They grinned at each other. A moment later they huddled together on the floor to reexamine their birthday gifts.

Grant was about to turn away and begin preparing the sandwiches. But he paused to watch Dahlia move into the living room as Arlen rose from the sofa. The boy towered over her, but she didn't look intimidated. She reached up and touched his shoulder.

"I wish I'd known your sisters, Arlen. They must have been special, too."

He nodded, easing away from her touch but saying nothing. Grant had a hunch he was still choked up.

"The twins are right." Earnestness filled Dahlia's

voice. "Your sisters loved you. They'd understand a mistake, whatever it was. We all make them. I did, too."

"You? But you're always Miss Perfect." Arlen frowned. "What mistake did you make?"

"I wasn't there when my brother needed me," she told him. "I got sucked up in my own stuff and didn't notice that he was desperate for my help."

"What happened?"

Dahlia explained, but Grant could see the words cost her. Grant knew she was still trying to make up for not being there for her brother just as Arlen was still punishing himself for his sisters' deaths.

"But can *you* forgive yourself?" Arlen asked after a long pause.

"I know that's what he would have wanted so I'm trying," Dahlia replied.

"Is that why you're pushing this go-kart thing? Because of your brother?" Arlen's question dared her to tell the truth.

"In a way." Dahlia's smile broke free, bringing Grant relief. "Partly it's to show my parents. They never thought I was strong enough to take his place."

"Why do you have to take his place? You have your own place." When she didn't answer, Arlen knelt down to talk to the girls.

Dahlia walked into the kitchen. She looked slightly dazed.

"Are you okay?" Grant asked.

"I'm not sure." She set napkins at each place, but her attention was elsewhere. "Did you hear what he said? He said I have my own place. I never thought of it like that before."

There were a hundred things Grant could have said to help her realize that she didn't have to earn anything, but he let her muse on it alone. Dahlia had spent a long time trying to make others proud of her, but what she really wanted was to be proud of the woman she was. He had a hunch that discovering that for herself would be a major milestone.

"Are the sandwiches ready, Daddy?" Glory tugged at his leg.

"Just about. You and Grace go and wash your hands." Grant flipped one sandwich, delighted when it landed perfectly in the pan.

"Daddy, look!" Grace squealed. "It's snowing."

Dahlia came back to life. She hurried to the window and peered outside. A groan seeped from her.

"Grace, will you ask Arlen to help you and your sister wash up?" He shut off the stove, waited until they were alone then walked over to Dahlia. "What is it? What's wrong?"

"I tried to tell you earlier. I got a letter from my mother today. They're going to come and visit to see the progress I've made." She gazed at him. She didn't need to say any more. He understood.

"You want to show them all you've done, to present a fait accompli," he guessed. "With the snow covering, you won't be able to do that."

"Because I haven't finished it, Grant. I've tried so hard but I just can't make it work."

"I know." He gathered her into his arms, pressed her head to her should and just held her as she wept.

A moment later they both heard the twins coming

and Dahlia broke free of his embrace, dashing the tears from her eyes.

"Please excuse me," she said, her voice full of heartbreak. "I have to go."

Though the twins and Arlen tried to persuade her to stay and eat with them, Grant said nothing as he helped Dahlia pull on her jacket. She said a quick goodbye then hurried away, trudging through the wisps of white that now covered the ground, a small, lonely figure in the vast outdoors.

Arlen said nothing for a few moments. When they could no longer see her through the window he glanced at Grant. "She's upset the track isn't ready, isn't she?"

"Yes," Grant said then added, "Her parents are coming soon. It's a big deal to Dahlia to show them what she's accomplished. Without the karts running on the track…" He wanted Arlen to seriously consider what this failure of this project meant to Dahlia.

"She asked me to help and I wouldn't do it. I told her I was busy," Arlen admitted, "but that wasn't true."

"Then why did you say it?" Grant asked.

"Because I was mad at her," he admitted in a rueful voice. "She has everything. At least I thought she did. Everybody's making a big deal about her and this track and how she's pulling it all together and I thought, 'Why should I make it easy for her?'" Arlen shook his head. "I didn't realize the track was about her brother and her parents."

"And now that you do?" Grant slid the sandwiches onto a plate and set them on the table along with a gallon of milk.

"I dunno."

"You can still help. It's not too late. There are still the tires to be painted. There's lots left to do." Grant didn't want to press the boy. He wanted Arlen to *want* to help Dahlia, but all he could do now was pray for God to soften the boy's heart. As they ate, the twins asked Arlen if he'd help them build a snowman tomorrow. Arlen shook his head.

"Sorry. I can't. I think I'll be painting some tires tomorrow." He winked at Grant. "Laurel says the first snow in Churchill never stays."

"I sure hope she's right," Grant said with a grin.

Arlen babysat while Grant went to the turkey shoot. By the time he returned home, the boy was sacked out in the spare room, where he'd stay until Grant took him back to Lives in the morning.

With everyone asleep, Grant sat in his darkened living room and stared out at the whirling snow, which had kept some of the turkey shoot crowd home. He worried that they hadn't made enough to make Dahlia's dream come true.

Grant struggled to pray as Rick had directed him. In the past he'd always held some part of himself back. Now he tried to release his distrust in God, for Dahlia.

Please, please make the snow melt so she can have her dream. Please? She's worked so hard. Let her have that much.

This desperate craving to see Dahlia's dream realized was confusing for Grant. Though he wanted the best for Dahlia, he was no longer sure that completion of the track *was* the best thing for her. He desperately wanted her to be happy. Actually he wanted to be the one to make her happy.

It had felt so right to comfort her earlier, to be there to support and encourage her.

But Dahlia deserved a man who could love her and Grant didn't have the ability to do that.

But oh, how he wished he did.

On Thanksgiving Day, Grant squeezed his eyes closed as he held the phone and listened. He had a lot to be thankful for today.

"Dahlia and the boys are going to be so happy," he said into the phone. "Thank you. And happy Thanksgiving," he said.

For a few moments he hugged the secret information to himself, relishing the response he knew he'd get when he made it public. Mostly he relished the thrill of telling Dahlia.

Grant stepped out the back door to inhale the crisp autumn air. The snow was long gone. Sunshine blazed across the land.

Dahlia. He could imagine the flash of gold that would shoot through her eyes before her dazzling smile appeared. He'd scarcely seen her since the twins' birthday, but that didn't matter. He just had to close his eyes and he could visualize her face. Somehow thoughts of her were always with him.

Grant had believed that keeping his distance would diminish his fascination with Dahlia, but he'd been so wrong.

Dahlia was embedded in every detail of his life. If he closed his eyes, he could breathe in her soft fragrance that reminded him of sunshine; he could hear her laughter. When his negative thoughts grew strong, he heard her voice chiding him to look on the positive side. The day dragged if Dahlia wasn't there to share it. It was Dahlia's smile he craved, Dahlia he wanted to be with.

What was this? Love?

No. Couldn't be. Grant was certain he was capable of feeling love again. So why was he so attracted to her? Dahlia hadn't coaxed him. By simply being herself, she'd become part of his life. Even if he wanted to, Grant couldn't forget her. Dahlia was unforgettable.

Confused, Grant went inside and poured himself another cup of coffee. Then he sank into his chair perched in the kitchen's sunniest spot.

Eva's Bible sat on a nearby stand. He'd planned to study the fragile onion-skin pages many times since her death to find answers and yet somehow he'd never gotten past the first page of Genesis. He felt so guilty every time he looked at it that he'd almost decided to put it away, store it for the girls.

But Grant needed somebody to talk to and according to Rick, God was the one with all the answers. So he picked up the Bible, held the covers between his hands and let the book fall open. The seventh chapter of Matthew.

If you, being evil, know how to give good gifts to your children, how much more will your Father in heaven give good things to those who ask Him?

Gifts. For their birthdays Grant had given the twins tiny silver lockets with their names engraved inside. He'd wanted something lasting to cherish, so they'd feel cared for. The girls had seemed thrilled.

This verse said that God was better at giving good

gifts than Grant was. Did that mean God could give the gift of love to him?

At the service yesterday, Rick had said that God was the giver of good gifts, that, "it gives Him joy to see His kids smiling and happy."

Until Eva, Grant had never felt loved. He still didn't understand it. How did one get to love another? To have love grow inside *him*—it seemed impossible. All he wanted was to make sure Dahlia was happy. Was that love? Grant read the passage again.

I don't understand, God. Why would you love me? How can I be loved when I can't love?

For the first time since Eva's death, Grant examined their relationship, compared it to what he'd seen and heard among his new friends in Churchill and was stunned. His feelings for Eva had their basis in insecurity. They'd never had that sweet sharing of kindred souls. He'd accepted all Eva lavished on him. But what had he given back? He'd been so afraid to push past *his* needs, *his* fears, *his* problems to find out hers.

What a terrible deal Eva had made when she'd married him.

Grant glanced at himself in the mirror across the room and reminded himself that whatever he felt for Dahlia, he couldn't let anything come of it.

The doorbell rang.

"Hi, Rick. Come on in. I was just thinking of you."

"All good, I hope. Are you busy?" Rick followed him to the kitchen.

"The twins are at the hotel with Laurel and Dahlia, making pies for the big Thanksgiving dinner tonight." He poured Rick a cup of coffee and freshened his own.

"I'm supposed to go there to peel potatoes in an hour or so but I've got time to chat till then. What's up?"

"You're on potato detail, too, huh?" Rick chuckled.

"I just got a phone call from Kyle and thought I'd share with you. He's got the final tally on the turkey shoot. We did well." The figure Rick quoted made Grant's brows rise. "Think Dahlia's going to be happy?"

"If she isn't, my news should do it. I had a phone call from a man who's willing to donate his garage for as long as it takes the boys to get the go-karts running, *and* he's offered his expertise as a former mechanic." Grant high-fived Rick. "Now all we need is enough money to pay for transporting the go-karts from Thompson."

"Taken care of, pal. Laurel approached the government to cover transportation of the karts to Churchill as part of therapy for the boys. They agreed." Rick grinned. "God is really blessing Dahlia's idea. Now, if the weather holds until the karts are operational, it might all come together before a freeze up."

"God giving good gifts to His children," Grant murmured. Seeing Rick's quizzical look, he explained the verse he'd just read. "But why? That's the thing that keeps stymieing me. Why would God love us so much?"

"Well, why do you love Grace and Glory?" Rick asked. "You're not related by blood. They must have made you change a lot of your life. As sweet as they are, I'm sure they aggravate you sometimes. So how can you love them?"

"I just do," Grant admitted, slightly surprised to realize how naturally those words came. "They're my kids."

"Same with God," Rick said. "Love is love. Giving of yourself, caring for someone else more than you care for you, being willing to let go of what you want most to make another happy—that's love. God gave it to us so we could enjoy each other. As much as we might think we must aggravate God by failing to understand His love, He doesn't give up. His very nature is love."

"And all we're supposed to do is accept it?" Grant felt stupid for asking, but he desperately needed to get this straight.

"Love is a verb. It *does*." Rick smiled. "Part of love is accepting it, but the most rewarding part of love is giving it." Rick raised an eyebrow. "What's troubling you?"

Grant needed to understand love as it pertained to a relationship with God. Maybe that would help him be the father God expected. Maybe if he understood love, he could figure out his feelings for Dahlia.

So Grant asked all the questions about faith and fatherhood he'd never dared voice. At first he was embarrassed to show his ignorance, but Rick's explanation about God as a loving father helped Grant come to terms with his terrible memories of life with his father. He also understood why Eva's love had been the start of his healing.

Because Rick offered quiet understanding, Grant felt able to reveal the deep-seated fear he kept inside.

"What if I've inherited the abuse gene from my father?" He looked down, disgraced that he even needed to ask. "What if I end up hurting the girls."

"You haven't so far, have you?" Rick asked in a stern voice.

"No. And I don't ever intend to, but I do mess up, forget things, have a short temper." He couldn't look

Rick in the eye. "I got angry at the twins the morning of their party."

"Why?"

"They spilled icing all over themselves, the kitchen and the floor."

"Did you hurt them or yell at them or make them cry?"

"No, but I scolded them," he admitted shame-faced.

"Because making a mess was something your father hated." Rick's gaze intensified.

"Yes. It was the same at Dahlia's when we were making cookies. Flour everywhere, cookie dough stuck on everything. I almost lost it."

"But you didn't lose it. You stuck it out." Rick shook his head. "That's the difference, Grant. That's why you'll never be an abuser. Abusers put themselves first and pretend it's for their kid. Real parenting is putting your kid's needs first and your own needs last. That's what you're doing."

"But it doesn't come automatically," Grant murmured in confusion.

"Why would you think it should?" Rick sounded amused. "You've never been a father before, have you? Or practiced on some other kid?"

Grant shook his head.

"Did you always know how to teach life skills?" Rick asked.

"I took lots of courses. But there's no manual for fatherhood. Everything is trial and error, and some of my errors might be bad for the twins."

"Then you'll apologize and do better."

"You don't understand," Grant muttered. "It's not

that easy. I'm not like Dahlia. Parenting comes so easy to her. I just mentioned the twins' birthdays and she was full of ideas. I didn't have a clue where to start."

"Nobody said fatherhood was easy. And Dahlia is amazing, that's true." Rick smiled. "But God didn't make her responsible for the twins. He gave you that job."

"Exactly." Grant huffed out his frustration.

"You're questioning God's decision?" Rick grinned at Grant's chagrined look. "Parenting isn't a sure thing for anybody. Take me. Cassie eased into parenting her son, Noah, but I didn't. The day I married her I became Noah's father. No training. But I *am* his father and I have to do my best for him. So every day I pray for God's leading, do the best I can and leave the rest in God's hands."

"Maybe I need to buy another book on parenting," Grant mused.

"You already have the best one there is. The Bible." Rick's face sobered. "Study it. Check your ideas against what it says. Consult with other parents. But most of all, pray for guidance. God knows what you're going through. He's a father, too, and His kids get into far more trouble than yours."

Grant's watch alarm went off. "My cue to start peeling potatoes," he said.

"Mine, too." Rick zipped his jacket while Grant pulled on his own. As they strode toward the hotel, Rick said, "If you ever want to talk again, I'm always available. Even if you only want to talk about Dahlia."

Grant stopped, paused then muttered, "What do you mean?"

"I mean your feelings for her. Buddy, I recognize the signs," Rick said when Grant would have argued. "You get the same goofy look I used to get when I met Cassie. You care about Dahlia, don't you?"

"Yes," Grant admitted. "But I'm not sure what that means."

"Can I offer some advice?" He waited for Grant's nod. "Dahlia has convinced herself she must manage on her own. She believes her project will show her competence, so she won't deviate from her goal no matter what it costs her."

"I know," Grant agreed. "That's why we've got to make her project succeed."

"My advice to you is, support her as best you can while helping her see that her competence doesn't come from what she accomplishes. It comes from who she is, a woman who has God on her side." Rick nodded. "That's the most powerful help any of us have."

Though he'd never especially enjoyed peeling potatoes, Grant walked inside the hotel with excitement building inside. Because this was for Dahlia, potato peeling had gone from being a chore to being a pleasure.

Was that what Rick had been talking about when he said those things about doing stuff for others? Because if it was, Grant would do a lot more than peel potatoes for the lovely Dahlia.

Chapter Twelve

On a Friday afternoon two weeks after Thanksgiving, Dahlia drove to Lives to ask Arlen for help. The trip was not a success.

"I painted the tires, but I'm too busy to help with the garage," he snapped.

"It's not hard work." Dahlia frowned at the anger in Arlen's voice. He'd put up barriers between them again. "The other boys have helped organize the shelves. I thought you might help me fill them. It won't take long."

"I said no!" The sharp response had barely left his lips when Arlen flushed. "Sorry, but I can't," he said in a quieter voice. "I'm tied up."

The way he said it made Dahlia frown.

"You don't have to look so suspicious," he said. "It's nothing bad."

"I'm sure it isn't. Thanks anyway." Dahlia conceded defeat as he sauntered away.

Two minutes later, the other boys rushed outside, eager to begin preparing the area Kyle would soon flood to make an outside hockey rink. Temperatures had dropped considerably in the past few days and now the frost took till late morning to dissipate. The signs were all there. Winter was coming.

Plagued by a sense of urgency to get the go-karts on the track at least once before the land was obliterated by snow, Dahlia couldn't rest. She pushed through her days at the store, desperate to steal every moment to work on another project detail.

A new missive from her mother suggested her parents' visit could happen any day. If they appeared, what would she have to show? A project half-finished?

She was reaching into the hall closet when she heard Arlen speaking in the next room.

"Hey, Rod. I just got a call," Arlen said.

"Oh. From who?"

"My probation officer. My mom's decided she won't make me a ward of the court. She wants me back."

Dahlia shook herself out of her trance and walked quickly toward the kitchen, anxious that Arlen not think she was spying on him. She sat there for a long time, stunned, trying to absorb the news that would certainly put an end to her plan to adopt.

"Hello. Come to join me for coffee?" Laurel poured two cups of coffee and handed one to Dahlia. "You look upset. Can I help?"

"Uh, I was trying to persuade Arlen to help me, but he says he's too busy."

"He's been meeting with Grant. I understand there's some homework involved."

"Oh, that explains it. I hope it helps him." She sighed. "I have to get this project finished, especially now."

"Why especially now?" Laurel asked.

"My parents are coming. I don't have a firm date, but knowing them, they'll arrive without notice." She made a face. "I sound like a whiner. Ignore me. I'm just concerned. The Weather Channel is predicting snow by the weekend."

"Which isn't unusual," Laurel reminded. "Sweetie, you always knew there was a risk you wouldn't finish before the snow arrived."

"But I've prayed so hard. We're so close." Dahlia forced a smile. "Why can't I get this done?"

"God's still in control though He may not do things the way you want." Laurel grinned. "Want proof? The karts will be on tomorrow's train and we won't have to pay a dime."

"Really?" A weight lifted off Dahlia's shoulders. *Thank You, Lord.* "I can't thank you enough for going to bat for us, Laurel."

"You're doing this for my boys. Of course I'll help." Laurel studied her. "But I get the feeling there's more on your mind."

"I feel like a failure," Dahlia admitted.

"Then, girl, you need to take a walk over that track again."

"I overheard Arlen talking to Rod," Dahlia admitted. "Is it true his mom rescinded her decision to make him a ward of the court?"

"It's true." Laurel's forehead furrowed. "She wants him to come home when his sentence here is finished, to try to rebuild their relationship. Arlen's all she has left now."

With those few words, Dahlia's dream to shower Arlen with the love she'd stored inside melted into ashes.

"I'm sorry, honey. But you'll be a mom in God's time." Laurel hugged her.

That tenderness was her undoing. Dahlia couldn't stem her tears.

"Why am I never enough, Laurel? What's wrong with me?"

"Nothing!" Laurel exclaimed. "It's just—I guess God has a different plan."

"So what is it? I've tried so hard to prove myself. And yet I keep failing." The lump in her throat blocked the rest of Dahlia's words.

"That's a lie." Grant stood in the doorway. His face flushed a rich red when Dahlia turned to him. "I didn't mean to listen in, but I have to say this." His gray gaze searched hers. "You haven't failed, Dahlia. You've achieved a lot. The go-karts are arriving. That's an answer to prayer."

"And if we need extra money to fix them? I will *not* go back to this community. They've already given so much."

"You're jumping the gun," he said, his voice gentle.

"I'm trying to be prepared," she shot back.

"Are you?" He sat down as Laurel quietly slipped from the room. "There's a verse I found. It says, 'Sufficient unto the day is the evil thereof.' In other words, let tomorrow take care of itself. Jesus said the same thing when he was talking about the birds, remember?"

"I'm responsible if this thing falls apart."

"Why just you?" Grant said, surprising her. "We're all involved in this project, Dahlia. We've set up fundraising, coaxed donations and talked about it nonstop. If it fails, it will be our faults, too." He arched an eyebrow. "Aren't you the one who keeps saying this is a *community* project?"

"Wow! You sound different." She saw a new confidence in his eyes.

"I'm learning who's in control." Grant stretched out his legs and leaned back, fingers meshed behind his head. "It isn't me and it's sure not you."

She kept her hands folded in her lap, wondering what had changed Grant.

"I believe God places things on our hearts that lead us to our goals. But just because our goals are directed by God doesn't mean we automatically get them. That'd be too easy."

"I wouldn't mind having things go easy with this project."

"I doubt you'd feel the same sense of accomplishment."

"So fighting through the problems is supposed to make me feel better?" She used her driest tone.

"Maybe it's supposed to make you question whether this is a worthy goal or simply an idea you aren't willing to pursue if the going gets tough," he suggested.

Dahlia studied him. "Any personal examples?"

"Not that I want to share right now."

Grant's words suggested a change in his faith. She wanted to know more and it seemed she would when he asked, "Will you come for dinner this evening?"

A faint smile shaped his lips. Dahlia remembered vividly what those lips had felt like on hers. Her heart began to race.

"I'd love to," she said without thinking, then realized it was true. "Can I bring anything?"

"Just yourself. Around six-thirty?" he asked.

"Sounds good."

"Okay. See you then." Grant rose, zipped up his jacket and grinned. "The twins are at story time so I'll use this hour to talk to the boys."

"What's today's discussion about?" she asked curiously.

"How striving to reach a goal teaches patience and purpose and a whole lot of other things we need to get what we most want out of life. That 'easy come' usually also means 'easy go.'" He arched an eyebrow. "See you later?"

"For sure." She watched him leave, noting a new assurance in the way he moved. Something had changed in Grant's world, and she couldn't wait to find out what it was.

Grant checked the oven for the tenth time. Everything looked good.

"I'm hungry, Daddy." Glory's plaintive voice joined Grace's just before the doorbell rang. "It's Dally!" they yelled as they raced toward the door.

"Hello, darlings." Dahlia scooped the girls into her arms, then leaned back to study them. "You look so pretty."

"Daddy got us new dresses." Grace twirled around so her flouncy skirt flared. Of course, Glory followed. "I like pink and Glory likes yellow."

"You both look beautiful." Dahlia lifted her lovely hazel eyes and smiled so warmly Grant couldn't look away. "I'm so sorry I'm late. My parents phoned as I was leaving."

She let him help her with her coat and his breath vanished. Dahlia looked like a queen in her black velvet pantsuit trimmed with satin piping. Her hair, ablaze in a cloud of auburn curls, tumbled from its updo to caress her pale neck.

"You look lovely," he said truthfully. "What did your parents say?"

"Not much. They've decided to go on a cruise. They've set a tentative date for their visit. A month from last Monday." Dahlia's irrepressible smile blazed. "I've got until then to get the track finished."

"Prayer works." Grant smiled and refused her offer of help in the kitchen. "Dinner will be ready shortly. Till then, you can relax."

The twins took that as carte blanche to get Dahlia into one of their favorite word games, leaving Grant to admire the three auburn heads bent close together, giggling as they built words on the game board. He'd have to thank Rick for his advice to show Dahlia he was no longer the man she'd first met. Tonight, Grant intended her to see him in a different light: as a competent and confident father.

Maybe then—he didn't allow himself to finish that thought.

Sufficient unto the day, he repeated mentally as he stirred the gravy. Tonight was also about building Dahlia's confidence because he sensed she'd begun to give up on her dream.

When dinner was ready, Grant could have called them to the table, but he let them play on, content to admire the tender way Dahlia coaxed the twins to do better. Did she recognize the gift she had for helping people be more than they thought they could be? For the hundredth time Grant thought what a wonderful mother she'd make.

"Are we holding you up?" She tilted her head, catching him watching her.

"I thought I'd let you finish your game. Nothing will spoil."

Grace pounced when Dahlia wasn't looking. "S-i-g-n, sign," she said with a big grin. "I win."

"That's a very good word. You do win." Dahlia pressed a kiss on her forehead then glanced at Grant. "Shall we come to the table now?"

Grant held her chair, then helped the twins tie on polka-dot aprons. "Ready, girls?" he asked.

They could hardly wait to show off. A burst of pride shot through him as they carried the rolls and salad to the table.

"Good job," he cheered. "Now the potatoes and the vegetables. Okay?"

"We can do it, Daddy." Their voices brimmed with confidence.

"Yes, you can." When they finished their tasks, he helped them climb onto their chairs then he carried in the meat and the gravy. "Okay, we're all ready."

"It smells delicious." Dahlia's smile made his heart race.

"Enjoy." *I made it especially for you.* "Shall we say grace?"

The twins clasped each other's hands. When Dahlia slid her smooth palm into his, Grant's breath caught in his throat again. The twins recited a poem of thanks. Her delicate perfume assailed him, sending him into a dream world where dinners with her happened every day. When he opened his eyes, he found them all staring at him.

"Amen." He tucked away the dream. "Enjoy."

It was the kind of family meal Grant had imagined having when he was a boy. He wanted it to last forever.

"Can we have our special dessert now, Daddy?" Glory asked when they'd all finished the main course.

"It's special because we all made it together," Grace told Dahlia with a proud smile.

"Then I'll love it." Dahlia's smile echoed in her hazel eyes. Grant felt trapped in her smile and loved it. The very last thing he wanted was to move.

"I'll clear the table."

He couldn't allow that. "Stay put. You're our guest." He glanced at the girls and they began removing dishes from the table.

Dahlia watched them walk away. "You're doing an amazing job."

"Thanks. Coming here has been great for them." *And me.*

The sound of a dish hitting the floor broke the mood.

"Excuse me." Grant caught the flicker of worry in Dahlia's eyes and knew she was remembering his unease the day they'd made cookies.

But all she said was, "Of course."

Grant walked to the kitchen, steeling himself for the mess. The old rush of irritation building inside vanished when he saw Glory on the floor, holding her bleeding finger.

"Let's see." He tenderly examined her hand. "It's

not too bad, sweetie. We'll put on one of those funny bandages you like."

"But we made a mess, Daddy." Grace's face wrinkled as if she'd burst into tears.

"You sure did. But sometimes messes happen. So we clean them up." He smiled at her. "Right?"

"Right," she agreed, happy—and perhaps relieved?

"Why don't you go keep Dahlia company? After I fix Glory's finger, I'll clean this up."

Maybe he'd been wrong to give the two so much responsibility. But on the heels of that worry came the reminder that parenting was trial and error. He refused to allow the rush of guilt looming inside to overwhelm him.

"Okay, Daddy." Grace skipped to the doorway. "We made a mess, but Daddy's going to fix it," she announced.

Daddy's going to fix it. And that was the sum total of his job, Grant mused as he lifted Glory in his arms and carried her to the bathroom. As long as he kept fixing their world, he would do all right.

It didn't take long to bandage Glory's finger. He sent her back to the table while he cleaned up the kitchen, only then remembering that the apple Betty was still in the oven.

"I'm sorry," he muttered, carrying the too-crisp confection with its blackened edges to the table. "I left it in too long." He felt like a fool for trying to show off. He'd wanted Dahlia to see that he'd changed, but that seemed like a dumb idea now.

"It smells amazing. Do you have any ice cream?" she asked.

Grant nodded. His heart bumped at her sweet smile, erasing the doubt he'd been feeling just moments earlier.

"Everything tastes better with ice cream," she said cheerfully. "May I serve while you get it?"

"Sure." Grant went to search the freezer. He returned with a half-full container. "All we have is maple walnut," he said apologetically.

"Walnuts and maple are perfect with apples." She placed a scoop of ice cream on each serving of apples from which the blackened edge had been removed. "Doesn't that make your mouth water, girls?"

Grace and Glory nodded, eyes wide. They tasted, then grinned.

"It's really good, Daddy," Glory told him.

"It's a com—com—" Grace frowned. "I can't remember the word."

"What does the word mean, Grace?" Dahlia asked.

"That we all did it together."

"Community?" Dahlia smiled.

"That's it." Grace's face lit up. "This is a community dessert."

"Yes, it is," Grant agreed.

Grant couldn't stop staring at Dahlia, wondering whether there was a way in which they could be more than just friends. And for once, that wish had nothing to do with the twins.

"They're so adorable." Dahlia accepted the cup of tea Grant poured for her now that the twins were in bed. "I see a big change since I first met them on the train. They're calmer."

"I'm not sure about that." He sat down opposite her. "But I agree they seem more secure."

"That's due to you," she said quietly. Her eyes met his. "You've changed, too."

"I still have my moments," he told her.

"Everyone does." She debated a moment before asking what was on her mind. "Do you still feel you're failing Eva?"

"Yes, but life goes on. I'm responsible for the twins. I do my best. If I mess up, I try to make it right." He shook his head. "I know you've been telling me that for a while, but I had to figure it out for myself."

"How did you?" She couldn't conceal her curiosity.

"You helped me see there is no right way to parent, though I guess I had to hear it again from Rick to have it sink in. I do what I can and keep praying for help." Grant shrugged. "I still doubt every decision I make. I probably always will. But that isn't going to keep me from acting."

"Good for you." Dahlia smiled at him. "I think Eva would be proud." After a moment she said, "It's hard to go on without someone you loved."

After a pause he said, "It's getting easier."

"But?" Dahlia heard an unfinished note in his voice.

"I'm not a person who knows much about love, Dahlia."

"I don't understand." Dahlia wondered at the strain underlying his words.

"Love is practically a foreign concept to me," he explained. "My mom left when I was very young. My dad was— He wasn't a loving man. He was probably angry because she left me behind, but I've stopped making excuses for his behavior."

"He was abusive?" Dahlia's heart sank as his expression confirmed it. "I'm so sorry you had to go through that, Grant."

She reached across the table and squeezed his hand. Tension shifted the lines on his face as he fought his past.

"My father demanded more than any kid should have to give and he took without ever saying thank you. He treated me like a servant. I doubt he even noticed when I left."

No wonder he'd struggled with fatherhood.

The desolate remark reached straight into Dahlia's heart, especially when he looked straight at her.

"There's nothing I wouldn't do for the twins. Why didn't he feel like that about me? How did I alienate him?"

Dahlia set her cup down and moved her chair next to his. She slid her arm around his shoulder. "You have to know it wasn't you."

"My head knows it, but—" He gave her a wry smile.

"Your father's problems had nothing to do with you, Grant. Maybe no one ever loved him the way he yearned to be loved."

Grant lifted his head. "I never thought of that."

"Perhaps your father never had anyone tell him he was worthwhile or that he mattered." Suddenly unnerved by her proximity to him, she eased her arm away and immediately regretted the loss of contact. "What about your mother?"

"I looked for her years ago. She died of cancer within

a year of leaving my father. Maybe she needed to get away to die in peace."

"It's odd how everything in our lives always harks back to our childhood," Dahlia mused.

"Eva said our minds are molded in those tender years," he murmured. A half smile tugged at his lips. "I once told her I never wanted to be responsible for anyone else, that I wouldn't marry because I couldn't be a family man."

"You didn't want more children?" Dahlia hid her surprise. "What did Eva say?"

"She said nothing was ever so bad it couldn't be changed by love. She kept saying she loved me." He glanced down at their entwined fingers. "In hindsight, I was dependent on Eva. I'm not sure I gave as much as I got," he admitted. "Eva made it comfortable for me to remain aloof from everything. She bore the load in our relationship. She should have demanded more of me. She deserved more." His fingers tightened on hers.

"I never realized how little I gave back until I noticed the couples around here. They depend on each other. In order to work, their relationship needs both of them fully participating."

Dahlia nodded.

"I never knew caring about someone could be so demanding yet so fulfilling." His gray gaze met hers.

"You sound as if you've now found someone else to love." A shaft panic ripped through her when he slowly nodded. Who had Grant found to love?

"The twins, of course." Grant grinned and she grinned back as relief flooded through her. He hadn't found a mom for the twins. Yet. "I know it's not romantic, but I'd do anything to keep them safe and happy. In fact, that's my new goal."

"You've given up on finding a mother for them?"

"Maybe loving the twins is the only kind of love I can have." Grant looked down. "Maybe I'm not capable of the kind of love others experience."

"I don't believe that," Dahlia told him firmly. "I think God wants His children to experience all the shades of love He created."

"Maybe." Grant eased his hand from hers and leaned back in his chair. "When I first started speaking to Rick a couple of weeks ago, he recited a verse to me that's echoed in my head ever since. 'God hasn't given us a spirit of fear, but of love and of power and of a sound mind.'"

"It's a good one."

"Rick told me that if I put that verse in the boys' vernacular, it would be, 'God didn't create any dummies.'" He chuckled. "I repeat that when I'm fighting my spirit of fear."

While Grant sat in silent contemplation, self-truth filled Dahlia.

She loved Grant.

She hadn't tried very hard to find a mother for the girls because *she* wanted to be the woman in Grant's life. She wanted to tell him her secret fears and desires, and hear his. She wanted to be by his side to help raise the twins.

But that dream was impossible. She wasn't strong enough to be a wife or a mother. Maybe that's why Grant no longer saw her as a viable partner. Maybe that's why

God hadn't answered her prayer about Arlen—because she didn't deserve those blessings.

She rose, hating to leave but she needed to get away and think about this.

"Thank you for a wonderful evening. You've come a long way from the dad who couldn't relate to his twins, Grant."

He rose to see her out. "Thanks, Dahlia."

A longing to share the burgeoning feelings in her heart swelled. Impulse overcame wisdom and without thinking, she leaned forward, touching her lips to his. After a momentary hesitation, Grant responded, deepening the kiss as he wrapped his arms around her.

This was what she wanted, to be with Grant like this. She wanted to share his hopes and dreams, and his fears. To be there for him.

And yet, she couldn't help it—doubts and worries flooded in. A moment later, as if Grant understood, he ended the embrace, his eyes searching hers as he stepped away.

"Thank you for coming," he said as he led her to the door and held her coat. Then, he pulled her back into his arms. "Don't you dare give up, Dahlia," he whispered.

She wasn't exactly sure what he meant but in the moment, she didn't have the strength to ask. It was enough to relish the joy of being in Grant's arms for the second time that night.

"Good night" was the best she could manage when she finally eased free of his embrace.

She drove home with her brain whirling with questions, her lips still tingling from that wonderful kiss.

Chapter Thirteen

On November 11th, after the Remembrance Day ceremony was finished, Grant walked into the garage and saw Dahlia dressed in shabby jeans, a red plaid shirt and boots that were clearly too big. He didn't bother to stifle his laughter.

"Are you really laughing at me, Grant Adams?"

"Actually—yes." He chuckled harder at the fierce frown she shot his way. "How much do you actually know about mechanics?" he asked, shedding his coat on a nearby box.

"Less than you, probably." Dahlia's indomitable smile appeared as she shrugged. "They've almost fixed this kart. Maybe we can try it on the track soon."

She looked so cute with that streak of grease on the end of her nose, her fist clenched around a massive wrench. Grant couldn't stop staring at her.

"I keep trying to tell her there's no such thing as almost fixed." Pete, the mechanic who was helping the boys repair the go-karts, winked at Grant. "You'd better take that away from her. She could do herself an injury,"

"You know me better than that, Pete." Dahlia gave him a mock glare.

"I know saying you can't do something is like waving a red flag in front of a bull, Dahlia Wheatley. But the boys and I need peace and quiet, and you're hovering." Pete pretended a glare. "Why don't you two go do something fun and leave us to work?"

"But I want to help," she argued.

"You'll be a bigger help if you leave us in peace," he said. An amused rumble of agreement came from the three boys beside him.

"I will be back," Dahlia assured him before she turned to Grant. "Want to go to the track? We could check that everything's good to go."

"I know very well that you did that yesterday, and the day before, and the day before that." It was a token objection because Grant knew he was happy to do whatever she wanted. "Okay, we'll go to the track if you want, but I'm not anxious to take the girls. There were two sightings of polar bears yesterday."

"Arlen's babysitting, isn't he?" Grant nodded. "So we'll take him along. You know you can trust him to keep an eye on the girls."

Grant remembered Rick's verse. *God has not given us a spirit of fear.*

"Hardly seems like rain, doesn't it? But that's what the weatherman predicts," Dahlia said as they got in his truck and headed toward Grant's.

"They're never right," Grant said, then wished he hadn't in case he'd raised Dahlia's hopes. He figured getting her project operational before winter hit wasn't likely, though he'd never say that out loud. "The ugly weather has to come sooner or later."

"Later is fine." She pulled into his yard. "Usually I love winter, but putting out sleds for the kids and snow-blowers for their parents at the store just isn't doing it for me this year."

"Dahlia, can we talk about that kiss?" Grant blurted and held his breath when her lovely hazel eyes stretched wide.

"Uh, okay." Her cheeks pinked when she glanced at him before quickly averting her face.

That was it? Grant shifted awkwardly, waiting, hoping she'd say something, anything more. She didn't.

"Why did you kiss me, Dahlia?" he asked finally, frustrated by her continued silence.

"I probably shouldn't have." She kept staring straight ahead.

"So why did you?" He desperately wanted to know what that gesture of hers meant, especially if their embrace had meant as much to her as it had to him.

"I guess I wanted to show you I cared," she mumbled.

"Cared?" He seized on the word. "Cared how?"

"You were hurting," she said. "You'd just told me about your dad and I..."

"You felt sorry for me?" Grant almost groaned. He so did not want her pity.

"It was more than pity." She did glance at him then. Her hazel eyes held a message that Grant couldn't decipher before she demanded, "Why did you kiss me back?"

"I—uh—you were—" he stammered to a stop while his brain searched for an answer.

Oh, why had he ever started this? His brain was so jumbled, his emotions all over the place. On top of that, he didn't want to say something without thinking it over carefully lest he later regret it. Most of all, he didn't want to hurt Dahlia in any way.

Relief flooded him when Grace peeked out the front door and waved them inside.

"Maybe we should continue this later," he suggested, seizing on the excuse.

"Sure," Dahlia hurriedly agreed. "Anyway, I have to focus on finishing my project."

She sounded like she was also glad for the reprieve that meant she didn't have to answer. Suddenly Grant wished that the track was finished, the karts were operational and she was finally free of the worry that dogged her.

Let her get one kart around that track, Grant prayed as he opened his door. *Just one. Please?* When had Dahlia's project become so important to him?

Since she'd taken over his world.

"It looks pretty good, don't you think?" Dahlia snugged her collar around her ears, turning her back on the wind that raced across the land.

"It looks ready." Grant smiled as the twins squealed in a game of tag with Arlen. "There's nothing more to do. It's waiting for a go-kart."

"I can't thank you enough for all you've done. This wouldn't have happened without you." She felt so close to him. If only she could have told him what was in her heart when he asked about that kiss. "I wish—"

She heard a noise before the wind caught it and

tossed it away. When she turned to look, Dahlia's blood froze.

"Grant," she hissed, grabbing his hand.

"I see it. So do the kids." He raised his voice a notch. "Don't move, guys." They both watched as a polar bear waddled near Arlen and the twins. "Let's move toward them very slowly." Grant's voice was hoarse.

They inched forward together. The closer they got, the more clearly Dahlia heard the twins' whimpers. She could also hear the bear's low-throated growl.

"No way," Arlen repeated, fiercely trying to stay between the bear and the girls. "You're not getting near them."

But the hungry bear knew how to maneuver.

"Get out of here!" Arlen suddenly yelled, flailing his arms. The bear backed off only for a moment, then shifted closer to Glory.

"What do we do, Grant?" Dahlia breathed.

"Don't make any sudden moves," he said. "We don't want to force it into defense mode. Ease up, Arlen," he said a little louder. "Keep calm, girls. Daddy's here."

Daddy's here. If Grant could only hear himself, he'd never doubt his abilities again.

Please help us, Lord. The repeated prayer left her lips over and over.

Grant moved cautiously but unerringly closer to the twins. He was steps away when the bear suddenly lunged. With lightning speed, Arlen stepped in front of Glory and swung his arm to swat away the bear's paw. But the claws sunk into his arm.

Arlen screamed with pain while Grant and Dahlia raced toward him and the twins. She grabbed the twins' hands and pulled them toward the truck. With the girls safely inside, she turned back to see what else she could do. Arlen was on the ground, clutching his injured arm. Grant stood in front of the snarling bear, yelling. He used a broken tree branch as a club, swinging it at the lunging bear.

"Daddy!" Glory's whimper forced Dahlia into action.

She started the truck, threw it into gear and raced toward Grant while honking the horn. While the bear was distracted Grant scored a direct hit to the bear's head and the animal backed off, but its eyes returned to Arlen, who was still on the ground.

Behind her, the twins whimpered. Dahlia hit the gas as Grant moved between Arlen and the bear. She pulled up and leaned over to thrust open the passenger door.

"Get in!" she yelled before hitting the horn again.

The bear stood fully upright, preparing to attack.

Dazed and bleeding, Arlen staggered to his feet. Grant thrust one arm around his shoulders and half dragged the boy to the truck. He boosted him inside and jumped in, too. As soon as the door closed, Dahlia backed away and took off.

Dahlia called the police, knowing that they would call the wildlife service. Then she called Laurel.

"There's a bear inside the fence. Keep everyone indoors until you hear otherwise," Dahlia told her friend what had happened. "We're taking Arlen to the hospital."

Laurel promised to meet them there. Dahlia hit the gas and raced to the emergency room.

"I think he's in shock," she explained to the attendants who hurried Arlen away as soon as they got him out of the car.

Grant shot her a questioning glance. She could see he needed to make certain Arlen was okay. She guessed he felt a bit of guilt because Arlen had been injured protecting his children.

"Go with him," she urged, feeling queasy. "I'll take care of the twins."

Dahlia led the girls to the waiting room and spent some time reassuring them that Arlen would be okay. A few moments later, Laurel appeared.

"Arlen?" she asked breathlessly.

"Grant's with him now." Dahlia glanced at the twins. "Arlen was a hero today." She shuddered at the thought of what could have happened.

"The area is fenced to stop this exact thing." Laurel was visibly upset. "I'll get Kyle to check the perimeter before anyone goes on the track again."

"Let the wildlife people do that." Dahlia realized she was still trembling.

"You two are okay?" Laurel asked the twins, who clutched one another, tear marks still on their cheeks. Glory and Grace nodded.

"Daddy and Arlen saved us," Grace said, her voice shaky.

"That's because they love you," Laurel said, hugging them. "I'm going to check on Arlen now. Will you pray for him?"

As Laurel left, both girls bowed their heads About to join them, Dahlia found she couldn't say a word. Grant had left his jacket on a nearby chair, and one sleeve was ripped. There was a large red stain around the tear.

Her heart squeezed so tight it hurt. Had the bear injured him, too? Had the doctors noticed? Were they treating him?

Oh, God, please, please don't let Grant be hurt. Because I love him.

"I'm very grateful for what you did, Arlen," Grant said in a gruff tone, unable to hide his relief.

"Twenty-two stitches isn't much," the boy bragged, glancing at his bandaged arm.

Dahlia smiled, but Grant couldn't. Not yet.

"You saved my kids' lives. Thank you," he said.

Arlen nodded and grabbed another slice of Polar Bear Pizza.

It had been Dahlia's idea to come here once the doctor had released Arlen. Grant had agreed. They needed time to relax, let the fear die down in a place away from the tense atmosphere at the hospital before the twins tried to sleep. To reassure himself, he took a second glance at the pair. They sat silent, watching Arlen, their eyes wide with fear still clinging to the depths.

"They're fine, Grant," Dahlia assured him softly. "And thank God, so are you. That blood on your jacket scared the daylights out of me."

"It was just a scratch," he assured her for the tenth time. "Nothing to worry about."

Her eyes met his. "I do worry about you, Grant. All the time." Then she shyly broke the connection.

Grant loved her concern for him. For just a moment he wished he had been injured enough that she'd fling her arms around him so he could feel Dahlia's embrace again and savor the sweet caring she'd lavished on him at the hospital, until the doctors had reassured her he wasn't injured.

Glory nestled against Arlen's good arm, as if to reassure herself that he was all right. Arlen patted her shoulder. A moment later Grace copied her sister, snuggling next to the boy.

"Why did you jump in front of the bear, Arlen?" Grace's blue eyes gazed at him with adoration. "You got hurt."

"Your dad was too far away," Arlen explained. "I knew he couldn't get there fast enough. I couldn't let that bear near you." He smiled and tickled her under the chin.

"He could have eaten us," Grace said in a whisper.

"Nope. You and Glory are too small to make a good bear dinner," he insisted.

"But your arm's hurt," Grace said.

"I'll be fine, I promise," he told the girls.

Grace peered up at him. "Did you save your sisters like that?"

"No." Arlen fell silent, staring at his food.

It seemed the twins understood his silence, for they simply rested against him. Then Glory soberly invited him to play with them.

"Maybe later." His smile didn't reach his eyes. "After I finish my pizza. But you two should build a tower with those awesome blocks. I'd like to see that."

They checked to be sure he was serious then nodded and, holding hands, walked to the toy area. "Will you tell us what happened to your sisters, Arlen?" Dahlia rested her hand on his arm. "It might help to talk about it."

Arlen studied her for a long time. But Grant saw no malevolence in his gaze, just inexpressible sadness.

"You can tell us," Grant urged.

Arlen finally nodded.

"We were going on a picnic." He pushed away his plate and leaned back against the seat. "Mom said I could fish. She only had a few hours off until she had to go back to work the late shift at the diner so we were hurrying, me most of all because I loved fishing and I could almost feel them nibbling on my line. It was one of those perfect summer days when it seems like nothing can go wrong." His voice cracked.

Grant noticed that Dahlia's eyes were already brimming with tears.

"I rushed my sisters into the car and told them to do up their seat belts while I got my tackle and stowed it in the trunk. I got in the front seat. I remember asking them if their belts were on," he said, then paused, his throat working as he fought to regain control of his emotions. "They said yes. Then Mom got in and we took off."

His voice cracked and he stopped. Under the table, Grant slid his hand into Dahlia's and held on. Neither of them said a word. This was Arlen's moment. They waited for him to regain his composure.

"We'd only gone a block when a truck ran a stop sign and hit us. My sisters were thrown from the car." He gulped. Tears coursed down his cheeks. "They died and it was my fault."

"Oh, honey, how could it be your fault?" Dahlia whispered.

"I should have known their belts weren't fully

latched. It happened before. I should have known to check even though they said they'd fastened them." He dashed the back of his hand across his face to obliterate his tears.

"Arlen, sweetie—" Grant loved the tenderness in Dahlia's voice.

"It *was* my fault. My mother said it over and over."

"Oh, sweetie." Dahlia reached out and touched his cheek. "Your mom needed to lash out at someone in her grief. She didn't mean it. It's just something she said in the heat of the moment."

"No." He shook his head. "After the funeral she told me she never wanted to see me again. She hates me. I hate myself!" He jumped up and rushed outside. The twins noticed and rose, frowning.

"Can you get the girls home and to bed, Dahlia?" Grant asked. "I need to talk to him, to help him deal with his feelings."

"Of course. The twins will be fine." She pressed his arm when he hesitated. "Go, Grant. He needs you and you can help him."

"Thank you." He squeezed her shoulder, and in a rush of understanding, he now knew the feeling hidden inside him was love.

Love for this wonderful woman.

He grabbed his tattered jacket and shrugged into it. As he pushed through the door into the pouring rain, Grant suddenly stopped.

What would he do when Dahlia found someone special to fill her life with? When he had to manage on his own without her behind him, backing him, supporting him?

Then Grant knew the truth.

He couldn't let that happen.

Somehow, someway, Grant had to keep Dahlia Wheatley in his life.

Permanently.

"Give me the right words for Arlen, Lord. And about Dahlia…" He let his heart speak for him, knowing God would understand.

Chapter Fourteen

"Thank heaven the rain has stopped." Dahlia rang up Grant's purchase order for the sleds he'd chosen for the twins for Christmas.

"When she offered me a job, Laurel never said anything about a rainy season. I think my house might float away if it continues," Grant teased with a smile.

"It's not normal for Churchill to have rain at the end of November, especially so much of it," Dahlia assured him. "Climate change I guess."

"There is a lot of water." Grant's smile bathed her in comforting warmth but it couldn't dispel the urgency she felt to get the project completed. "I guess it'll eventually sink in."

"All I need is one nice warm day to dry off the track. Then we can get a kart on it. It's not for me," Dahlia defended when he grinned. "Everyone who has contributed to the project needs to see results for all their fund-raising efforts."

Grant didn't say anything as she handed him back his credit card. His odd expression confused her. Why did he keep staring? She reached up and patted the combs that held her curls in place. Grant's steady regard was scrambling her train of thought.

"I never did get a chance to ask you about your talk with Arlen," she said. "How did it go?"

"He struggles to forgive himself, so of course he doesn't believe anyone else can. But I believe he's changed enough during his time at Lives that he'll be able to accept what happened. Perhaps one day soon he'll be able to let it go."

"You have quite a talent for reaching kids' hearts, Grant Adams," she said in a soft voice but meaning every word. "We're blessed to have you in our town."

"I'm a blessing to you, Dahlia?" he teased with a wide-eyed, pretend-innocence look.

"Oh, stop. And yes, you are. And you could be even more of a blessing," she told him, loving this repartee between them.

"Tell me more." He leaned his elbows on the counter and cupped his chin in them.

"I'm planning on going to Lives early tomorrow morning before the store opens. I'll check out the track. If it looks okay, the boys can take out that kart they've repaired and give it a run on Sunday afternoon. Want to come with me?"

Grant smiled. "To see your dream become a reality? I wouldn't miss it."

His words nearly made her heart sing. "Want to bring the girls over for dinner?" she asked without thinking.

"Tonight? But you've been working all day," Grant protested.

Dahlia shrugged. "I put a chicken in the slow cooker

at noon so making dinner isn't a big deal." His hesitation made her add, "Please come. I'd appreciate the company." She swallowed past the lump in her throat. "My brother died twelve years ago today."

"I'm so sorry, Dahlia." He reached out and covered her hand with his. His reassuring voice warmed the cold, sad part of her heart that still mourned.

"Of course we'll come," he said, adding, "The girls will love it."

Dahlia found herself hoping that he was going to love it, too.

Her mind drifted back to the night he'd asked her to marry him. It seemed like a long time ago now. How long would their friendship last if another woman came into the picture? How would she feel?

What were they doing?

Dahlia drew her hand away on the pretext of handing him his receipt though she really wanted to hang on and pretend she had the right to.

"I hope Glory and Grace love the sleds," she said, trying to get her mind back on track.

"They will. Christmas is coming so fast." He smiled. "A year ago I couldn't have imagined how my life would change."

"Neither could I."

How could she have imagined the difference Grant and his twins would make to her world? His gaze held hers. "Your staff is watching us."

Dahlia grinned. "I know." Let them stare. Grant made her feel special and Dahlia didn't want that to end.

"You probably need to get back to work if you're leaving early. And I have some more errands to run while the twins are practicing for the Sunday school Christmas concert. See you at six-thirty?" He murmured the last part in a whisper so her staff couldn't hear.

Her heart thumped at the gentle glow in his eyes.

"Perfect." Dahlia kept her gaze on him until he went out the door. She busied herself counting receipts, urging the clock to hurry toward six-thirty.

Her eagerness to have dinner with Grant was silly. She wasn't what he needed. But she ached to share his life, to know he'd always be there. Until he distanced himself, Dahlia intended to enjoy every moment she had with him.

She locked up the store a few minutes before six, something she'd always before refused to do. At home, she hurried to shower and change, choosing her most flattering outfit. She set the table carefully, with candles and Granny Bev's best dishes, to make the evening special.

Everything Dahlia did now was for Grant. He was in her heart.

When she opened the door and saw him standing there, her pulse skittered. "Welcome!"

His hand rested against hers when he handed over his coat. The contact sent a rush of longing straight to Dahlia's heart. She hid her emotions as the twins enveloped her in hugs. If only this was her family. If only she deserved them.

"Are you sick, Dally? You look funny." Glory peered into her face.

"You're supposed to say she looks nice," Grant said with a rueful shake of his head.

"I'm fine, Glory. Just thankful to have you here." She brushed through the silken curls with her fingers. "Did you have a good day?"

The twins told her about the concert practice at church, and their parts in it. It was a glorious meal, full of intimacy and sharing, as if they were a real family. And through it all, Grant sat watching her, his gaze warm. But when Glory could no longer smother her yawns and Grace nodded off while eating her last bite of the chocolate cake Grant brought, Dahlia knew they'd soon leave.

Loneliness waited to engulf her.

Grant went out to warm up the car and returned shivering.

"The car's thermometer says it's minus thirty-two," he said frowning. "Can that be right?"

"Of course not." Dahlia chuckled. "It was raining when I got up this morning. Even in Churchill the temperature doesn't drop that fast."

"I guess I should get it checked." Grant started to dress the weary twins.

"This will keep you warm, Grace." Dahlia tied her scarf. "Can I have a hug good-night?"

Tiny arms slipped around her neck as a tired voice mumbled good-night. Glory, who usually wiggled non-stop, barely moved between yawns.

"Poor things." Dahlia let them go and rose. "Time for bed. Thanks for coming, Grant."

He stared into her eyes for a long moment. Then he stepped forward to lay his hand against her waist. "Thank you for a wonderful evening, Dahlia."

He kissed her—a gentle, bittersweet kiss that made her want to weep when he finally drew away.

Dahlia could barely catch her breath as she stared into his gentle gray eyes.

"I'm tired, Daddy. Does Dally need another good-night kiss?" Glory asked.

Dally did, but she only smiled as Grant gathered one girl in each arm and went out into the cold.

Then the door closed behind him and she was left alone with one question.

Why had Grant kissed her like that?

Kissing Dahlia like that had rocked Grant's world so badly, he held an all-night vigil to figure out the state of his heart. By morning he was no clearer on how he'd fallen in love; he only knew that it would not go away even if he wished it so, which he didn't.

His feelings for Dahlia were not the same as those he'd had for Eva. He'd lost the desperation that once plagued him. He didn't need Dahlia to rescue him or teach him or save him. Grant needed Dahlia because his life wasn't complete without her. He wanted to share special moments with her. But mostly Grant wanted to fill her world with joy as she filled his.

He loved her.

With a sense of wonder, he prayed for understanding. He knew that God had blessed him because he'd never expected to feel like this about anyone.

Wasn't it about time he told her how her felt?

While the twins slept, Grant savored his first cup of morning coffee and planned how he'd tell Dahlia what lay in his heart. He wasn't a romantic man, but romance was what he wanted for her.

He stood to put his cup in the sink and checked the thermometer. Minus forty degrees? Immediately his thoughts went to Dahlia's track. How had it fared in such cold after so much rain?

Grant set down his coffee. He couldn't let Dahlia go look at it by herself. If something had happened she'd be decimated. He needed to be with her, to support her, to do whatever he could to help.

How quickly Dahlia had become part of his heart, his world, and hopefully his future.

He picked up the phone and dialed. "Lucy, would you be able to come watch the girls this morning?" Only after her groggy voice agreed did Grant realize that it was far too early to phone anyone on a Saturday morning.

But Lucy made it in half an hour, and Grant arrived at Dahlia's house just before eight o'clock. Her truck was running, the windshield clear of frost. As he waited for her to emerge, Grant prayed wordlessly that when he told her how he felt, she'd return his feelings.

In the midst of his pondering, Dahlia stepped outside and pulled her front door closed. She was drawing on thick gloves when she saw him. Her eyes widened. Grant climbed out of his car and tromped over the icy ground toward her.

"What's wrong?" she asked.

"Nothing. I'm going with you to check out the track. Okay?"

"Sure." She didn't look at him as they climbed in the truck, but Grant put it down to shyness after their kiss.

"The ice will come into the harbor now," she murmured. "The polar bears will soon hibernate. Then they won't hurt anyone else."

"Yes." Grant hated the thread of worry in her voice. *Oh, Lord, help,* his heart begged.

As they drove to the track, Grant was conscious of tension between them. In silence, they bounced and jounced over the frozen hillocks of tundra until they came to the track. Carefully Dahlia eased her truck onto the asphalt they'd resurfaced. She drove slowly.

"Everything seems okay."

Grant thought so, too, but worry lingered. As faint traces of morning light began to penetrate the gloom, he peered through the windshield, trying to more fully assess the condition of the track.

Suddenly Dahlia jammed on her brakes. She struggled for a moment to control the sliding vehicle until the wheels found traction and jerked to a stop.

"Oh, no," she gasped.

Grant's breath stopped. Unwilling to accept what he saw, Grant got out of the truck and walked several yards. His heart sank to his toes. A huge section of jagged pavement had heaved upward, probably due to freezing and swelling in the soggy permafrost beneath. The track would have to be completely rebuilt and re-paved.

Dahlia's voice was stark with pain. "I couldn't make it happen."

"Now you're responsible for the weather?" Grant couldn't stand to see her so defeated. "You did your best."

"It wasn't enough. It never is." She trudged back to

the truck, climbed inside and waited until he joined her before she turned around and drove back.

"So you don't believe God's in control?" he asked when they'd reached the edge of town.

"If He is, where is He now?" Anger tinged her voice.

"Right here. Always has been." Grant couldn't bear to see Dahlia's faith weaken when she'd been such a bulwark to him in his worst moments. "Just because this didn't turn out as you wanted doesn't mean He isn't in it. God has a plan, Dahlia. You helped me see that, remember? Nothing you've done for the boys will be wasted. Somehow He will use this."

She pulled up in front of her house, shoved the gearshift into park and turned on him.

"I don't need platitudes, Grant," she said, her voice tight. "That track was my dearest goal and God abandoned me when I counted on Him most. It's just like with my parents, all over again. They'll arrive to see that once more, poor Dahlia wasn't strong enough."

"But you haven't failed," Grant insisted. "This isn't over yet. You're talking yourself into defeat before the game is finished."

"I am finished. I'm out of money and time."

"God isn't." He grasped her shoulder, turning her to face him. There were tears clinging to her lashes. He caught them on his finger, feeling her pain as his own. "Dahlia, this is the job God laid on your heart, right? Don't be intimidated because things haven't gone the way you wanted."

Her lips pressed together. "I didn't do this only for me— The boys are going to be crushed, Grant."

He pressed his finger to her lips.

"If *God* is for you, who could be against you? It's not you who can make this project succeed, but Him. You have to trust Him. You can do that."

"You have a lot of faith in Him, and me."

"Yes, I do." He cupped his hands around her face and leaned forward, pressing his lips to hers. "Don't give up. Trust Him to come through for you. You're so precious to God." Grant took a deep breath. "And to me, too, my dearest Dahlia."

Dahlia seemed to freeze.

"Wh-what are you saying, Grant?"

He grazed his fingertip over her lovely cheek, quelling his nervousness.

"My feelings have been growing since I first met you on the train, only I didn't know what they were. I've admired your generosity and dedication, the way you challenge and uplift, the way you've taught me how to open myself to what God has given me. You're part of my life and my heart."

Dahlia seemed speechless so Grant continued.

"You are a champion. You're pure and gentle, but you endure like steel." He gazed into her gorgeous eyes, willing her to see how much he cared. "You've become my best friend, the person I want to run to when life overwhelms me. I want to be there for you, Dahlia. I want to share your goals and dreams and your future. You're very special to me, and… I love you."

Dahlia didn't say anything. Grant's nerves stretched piano-wire taut. He needed to hear the words his soul craved—that she loved him.

Finally he asked, "Do you feel anything for me, Dahlia?"

Her slow smile brought joy to his heart. "I've come to treasure you, Grant." Her smiled faded. "But I'm not who you need for the twins."

Grant clasped her hand in his. "Don't talk to me about the twins or anything else. Just tell me. Do you love *me?*" Grant wasn't giving up. Dahlia mattered too much. He felt as if he was holding on to a cliff by his fingernails. One wrong word and she could send him crashing down.

"I do love you, Grant. I love you very much."

Dahlia loved him! His soul sent a praise of thanks-giving. But when he moved to wrap his arms around her, she held up a hand.

"But that doesn't matter."

"It matters more than anything."

"I have a business that takes a lot of time. I—"

"Stop, Dahlia." He frowned. "Tell me the truth."

She bowed her head. Her words came slowly.

"I can't be who you need, Grant. For so long, I felt like I was under Charles's or my parents' thumb, like I needed them to fall back on because I'm not strong. My parents were right."

"You are the strongest woman I know," Grant in-sisted.

"You think I'm strong because I helped you with the twins." She shook her head. "But inside I'm not like that, Grant."

"Dahlia—"

"I pretend I'm strong because that's the only way I know to get through things. But it's a lie. I don't have the strength to…share my heart with you."

Grant was feeling so much, he hardly knew where to start. And then it became clear.

"Can I say one thing, Dahlia?" At her nod, Grant brushed a curl off her beautiful face. "The reason I said I love you has nothing to do with my daughters. I didn't fall in love with you because you inspired confidence in me, or because you showed me that God is not like my father and that I don't have to try to attain His attention or worry that I'm not a good enough son. I do love you for doing all those things," he said, pressing a kiss to her hand. "But that's not the reason I need you in my life."

She frowned at him, uncertainty coloring her eyes.

"I love you and want you in my life because I can't visualize a future without you, Dahlia. You are the most important part of my world." He pulled her into his arms and held her tightly, breathing the words into her ear. "I don't need you to be strong. And I understand what it's like to be scared to love. But I need *you,* Dahlia. I love you."

Grant eased her away and then, pressing his lips against hers, tried to show her the depth of his feelings. Gradually Dahlia began to respond, her lips melting against his, sharing the love that surged in his heart. Hope built. Maybe, maybe—

Suddenly it was over.

"I'm sorry, Grant. I can't. I'd fail you, too." She pulled away from him, her face averted, her voice hoarse. "And I couldn't stand that."

She had to get to work so Grant decided to let it go. For now. He climbed out of her truck. "If you need me—" he began.

"I won't. I can't. In fact, I think it's better if we don't see each other," Dahlia whispered. "I'm sorry."

His heart aching, he closed the door and watched her drive away.

At first loss overwhelmed Grant as he pushed through days without Dahlia. But talking to Rick helped him realize that he could no more force her to accept his love than she could force the weather to change. Grant would have to trust God to work on Dahlia.

Meanwhile, Grant was going to prove his love to her.

He gathered together leaders in the community to brainstorm how they could make Dahlia's go-kart track functional. Everyone brought their best ideas, but no matter how hard they tried, they could not figure a way to finish the job.

"There has to be something else we can do," Rick said.

"I agree. We can't just let this die." Laurel studied him. "Are you sure you've thought of everything?"

"Maybe there's a way we could honor her," Mindy suggested.

"Yes. Because her project can't just die," Eddie, the miner, grumbled. "Isn't there someone whose opinion Dahlia values, someone who could help her realize how strong she is."

Then Grant had idea. That night, after the twins were in bed, he made a call.

"Hello, this is Grant. I'm a friend of Dahlia Wheatley's. You're Dahlia's mother, correct?" He held his breath, wondering if the woman would even speak to him. This was his last hope, a desperate move to prove his love to Dahlia.

"She misses you and your husband very much. I know there was a rift between you. I'm hoping this might be the time to repair it."

"Who are you?" the querulous voice demanded.

"I'm the man who loves Dahlia more than anything else in the world. I want her to be happy and I don't think she will be as long as she's estranged from you." Grant took a deep breath. "I'm hoping we can work together to make a very big dream of hers come true."

No response. Defeated, he was ready to hang up when another voice came on the line.

"Tell us what our daughter needs," a man ordered.

Praying for help, Grant explained Dahlia's goal.

Chapter Fifteen

For Dahlia, Christmas had always been a season of joy and excitement. But as December passed, she couldn't find her Christmas spirit. Each day she forced herself to smile and wish her clients merry Christmas while inside her heart shriveled a little more.

Every day, she questioned her decision to refuse Grant's love, but she knew in her heart it had been the right one. She couldn't be a wife and a mother without love, not even for Grant whom she loved deeply. And Grant didn't love her. He couldn't. Not the real, weak her.

Dahlia decorated the sleds he'd ordered, wrapping them with giant shiny bows, green for Glory, red for Grace. When he came to pick them up, she stayed in the stockroom until he left because it hurt too much to see his handsome face.

She'd taken to slipping into church at the last minute and slipping out again before the services ended to avoid him, too. At the choir cantata featuring the Lives boys, tears welled at the sight of Arlen glowing with happiness because his mother had come for a visit. His deep bass voice underpinned the others', his confidence obvious. She knew he would leave soon to be with his mother. It was best for him, but it was like the final nail finishing her dream to adopt.

"We're caroling tonight." Marni's morning call had come just as she was leaving for work. "You're coming, right?"

"Sorry, I'm too busy." Dahlia didn't have the heart to sing with her friends. "Next year," she promised.

The night of the Sunday school concert, Dahlia crept into church after the lights dimmed. She'd planned to stay away until the twins phoned.

"Please come and see us, Dally," they'd begged. "We have new dresses and we're going to say a poem. Please?"

She couldn't refuse. She smiled, her heart aching when Glory and Grace walked onto the stage. Grant had dressed them in white lacy dresses with green trim and white patent-leather shoes. They looked adorable. Her heart swelled with pride as they recited a sweet, funny poem about love. The poignant words hit deeply, especially the part about trusting that God would make the bad parts better. If only He would.

Dahlia praised them on her way out. But then they begged her to stay and taste the cookies they'd made with their dad. Dahlia couldn't leave, not when Grant added his urging.

"I didn't think you'd come," he said, staring into her eyes.

"I couldn't disappoint the twins. Besides, I wanted to see their new dresses."

"You wanted to see them, but not me."

Another time she might have pretended it wasn't true. But the stark sound of hurt in his words silenced her.

"When will you trust, Dahlia? What do I have to do to prove I love you for yourself? Christmas is a time to believe. Can't you believe in me, just a little?"

"Believing in *you* isn't the issue," she murmured.

"I'm not giving up. Not ever," he said tenderly. "If you can't be strong right now, that's okay. I'll be strong enough for both of us." He kissed her lightly, then drew away. "I love you, Dahlia. Trust God. He won't let you down."

Scarlet-cheeked and aware of interested stares, Dahlia hugged each girl, then hurriedly left, racewalking home through the snow to stop her thudding heart.

Oh, why did he have to kiss her?

She couldn't shake off the ache that kiss engendered. Nor could she sleep later. Overhead, the northern lights danced and twirled in a vortex of green and silver. God had made them. He'd made the universe. He'd made her. Why wouldn't He help her?

Frustrated Dahlia finally flicked on her bedside lamp and grabbed her Bible. An old church bulletin fell out on the floor. Curious, she picked it up. The verse on it blazed at her.

Despite all these things, overwhelming victory is ours through Christ who loved us.

Despite all these things—what did that mean? She turned to Romans 8 and began to read. *For his sake we must be ready to face death.* God wasn't asking her to do that, but Paul had and still he'd been able to say that victory, actually *overwhelming* victory was his.

Dahlia continued reading to the last verse of the chapter. *Nothing can ever separate us from the love of God.*

The strength in those words hit home. She wasn't alone. God had given her work, friends and—dare she believe it?—the love of a man whose integrity was unquestionable. The problem wasn't Grant or the go-kart track or anything else. The problem was her.

God loved her. If she loved Grant, God had blessed her with the love she'd longed for her entire life. Why not embrace it?

"Because I'm scared I'll fail him, drive him away," she whispered.

Dahlia finally saw the truth. When she didn't get her way, when things didn't go the way she wanted, she blamed God! God didn't need her or the track. But He could use them for His glory, if she let Him.

"I've been a spoiled child." She gazed at the whorls of color that danced in front of her window. "If it doesn't go my way, I don't want to play. I'm running away, just like I did before."

Saying the words aloud brought home the truth. In that moment, Dahlia begged forgiveness.

"The project is Yours, to do with as You please. I relinquish all control. Your will be done."

Grant's face swam into view, his silver-gray eyes brimming with love—for her.

"You know how much I want to trust his love. So I'm asking You to work things out. I will trust You."

Dahlia opened her eyes. Outside, the heavens glowed.

A shooting star arced overhead as if to celebrate her surrender. Her fears drained away.

She watched the lights far into the night, glorying in the freedom she now felt. Over and over Dahlia gave her inadequacies to God, clinging to one verse as she finally allowed herself to bask in the true joy of Christmas.

Overwhelming victory is ours.

Grant was worried. He never should have done it. He was risking everything. If it went badly, he'd lose her forever.

Please don't let that happen.

As he drove to the airport on Christmas Eve morning, all he could do was pray that God would work everything out and that Dahlia would forgive him.

Behind him, the twins chattered gaily. At the airport, they asked questions. He shushed them, promising to explain later. Then the plane pulled in and it was too late to second-guess his actions.

"Hi, I'm Grant," he greeted them inside the tiny airport.

"Good to meet you." Dahlia's father, a tall thin man, held out his hand. His grip was firm. "Where's my daughter?"

"She still— uh, doesn't know you're here," Grant explained.

"I expect she's still angry," her mother said. "We hurt her badly, I'm afraid."

At least they regretted what the past had done to Dahlia, Grant thought, liking the pair but still nervous about their reunion with their daughter. Dahlia's parents gushed over the twins. He drove the couple to the hotel where he told them his plan and their part in it before he took the twins home later to prepare for the Christmas Eve service.

"Daddy, will Dally be happy her mommy and daddy are here?" Glory's forehead furrowed in concern.

"I hope so." Grant prayed fervently that "Dally" would soon be very happy.

Dahlia ached to talk to Grant, but he hadn't answered her messages. In the flurry of last-minute shoppers, Dalia wondered if her hesitation with Grant had cost her everything.

Heart aching, Dahlia reminded herself that God had everything under control. She kept a smile on her face, wishing everyone a merry Christmas. Around three o'clock, the last customer left. She was closing up when Arlen walked in.

"Arlen! I thought you'd gone home. When will that be?" she asked.

"New Year's. My mom's here for Christmas."

"That's nice." Dahlia frowned. Arlen seemed oddly uncomfortable, and wouldn't quite look at her. "Is anything wrong?"

"Kind of." He pulled a package from behind his back. "I really want to see the track again before I go, just to have a memory to keep. It got be pretty important, you know. My run-in with that polar bear really got me thinking about the future. I'm sorry it's ruined 'cause it would have been cool, but I was wondering—"

"Of course I'll give you a ride out there though I don't know if we'll see much. The days are so short now." She finished closing up and followed him to the front door. The streets of Churchill were nearly deserted. "I guess everyone has finally finished their shopping," she said with a smile. "I've never seen the town look so deserted."

Arlen was silent during the drive but seemed to come alive when she pulled through the fence gates he opened.

"We won't be able to stay long," Dahlia warned. "You guys are singing in the Christmas Eve service tonight and I know you—" The rest of her words dropped away as she turned into the track site and saw the number of cars parked there.

"Come on," Arlen said. "Let's go see what's happening." A funny grin creased his stern face. "Look."

Dahlia followed the direction in which he pointed. The last rays of sunlight highlighted a figure coming toward her. Grant. She'd know that stride anywhere. Her heart swelled with love and then pain. Her fingers tightened around the steering wheel as she fought the urge to put the truck in gear and leave.

Hadn't she promised God she was trusting him?

Arlen climbed out of the truck, and suddenly Grant was there, opening her door, smiling that gorgeous smile. He held out a hand to help her out of the truck. His fingers tightened around hers. And now she recognized the light in his eyes. Love. For her.

"I have a surprise," he whispered.

She gulped then slid her hand in his and stepped down.

"Your parents are here. Everyone is." He turned her to face them. Her parents stood in front of the group, and to Dahlia's astonishment they began to clap. Everyone did. "They're here to honor you."

"Me?" She frowned at him. "Why?"

"Because you're Churchill's citizen of the year, a designation given to the person whose efforts have contributed greatly to the community and its spirit."

"But…" she whispered, trying to understand.

Grant drew her forward, helping her onto the track. The spot where it had heaved had been cleared.

"Grant asked us to come and celebrate your achievement." Her father stepped forward. "We're grateful to him for inviting us to celebrate your honor, Dahlia."

"But the track isn't finished," she sputtered in confusion. "We—I ran out of money."

"In a community like this where the spirit of caring is so strong, money is the least of your worries," her father said. "This track is work to be proud of, Dahlia. It's a goal your mother and I would like to share in, if you'll allow us."

"How?" Dahlia asked, not quite able to grasp all that was happening.

"We'd like to make a donation that will see the completion of your track," her father explained. "If you agree, a paving company will arrive in the spring and lay as much new track as necessary for your go-karts. We're making this donation as a tribute to you, Dahlia, and to Lives Under Construction, because we love you and support you."

The tenderness in his voice stunned her.

"You're a daughter to be proud of." Her mother stepped forward. "We've always regretted that we never gave you enough credit." She shook her head. "We're so sorry, honey. And so proud. You moved here and used that indomitable inner strength of yours to create something lasting." Her mother's eyes filled with tears.

"Your Granny Bev must be celebrating in heaven over you, Dahlia." Tears glittered in her father's eyes, too. "Will you forgive us? Will you allow us to share in this project of your heart?"

"Of course," Dahlia said. "You're welcome here." She threw herself into her parents' arms as peace filled her heart. "I love you guys."

Around her, the crowd cheered. Finally Laurel managed to be heard. She thanked Dahlia for all her hard work, presented her with a plaque on behalf of the town and then invited everyone to Lives for a celebratory snack before the Christmas Eve service at the church.

At Lives, Dahlia was stunned to learn the lengths Grant had gone to in order to locate her parents in Florida without her assistance, and bring them here.

Dahlia couldn't stop smiling. Grant had done this for her because he truly loved her. And she loved him. She ached to tell him so. Her heart sank when Laurel told her he'd already left to get the twins ready for the service. She hadn't even had the chance to properly thank him yet for all that he'd done.

"We should go, too, honey," her mother said. "We don't want to miss Churchill's Christmas Eve service. We've heard it's very special."

"It is," Dahlia agreed. Just then, Arlen appeared with a box.

"I want to give you this." He opened the lid and lifted out a rose bowl with a gorgeous tangerine rose nestled inside. "To thank you. You and Grant helped me change.

I came here believing I was alone, but how could I be alone when you kept pestering me?" He grinned.

"Oh, Arlen." Dahlia inhaled the rich scent of the gorgeous flower. "I'm really glad you're going home." She had no regrets. God had a plan for Arlen, too. "Come back and visit us," she said, giving him a hug.

"I'll be here for the opening of the track." He tolerated her hug, then hurried away, red dots of color on each cheek.

"What a lovely boy," her mother said.

Dahlia smiled, remembering how unlovely Arlen had been.

As she drove her parents to her house, her thoughts turned to Grant, and everything he'd done for her.

She couldn't wait to tell him how much she loved him. She only hoped it wasn't too late.

Grant pulled up in front of the church.

"You can't tell anyone," he reminded the twins.

"We know what to do, Daddy," Glory promised.

"We won't tell anyone." Grace's nose wrinkled. "Not even Miss Lucy?"

"Not anyone. Okay?" He tried to be satisfied with their nods.

Praying his scheme would work, he helped the twins from the car and escorted them backstage. Then he found a seat where he could watch Dahlia, who was up front with her parents. His heart hurt from the burgeoning love inside, but, as Glory would say, it was a good hurt.

The kids' choir filed in, backed by the teen group of mostly Lives boys. Rick led everyone in "Silent Night."

When the congregation was seated, the lights dimmed and the choir filled the little stone church with glorious music.

Grant imagined that night when God the Father had sent His son to earth. For him. A sweet certainty filled him. He *could* be the father the twins needed because he had his Heavenly Father to lean on. He *could* be what Dahlia needed—with God's help.

When the service ended everyone rose, took a cup holding a lighted candle and paraded through the town to the huge Christmas tree in the square. The group circled the big, lit tree singing "O Holy Night." After wishing each other merry Christmas, the crowd dispersed.

"You know what to do?" he asked the twins as he took their candles.

"We know, Daddy." They waited until he'd moved out of sight before racing toward Dahlia. "Merry Christmas, Dally." Their voices rang out in the frosty air like joyful bells.

Grant hurried toward the manger scene in front of the church to wait.

Dahlia took her time arriving. When she saw him waiting by the wooden donkey, she paused before continuing toward him.

"Your parents took the twins?" he asked, just to make sure the girls followed orders to go home with Dahlia's parents as soon as they'd delivered their message to Dahlia.

She nodded.

"Good." He took her hands in his, strong hands that gave so much. He placed a kiss in each gloved palm, then pressed her fingers around it. Dahlia's eyes widened, but she said nothing.

"My beloved Dahlia." He couldn't stop staring at her, so lovely in her long green coat and matching beret. "Do you know that you make my world live? You've taught me to see my possibilities in God, to understand that with God's help, I can be the man He wants. But what you doubted is that with God's help, I can also be the man you need."

"Grant—"

He leaned forward and kissed her, lightly, tenderly.

"Let me say this," he begged and waited for her nod. "I love you. You, Dahlia. If you'll trust me, I can change to be what you need."

"No." Dalia shook her head, her hazel eyes glossy with tears. When she tugged her hands from his, Grant thought his heart would crack, until she cupped her fuzzy white gloves against his cold cheeks and pressed a kiss to his lips. "Don't change, Grant. Don't ever change. You're the man of my heart, the one I trust completely."

He was speechless.

"I was wrong, Grant. I was afraid and hurt and so scared to trust that you could love me. But I know now that with you and God, I can accomplish whatever God wills."

She kissed him again, showing her love so sweetly.

"I thought I had to be strong to be used of God. I've come to understand that God works with weakness to make great things. My future plans are now subject to His approval," Dahlia whispered.

"Am I part of your future plans?" he asked softly.

"Without you, I don't have any plans."

"I love you, Dahlia Wheatley." Grant drew her into his arms and kissed her. His dearest wish had come true.

It was only when she finally drew away that Grant noticed it was snowing, hard. As in blizzard. Dahlia's gorgeous auburn curls were covered in white crystals. She looked like a snow princess.

He felt like her prince.

"Are you going to marry me, Dahlia?"

"Yes." She laughed before sliding her hands around his waist. "Is the deal off if I tell you I want brothers or sisters for the twins?"

For a moment, Grant's heart raced. How could he be a father to more children when he struggled so much with being the right father for the twins?

Then he saw the manger scene and the spotlight shining on it. God would supply all the knowledge Grant would need to raise a family. Hadn't He done that so far?

"My darling Dahlia, you and I are going to have the family that God gives us, whatever its size," he told her as assurance swept through him.

After one last lingering embrace, they hurried arm in arm through the whirling snow to Grant's house, where Dahlia's parents sat reading to the sleepy twins in front of the fire.

As Grant sat beside Dahlia, their hands entwined. They listened to the age-old story of love from heaven. He could hardly wait for tomorrow when Dahlia would open her Christmas gift and find the engagement ring he'd bought for her. Their future would be anchored in the Father's love. Nothing from Grant's or Dahlia's past could ruin that.

Epilogue

On the longest day in June, Dahlia clung to her father's arm as they followed Grace and Glory down the aisle—the aisle being the now-finished Damon Wheatley Go-Kart Track.

The girls had chosen pink dresses and pink shoes. They carried little nosegays of palest pink rosebuds. Dahlia wore a blush-pink ankle-length dress with a silk organza overlay. She carried one bright pink rose.

With the community in attendance, Rick officiated as Dahlia and Grant pledged their love to each other.

"I promise to love you, cherish you, honor you and always believe in you. I promise that together we will teach our children to love God. I love you, Dahlia."

"I promise to trust you no matter what and to love you forever. I promise to be by your side through whatever God sends our way. I love you, Grant."

When Rick pronounced them husband and wife, the audience rose and clapped. A sudden roar of an engine came from the end of the track. Then Arlen, who'd returned for the wedding by special request of the couple, burst over the smooth pavement to run the first lap of the new track in a freshly painted, perfectly humming go-kart.

"Did you know?" Dahlia asked her new husband.

"No clue. Pretty cool way to open the track, huh?"

"Way cool," she agreed as everyone clapped when Arlen returned, grinning from ear to ear.

Dahlia and Grant celebrated their marriage in a reception at Lives, reveling in the support they received, but eager to be alone together. They snuck away after cutting their cake. Dahlia's parents drove them to the train station.

"You have our phone numbers," Dahlia said to her parents. "If anything happens with the twins, you promise to call?"

Glory tugged on her new grandmother's skirt. "Do they know about the boat ride we're going to take?" she whispered.

"Boat ride?" Grant asked carefully. "What boat ride?"

"To see the whales," Grace explained. "It's a blow-up boat. A Zoe-something. I hope the whales don't poke a hole in it."

"I hope you don't fall out," Glory said.

Grant opened his mouth just as the train whistled. Dahlia leaned over, kissed his cheek and reminded him, "We're leaving things up to God, remember? He surely knows how to care for two little girls."

"I have a hunch it's your parents who will need looking after," Grant told her.

They got on the train in a flurry of confetti and took seats by the window, where they could wave goodbye until the train slowly pulled out of the station.

"I love you," Dahlia whispered.

"I love you," Grant replied.

The bride and groom were oblivious to the other passengers as they stared into each other's eyes while the train rumbled over the tracks, taking them away from the tiny town where they would create their first home together.

"They're all looking at us, you know," Dahlia whispered after a quick glance around the train car.

"They're looking at you, the most beautiful woman in the world," Grant corrected.

"Thank you, darling." Dahlia returned his kiss then laid her head on his shoulder to watch the taiga give way to trees as the midnight sun shone on. Suddenly she sat up. "I never did find out where you're taking me for our honeymoon."

"Banff." He waited for the smile to light the flecks of gold in her eyes.

"Really?" A smile spread across her lips.

"I know how much you love nature, and I have it on good authority that the stargazing is unbelievable." Grant snugged his arm around her.

"'The heavens declare the glory of God.' They're a marvelous display of His handiwork," Dahlia murmured. "It's the perfect place to thank God for all He's done for us." She leaned over to kiss Grant's cheek.

Grant turned his head just in time to catch her kiss. When it ended, they heard the woman behind them sigh and say, "Love. Nothing can beat that gift from God."

Grant smiled at Dahlia, who nodded in perfect agreement.

* * * * *

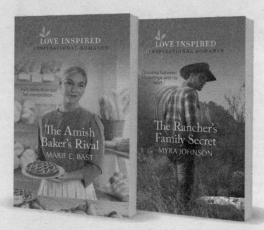

HARLEQUIN
PLUS

Announcing a **BRAND-NEW** multimedia subscription service for romance fans like you!

Read, Watch and Play.

Experience the easiest way to get the romance content you crave.

Start your **FREE 7 DAY TRIAL** at
<u>www.harlequinplus.com/freetrial</u>.